Songbird's Sorrow

L.S. TAAL

L.S. Taal Publishing

ISBN: 978-1-7381227-1-4

Dedication

To all the dreamers . . . Never stop believing.

Note From The Author

SONGBIRD'S SORROW IS AN adult fantasy romance novel, book 1 in the Celestial Songbird Series. Although I would not consider it a dark fantasy, it does contain darker content worth mentioning: depression, attempted suicide, attempted sexual assault, child abuse. It also contains crude language and explicit sexual content.

That said, I promise the story will enchant you, whisking you away to a fantasy world where you can escape for a while and get wrapped up in the adventure that only books so magically provide.

Happy reading, dear reader, and welcome to the world of Ariadna!

Contents

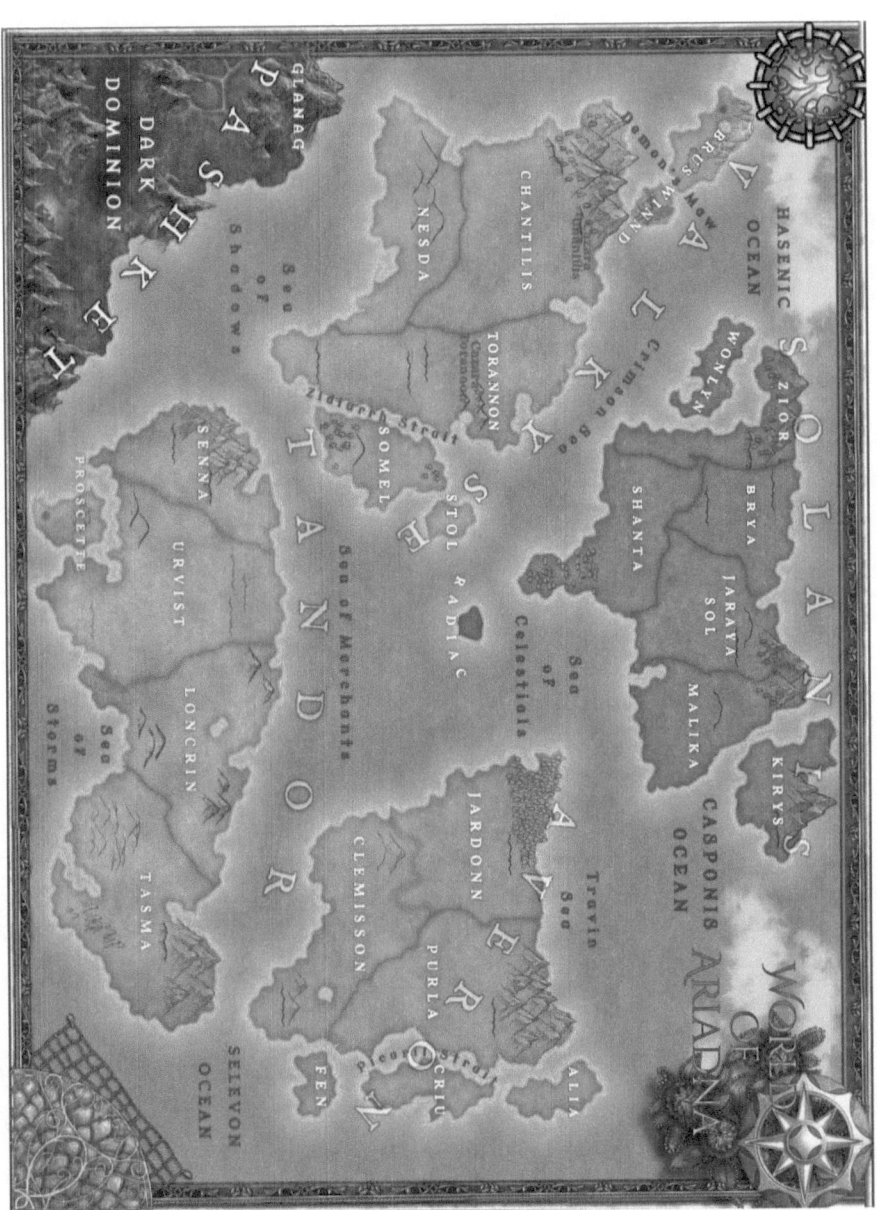

Prologue

PAIN RIPPED THROUGH ME with ruthless ferocity as I sat at my piano, jagged shards stabbing into my heart with the prison-yard efficiency of a grimy, blunt shiv. Funny that a soul so completely void of life could still feel such shattering agony. If only I could just die.

Outside the tall windows of my sunroom, the wind howled, angry streaks of lightning arcing through the night, followed by booming peals of thunder. Talk about symmetry. It was a mirror reflection of the storm raging inside me. And just like the torrent outside, I was ready to combust.

She's such a cold bitch.

Five words. I couldn't get them out of my mind. She's. Such. A. Cold. Bitch. That's all it had taken to set me off this time. And the sad thing was, the stuck-up work colleague who'd said it—someone I gave zero shits about—wasn't wrong. I was a cold bitch. And I hated it.

To anyone looking in, on the surface, my life probably seemed idyllic. Upper middle class woman in her late twenties living in a vibrant North American city, moving up the corporate ladder at work, killing it on her own.

Dig a little deeper, though, and it all fell apart. I was my own worst enemy. My depression had seen to that.

Major depressive disorder.

The disease was just as ominous and dark as it sounded. Oppressive, all-consuming, leaving me powerless to break free—crippled with a cruel self-awareness that sent me burrowing deeper into myself and shrouding me in the most sickening melancholy and emptiness.

I understood the reality. The world in general was unforgiving and harsh to those gripped in the clutches of despair.

Snap out of it. Turn your life around. Just be happy.

As if it were so simple. Heck, most days, I fought with myself just to get out of bed. I was entirely aware that no one in their right mind would want to spend any length of time with a Gloomy Glenda like me. Negativity was draining and toxic, and I was both of those things. It hurt so fucking much.

My fingers gripped the stiff, worn leather of the piano bench under me as I fought for control. Digging in hard, I pushed my nail beds back, wincing at the sharp sting against my tender skin. I was used to the pain though; it was always there, very much like the mangy, cross-eyed cat who chased me home from my run every day. I wished they'd both fuck the hell off.

Meditation sometimes helped when things got really ugly—well, my version of meditation anyway. I'd find a quiet place, close my eyes, and relax into my breath. Sinking deeper into myself, I would visualize slowly reaching into my chest, ripping my heart out, slamming the blighted thing onto the counter, and pulverizing the shit out of it with my kitchen mallet. The spiky side. It was grisly but effective, oftentimes dulling the pain that battered me into submission.

Not tonight, though. Tonight, I was beyond that. No amount of pulverizing would help. I clenched my fists and lowered my head as snippets of Liam flashed through my mind—his gleeful laughter, his sparkling brown eyes, his mischievous grin, his unbridled love for life . . . and for me.

It wasn't fucking fair. A random trip to the grocery store should not have resulted in sickening tragedy, should not have robbed me of the man I was about to marry. My best friend, my love—violently taken from this world in the time it took for me to decide on a bag of bloody potato chips.

It was hard to believe two years had passed since then. I was stuck in a never-ending loop, unable to move on, grief taking up permanent residence in my heart. Again and again, life had raked me through the coals and stripped me of love. From the age of five, this had been my reality. First my parents, then my beloved aunt, Mags, and finally my rock, Liam.

All four of them gone.

Dead.

Leaving me with no one.

Fuck never having to worry about money for the rest of my life. I'd give it all away if it meant I could have them back.

The hastily scribbled sheaf of sheet music blurred in front of my eyes as I swiped at the tears spilling down my cheeks and dripping onto the frigid ivory of my piano. My chest constricted, and I inhaled a frantic breath, clawing at my skin in a demented attempt to rip the hurt out.

I closed my eyes, my fingers gliding softly across the keys, the notes second nature, springing to life as I formed them, music—as always—the balm that soothed the wicked storms churning inside me.

I needed to get the words out—out of my head and out of my mangled heart. I opened my mouth and unleashed them into the world, cradled in an agonizing melody.

Death taunts me, he's like a stealthy beast of prey

Lurking deep in the shadows, where I never go to play
I'm scared of the darkness there, deep inside I'm filled with so much fear
Drifting outside myself, I see the veil of twilight draw near

Tonight I had a dream, and he was standing next to me
On his face the moonlight gleamed, the truth bared transparently
He was so cold, his glittering eyes so wise and old
Gripping my soul, his words so dark and bold

"I come for the meek, I come for the wild
The frail and the old, the sweet little child
The rich and the poor, the sinner, the saint
The fed and the hungry, the strong and the faint
I'll come for you one day, I have no choice
In the end I come for everyone, they all hear my voice."

My fingers skidded to a stop, and I dropped my head, collapsing onto the piano in a deluge of sorrow and rage. My cries echoed in my ears, a pitiful, wounded dissonance. "Please," I pleaded. "Please, for the love of God, come for me. Make it stop. I can't do this anymore."

Ever so gently, as if lifted on a tremulous breeze, the tender caress of fingers tangled in my hair and the warmth of a soothing whisper fluttered against my cheek.

Be strong, Elle. Live. Fight the darkness . . .

Tenuous and phantasmal, the words floated in the air around me, and I lifted my head abruptly.

"No!" I screamed, my face hot and flushed. "I don't want to anymore!"

The cold rushed in around me, smothering whatever wistful

illusion of comfort I'd just felt. Silence bounced off the walls and back at me, resounding and intolerant, and the emptiness of it all seeped through my bones into my very core, a mocking reminder that even Death—the Reaper, that unprejudiced asshole—had chosen to abandon me. I was truly and utterly alone.

I slammed shut the top on the piano and grabbed my acoustic guitar from its stand next to the piano bench. In a fit of rage, I hurled it across the room, only to have it land soundlessly and undamaged on my couch.

Pathetic.

I couldn't even break shit and make a scene like a normal person.

I clenched my fists and gritted my teeth. I was calling it. Time of death? *Now.* My lifelong love affair with music was done. It just hurt too goddamn much. I couldn't do it anymore.

I paced the floor restlessly before making my way to my kitchen island. Grabbing the bottle of pills on the countertop, I unscrewed the cap. Maybe this would be the last night I spent on this earth. Maybe . . . I wasn't that optimistic, though.

It wasn't the first time I'd played this sick game of Russian roulette. Technically, the first time should have been the last, but ingesting an entire bottle of pills had done nothing that desperate night almost a year ago, had borne no ill effects—I'd simply gone to bed and woken up again the next day, completely unaffected. Unbelievable! And ever the picture of health, I'd gone on with my life.

A few weeks after that, I'd ventured out into the middle of bustling traffic, walking from one side of the highway to the next—as leisurely as a high-society lady of old with her frilly parasol taking a stroll around the promenade—and not a single vehicle had even touched me. As well, no one had been any the wiser. Seriously—how was that even possible?

Fast forward to a month later when I'd jumped off a suspension bridge into the river more than a hundred feet below. All I'd managed was a weak splash—no word of a lie—and the currents had quickly towed me to the river bank, drenched like a drowned rat, but nevertheless unharmed.

All in all, as crazy as it sounded, I'd tried nine times, hoping each time that death would take me, but it was clear I was the brunt of some twisted and sadistic joke that God—if the bastard even existed—had chosen to play on me.

Only the ones I loved had felt the blade of death's scythe.

Never me.

I didn't understand. Had I done something terrible in a previous life to deserve this kind of enduring torture?

Tears stung my eyes as I dumped the contents of the bottle into my hand. Maybe the tenth time would be the charm. The potency on these was stronger than the ones I'd taken the first time. It had to work, it just had to. I was tired of living like this.

Grabbing the glass of water I'd left on the counter, I stuffed the pills into my mouth and took a drink to wash them down. Slowly, I made my way to my bedroom, my body drained and numb. I just wanted for it to be over, to close my eyes and lose myself to the darkness.

I wasn't alone.

I couldn't see anything, but I felt the presence of something . . . extraordinary. An odd sensation, as if my conscious self was floating above my slumbering self in a transitory realm.

My heart thudded excitedly, my body overcome with giddy

anticipation. A haunting melody floated around me, seeping into my mind, my soul, each spellbinding note clawing into me as if it belonged there. It was like . . . coming home. As if some part of my twisted soul claimed a kindred affinity with this wondrous and mysterious presence.

God Almighty! Had I succeeded this time? Was this at last the end of my suffering? Had I crossed over into the land of the dead to be reunited with the ones I loved?

The melody rose to a crescendo, and I shivered as a dusky glow appeared in front of me, moving and swaying mellifluously in a ripple of color. A woman appeared from within the undulating light, her hair a riot of violet curls, her eyes flashing silver as she approached me. She was the most majestic creature I'd ever seen. Surely, I was an unsightly hag in comparison. One with the light and the music, her body was wrapped in the soft, glowing mass, the melody springing forth from inside her.

Frozen, I stood, my legs wobbly and unsure as I beheld her magnificence. Her face was filled with raw joy as she regarded me intently. Coming to a stop in front of me, she took my hands in hers. A rush of power coursed through me at her touch.

"We do not have much time, cherished one," she whispered, her voice melodic and tinged with sadness. "For more than a century I have slept, and in so doing, I was robbed of what I awaited with bated breath for thousands of years. Your entire life was lost to me, but strangers no more we shall be. Long have I waited for this moment."

Wait, what? Thousands of years? What, for the love of God, was she talking about?

"Who are you?" I asked, my voice filled with confusion and wonder as I beheld the being I could not tear my eyes away from. "Where am I? Am I not dead?"

"No, my child. You are back where it all began—in the In-Between. As for who I am, what does your heart tell you?" She placed her hand on my chest, and my pulse quickened and reverberated through my body. Vivacity and strength exuded from her touch, and her presence made me feel alive and safe. I didn't know who she was, but as for what she made me feel—that was something else entirely.

"It tells me that you are life . . . redemption."

She smiled, her eyes shining with warmth and affection. "Tell me, do you know who *you* are, Eleyse?" Her gaze penetrated mine, as if searching deep inside me for the answer.

I wasn't sure how to respond. Who was I? What kind of answer was she looking for? "I am Eleyse Maren," I said, my mind at a loss. Geez, I was simple.

"The truth of who you are is much more than a name, my sweet Eleyse." She stroked my cheek gently and touched a tendril of my hair. "You are the Secret of the Gods."

Secret of the Gods? Was this a joke? What did that even mean?

She placed her palm on my heart and gazed at me, her eyes blazing silver. "No more seeking out the end, my heart. Your entire life with a paramount future awaits. All will be revealed in due time. When everything is laid bare, accept the truth of who you are. Claim it as your birthright. You will be many things to many living beings, but to yourself, you are whomever you choose to be. Never forget that. That omnipotence lies within you."

Wide-eyed, I looked at her, my heart aching, although I couldn't understand why. Something about this woman was soothing, causing every cynical, deprecating thought in my mind to shrivel up and die. I clung to her essence like an emaciated leech on supple, warm skin.

"And you?" I asked, my eyes lost in the silver fire of her eyes.

"What am I to you?"

She smiled tenderly and pulled me to her in an embrace. "You are to me what you've been from the moment I first learned of your existence: cherished. Leida mata." She pulled back and placed her hands on either side of my face. Pressing her lips against my forehead, she looked at me, her eyes filled with sadness. "Hold firm, precious one. This world will not break you. *He* comes, and on his heels, your future. It's almost time to soar again, Renala Cielta. To take to the heavens and fly."

I awoke with a gasp, the charged tendrils of energy that had riddled my dream still pulsing through my body. My heart hammered in my chest, at odds with the lingering silence that clung to my bedroom walls. Sunlight streamed in through the windows, swallowing the shadows from every corner of the room. The air around me felt lighter, less . . . dismal?

Okay. Clearly, I didn't die. But what had happened? Some kind of supernatural experience? Who was she—the magnificent woman in my dreams? Calling me by my name. Calling me other things—things that made no frigging sense. *Secret of the Gods. Leida mata. Renala Cielta.* What language was that even? What did it all mean? She'd entranced me, speaking to me with warmth and affection, like she knew me, cared for me.

Was she an illusion conjured by my mind or was she real? Perhaps she was an angel of light, dispatched by the heavens to curtail my destructive, hell-bound aspirations. Beseeching me to stop seeking out my end, her words had been tinged with sorrow and something else . . . desperation?

When she'd looked at me, her eyes had shone with untold emotion. In those silver depths, I was someone to be revered, treasured. I mattered. For as long as I lived, I would never forget that look.

He comes. A simple proclamation. Who in blazes was *he*? And what was my future?

I didn't know much of anything, but I knew one thing—knew it deep in my bones. She felt like hope. And hope was the one thing I no longer had in my life, but desperately needed. It had long since faded to dust, had been gathered and ground up with the dirt I'd crumbled in my fingers to scatter onto the graves of my dead loved ones.

I sat up and swung my legs off the side of the bed, padding softly to the bathroom. Staring at myself in the mirror, I touched my black, wavy hair—a god-awful tangled mess—and frowned at my gray eyes, still swollen from crying.

No more seeking out the end, my heart.

A trickle of resolve coursed through me. No more. Death didn't want me anyway. I'd try to give life a chance.

Your life with a glorious future awaits.

Hope. Longing. Possibility. I wanted it so much I could taste it. I would do it. I would try to live.

Chapter 1

THREE YEARS LATER . . .

The sound of crude laughter seeped into my consciousness, jarring me awake. What the—

Disorientation quickly gave way to panic at the feel of rough hands groping wildly at my breasts. Bloody hell, what kind of sadistic nightmare was this? Instinctively, I flung my arms and legs out, but my body was frozen in place, unable to move.

"She's a lovely thing, this one," a voice cackled from somewhere above me. "Look at the tits on her."

Brusque and hoarse, the words reverberated in the stillness as I struggled to open my heavy eyelids. Not even a flutter followed.

"I get to go next," another voice leered from behind my head.

"You'll get your turn after I've had my fill," the first voice snapped in response.

Gah! My body refused to obey me, as if mired in muck, lost in a nebulous fog, unable to find my way to safety.

Where the hell was I?

Beneath me, the ground was uneven and hard, with not an ounce of give. Cobblestone? The air smelled stale and musty, but there was nothing distinguishable to trigger my senses. A soft breeze stirred strands of hair on my face, and the ever-so-faint sound of crows cawing in the distance drifted to my ears.

Outside. I had to be outside somewhere. My heart pounded in

my chest. Not being able to see or move was terrifying.

Again, hands grabbed at my breasts, and a putrid smell invaded my nostrils as a mouth slid over mine, a slippery tongue prying my lips apart.

Oh fuck, no.

Strangely, my body responded, convulsing at the stench, and I dry heaved.

"You stupid creya!" the voice bellowed, and a flash of pain registered as a sharp blow connected with the side of my head.

Son of a bitch!

"Don't be greedy," the second voice piped in. "Let me have a go."

"No! She's mine until I'm done with her. Just hold her hands in place; she's coming to."

Two hands grabbed my arms, pinning them down, and to my horror, a knee ground into my thighs, prying my legs apart. I struggled to move, mentally pleading with my body to comply. Apart from the reflexive heaving a moment before, I had no control. My heart pummeled a wild staccato as the clink of a belt unbuckling reached my ears, and rough hands forced my legs open.

No, please, no! Not this! I begged the words to spill from my lips, but they remained shackled in the confines of my mind. I was powerless, my body a flaccid and gelatinous blob.

"Get away from her!" a voice commanded from the muffled periphery of my aural consciousness. A woman's voice, spoken with calm authority.

Relief washed through me. Oh, thank God!

"You want to join in, love?" the one on top of me asked, snickering loudly. "There's plenty of me to go around."

"Not anymore, there isn't," the woman replied softly, yet matter-of-factly, and just like that, there was silence.

The weight on top of me disappeared, and the hands pinning my arms down—they too were gone.

Holy shit! What had just happened? Where did the men go?

The unmistakable clicking of stilettos drew closer, and two hands gently lifted me to a sitting position. "Medra, you're in no shape to move," said the same woman from before. The tender brush of fingers lingered against my brow. "Let's get you safe."

Safe? For a brief moment, the fog cleared, and I opened my eyes to catch a glimpse of eyes the color of amethysts gazing intently at me. Then the blackness engulfed me once more, and I free-fell weightlessly into its welcoming arms.

Chapter 2

Bells—no—a clock was chiming somewhere in the distance.

What the— Where was I? My mind was foggy; vaguely, I remembered slipping in and out of consciousness, my dreams troubled and turbulent. Unable to tell night from day or to discern the passing of time, I was incapable of breaking free of the slumber that claimed me so completely however long ago it was.

Beads of sweat prickled my brow, and I opened my eyes fully as the haze dissipated. My lips tingled as a blast of something cool and minty swirled in my mouth, coating my throat. What the hell? I ran my tongue over my teeth. Why did it feel like I'd just left the dentist? Strange.

I moved my arms and legs slowly, a surge of triumph coursing through me when they obeyed. As my heartbeat slowed and returned to normal, I looked up cautiously at my surroundings.

Holy lap of ostentatious luxury! I was propped up by soft, fluffy pillows in an enormous four-poster bed, the likes of which I had never seen before. The pillars on each corner of the bed were monstrous, with intricate carvings chiseled across the entire length of the dark wood. I wiggled my feet against the cool sheets on the plush mattress, savoring the softness against my skin. A girl could get used to this. But where in blazes was *this*?

Against the wall in front of the bed stood a magnificent stone fireplace where a warm flame crackled quietly in the hearth, throwing heat in my direction. The fireplace mantel and stone pillars, like the four-poster bed, were covered with ornate carvings. I drank in the beauty of the workmanship and marveled at the detail that adorned every part of it. Whatever this place was, it screamed wealth. Which begged the question—how the hell did I end up here?

I squinted at the large, gilded design piece that hung above the mantel, my brows furrowing as I tried to make sense of it.

Round.

Clock-like.

But all along the inside edge, instead of *numbers*, *words* were carved in exquisite print.

I scratched my head as I read them. Strange. They were all *feelings*.

Happy. Sad. Angry. Pensive. Brave. Lonely. Amorous. Spiteful. Playful. Afraid. Cautious. Lost.

In the center were three silver stars. My gaze drifted up to the top of the peculiar object where a golden arrow was affixed, pointing straight up.

As I continued to study the piece, a soft whirring sound broke the silence, emanating from the object itself.

Crap. What was happening?

The arrow at the top began to glow, the stars in the center moving outward toward the carved words. Each star came to settle in front of a particular word, lit up in bright silver.

Pensive. Cautious. Afraid.

What the heck was this used for? And what did it even mean?

My attention snagged on the tall cylindrical object next to the fireplace—about as tall as I was, long and slender. An hourglass of sorts. The sand at the top was an incandescent silver, but the sand that sifted through the neck and collected into the crystal chamber below was blue. I'd never seen anything like it before.

Seriously, what was this place? It was so peculiar, I half expected an eccentric wizard to come floating through the door, pointy hat askew and wand in hand.

The coffered ceilings in the room had to be at least twelve feet tall, and the moldings mirrored the workmanship displayed throughout the entire space. On the other side of the fireplace, two massive wooden doors flanked the entrance to the room, and on my far left stood another door, leading to what I presumed was a bathroom. Whoever owned this house definitely had money. Every inch of this place was spectacular.

To my right, two floor-to-ceiling glass doors opened onto an uncovered, circular balcony. One of the doors was slightly ajar, and from the pale light filtering in from outside, I surmised that it was either close to sunrise or sunset.

I closed my eyes and breathed in the air. Crisp and fresh. Although a fire burned quietly in the hearth, a cool breeze drifted in softly from outside. The aroma was heady—lavender and jasmine, mingled with wisps of dew-kissed evergreen—and as I inhaled deeply, a strange tug pulled inside me—an unexplained sense of connection to what lay outside, beyond the walls of my room.

It was morning; I inexplicably sensed it. With my eyes still closed, I gave myself over to an onslaught of feeling, and in the stillness of the new day, the soft trill of a songbird echoed outside my window. The melody was bewitching and sorrowful, my emotions shifting as the bird continued its song.

In my mind's eye, a creature took form. A beautiful woman in a silver and lavender gown, her head adorned with a crown of sapphires and amethysts, stood at the edge of a precipice. With one step forward, a pair of wings unfurled across her back—an intense riot of shimmery color—and she leapt off the edge and soared majestically through the air into the night.

The bird outside stopped singing, taking the vision of the woman with wings with it, breaking the connection.

My mind reeled.

This was all very . . . trippy.

Had my imagination conjured the image of the woman with wings? And what about the melody? Surely I hadn't imagined that too? It was raw and primal, stirring waters deep and restless inside me.

As I pulled my body into a sitting position, a twinge of pain shot up my left leg. I slid the duvet down, gasping at the thick bandages wrapped around my thigh.

What the hell? How had I gotten hurt?

The throbbing was dull and intermittent, but I could still move my leg without too much discomfort. Touching the area gingerly, I grimaced as the soreness deepened, but I couldn't gauge the nature of the injury without undoing the bandages.

Before I could assess the wound any further, soft shuffling outside my room drew my attention, followed by a gentle knock. With a quiet creak, the door opened.

A beautiful woman with bright amethyst eyes strode purposefully into the room. Lips parted, I stared at her in wonder.

Those eyes . . . Strikingly familiar.

She was movie-star gorgeous. Inky-blue hair cascaded down her shoulders in shiny waves, bouncing softly around her face as she made her way to the bed. Fitted, black pants molded to her legs like a second skin, her feet decked in high-heeled ankle boots. A red silk blouse clung intimately to her body.

Exuding confidence with each step she took, her presence filled me with a reassuring calm I couldn't understand. Teeth gritted, I wrestled for control of my emotions, my subconscious's immediate acceptance of her presence only serving to incite my rational mind, sending it on guard.

"I am so happy you're awake." The woman's smile was warm as she sat on the edge of the bed and took my hand. "When I found you in the alleyway, I feared the worst."

Wow. She was bubbly. And airy. And . . . sunny. Every cell in my body leaned in, basking in the warmth she exuded, longing for even a fraction of her energy to seep into me. I mentally slapped myself, shoving the reins of control back to my cold, rational mind. I needed to focus.

What did she say? The alleyway . . . Right. The memory of my two attackers came flooding back.

I furrowed my brows. "You . . . you rescued me."

"Yes. My name is Gwynn." Her amethyst eyes crinkled as she regarded me.

Gwynn. I struggled to remember my own name, but then it came to me, as if out of a dream. "I'm Eleyse." I sat up higher in the bed. "Where am I? What is this place?"

"Do you remember how you got here, Eleyse?" Gwynn asked gently.

"In this bed?"

"Oh, Medra, no. I brought you here. I mean, do you remember how you got to Ariadna?"

Medra? Ariadna? What the— "I'm sorry. I don't understand. I've never heard of them before."

"Eleyse," Gwynn said, her forehead creasing as she regarded me, "do you remember where you're from?"

My mind was a jumbled mess of thoughts. Why was she asking me that? And how had I gotten to this Ariadna she spoke of? I didn't even remember leaving the city.

My gaze flitted to hers. "I'm from Hargrove, a city in central Canada. Is Ariadna near there?"

Gwynn pursed her lips in a thin line, the muscle in her jaw clenched. "What do you remember from before the alley?"

I opened my mouth to speak and immediately shut it, my lips quivering in confusion.

What *was* the last thing I remembered?

Staying late at the office and then deciding to go to Crusoe's for a drink before going home.

Yes—wait, no. That wasn't right. There was more.

But what?

I bit my lip and tried again. I searched my mind, but no matter how hard I tried, I couldn't remember what happened after I got to Crusoe's. Dammit, it was right there, on the periphery of my consciousness, but I couldn't grab hold of it.

"I remember going out to the bar near my office for a drink," I said aloud, "but after that, it's all fuzzy. I mean, I know there's more, but I can't remember. It feels . . . strange. Like a chunk is missing."

"All will be well, Eleyse." Gwynn squeezed my fingers. "I will help you in whatever way I can. I promise."

Promises. Someone had promised me something very important and didn't keep it. I shook my head and tried to remember more.

Crap. Nothing.

"Did something come to you?" Gwynn asked.

"Just a flash," I answered. "In my mind, it feels like it's right there, but it's just out of reach."

"What about we start with your age? How old are you?"

My age . . . My mind went blank, and a wave of panic surged.

How old was I?

"Umm . . ." I said, waiting for it to come to me. "I just turned twenty-eight."

Yeah. That sounded right. Right? But if some of my memories were missing, it meant I was older than twenty-eight. But how much older? This was infuriating. What was wrong with me?

Gwynn smoothed her hands over her pants, her glossy red nails a stark contrast against the black fabric. "Well, my uncle, Andreo, should be back later today, and if there's anyone who will be able to help you, it's him."

Anxiety crept over me, heat rushing to my head with each breath I took. How could her uncle help me? Where was this place? How did I end up here? And how did I get hurt? The gaping hole in my mind riled my frustration, raising my hackles.

"Do you know what happened to my leg?" I asked, pushing the duvet aside to look at my bandaged thigh.

Gwynn frowned. "I'm sorry, but I don't. In the alleyway, when I found you, you weren't wearing any clothes, and the stitches on your wound were ripped open, probably during the assault. I applied some healing ointment and re-bandaged it when I brought you here. The gash was pretty nasty and swollen."

"Hold on. I didn't have any clothes on?" Had the sickos who assaulted me taken them off? What the hell was going on? Again, I tried to go back in my mind past the alleyway, but I slammed into a wall of unnerving silence that stretched all around me, trapping me in a sea of shifting fog and shadows.

My emotions must have been projected on my face because Gwynn squeezed my hand gently. "You've been through a terrible ordeal, Eleyse. I know this must all be very confusing. Please rest assured that you are safe here. Why don't you have a warm bath and then join me on the terrace for breakfast? Your bandage is water resistant, so you don't have to worry about getting the wound wet. The bathroom is right through there." She pointed to the door I noticed earlier. "Pick out anything you want to wear. All the clothes and accessories in the closet should fit you. If you need anything, just touch the orb near the wall, and I'll come to you."

She inclined her head toward a crystal orb above me, adjacent to the bed. It hovered in mid-air, peculiar splinters of blue light floating around inside. This was technology I had never seen before, reinforcing my earlier thoughts that whoever owned this house was stinking rich.

"Are you going to be all right?" Gwynn asked.

I nodded, even though I wasn't sure of anything at the moment. Everything felt . . . different.

I shifted my weight and turned to look at Gwynn. Although everything I knew about her could comfortably fit on the tiny freckle on my thumb I was always poking at, I instinctively felt I could trust her. That in itself scared the shit out of me given how guarded I was when it came to people I didn't know. The moment she had breezed into the room, trailing warmth and charisma behind her, she'd slipped past my defenses, and I couldn't help but feel at ease around her.

My head swarmed with questions. I closed my eyes, forcing myself to inhale slowly. A bath would do me good, give me a chance to clear my mind and regroup. I nodded once more, coaxing a smile to my lips.

Gwynn patted my hand and rose from the bed. "If you need anything, touch the orb, okay? I'll see you downstairs for breakfast when you're ready." She squeezed my fingers lightly before heading toward the door.

Chapter 3

I GOT OUT OF bed and cautiously made my way to the bathroom. The sound of running water greeted me, and I stopped short at the door, my jaw dropping open at the sight before me. A fricking pool? This was pinch-me-I'm-dreaming decadent! Steam rose off the water in billowing wisps, beckoning invitingly.

I looked around the chamber. Polished marble floors. Same material on the countertops and pool. Gilded sconces adorned the soft gray walls, all lit with a blue flame—the same type of light in the orb earlier. An ornate chandelier hung from the ceiling over the center of the pool. What the hell was this place? I had never been anywhere this opulent before.

Of their own accord, my legs moved across the room, and my eyes greedily drank in everything within their line of sight. A beautiful vanity was ensconced opposite the sink, complete with a velvet cushioned bench on weighty oak legs.

Across from the bathing pool, double doors led to a massive walk-in closet showcasing a large collection of clothing, undergarments, accessories, and shoes. Everything was organized neatly and laid out with exacting precision. I was in heaven. Seriously! Did people really live like this?

I made my way back to the pool and slipped off my nightdress. Dipping one toe into the warm water, I slowly made my way down the steps and sank backward, sighing in contentment as the water enveloped my body. The moment I was immersed, jets around the tub came to life, massaging me gently. Soapy bubbles coalesced in thick, foamy waves across the water.

Yep. Definitely filthy rich.

Easing my body onto the curved marble chaise that was built into the pool, I let my thoughts carry me away. What had I gotten myself into? Gwynn didn't seem to know how I had gotten here, and I couldn't remember. Something had to have happened for me to end up in that alley. And why couldn't I remember anything after walking into Crusoe's? How long ago was that? It was the very last thing I had any clear memories of, but I *knew* there was more to it. But how much more?

I finished my bath hurriedly, wrapped myself in a bathrobe, and stepped into the closet to get dressed. Gwynn was right. Everything in the closet was just my size. I settled on a soft, ankle-length floral sundress that hugged my curves and flowed softly around me as I walked. It reminded me of one I owned. Belting a braided silver cord at my waist, I eyed the collection of shoes at the far end of the wall. I picked out a pair of white leather sandals and slipped them on.

I sat at the vanity, my eyes immediately drawn to the assortment of earrings that lay open in a jewelry box. Choosing a pair of jade-colored ones in the shape of a crescent moon, I slipped them into my lobes and gingerly picked up an ornate, gilded hairbrush with hand-carved blossoms all over it. I admired it for a moment before running it through my long, wavy hair. As my eyes made contact with my reflection in the mirror, I almost slid off the bench.

My hair was a deep shade of violet. Violet! What the actual fuck? How had I not noticed it before? It looked so unnatural on me. When the hell did I dye it that color? My hair was always as black as night. Once in college, I'd experimented with highlights, but had quickly decided it wasn't for me, and after my hair grew out, I'd left it my natural color and hadn't changed it since.

My eyes were still gray, but peculiar silver flecks were peppered amid their depths. Prickly tendrils of unease trailed over me. Something was very wrong, and I couldn't make sense of it.

My face itself, mercifully, was familiar to me—almond-shaped eyes, tanned complexion, full mouth, and slightly upturned nose. My fingers were long and—

A flash of my fingers intertwined with what were definitely a man's fingers flitted briefly across my mind. I was sitting at a piano, and a masculine forearm draped down my shoulder, fingers interlaced with mine.

I dropped the brush and stared at myself in the mirror, my eyes wide with alarm. *What the hell was that? Remember! Remember!* To my frustration, the veil of forgetfulness quickly slipped back into place, shrouding my mind in haze and disarray again.

A mistake for sure. That couldn't have been a flash of me. I certainly would not be cozying up with a man that way. Especially not seated in front of my hallowed piano that I hadn't touched in a year. And why, for the love of God, did the image of those fingers make me feel excited . . . aroused? Something was definitely wrong.

Abruptly, I got to my feet and padded over to the bathroom sink. As my hands absently drifted into the basin, the faucet automatically turned on, warm water splashing onto my skin. In the next breath, with no assistance from me, my hands were worked into a soapy lather, then quickly rinsed off. A blast of cool air shot onto my fingers, drying my hands in less than a second. I stared at them in confusion. Holy frig. It truly was incredible the shit rich people could afford.

And yet, there was no toothpaste or toothbrush. Or any kind of lotions. My skin was incredibly soft after my bath, though, so I couldn't complain. I ran my index finger across my teeth, recalling the cool, minty taste in my mouth when I woke up. I stared in the mirror, my perplexed expression staring back at me.

I slowly made my way back into the bedroom. I needed to get answers. What had Gwynn said about using the orb to summon her? I didn't even know where the terrace was. I walked to the edge of my room and opened the balcony doors.

Sweet, merciful God! The view outside stole my breath away.

The house was built at the top of a mountain overlooking a deep valley. As far as my eyes could see, the trees were a kaleidoscope of color—blue, silver, lavender—screaming out for notice, but the colors were not just vibrant, they *shimmered*. The shimmer was amplified by the bright sunlight streaming onto the expansive vista.

My jaw dropped open. What kind of trees were these? Where the hell was Ariadna?

The fragrances that had softly wafted into the bedroom earlier were now intensified out here in the open. I closed my eyes and inhaled, like a cat sniffing the air in successive bursts, unable to get enough. Just like before, a strange tug at the center of my body drew me in, connecting me to my surroundings. It was as if I was seeing and breathing for the first time in my life.

A large terrace spread out on the grounds below me, winding a path to a rectangular-shaped infinity pool. From my vantage point, the water sparkled like diamonds in the dappled sunlight. To my left and right were several other balconies with views of the valley, and I shifted my gaze to the floor above me that boasted a lone balcony several times the size of the one I stood on now. Whose was that?

On the terrace below, I glimpsed Gwynn walking toward a table laden with food. Answers. That's what I needed. And she was the one who had them. It was time to find out what was going on.

I made my way out the bedroom door Gwynn had used, stepping onto a wide, long, circular landing. Two curved staircases beckoned on both ends of the floor, and I headed for the one closest to me. Overhead, an enormous crystal chandelier—fashioned out of what looked like a single slab of crystal—was suspended from the top of the vaulted ceiling on the third floor, extending all the way down to the second floor, refracting shards of light throughout the sweeping interior. It was magnificent. My mouth gaped open in amazement. This place was nothing short of palatial.

At the foot of the marble staircase, I spied the terrace on my right and made my way toward it. Gwynn, seated at the table, waved me over as I stepped out into the sunshine.

"You look lovely," she said, beckoning to a chair next to her. "I love those earrings on you."

"Thanks." I sat down, and Gwynn quickly offered me a plate.

"Please, eat something. You must be famished. You were in bed for two days, and except for some water and broth, you haven't had anything to eat."

At the sight of the feast on the table, my stomach grumbled loudly. I surveyed the spread in front of me, trying not to drool: pastries, toast, eggs, sausages, ham, bacon, cured meats. An array of fresh fruit was arranged on a platter—some that I recognized, and others that were strange to me.

"You must try the lendelwin." Gwynn pointed to a heart-shaped turquoise fruit. "It grows exclusively in the Sangwene Valley here and is in season right now. Our housekeeper, Ezla, makes the most delicious spiced jam from it."

Lendelwin? What on earth? Was I in a different country? Blue and silver trees. Strange fruit. There was nothing like this in Canada. This place was different. It *felt* strange and new.

I reached across the table and picked up the fruit that Gwynn had pointed to, turning it around in my hand, tracing the heart shape with my fingers. Almost perfectly symmetrical. The skin was soft and fuzzy, like a peach, indenting as I pressed on it.

Gwynn reached for one and took a bite, sighing in contentment as she chewed slowly. "I hate that the season for these is so short," she said between bites. "They're my absolute favorite."

Following her lead, I slowly brought the fruit to my lips. I mean, she'd just eaten it, so it was clearly safe to eat. Right?

I took a bite, my mouth exploding with flavor. Oh my God. What devilry was this?

The lendelwin was sweet and tart at the same time—like orange infused with chocolate and ginger, and the smell was glorious—citrus and something else I couldn't quite place. The juices trickled down my fingers as I bit into it, and I licked them off, wiping the residue on a napkin.

I stared at Gwynn, mentally organizing my thoughts. "What is this place?" I set my napkin aside. "You said that we are in Ariadna, but where *is* Ariadna? These trees . . ." I gestured to the valley in front of us. "I have never seen trees with such magnificent colors that take my breath away."

"I can only imagine how confusing this must be, Eleyse. I'll try to explain things as best as I can." Gwynn squeezed my hand gently. "But you must understand that there are some things about your predicament I don't have the answers for. I will, however, do my best to get to the bottom of it all."

"Okay . . ." I said cautiously.

She smiled and furrowed her brows thoughtfully. "Well then, where should I start?" Her foot tapped soundlessly on the cobblestone. "You are from the human world, Earth. Correct?" Her eyes were guarded as she studied me.

I stared at her blankly and narrowed my eyes. "What do you mean?" Why was she looking at me like that? Like I was slow. And why the "You are from the human world?" Where else would I be from?

"You see, Eleyse, Ariadna is an entirely different world."

I blinked, my mind drawing a complete blank. "I'm sorry, what?"

Good God. What was in the lendelwin? Did it have hallucinogenic properties?

"Ariadna exists in a neighboring galaxy to Earth," she went on, "in a distant sliver known as the Sangelis. I'm sure you know that in the vast expanse of the universe, billions of galaxies abound. Well, some of them contain worlds with civilizations of life-forms; others are barren and void. Are you with me so far?"

Oh. She was being serious! I gawked at her—wide-eyed and slack-jawed—as if she had spoken another language. Really? This had to be some kind of joke. What nonsense was this?

But even as my rational mind exploded with disbelief and confusion over the utter lunacy of what she'd said, a soothing hum vibrated inside me, lulling me, placating me, as if whispering, *There, there, don't be so closed-minded.* Or maybe that was the yawning emptiness in my soul talking, grasping at straws for any sliver of excitement to cling to. Whatever it was, I swatted it away.

"I have no idea what you're talking about." I swallowed down the rising bile creeping into my throat. "I don't know of any other civilized worlds in existence. And *if* what you're saying is even true, how do you know which world I'm from if there are other worlds with life-forms out there? We look the same physically. Even your clothes look like clothes I'm used to seeing."

Gwynn hesitated, chewing on her lip and tapping her fingers against her cheek. She leaned forward in her chair. "Well, a couple factors led me to that conclusion. First, humans are the only species from another world that bear an almost-identical physical resemblance to Ariadnans. At least from the civilized worlds that we know of. I know you're not Ariadnan because you don't have a Drukhiu." She lifted her blouse to reveal a crescent-shaped, red birthmark on her right hip. "Every child in Ariadna bears the mark of the dominion in which they were born. I also did an origin scan on you, and it confirmed your human descent."

"Origin scan?" I asked.

"Yes, it's an assessment we can do here to cross-reference beings from known worlds."

My head spun with the incredulity of it all. A different world. Identifying birthmarks. Origin scans to cross-reference beings from other worlds. Geez. This was something plucked straight from a sci-fi movie.

I shook my head, trying to ground my thoughts. "Are you being serious right now? Or is this all an elaborate prank someone is playing on me?" I glared at her, looking for any signs of deceit or trickery.

A flash of what looked like hurt flickered in her eyes for a second before shifting to something else—kindness, sympathy. "I can assure you, this is not a joke, Eleyse. I would never do something so cruel." Her words were firm, filled with resolve. "Do you really mean to tell me that you don't believe it could be a possibility for life to exist outside of the human world? That you haven't thought about it?"

Well, of course I'd thought about it before. Instinctively, I wanted to believe her, to trust her, but . . . well, what she was saying went beyond the realm of possibility of everything I *knew* to be true.

Gwynn leaned forward in her chair, her eyes flaring with intensity. "There is something special about you, Eleyse, that I can't explain."

"What do you mean?" I asked.

"Well, you're human, but you can communicate in Valkyn, one of the languages spoken here in Ariadna. You speak it fluently, without any trace of an accent in your voice."

"Wait," I blurted out, my voice shrill and panicked. "What do you mean I'm speaking another language? Are we not speaking English?" In my head, that was the language I was hearing and responding in. Wasn't it?

Holy shit, that lendelwin *was* something else.

Gwynn shook her head. "No, you're definitely speaking Valkyn, one of the four main Ariadnan languages."

"How is that even possible?" This was beyond weird. For the life of me, my brain was still understanding everything she was saying. It had to be English. Had to be. I looked at her in confusion. "English is the *only* language I speak, Gwynn. I mean, I know a smidgen of French, but I can barely string a full sentence together, if you know what I mean."

She lightly touched my hand. "That's why I'm convinced there is more to you than meets the eye. That you are a human and can communicate here seamlessly defies explanation."

At the sound of footsteps behind me, I turned to see a tall, fair-haired man approaching us. He was wearing a worn leather jacket, a gray shirt unbuttoned at the neck, and dark, form-fitting pants. His blond hair was tousled and fell in soft waves around his face. He walked with a confident swagger, and as he drew closer, I was struck by the color of his eyes—a piercing silver-blue that held my gaze hostage for a moment.

"Far!" Gwynn shrieked with delight, jumping up to embrace the stranger.

He lifted her off her feet in one swift movement and twirled her around. "You're a sight for sore eyes, Gwynnie," he said, planting a kiss on her brow. "Medra, I've missed your gorgeous face."

That word again. Medra. Must be slang for something.

"I've missed you, too, you handsome devil," Gwynn replied fondly, mussing his hair. "Did you come from Torannon?"

"No, I came straight here from Nesda after I got your message." He looked over at me questioningly, and my gaze dipped to the jagged, faded scar on his upper lip that ended at the base of his nostril, marring his otherwise perfect features.

"This is Eleyse. She's the one I told you about." Gwynn turned to me and touched my shoulder. "Eleyse, this is Faron Cardinin. He and his twin sister, Astrid, are very close friends with my brother and me." Her voice and her face were filled with affection as she made the introduction.

"It's a pleasure to meet you, Eleyse," Faron said, extending his hand. "Gwynn mentioned the regrettable circumstances under which you both met."

I shook his hand, unsure what to say, my eyes flitting across his frame. Like Gwynn, he was gorgeous—smoking hot, but in a ripped, sexy surfer sort of way.

"Eleyse and I were just talking," Gwynn said. "She doesn't remember anything about how she ended up here."

Faron looked at me sympathetically and slipped into the chair next to mine. "I'm sure Andreo will be able to help you," he said reassuringly. "If there's anyone who can find answers, it's him.

Have you received word from him yet?" he asked, turning to Gwynn.

"Yes, he should be here later today. What of Ash? Any word?"

"No, I haven't seen him since Torannon last week," he said. "I'll deny it if you tell him, but I'm starting to get worried. It's been quiet on the Kaliope front, and that makes me nervous about what might be brewing. It's not like Ash to disappear like this without telling one of us where he was going."

Ash. My heart fluttered at the name. There was something familiar about it. I tried to make the connection, but the knowledge hovered somewhere on the outskirts of my memory, dangling just out of reach. A flash of piercing emerald-green eyes flitted across my mind. To my utter bewilderment, that same feeling of carnal excitement from earlier bubbled to the surface again, leaving me aching for something I couldn't make sense of.

"We both know my brother can take care of himself," Gwynn said. "Especially from *her.*"

"Oh, I know. That's not what I'm worried about."

"Do I know Ash?" I blurted out loud, my heart tittering in excitement at the sound of his name on my lips.

"Asher is my brother," Gwynn said, the shadow of a frown on her face. "Is everything all right?"

"I don't know," I said. "It's just that when you said his name, I felt something—a burst of happiness, and then . . . Maybe it's nothing. Perhaps I just know someone else by that name."

Faron exchanged looks with Gwynn.

I studied them silently. An elaborate ruse . . . Gwynn had seemed offended at the semi-accusation, but what else could it be? Was Faron in on it too?

I crossed my arms across my chest. "Let's just say for a moment that this isn't all a joke. You said earlier that every child bears the mark of the dominion in which they were born? What's a dominion?"

Gwynn leaned back in her chair. "Four dominions rule over Ariadna: Valkyse in the west, which is where we are now; Averon in the east; Solanis in the north; and Tandor in the south."

Valkyse. I knew that name. But how?

I twisted the napkin on the table between my fingers. "If Ariadna is an entirely different world, how did I get here?"

"That's an answer I don't have, unfortunately." Gwynn leaned forward in her chair. "Ariadna is known as the Medial Realm; it acts as a gateway, so to speak. Portals exist here that open to other worlds, but they are heavily warded, and travel between worlds is not a common occurrence. Travel between worlds is also one-sided, meaning that the portals open from Ariadna into other worlds, not the other way around. Which makes your presence here all the more intriguing."

Gateways. Portals. Travel between worlds. This was getting more far-fetched by the moment, but for the life of me, I couldn't ignore that tiny whisper inside me that chirped, *Truth, truth.* What was happening to me?

Faron leaned forward in his chair, his body angled closer to mine. "Trust me, Eleyse, if I were you, I'd be wondering what fuckery this was too. It's a lot to wrap your head around. As skeptical as you might be, for what it's worth, just know that you are safe here in the Dominion of Valkyse." He smiled, his eyes shining with sincerity.

"And that's another mystery by itself," Gwynn said. "How you came to be here. No human has ever crossed over into Ariadna, which makes me think that divine intervention is at play."

"Divine intervention? What does that mean?" I shook my head and rubbed my temples.

"I fear that I am overwhelming you." Gwynn pursed her lips. "I know it's a lot to absorb."

"You said that this place—the *dominion* where we are—is . . . Valkyse?" I looked around, absorbing everything in my line of sight.

"Yes. I am Gwynnis Valkyse. My family has ruled over Valkyse for thousands of years."

"Hold up. You're . . . a queen?" I asked, my eyeballs threatening to pop out of my head.

"No, I am a Valkyse," Gwynn said simply. "My brother is the Sovereign of Valkyse. He inherited the rule after our parents were killed over a century ago."

Oh God, this was the end of the road for my poor eyeballs. I shut my lids quickly and shook my head. "Come again? Did you say they were killed over a *century* ago? How old are you?"

"I am forty-eight years into my second century," she said, then inclined her head toward Faron. "Faron is a year into his third, as is my brother."

My mouth dropped open, my eyes darting between them. "You're fucking kidding me, right? You both look the same age. And you don't look any older than I do."

Faron smiled, reaching for a cluster of grapes from a platter on the table. "Life spans are different here than what you know to be normal in the human world. The Ethereal Harmonies keep Ariadna preserved with their magic and give the gift of longevity."

"The Ethereal what?" This was unreal. My mind was on overload. This defied everything my rational mind knew to be possible. Preposterous.

Gwynn shifted her legs and leaned closer. "The Ethereal Harmonies are the life source of the Sangelis. They exist within Ariadna's core and are the source of all life, power, and magic in Ariadna. They are also responsible for keeping the Sangelis in balance."

I blinked rapidly, trying to put what she just said into context. I just didn't have any frame of reference to compare these Ethereal Harmonies to. Life source. Balance. Was it like the concept of God?

"So they're a real thing? Like, can you see them?"

"We can certainly see manifestations of their power," Faron answered, crossing his ankles as he stretched his long frame in the chair. "But no one, as far as we know, has actually been to the true source that is contained within the heart of Ariadna."

"Unless you believe Nezra Reardon's stories," Gwynn said, cocking her head.

Faron snorted. "Nezra Reardon is as batty as they come, Gwynn. Too much fleha mushroom tonic has melted the old bird's mind."

I stared at them, observing their relaxed rapport with each other, which truth be told, was putting me at ease.

"What do you mean you can see manifestations of their power?" I asked, narrowing my eyes.

Faron's brows knitted. "Well, for starters, the majority of power and magic in this world come from the Ethereal Harmonies. And that is manifest everywhere throughout Ariadna."

"There is truly magic in this world?" My voice crackled with disbelief.

Gwynn and Faron both nodded.

"Yes," Gwynn said, "but only the celestial beings and Sovereign bloodlines can wield it. There are many artifacts of power that allow those without magic to harness special abilities, but most of them draw strength from the Ethereal Harmonies."

Holy crap. This was surreal. There had to be another explanation for my predicament. People didn't just wake up in different worlds filled with magic and mysterious power sources. But what other explanation could there be? Maybe I had hit my head and was lying in a wild coma somewhere dreaming this all up? Or maybe I was hopped up on some pretty insane drugs and hallucinating my ass off? Without my memory to tell me what had happened after I walked into Crusoe's, I had no idea what the hell was going on.

Everything Gwynn and Faron had said sounded completely bonkers. Like loony-bin, lock-me-up-and-throw-away-the-key bonkers.

So why then, why for the life of me, could I not shake the blistering persistence inside me exhorting me to believe?

Faron leaned back in his chair and folded his arms across his chest. "As the Sovereign of Valkyse, Ash wields the most magic of anyone in the Dominion of Valkyse. The Ethereal Harmonies imbue their power directly into him."

Ash . . . Asher Valkyse. Yes. That sounded right. I did know that name. A sense of security and wild longing brushed against the recesses of my mind, soothing the unease and confusion rattling around inside me. Another flash surfaced—full lips tipped in a smile; deep, throaty laughter. Who was Ash to me? Deep inside, something reared its head in a restless frenzy, chomping at the bit to be set loose, to bolt and run, but where? Why?

My frustration mounted as a sense of helplessness washed over me. A sudden burst of pain ripped through my temples as flashes of light pulsed in front of my eyes.

"I . . . I'd like to lie down now." I hunched forward as a wave of nausea rolled over me. "I think I'm going to be sick."

"Oh, certainly, Eleyse," Gwynn replied, a look of concern lining her face as she got to her feet. "Get some rest, and if you need anything, touch the orb in your room. I'll let you know when Uncle Andreo gets here."

I stood and smiled shakily at Faron. "It was lovely to meet you."

"I'll see you again soon, Eleyse," he replied, standing and taking my hand once more, and with that, I left the terrace and walked back to my room, my head pounding with each step I took.

I crawled into bed and covered my face with a pillow to block out the light, and although a million thoughts were racing through my mind, pain tore through my skull. My eyes went heavy and slack, and as quick as a flash, the ferryman of dreams bade me welcome and carried me away.

Chapter 4

"WAKE UP, ELEYSE," A voice whispered through my slumber.

I moaned and slowly opened my eyes. The pounding in my head was gone, and I rubbed my temple slowly as I slid the pillow off my face.

Holy mother of God! I gripped the sheets beneath me, my body taut and unmoving. The woman I had seen in my mind earlier that morning, the one wearing the lavender gown and the crown on her head—the songbird with wings—was sitting on the edge of my bed! As casual and serene as a gentle breeze . . . or an axe murderer sweetly gazing upon their prey, depending on how you looked at it. My mind flitted between the two visuals, sending my heart rate soaring.

I quickly flashed back to the strange dream of another mysterious, beautiful woman. How long ago was that? A year ago? Based on the last thing I remembered, it would be thereabouts. I never forgot about her. Was this connected somehow?

"Don't be afraid," the woman in front of me said, reaching out her hand toward me. "You have nothing to fear from me. We are bound by fate, you and I."

Bound by fate? Oh God, should I let her touch me? To my bewilderment, as her fingers closed over mine, warmth seeped through my skin, and the uncertainty and fear drained out of my body, leaving me with a curious calm and sense of kinship.

Again, my mind conjured up the woman from my long-ago dream. It was clear that it wasn't the same woman; the one standing in front of me was more slender and not as tall, her hair and face different. There was, however, something eerily similar in nature to both their auras and appearances.

"Are you an angel?" I asked, spellbound by her magnetic presence.

The woman squeezed my fingers. "I am a phantom of Ariadna's past, here to bear witness and usher in its future."

Okay then. Phantom. Like, was she a literal phantom? A ghost? Or did phantom mean something else here? Seriously. How much more cryptic could she be?

Despite the vague response, something inside me churned restlessly, urging me to go to her. My indecision lasted all of two seconds, the burning compulsion winning out over my fears. Fingers crossed she wasn't an axe murderer, I rose from the bed and followed her through the open door onto the balcony. Her silver-blue hair fanned out behind her as she walked, and when she turned to look at me, her eyes glittered in the moonlight. My hand flew to my mouth as I stared at her. *Her eyes.* They were silver, just like the eyes of the woman from my dream. Two beautiful, mysterious women with flashing silver eyes. It *couldn't* be a coincidence.

The woman transformed into the being with wings, and I was struck again by how magnificent she was. She still retained her womanly form, but a crystal mask of sorts, embedded with gemstones, now covered the top half of her face. Her wings unfurled behind her in a shimmer of color, and she beckoned for me to come closer.

"Is this a dream?" I asked, completely in awe of her splendor.

Her eyes twinkled as she smiled at me. "You physically sleep, but your consciousness is here with me. Do not be afraid."

Caught up in her spell, I took her hand, and to my amazement, my body shifted into mist and seeped into hers, my form encapsulated somewhere within her, like a genie in a bottle. Together, as one, we leapt over the edge and took to the skies, soaring across the mountains.

A rush of adrenaline coursed through me, my heart racing with excitement. So unbelievably free. I was fucking flying! The moon—mammoth and lambent—hung low in the valley and lit up the night with an ethereal glow. It was breathtaking.

Suddenly, I was struck with the most intense feeling of déjà vu. The wind whipping around me, the rush, the world stretched out before me, the freedom—so familiar, swooping in to settle around me like a favored cloak. It made absolutely no sense.

Up ahead, a cliff loomed in the distance, and we turned in that direction. Closer we came, heading straight for a shadowy escarpment, and with one swift move, we landed on a ledge jutting out of the cliff face.

As the woman with wings stood on the rocky surface, I separated from her back into my own form, and she gestured for me to follow her. The ground rattled beneath my feet, and before my eyes, the cliff face above the ledge opened to reveal a cave. Trepidation and anticipation tangled together, heating my blood. What was this place? Some kind of secret lair?

The woman stepped inside and inclined her head toward me. Shockwaves of excitement pulsed under my skin as I followed her in, and as we walked, golden lanterns of blue flames came to life to light the path on either side of us. A low, melodic humming lilted through the emptiness of the cave, each note holding my mind hostage. I had heard this cadence before.

Deeper into the belly of the cavern we walked until I saw a

floating platform above us, flooded with blue light. As we drew closer, a crystal staircase materialized, and the woman turned and took my hand, leading me up to the platform. The humming grew louder as we climbed up, the wistful assonance assuming control of my mind with each step to the top.

Music had always been in my blood, but this was far beyond that. This melody resonated within the depths of my soul, piercing through me, nestling in deep. It was the same melody that had spilled forth from within the woman from my dream a year ago.

A crystal dais hovered in the center of the platform, above which a crystal formation spiraled down from the roof of the cave. Shit. It looked just like the chandelier hanging from the vaulted ceiling of Gwynn's house. They were both remarkably similar in likeness.

The woman stepped onto the dais, and a translucent cloak—spun with what looked like threads of silver, and infused with light—materialized and encircled her shoulders. She unclasped the mantle at her neck and turned to me.

"Come forward," she said softly, and at her words, the walls of the cave began to shake and rumble.

I stopped in my tracks. Were the walls caving in on us? A healthy dose of fear shook me, but as I watched, a grotto emerged from the base of the floating platform. It was crafted entirely out of gemstones. At the center of the grotto, a stream of rippling blue light swirled radiantly, and I gasped when I glimpsed a living being hovering there—feminine in form, but indistinguishable in features.

I stepped back in alarm. What the— What was I looking at? Some kind of strange fairy life-form? This was off-the-charts nuts. My heart thudded faster in my chest. The melody was emanating from the creature. My body stood paralyzed from the power radiating from the grotto. From one moment to the next, the being shifted from a material presence to something fluid, and then to incandescent blue mist. I half expected the being to transform into the violet-haired woman from my dreams, but the form remained as it was.

The woman with wings stepped off the dais and stood in front of me, removing the cloak from around her body. She placed it around my shoulders, clasping it at the base of my throat. "Step onto the dais, Eleyse, and be deemed worthy." She took my hand and guided me toward the crystal podium.

Deemed worthy? What did that even mean? Bloody hell. Did I want to do this? I stood there like a frozen blob, uncertainty bolting me in place, but at the gentle encouragement in the woman's eyes, coupled with the roaring compulsion inside me and a burning curiosity, I carefully stepped onto the dais facing the grotto.

A shiver snaked down my spine as the being in the grotto shifted back into its material form, settling its unworldly gaze on me, slipping stealthily into my mind. Slowly, the air siphoned out of my body, compressing my insides. I grimaced and gritted my teeth, struggling against the pressure suctioning my eyes and throat and slowly tightening. Shit. This was it; I was going to be crushed from the inside out.

Abruptly, I was released, and I gasped loudly, gulping in deep breaths. God, that hurt like a bitch! I massaged my windpipe, glaring daggers at the grotto.

"Hallowed one, you are known to us," a myriad of voices declared from inside the being. "The fire coursing through your veins proclaims the truth of your identity. We have found you worthy. Choose wisely when the moment is at hand. Your broken spirit holds the fate of this realm in the balance. In the depths of your dark heart, a grain of hope flutters inside you, floundering to survive. It must thrive."

What. The. Fuck. My heart hammered like a monkey on crack playing bongos. What the hell did any of that ghostly fairy's proclamation mean? Who did she . . . it . . . they think I was?

The being's gaze swept over my face, its piercing silver eyes peering intently at me for a long moment. A cool flutter of energy coursed through my body, and for a fleeting moment, I swore a flicker of emotion stirred on that imperial face, but it was gone as quickly as it appeared. The being faded into mist, and the grotto sank into the platform and disappeared.

I stood trembling on the dais, frozen and bewildered. That was . . . utterly terrifying. What just happened? What did it all even mean? The fate of the realm . . . fire in my veins . . . my dark heart? Many voices had come out of that . . . creature. It/they said they knew me. How was that even possible?

Even as my head spun from all the questions screaming out at me, something deep inside—that goddamn compulsion—urged me to relax, to not panic or lose my shit over everything that was happening. I was so conflicted and confused.

Two warring sets of emotions were battling it out inside me. There was the me that I knew—me, Eleyse—who felt skeptical, bewildered, scared, wary, but something else was emerging—and its whispers were growing into rumbles. A voice that sounded remotely familiar—calm, accepting, and frigging jubilant with everything that was unfolding.

The feeling of connection to this place, the sense of ease with Gwynn, the kinship with the woman with wings, the firm belief that everything Gwynn and Faron explained earlier was the truth—they all came from that same place inside me that claimed some kind of belonging with the world of Ariadna. For the life of me, I couldn't reconcile the two parts. It was just all so incredibly surreal.

The woman with wings stood in front of me, drawing me out of my thoughts. She took both of my hands in hers, her strength seeping into me, warming me on the inside. Gathering me close to her, she rested her forehead against mine. "He filled my heart with so much love, but his heart was always meant to be yours. Don't hold back."

I blinked in confusion. Who was she talking about? Here was another woman talking about an unknown *he*.

The woman kissed both of my cheeks, her eyes filled with bittersweet emotion, and as I watched, she faded away, and I was left standing alone in the cavernous chamber.

Chapter 5

OUTSIDE ON THE BALCONY, the sky before me was ablaze with the colors of a magnificent sunset. I had slept the day away. Strange thing, though. It was night when I was with the woman with wings, so it only stood to reason that my encounter with her probably *was* all just a dream. And really, a dream made more sense.

I had awakened soon after the woman left me in the chamber, and floundering in restlessness and unease, I'd made my way onto the balcony to get some fresh air and process everything. That's where I was when Gwynn knocked on the door and walked into the room.

"How are you feeling?" she asked, stepping onto the balcony, brows drawn together as her eyes swept over me. "Were you able to rest?"

"Yes," I said, running my hand through my strange violet hair. "The throbbing in my head is gone too."

"I'm happy to hear that." A sunny smile lit up her face. "Are you feeling well enough to meet with my uncle, Andreo?"

"Yes," I said, perking up. If her uncle was able to shed some more light on everything, I was all for meeting him.

I followed Gwynn as she made her way out of the room. "You are close to your uncle?"

"Yes. He is my father's younger brother. After my parents were killed, Uncle Andreo became a father figure to my brother and me. He is Asher's closest advisor and is also the head of the Valkyse Council of Governors."

"Why do you think he will be able to help me get my missing memories back?"

Gwynn looked over her shoulder as she walked down the stairs. "Remember when I said earlier that there is magic in this world that can be wielded by Sovereign bloodlines?"

I nodded.

"Well, my uncle has various special abilities, one of which is the power of healing. Many times over, he has repaired broken bodies and minds."

My eyes widened. "What an extraordinary gift to have. Do you have special abilities too?"

"I do. I have the power of perception, and the power of banishment."

"I don't know what either of those mean," I said, shaking my head.

She stopped walking and turned to look at me. I skidded to a stop, and a twinge of pain arced through the wound on my leg. I rubbed it absently as I waited for her to answer.

"Do you remember in the alleyway how those men disappeared?"

I recalled the silence and the weight that was lifted off me when Gwynn interrupted the attack. I nodded slowly.

"Well, I banished them to Pashket, the shadowlands of Ariadna, also known as the Dark Dominion. It's where we expel evildoers to in Ariadna to await judgment. I can only banish, and so can Uncle Andreo. Ash has the ability to destroy completely. All four Sovereigns do."

Shadowlands. Dark Dominion. It sounded ominous and dangerous. And there was that name again. *Ash.* My heart skipped a beat at the sound of it. I swore a guttural growl rose from somewhere inside me.

We stood in the foyer at the bottom of the stairs, the enormous crystal chandelier casting slivers of light all around us. It was even more magnificent lit up.

"As for the power of perception," Gwynn was saying, "I can see into minds—feel emotions, gauge general insights about certain situations, see memories sometimes."

My spirits soared. "Are you able to see into my mind?"

"No," Gwynn replied with a sigh. "Your mind is locked to me. Something is blocking me from seeing into your past. It's my suspicion that there is strong magic at work. That's why I'm hoping Uncle Andreo will be able to help."

Strong magic. Special abilities. It was unbelievable.

"I have a stupid question," I said.

"There are no stupid questions," Gwynn said with a smile. "This is all new to you."

I nodded. "The bath and sinks coming to life by themselves, even the taste of cool mint in my mouth when I woke up—is that all magic?"

Gwynn smiled. "Yes. It's simple magic. A lot of personal care can be handled with magic. For instance, you can clean your body without taking a bath or shower by using magic. But showers and baths are relaxing, so many people choose to take them. Magic provides many conveniences here, but we still have the choice to use it or do things the manual way."

Interesting. Completely mind-blowing, actually.

Past the foyer, Gwynn led me through a long corridor to a solarium with floor-to-ceiling views of a secluded hot spring at the back of the house. Outside the windows, the steam rose off the water in soft, opaque wisps. Blue and silver trees lined the perimeter of the spring, their branches fanning out in resplendent canopies over the water. It was the picture of tranquility.

"What's wrong with that tree?" I asked, pointing to a gnarled, white tree at the edge of the hot spring. It was completely bare, save for a few silver leaves and violet blossoms on a low-hanging branch. "Is it dying?"

Gwynn turned to look at the tree I was pointing at, and her jaw dropped open. "New growth. It can't be," she whispered. For a moment, she was lost in her own thoughts, her eyes rooted to the tree. "That's an ancient angorn. It has been barren since my mother's death." She looked at me with puzzled curiosity, but before she could say anything more, a distinguished looking man with dark hair entered the room.

Tall and broad-shouldered, an authoritative air emanated off him. He didn't look old enough to be Gwynn's uncle, but given what Gwynn had explained earlier about the longevity of life here, it was probably normal for him to look young. The wisdom in his eyes, though—they bespoke experience and age. His eyes were a muted shade of blue, his hair dark and wavy, with a few streaks of silver throughout. He had high cheekbones and shared the same shape of nose as Gwynn's—straight and patrician.

He was clad in a dark blazer, powder-blue shirt with the top button undone, and a pair of charcoal-colored trousers. As I studied his attire, I was struck once more by how similar the clothing here was to clothing I was familiar with seeing. Style, fabrics, fashion—if Gwnn hadn't told me this was a different world, the manner of dress would not have raised any red flags to me that something was different. Not at first glance, anyway.

A mix of concern and wariness flashed across his handsome face as he regarded me for the first time, and my skin tingled with unease under his scrutiny. "Hello, Eleyse," he said, his voice gentle and kind—at odds with what I had seen on his face. "I am Gwynn's uncle, Andreo."

"Hello," I replied cautiously.

"Gwynn has told me about your plight. I'd like to help." His eyes were warm and his smile earnest. "Did you know that no human has ever stepped foot in Ariadna until now?"

I stared at him, unable to tear my eyes away. Was I ready to face it? Did I believe? Was I convinced I was no longer on Earth? Everything inside me was screaming out that this place was different, a far cry from the world I knew. Where my life on Earth was a dark and depressing wasteland, this place was vibrant, teeming with life and power. It called to me, rejoicing in my presence here. And inside me, something returned the call. I couldn't deny that. What I felt here was unlike anything I'd ever experienced.

"Why has no human been here before?" I asked.

"Well," Andreo explained, "the human world is far removed from the Sangelis, and no portals exist that would allow a human to travel here."

"And yet here I am," I said, arching a brow.

"Yes, here you are. An anomaly indeed." He reached his hands out to me, and cautiously, I placed my palms in his.

"Why me?" I asked, searching his face for an answer.

He squeezed my fingers gently. "That is yet to be revealed. We'll find out the truth, Eleyse. I promise." His eyes flitted to my thigh. "Gwynn mentioned that your leg is injured?"

I glanced down at myself, nodding.

"Let me help." He placed his index finger on my left temple and closed his eyes. A tendril of warmth spread from his finger into the side of my head, trailing its way down my body. Bloody hell. He was actually healing me! I could feel it happening in real time. The dull twinge in my leg receded, replaced by a tingly heat that wrapped around my thigh. Andreo's finger lingered on my temple for a few more seconds before he opened his eyes and removed his hand.

I touched my thigh. No pain. Sitting in the chair near the window, I reached under my dress to remove the bandage and ran my palm over my quad to find the skin smooth and unbroken. Massaging the area with my fingers, not even a trace of discomfort or pain lingered. I looked at Andreo in amazement. This was no joke. He really did have healing powers. Magic truly did exist here.

"Thank you," I whispered, getting to my feet.

"You're most welcome, my dear." He placed both hands on either side of my face. "Now, let's see what can be done about your memory." He placed his thumbs on my temples, then trailed them across my forehead to rest between my eyes. "Close your eyes for me, Eleyse," he directed gently. "And relax. Quiet your mind and focus on the sound of my voice."

I closed my eyes and willed myself to be calm. Andreo continued to talk to me soothingly as his fingers traveled slowly across my face and head. After a minute or two, he pulled away.

"You're right, Gwynn," he said, turning to look at Gwynn in the corner of the room. "There is strong magic here, dark magic—a rebounding curse."

Gwynn gasped. "What? Can you remove it?"

What the hell was a rebounding curse? Clearly something terrible, based on Gwynn's reaction.

"Not without Ash."

Ash. The same jarring tug from earlier when Gwynn and Faron mentioned his name flared to life again. Then a flash of something—a laugh, a look of pure desolation. Desperately, I reached my mind out to capture more of the memory, but a sharp pain ripped through my temples, and I grabbed onto the chair next to me to keep my balance.

"Eleyse!" Gwynn cried out, and Andreo grabbed my arms to keep me from falling.

He lowered me gently onto the armchair behind me, and Gwynn rushed to my side.

"The same thing happened earlier today on the terrace," she said.

Andreo was silent, staring at me intently.

Whatever dark magic they were talking about was responsible for the gap in my memories. Which begged the question—how big was that gap?

"Is there any way to tell how much of my memory—how much time I lost?" I asked.

Andreo's brows knitted together. "Because you are not from this world, it's hard to say."

Of course. The last thing I remembered was deciding to go to Crusoe's after work on the Friday night of the Victory Day long weekend. It's not like they would even know what that meant. And did time even flow the same here as it did on Earth?

I looked between the both of them. "Gwynn explained that aging is a lot slower here, with much longer lifespans, so does that mean that there is a disconnect between how time flows here and in my world?"

"It's actually quite extraordinary," Andreo said. "Although Earth is far removed from the Sangelis, the flow of time there mirrors Ariadna's closely. That has more to do with the magic of the Ethereal Harmonies than anything."

This was all a lot to wrap my head around. "I need some air," I said, feeling suddenly light-headed.

"Of course." Gwynn placed her hand on my shoulder. "I'll take you out onto the patio."

She led me out through the side door in the solarium and we

stepped out onto the flagstone path that led to the hot spring. The air was cool, and I inhaled deeply, savoring the burning in my lungs. I moved toward the angorn tree and touched the trunk gently. Instantly, I recoiled as a sharp current jolted through my body. I stumbled backward and Gwynn reached out to steady me.

"Medra, Eleyse, you are having a rough—" She stopped abruptly as her hands pulled me to a standing position. Her mouth was agape, her eyes wide with surprise.

"What is it?" I asked. "Are you all right, Gwynn?"

"I . . . I . . .um . . . I'll be right back." Her cheeks and neck were flushed as she backed away from me and hastily made her way back into the solarium where Andreo still stood.

From outside, I could see them talking to each other, the animated movements of Gwynn's hands pronounced as she spoke. Every now and then, she and Andreo both glanced in my direction, making me uneasy and out of place. As if I'd committed some offense.

A pang of desolation coursed through me as loneliness gripped me with viselike fingers, refusing to let go. A sudden longing for home flooded me; I didn't belong here in this strange and unfamiliar place. But even as the thought left my mind, from that place inside me, a stirring of emotion—a whisper brushing against the edges of my mind—rose from the depths, the words unearthly and sanguine.

You have only ever belonged here, Eleyse.

I shivered involuntarily as gooseflesh peppered my skin. My mind was unraveling. I was seeing things and hearing voices in my head. How could I belong here? I didn't even know where *here* truly was.

I hated not having all the pieces to connect. Between my memory loss and finding myself in this new world, my blind spot was enormous. There were just so many unknowns. And that made me uneasy. All this business with the rebounding curse and dark magic, as well as the encounter with the woman with wings and the creature in the cave—what had I gotten myself into?

Chapter 6

A FEW MINUTES LATER, Gwynn stepped onto the patio, composed and collected. "Eleyse, you've had a long day. Why don't we go in for dinner?"

"I'm not hungry," I replied, fighting back the emotions threatening to spill over. "I think I'll just go back to bed."

The gurgling of the water in the hot spring, punctuated with the chirping of insects and other unknown night creatures, played out around me in a calming night symphony. A noted contrast to the clamoring of my thoughts.

"No," Gwynn said firmly. "You've been confined to your bed long enough since you've been here. Uncle Andreo has gone to the library upstairs to see what he can find on your unique situation. Why don't you and I have our dinner in the solarium and then we can go for a soak in the hot spring? The minerals in the water have healing properties and will be sure to rejuvenate you, both physically and mentally." Before I could make an excuse, Gwynn touched my elbow and looked at me beseechingly. "I'm sorry about earlier. When I touched you, I just saw something that threw me."

"What did you see?" Dueling feelings of hope and dread drenched me at the same time. "Was it something bad?"

"No," Gwynn reassured me. "It just surprised me. I don't want to say more until I know more. Is that all right?"

I sighed. "I suppose so. I just feel so lost and alone here."

"That's exactly why I won't let you go back to bed. Let's go in, and I'll have Ezla bring us some dinner."

"What's a rebounding curse, Gwynn?" I asked as we headed back inside. "Andreo said dark magic was involved. What does it all mean?"

Gwynn shifted her stance, her face fixed in concentration. She turned her gaze back to mine, her expression unreadable. "I know you must be anxious to get your memories back and get back to your life, Eleyse, but the truth is, it may not be safe for you to go back just yet."

I almost laughed out loud when she said I was probably anxious to get back to my life, but my self-deprecating humor quickly dissolved with the last part of her statement. "Why would it not be safe for me to go back?" I asked, narrowing my eyes.

Gwynn hesitated, her expression dark and somber. "Because of the rebounding curse. It is steeped in powerful dark magic." Her voice was barely a whisper. "Magic that was directed at you for one specific reason. To kill you."

I blinked, my eyes wide with shock. "Kill me? Who would want me dead?"

The air around me was suddenly suffocating, pressing in from all sides, making it difficult to breathe.

"That's what we're not entirely sure of, which is why I don't think it's safe for you to go back yet. I don't think it's a coincidence that you ended up here, Eleyse."

Someone had tried to kill me. Why? Wait. What did she say?

"What do you mean you're not *entirely* sure?" I asked. "Does that mean you might have an idea?"

Gwynn frowned as she pushed on her lip with her index finger. "It's more of a suspicion than anything, but until we know more, I don't want to speculate."

Icy tendrils of unease scraped down my spine. Oh, God! Someone wanted me dead. Did this psychopath even know me? I mean, they had to be a psychopath to want an innocent woman dead, right? What did I do to get on their shit list? Did this have something to do with how I ended up here?

I couldn't help but shake the feeling that everything was connected—my memory loss, how I ended up here, my feeling of connection to this place. In my mind, if was as if random pieces of a jigsaw puzzle were spread out in front of me, but I didn't know where to start because I had no frigging clue what the picture was supposed to look like, or if I even had all the goddamn pieces.

Gwynn took my hands in hers and squeezed them. "I know it's easier said than done, Eleyse, but for now, I'm asking you to try and not stress about it until Uncle Andreo can get more answers. There is not much I can tell you without creating unnecessary angst for you, and we just don't know enough about what is going on with you to decide on the right course of action."

I stared at her blankly. "How can I not stress? You just told me someone tried to kill me!"

Yes, in the past, I had longed for death, but geez, that was by my own hand! My choice. That someone else wanted me dead was sinister and terrifying. I felt numb inside.

Gwynn's gaze was intense, imploring me to trust her. "My uncle will get answers, I promise. He and Ash will set this right."

Ash—another piece of the puzzle. Sovereign of Valkyse, ruler of this dominion, and somehow, every time his name was mentioned, it poked and prodded at some unknown, shuttered chamber in the scrambled recesses of my mind. Familiar, yet completely unfamiliar, both at the same time.

What was he to me? My heart silently proclaimed that the weight of his worth was proportionate to the engulfing emptiness that had settled inside me as a result of my memory loss, but I didn't have any way to measure that.

"We won't let anything happen to you, Eleyse," Gwynn said. "You are in Valkyse, a guest in this dominion. My brother is powerful. He won't let any harm befall someone under his protection. You are safe here."

The conviction of her words bolstered me, but the mere mention of her elusive brother wreaked havoc with my senses. Something inside me was agitated, bursting at the seams to be set free, to conjure him, to kiss, to touch, to claim him . . . Oh God, I couldn't explain what the hell was going on—I was restless, excited, and impatient, all at the same time. No question about it, I knew Ash. If only I could remember him.

I sat in the solarium, waiting for Gwynn. Night had fallen, and as I looked outside, my spirits lifted at the twinkling lights hovering throughout the trees over the hot spring—a canopy of stars shining down on a silver, translucent lake.

Gwynn returned, balancing two bowls, wine glasses, and a bottle of wine on a serving tray. "Dinner is served," she said, handing a bowl to me. "Ezla is an amazing cook."

I studied the rich stew brimming with meat and vegetables. The aroma was heavenly, and as I took a spoonful, my stomach rumbled in response. I greedily dug in, then picked up the glass of wine that Gwynn poured me and took a sip. It was the perfect complement for the meal.

"Does your staff live here?" I asked, forcing myself to change the subject as I took another sip of wine.

"Ezla and her husband, Dialo, look after the place," Gwynn said, lifting her wineglass. "They have been here ever since I was a little girl."

"It's so beautiful and peaceful here. Truly magnificent."

"This is Cazara Chantilis. One of the four Sovereign residences in Valkyse."

"Cazara Chantilis," I repeated softly to myself.

"Cazara is the term for a Sovereign residence. You will find that all the Sovereign residences in Ariadna are named like that. The region we're in right now is called Chantilis."

"What are the other cazaras like?"

"They're all very different, to be honest," Gwynn said thoughtfully. "They're all a reflection of the region they belong to. Cazara Somel is in Somel, a very warm and tropical region. The residence is at the top of a cliff that overlooks the ocean. A beautiful beach sprawls for miles at the base of the cliff. I think you'd enjoy it. It's also very peaceful, but in an entirely different way. It was Ash's and my second favorite place when we were younger."

She paused for a moment, a faraway look on her face. Lost. Reminiscing.

She shook her head, as if to chase her memories away. "Then, there's Cazara Nesda. That one is located in the heart of Nesda, an idyllic region with miles and miles of rolling hills and countryside, teeming woods and farmlands, and beautiful flora and fauna. And Cazara Torannon is very different from the other three. While Cazaras Chantilis, Somel, and Nesda all have a tranquil feel to them, Cazara Torannon is bustling and noisy, full of life and energy. It's in the heart of Torannon, the capital city of Valkyse."

They sounded breathtaking, but really were they that different from places on Earth? A pang of longing for home filled me. But even as it washed over me, I didn't know what I was longing for. The familiar, perhaps? It's not as if I remotely liked or enjoyed my life; for as long as I could remember, each day had faded into the next, and I'd eked my way through them in painstakingly slow motion. I was dispassionate about life, to say the least.

That's not entirely true, that voice from before—the stirring deep inside—objected, whispering with conviction. The words jarred me; I didn't know what to make of them.

"I wish there was something I could do to make you feel better," Gwynn said, squeezing my hand. "I can only imagine how unnerving and scary it must feel to be in a strange and unfamiliar place."

"You have, Gwynn." I squeezed her hand in return. "You took me in and showed me kindness. It makes me sick when I think about what would have happened to me if you didn't intervene when I was with those men."

"The more I think about it, I don't think it was a coincidence that I found you in that alleyway," Gwynn said. "I wasn't even supposed to be in Torannon that day. I was running an errand two streets over when I felt you—your pain and your fear—and I followed my senses to where you were."

That threw me. She was able to sense my pain and my fear? Right. She said her abilities allowed her to feel emotions. What were the odds of her being in that place at the very same time I needed help?

"Well, I'm very grateful," I said. "You have my heartfelt thanks. I didn't realize that you found me somewhere else."

"I did. And I immediately brought you to Cazara Chantilis, away from the bustle of the city, where you could rest quietly, away from prying eyes, and where I could try to figure this all out." She poured some more wine into our glasses and turned to me. "Why don't we take our wine glasses and go outside to the hot spring?"

"Dressed like this?" I asked, looking down at the dress I was still wearing.

"No, there's a change room through there," she said, inclining her head to the door on our right. "You should be able to find something that fits you. We're about the same size, you and I. I'll meet you out by the spring. Let me just take these back to the kitchen."

She walked off, arms full, as I made my way to the change room. Sure enough, there was a wide selection of swimwear to choose from, and again, the fashions were very similar to what I was used to. I picked out a one-piece, emerald-green swimsuit with a plunging neckline, and after changing, I wrapped myself in a thick, fluffy robe and headed out onto the patio.

Walking over to the edge of the hot spring, I sat down, slipping my legs into the heated water. Under the canopy of trees, with the twinkling lights shining down on me, the warm steam rising off the spring, and the cool breeze drifting through my hair, I embraced the quiet peace, the connection to something bigger than I was.

My mind shifted to the woman with wings. As much as I tried to convince myself it was only a dream, I *knew* it wasn't. *We are bound by fate, you and I,* she'd said. My entire life, I had approached the topic of fate with disdain. Fate, if such a thing existed, was only ever cruel to me. It had brought me nothing but heartache and loss. What kind of fate did she believe bound us?

And what about her parting words to me? *He filled my heart with so much love, but his heart was always meant to be yours. Don't hold back.* I couldn't help but feel that this was related to what happened to me every time Ash's name was mentioned. My heart recognized him—was giddy at just the sound of his name. I knew him; I *felt* it. But it didn't just end there; it wasn't just my heart. My body, too, had a visceral reaction every time his name was spoken, forcing me to relinquish control and submit to a hedonistic and primitive need for him. It was absurd. I didn't even know what he looked like.

This *he*—even if it was Ash—the woman had said his heart was always meant to be mine, but who was she to him? She'd admitted to loving him. Was she a past love?

And then there was the spectral being in the grotto. Proclaiming that my broken spirit held the fate of the realm in the balance. Looking into my soul and seeing my dark heart. That my heart was void of light was an understatement. For so long, darkness had been the greater part of my identity.

But the being in the grotto had said that there was a grain of hope. Was she talking about the violet-haired woman from my dream? The night she had come to me, I was at my very lowest, but her words were transformative, made me believe that there was hope for me yet. She'd hinted at a future for me filled with promise.

After that night, I'd abandoned my quest to find a way out. She gave me the strength to go on, planted the seed of hope that my life contained purpose. What she said about me being the Secret of the Gods still made no sense, but neither did a lot of the other things she said. One thing was clear. She was pretty certain about the truth of my identity. As was the being in the grotto, and the woman with wings. Which begged the question—who the hell did they think I was?

Gwynn returned about fifteen minutes later wearing a black and white checkered swimsuit, and I admired her perfect physique.

She was slim but muscular, her skin tanned and flawless.

"You look incredible for someone over a century old," I said, smiling.

Gwynn laughed. "Thanks for the compliment." She lowered herself into the water and sighed in contentment. "Relaxing in here is the best part of my day."

"I can see why." I stood, slipping my robe off before immersing myself in the hot spring beside Gwynn.

"This was my mother's favorite place in the world," Gwynn said quietly. "She loved it here, and when she was alive, it was so full of life. She's been gone for more than a hundred fucking years, and still, sometimes it feels like just yesterday she was here, singing as she worked in the garden with her flowers and her beloved mountain creatures twittering and fawning over her. What I wouldn't give to have just one more moment with her."

My heart ached for her, grief rendering me breathless with a kick to the gut. Not a day went by when I didn't ache for those I lost. "What was her name?" I asked quietly.

"Harwen," she answered, her voice thick with emotion. "My father's name was Arlon. They loved each other very much, and the people of Valkyse loved them." She paused for a moment, tendrils of steam curling around her face.

She inclined her head toward the white tree at the edge of the hot spring. "Earlier, when you asked about the angorn, it surprised me to see that it was blooming again. Not since my parents' death over a century ago have there been blossoms on the ancient tree." Her eyes filled with sadness. "It was special to my mother, connected to her. While she was alive, it was a thing of beauty—vibrant and magnificent. I can still remember standing under those branches the day after that dreadful tragedy, the pain of losing my parents so soul-wrenchingly unbearable. With tears streaming down my face, I looked down to see waves upon waves of silver leaves and soft violet blossoms pooling at my feet, as if the angorn, too, was in mourning and shedding tears for the beloved Queen Consort of Valkyse."

I gazed at the angorn tree, an overwhelming sense of loss engulfing me. I knew the sting of that kind of pain intimately.

Gwynn turned sad eyes to me. "What about you, Eleyse? What's your family like?"

Her question caught me off guard and I swallowed, trying to dislodge the lump in my throat. "I don't have any family," I answered quietly. I sank lower into the water, willing the heat to sear the hurt away.

"Oh no. I'm so sorry, Eleyse."

"It's okay." I crossed my arms around myself, rubbing my shoulders with my thumbs. My chest was tight and heavy. It had been a long time since I'd talked about my family, but for some reason, sitting here with Gwynn, hearing her talk openly about her parents, made me want to share my story as well.

"My parents died in a car accident when I was five." I closed my eyes and sighed softly, flitting my fingers over the surface of the water. "After that, I went to live with my father's younger sister, Mags. She raised me, and I loved her so completely, but she died in a tragic accident when I was nineteen. She was the only family I had left." As hard as I tried to keep my emotion in check, my eyes welled up.

"Medra, Eleyse," Gwynn said, reaching for my hand. "You were so young when you lost your parents. And even your aunt. Was there no one else in your life?"

I nodded. "The only two people in the world I had left were my best friends, Liam and Charlotte. The three of us became friends when we were twelve. Liam and I fell in love when we were teenagers, and we got engaged years later, but a year after our engagement, he was killed in an accident as well."

Gwynn gasped. "Oh no, Eleyse." Her eyes shone with sympathy and understanding as she looked at me. Of course, she understood—her parents were lost to her as well—but even so, shame and guilt scoured me, like a steel brush shredding my skin. Four deaths, all tragic accidents? You didn't have to be a genius to see that I was the common thread. What was the likelihood of that being a coincidence?

"What about your friend, Charlotte?" Gwynn asked, moving a little closer toward me. "You still have her, no?"

"I haven't seen Charlotte since Liam's death," I said quietly, not willing to say more, fixating on the sound of water lapping quietly around us. How could I tell Gwynn that Charlotte, too, had almost died in a freak accident after she came to visit me after Liam's funeral? What would she think?

That terrifying incident had been the final straw for me. Everyone who loved me had paid for that love with their lives. I wasn't willing to let the same goddamn fate befall Charlotte. And so, I'd packed my things and moved across the country to Hargrove without a word to my friend. It was one of the hardest things I'd ever done, but knowing that Charlotte was alive and safe was worth it. I was a curse, a blight, and being alone was the only way to protect others from me.

Gwynn looked at me with knowing eyes, eyes that saw more than I wanted her to see, and I looked away. My entire life was defined by those exact types of glances—looks that said, "What a sad, sorry human being. To have lost so much, so young." Those looks had enraged me, filled me with self-loathing and disgust. Even now, I felt the same way.

Being alone was my choice. Running away had allowed me

to escape the wretched murmuring and whispers, the eyes that burned with sadness for my pain—and in the same breath, relief that it wasn't their lives ripped apart by death, their loved ones lost.

Fresh slate, wiped clean. It was perfect, this loneliness I'd imposed on myself; my life was predictable and safe. *You can't lose someone if you have no one.* That was the mantra I lived my life by.

"You know that none of those tragedies were your fault, right?" Gwynn said quietly, placing her hand on my shoulder.

I didn't answer her. Tears burned my eyes, and I wiped them away.

"You had absolutely no control over any of those things happening. They were just tragic accidents."

I nodded, avoiding her gaze.

"I can see it on your face, Eleyse. You've shut yourself away from the world. You remind me so much of my brother. He blamed himself for our parents' deaths and it almost destroyed him. He completely fell apart after they were gone. For a while afterward, he became so self-destructive. I see the same haunted look in your eyes—the same anger and self-loathing. I'm going to tell you the same thing I told him. Even in the darkest moments, beauty and purpose in life can be found if you look for it. Reach for the light and it will find you."

"And did he find it?" I asked. "That beauty and purpose in life?"

Gwynn tilted her head to the side. "It took him a couple years, but yes, I think he found a reason to live again. Perhaps it was fulfilling the legacy that our parents left him as Sovereign. Ash has a deep love for the people of Valkyse, and making our parents proud drives him to excel in everything he takes on."

"Maybe I will also find that kind of purpose in life one day," I said quietly. "God knows I desperately need one."

"You will, Eleyse," she said. "Just hold on to the hope that the light will come again." She reached for my hand and pulled me to her in a hug, and I let her. I couldn't remember the last time I'd accepted compassion from someone.

"Thanks for your kind words, Gwynn," I said, wiping my eyes. "I think I'll go up to bed now. I feel drained."

"Okay. I'm going to stay out for a little while longer," she replied. "Good night, Eleyse."

"You too, Gwynn. And thanks for making me stay."

"You're welcome. Please try and get some rest," she said, her eyes full of concern.

"I'll try."

I turned around and climbed out of the hot spring, grabbing the bathrobe I'd dropped on the ground. Slipping it on, I pulled it around me and patted myself dry as I walked away, the strands of my resolve quietly knitting back into place.

Gwynn meant well, but she couldn't truly understand. It wasn't as if I *wanted* to live my life alone. Of course not. I wanted to be happy—surrounded by friends and family who loved me—but that was not in the cards for me. Those desires were selfish. Especially given all that I had lost. My mantra still held true. *You can't lose someone if you have no one.*

Chapter 7

I STARED AT MYSELF in the mirror as I brushed out the tangles from my damp hair. Even wet, the dark violet shade was jarring, a reminder that I was not who I remembered myself to be. The silver flecks in my eyes proclaimed the same.

I'd left Gwynn in the hot spring about half an hour ago and had been replaying the events of the day in my head ever since I got back to my room. My mind still refused to relent, the rational part of my brain holding on to the assuring belief that this was either all a dream or some kind of mistake. That was the easy path, after all. Everything that had unfolded since I opened my eyes this morning was still too farfetched, too much to make sense of.

Despite the doubt swirling around in my mind, I couldn't stop thinking about one thing. If everything I had learned today was indeed true, the only familiar thread connecting my world to this one was Ash. Brother of Gwynn, Sovereign of Valkyse. How did I know him? How had we—worlds apart—come to know each other? I didn't remember anything about him, but with an innate conviction, I *knew* he meant something to me. And that, in itself, was very strange, because there was no one in my life who meant anything to me anymore.

My hand stilled on my hair as a peculiar noise pierced the air. Setting the hairbrush down quietly on the dresser, I tiptoed to the door, slowly poking my head out of the bathroom. I peered at the fireplace where the embers flickered languidly in the iron grate. That was the direction the noise was coming from. A constant chime, pealing through the silence in steady intervals.

My eyes flew to the circular gilded object above the mantel, the entire thing bathed in hazy light. The golden arrow at the top that was pointing straight up this morning was inching slowly to the left with each chime that rang out. After a few moments, the chiming stopped, the golden arrow frozen in position as the silver stars in the center began to move. The carved words along the circumference flashed in pulses as the stars flitted back and forth, until finally, three words flared brightly in silver when the stars stopped in front of them: Sad, *angry, lost.*

What the hell? Was this supposed to mean something?

I climbed onto the bed, clutching the blanket to my chest when a roaring sound—like a rush of wind through an empty cavern—filled the room, originating from the gilded object. Before my eyes, the entire thing melted in on itself and shifted to a rippling mass of gold, swirling in a circular pattern, until finally, it began veering away from the mantel, toward me, the size expanding with each rotation. It came to a stop at the foot of the bed, the size of the orb at least seven feet in diameter.

A soft squeak escaped my lips, and I watched in frozen astonishment as the gold parted in the middle and spiraled toward me with silken fingers. Terror trickled through me, blood thrumming hot and loud in my ears, but it was overpowered by something else: curiosity and a waxing excitement.

The surface of the circle grew calm, slowly growing more translucent until I could make out obscure shapes and colors behind it. Something lay on the other side; I was sure of it. Unable to stop myself, I crawled to the end of the bed on my hands and knees, peering into the depths of the sphere.

A cool flutter of air grazed my skin, and I shivered, reaching for and slipping on the robe that hung on the bedpost. Slowly, I swung my legs off the side of the bed onto the floor and padded toward the glistening orb in front of me. A quivering twinge of excitement blossomed across my flesh as I moved closer.

In a spray of shooting sparks, the orb yawned open at the center, and as I stood there, gripping my robe around me, a figure emerged from inside. I gasped, recognizing the woman from my dream that depressing night I'd tried to die.

It *was* all connected.

The woman before me had crossed my mind a number of times already since I'd woken up here.

Her curly, violet hair framed her beautiful face, and those eyes—flashing silver—found mine instantly.

"Wh—wha?" I stuttered, unable to think clearly.

Her presence filled the room, warm and calming, that haunting melody I remembered from before still resonating from inside her.

"Leida mata," she said, reaching for me with arms outstretched.

My treasure? I didn't know what it meant when I'd heard her say it in my dream, but here—in this moment—as soon as the words left her lips, understanding registered.

She embraced me, pressing a kiss to my forehead.

"Wh— who are you?" I asked, my voice a ragged whisper.

"I am the gatekeeper, Eleyse," she answered with a smile. "Long have I guarded the secrets of your identity, and tonight, I unlock the gate and set you free. The future you were born for is finally upon you. This world contains the very essence of who you are."

Like that night in my dream, my entire being responded to her in a way that I couldn't understand—with belonging, acceptance, and validation. Not a single part of me entertained any rebellion or doubt over her cryptic words.

She lifted her hand. "Through the eye of this vortex, past, present, and future converge. What awaits you is a pivotal moment—one that sets it all in motion and unites two ravaged hearts. Listen to the wisdom of your senses, Eleyse; it will not lead you astray. You have until the vortex reappears, after which you must make haste and return through the eye, back to this room. Lingering on the other side could corrupt the timeline and chain of events. Only the time granted is protected."

Holy shit! She wanted me to go through that thing? I stared at her, a flicker of uncertainty rooting me where I was, even as inside me, I burned with anticipation.

"Go, Eleyse," she said with a smile. "Trust your feelings, and trust your heart. You have nothing to fear."

Tentatively, I reached out my hand, and a frisson of energy arced through my fingers as they breached the surface. I looked back at the woman one more time, and before I could give my mind time to talk me out of it, I stepped forward and slipped through the orb to whatever lay on the other side.

Music swirled around me. The low, thumping bass of a slow, sensuous melody reverberated softly through the barely lit room where I stood. My entire body was rigid, wary of what I'd willingly stepped into. A massive bed stood in front of me, the room even more expansive than the one I'd just left.

To my right, a frameless floor-to-ceiling window heralded uninterrupted views of a glittering city sprawling on for miles beneath me. It was not that different from the nighttime views of cities I was used to seeing on Earth. Even the soft music filling the room was similar.

Wait, where was I? Could the sphere have transported me back home?

Of course not. The blue orbs of light on the wall in front of me—identical to the ones in the room I just left—quickly doused any speculations of where I was—world-wise anyway.

My heartbeat quickened as sprigs of anticipation skittered across my skin. I inhaled deeply as an avalanche of feeling toppled my senses, my knees almost buckling from the weight of it. The tempo of the music, the low lighting, the intoxicating smell of something dangerous and powerful in the air—my mind and body were trapped, as if under the snare of a compelling spell.

A flash of movement in the periphery of my vision snagged my focus, and I turned my head to see the outline of someone sitting in a dark armchair next to the window, legs open and stretched out in casual repose. A man, shrouded in faltering light and shadow.

My heart thudded in my chest, an urge to turn around and scramble back through the orb gripping me. But that calm certainty inside me rushed in, erasing all conflict and anxiety. Even if I wanted to leave, I couldn't; the vortex was already gone. I inhaled deeply, the music slowly working its way into my mind, relaxing me, drawing me in.

"The Gods are answering summons now, are they?" a deep, sultry voice drawled from the chair, the promise of mayhem dangling from each word.

Gods? Summons? What the hell was he talking about? And yet . . . his voice—it was resuscitating, sparking the lost partitions of my memory in recognition. It was familiar, welcomed.

What awaits you is a pivotal moment, the woman had said. *One that sets it all in motion and unites two ravaged hearts.* My heart flared with expectant jubilation.

The clink of ice jangled as the man lifted a glass to his lips and leaned forward to rest his arms on his knees. His eyes—predatory and silent—tracked my every movement, and I pulled my robe tighter around me as I bravely took a step closer.

Everything about him was familiar—the poise with which he sat, the graceful way he moved, the aura of his magnetic presence.

He shifted closer to the edge of the chair, and a shaft of light kissed his face, baring his features to me. I stopped in my tracks, staring at him. Recognition, confusion, and wariness rushed through me all at once.

Friend. Lover. Savior . . . Ash.

I shook my head, trying to unscramble my thoughts, desperate to reconcile my memory with what I innately felt and knew to be true.

I couldn't tear my eyes away from his; he was breathtaking. I basked in the intensity of his gaze, feeling him devour me the same way I was feasting on him. That there was no recognition in his eyes did not escape me. His fascination and curiosity, on the other hand, were unmistakable.

A flash of pain ripped through my head as I tried to summon my memories by force, willing myself to remember, to reconstruct the particulars of how, where, and when he fit in.

"Is everything all right?" he asked, his voice soft and hedonistic as he appeared in front of me before my mind could even register how he'd bridged the distance between us so quickly.

I looked up. Fuck, he was tall. And broad. And so incredibly sexy. The warmth radiating from him was making my head spin. My eyes made contact with his muscled chest, and my face heated as I drank him in. His shirt was unbuttoned and untucked, the waistband of his pants undone. I forced myself to keep my ogling gaze from drifting lower.

He cleared his throat, and I looked up at his face, noting the smirk tugging at his lips. Without thinking, I lifted my hand and touched his cheek, my fingers on fire where his flesh touched mine. A spark of surprise ignited his gaze.

Shit. I *knew* this face—memory loss or no. His face was as familiar to me as my own. Every contour and angle, the shape of his lips, the planes of his cheekbones, the ever-so-slight tilt of his perfectly shaped nose, the enviably long lashes, those depthless emerald eyes—I was intimately acquainted with them all.

And yet, there was something different. Something *off* that I couldn't place.

I rested my hand against his bare chest and closed my eyes, following the pull of my senses. Recklessness and simmering anger vibrated inside him, and at his core, an aching sorrow.

He placed his hand over mine, his fingers stroking the inside of my palm. "I assure you, I'm real," he said, his voice a guttural caress. "Which, if I'm honest, I'm still questioning about you." Lifting my hand, he brushed his lips across my fingers, his eyes never leaving mine.

His brashness excited me, my body savoring the uncurbed intimacy of his proximity.

His voice was low and seductive when he spoke. "No one enters this room, except by invitation or request, and yet, here you are, uninvited, but nevertheless an enchanting surprise."

My heart skipped a beat at his words, the feel of his mouth on my skin sending a current of pleasure hurtling to my core. I closed my eyes, lost in the feel of him and the music enveloping us in its entrancing rhythm.

He smiled seductively. "Dance with me."

A command, not a request.

He lifted my hand to his neck and pulled me closer, gripping my waist with his hand, his arm nestled tight against my side. I was powerless to do anything but obey. I craved his nearness, his touch, with everything inside me. My heart rejoiced, and at the same time wept, at being in his embrace.

I wrapped my arms around his neck, moving slowly against him as we swayed intimately, the thrill of carnal surrender a wanton suggestion in the air between us. Our bodies molded together seamlessly, as if we were crafted for each other. I pulled my head back to look at his face, unable to get enough—to be close enough—yearning to drown in the liquid fire burning in his eyes.

Everything about who I was up to the moment I looked upon his face ceased to exist. Here, there was only him; I was completely undone. He was the sun—magnificent and blazing in all his glory—and I was a speck of dust trapped in his orbit.

His finger traced my cheek as he studied my face. I swallowed and licked my lips, and his eyes flew to my mouth, his green irises dark and turbulent.

Oh God. This was insane. I was losing my goddamn mind under his scrutiny.

"I would have your name." His voice was a throaty murmur, his fingers continuing their exploration of my face, trailing across my jaw.

I stared at him, lifting my head a notch higher. "I was told once that I am much more than a name."

His eyes crinkled as he smiled. "I don't doubt that for one second, Tialla."

My eyes narrowed. "I'm no Goddess."

"Interesting," he said, brows arched. "A non-Goddess who has the commanding presence of a Goddess and also understands the language of the Gods. Seems a little contradictory."

"Language of the Gods?" I asked, squinting.

"Come, don't feign bewilderment now, Tialla."

I couldn't deny that I liked the sound of that name on his lips; the way his voice uttered the word was entirely sinful. Although in all sincerity, he could call me a tramp, and I was sure my ears would lap it up the same way.

"What about *your* name?" I asked, trying to untangle my train of thought. "Do I get to know it?"

His body stilled and he looked at me more intently, his brows creased. "Do you really expect me to believe that you don't know who I am?"

I know you. I just don't remember you.

I shrugged. "All you are to me is a presumptuous man in a grand room."

He laughed, and my heart soared at the sound of it.

"You find me presumptuous?" he asked, pulling me closer against him.

"Incredibly so."

His eyes widened slightly. "And yet, here you are, tangled in my arms, your body denouncing you as a liar. A beautiful one at that."

"My body is a traitorous wretch," I whispered, even as I strained to get closer to him.

His thumb lazily traced my lips, and it took all my willpower not to open my mouth and taste him.

He began moving again to the music, taking me with him. "So am I to believe that in coming here, it wasn't your intent to fuck a Sovereign on the eve of his coronation?"

My eyes widened, and I stiffened, pushing away from him. "I didn't come here to fuck anyone."

He reached out and twirled a tendril of my hair around his finger, a small chuckle escaping his lips. "Given your boldness to touch me and be touched by me, it surprises me that you are so easily offended . . . and vehement in your denial. Most women usually want one thing from me, and it was the only logical conclusion I could draw from you being here."

I looked at him, trying to compartmentalize what I was feeling. What he asked had surprised me, but I could see how he might think that's why I was here, dressed only in a robe and thin nightgown, throwing myself at him, delirious to be in his arms. Any man who looked the way he did had to have women lining the streets to be with him.

"Are you afraid of me, Tialla?" he asked when I took another step back. His body was still and his eyes grew serious.

Afraid of him? I was thrown by what he'd said about my intentions. Hearing him speak so inelegantly to someone *he'd* just met struck me as . . . unfamiliar. Surprise, confusion, disillusionment even, coursed through me, but not fear.

I stepped closer, and he reached for my hand and pulled me to his chest, his eyes flaring with curiosity.

My hand trailed up to touch his jaw. "I could never be afraid of you." Instinctively, I knew that was true. Fear was not an emotion that was tangled up with what I sensed existed between us.

"You should be," he said, his expression suddenly grim. "Sometimes, even I am terrified of the darkness inside me."

I cocked my head for a moment, and then wound my arms around his neck. "Well, I am well acquainted with darkness, and I don't scare easily."

A flash of surprise lit his eyes, and his touch was gentle as he tucked some strands of hair behind my ear. "What a pair we make, then," he whispered, a wistful smile lifting his lips.

A knock on the door jolted us back to reality, and the music immediately came to a stop.

"My lord?" a voice called from the other side. Sensuous. Female.

Tone of hopeful expectation.

I narrowed my eyes and glared at him. "Your entertainment for the night?" A tidal wave of jealousy overcame me, the bitter tang of it burning my throat. God, I was out of control. What the hell was happening to me? He was a stranger to me . . . and yet he wasn't. I felt febrile and possessive when it came to him.

"She's been informed that I'm indisposed," he said, and the music resumed, the slow, undulating tempo and melody gathering around us once more.

"What do you mean?" I asked.

He kissed my fingers. "I sent her away."

"How? You didn't even leave the room."

He tilted his head to the side. "Magic. That should be no secret to you, Goddess."

"Oh. Right." I didn't know what else to say. Not understanding how magic in this realm worked, I had no idea what he meant. "Why did you send her away if you were expecting her?"

His hand tangled in my hair and he lowered his face closer to mine. "So many questions."

"What can I say? I'm a curious woman."

He chuckled, dipping his head to my throat, where his teeth grazed against my pulse. The warmth of his lips and the flicker of his tongue against my skin sent shockwaves through my body, and I arched into his touch, my hands reaching out to pull his head closer.

"First of all, I wasn't expecting her," he said, his voice a raspy whisper. "And second, why would I want anyone else when I find myself in the presence of a creature so unbelievably bewitching and delectable?"

My body flushed at his words, heat stampeding through me like a herd of wild horses free of their corral. "How do you know I didn't come here to harm you?"

He lifted his head and looked at me, his eyes sparkling with amusement and a gripping intensity. "The moment you appeared in this room, I knew you were not a threat."

"You sure of that?" I asked, arching a brow as I trailed my fingers up a hard, muscled arm.

"Certain. I can sense the true nature of any living being I encounter."

My fingers paused their exploring as I studied him. "How is that possible?"

"It's one of my abilities." His hands gripped my torso and his thumbs grazed the underside of my breasts, the contact electric.

"One of many, I'm sure," I said, my heart racing as I struggled to focus on what I was saying. "What do your senses tell you about me?"

His brows furrowed, and he was silent for a long moment before replying. "What I discern with you is more intense than I've experienced before. Your aura is sharper. More vibrant. All-consuming. You possess a unique . . . essence."

I boldly met his gaze, and there was no mistaking his desire for me. His eyes were ablaze with hunger—hunger that I knew with certainty was mirrored in mine. All rational thought abandoned me, replaced with a relentless need to slake and feed the beast that had awoken inside. My body rippled with excitement.

"Is that a bad thing?" I asked, my breath fluttering as it escaped my lips.

He shook his head and cupped the back of my head as he pulled me even closer, his gaze locked onto mine. "Not in the least."

His thumb trailed a path across my jaw, flitting back up to trace the outline of my lips. I shivered, his touch driving me wild.

His body stilled, his gaze holding mine hostage. "As for what my senses tell me . . ." he whispered, and I angled my face closer to his. "They say that you are a promise and a storm. And that heart, body, and soul, you are meant for me."

Fuck. I was screwed.

He lowered his head and his mouth claimed mine. It was a blessed reunion, my body welcoming him home with devoted supplication. My tongue tangled with his, the intoxicating taste of spiced liquor causing my mouth to tingle. He deepened the kiss, and I threaded my fingers through his dark hair, my body arching into his, a low moan escaping my lips as the heat of his erection throbbed against my torso.

He reached down and grabbed my thighs, lifting me to his waist. I wrapped my legs around him, pushing the shirt away from his body. He shrugged it off, letting it fall to the floor, and I ran my hands across his muscled shoulders and chest, the heat of his skin driving me wild with need. I tore my lips away from his to look at him. He was glorious.

My eyes fastened on the silver cuff he wore on his wrist, pulsing slowly with a strange, blue light. An intricate design curved along its length, and I caught a glimpse of a crescent moon along the top just as his hard arousal ground against me, recapturing my full attention. I continued with my bold perusal of him.

Like his face, I *knew* his body. I had touched and kissed every inch of him before. My body possessed a memory of its own, and although my mind was locked to me, my body knew him as the one who had claimed mastery of it. Nothing had ever felt more right.

Yet in the rightness of it all, there was something different. Something harsh and untamed in his eyes that I didn't recognize. I didn't care, though. I wanted him so much that I hurt, the need to be with him superseding everything else.

I trailed kisses down his neck and across his shoulder, my hands roving down his chest and taut stomach, unable to get enough of him. *More! More! More!* my body screamed, every nerve ending on fire.

He carried me to the bed, laying me gently on top of the thick blankets. Covering my body with his, he rested on his forearms and intertwined his fingers with mine. "You have it reversed, Tialla. You are the Goddess. I worship you, not the other way around."

I looked down to see that all my clothes were gone and I was bare beneath him. He'd used his magic. I wasn't complaining.

He sat back on his heels and looked at me, his eyes a vortex of lust and primal desire. My body heated under his ravenous gaze, and I ground my thighs together to stop the pulsing between my legs.

"No. Let me look at you."

Of their own volition, my legs drifted open, and his gaze heated as he devoured me.

"Is compulsion one of your abilities too?" I asked, my body aching for him to touch me.

His eyes flew to mine. "It is, but I have not once used that tonight. Your willingness to do whatever I say is all your own doing." He flashed a devilish grin. "Compulsion wouldn't work on a Goddess, anyway."

I reached my hands out, my desperation spiking at not being touched by him. The tempo of the music changed—a slow and erotic number—the breathy vocals of an unknown female singer floating in like a siren's call around me. I closed my eyes, liquid heat snaking down my entire body.

"What is it?" he asked, his fingers swirling slowly across my collarbone.

My eyes fluttered open and I looked at him, a rush of heat coursing through me. "Music," I rasped. "It has a way of intensifying the mood, heightening my arousal. This song . . . it's seeping into my skin . . . my blood. I want . . . I . . . I . . . burn everywhere. My skin feels like it's on fire." I licked my dry lips.

Although his body was still, a maddened inferno of need churned in his eyes. "What do you want, Goddess?" he asked, shifting his frame onto his side next to me.

I shivered, reaching for him. His index finger trailed over my lips, and this time, I opened my mouth and closed it over the tip, swirling my tongue against his skin.

He sucked in a breath as his pupils dilated, only a thin ring of green visible as he looked at me. His other hand framed my cheek, his body still and rigid. "Tell me how I pay my tribute."

I lifted his hand from my mouth and dragged it down my body. "Incite the storm. Consume me."

He needed no further invitation. He parted my legs, his body hovering over mine as his mouth trailed a fiery path down my neck to my chest. He cupped my breasts in his hands, kneading gently as his thumbs grazed my nipples. I swallowed a moan, my nails digging into the sheets beneath me.

"Do you like it when I touch you here?" he asked, his eyes glued to mine as his fingers coaxed my nipples to stiff peaks.

I moaned, thrusting my chest out toward him. "I'd prefer your mouth there," I said boldly.

His eyes flashed, and he chuckled softly. "Only a Goddess could be so direct."

"I'm not one to mince words when it comes to my own pleasure."

"You command, Tialla, and I will obey." He lowered his head to my breast, his mouth closing over my nipple.

My back arched off the bed, and I moaned as his tongue swirled around the peak. He closed his lips and sucked gently, his eyes finding mine as he moved his head to my other breast, paying it equal attention. I lifted off the bed and reached for him, wrapping my arms around his neck as I kissed him, tugging on his lip with my teeth. My hands slid down his stomach to the waistband of his pants, where I gripped the fabric and began yanking.

"Impatient, are we?" he whispered against my lips.

"Use your magic to get rid of them," I demanded, my voice breathy and rife with mindless need.

"Done," he said. "I like it when you command me."

I tore my eyes away from his and looked down. I bit my lip to suppress the moan that escaped at the sight of his arousal. His cock was just as impressive as the rest of him. Shit.

I reached my hand out and wrapped my fingers around the thick length of him, reveling in the satiny feel of his rock-hard flesh.

He reached for my hands and held them against his chest. "Come now, I'm not done with my show of devotion," he said, a trace of amusement in his voice. "There is still so much of you to be worshipped."

"Ash," I whispered breathlessly, the name slipping past my lips in a rush, as if it had been coiled on the tip of my tongue all along, waiting to spring free.

His brows lifted. "So you do know who I am after all. I quite like the way you moan my name."

Every time I'd heard his name since this morning, something inside me had rolled over and purred with excitement. The moment I entered this room and spotted him in that chair, my heart had recognized him, even if my mind didn't. In this moment, the only thing I understood was that my body and soul claimed him as mine. And hell. Right now, I wanted him to claim every part of me.

I kissed him again, my lips moving against his in a feverish onslaught. He caught my bottom lip between his teeth and nipped gently. His mouth pulled away from mine, traveling lazily down my body, licking and kissing every inch of me he touched.

My entire body burned for him, screaming out for more.

His head dipped lower, settling between my thighs. "Fuck," he growled. "You are so gloriously wet." And with that, he lowered his head and tasted me, his mouth closing over the throbbing source of my need, his tongue swirling over my swollen clit. I gasped at the contact, moaning loudly as pleasure jolted through me.

He slipped a finger, then another, inside me, sliding them in and out slowly as his mouth continued to circle my pulsing flesh. I lifted my hips and rocked against his face and fingers, losing control of myself as heat swirled through my body. My breath hitched and my pulse raced as it approached the onset of my orgasm, and I whimpered and moaned, grinding my pelvis against his face in shameless abandon.

He lifted his head for a moment and I screamed, gripping his hair and pushing him back down. "Don't you dare stop," I panted. "I'll use those so-called Goddess powers you think I have to turn you into a toad if you do."

His breath tickled my skin as he laughed, but his tongue and mouth found me once more, swirling faster, coaxing my orgasm from me. I gripped the sheets, my body hot and agitated as the pleasure came roaring in, erupting like a volcano inside me. I screamed his name as my body reared and convulsed, my nipples tingly and tight as waves of release washed over me.

Slowly, he drifted up my body to hover over me, slipping the fingers that were inside me into his mouth and sucking them clean, his eyes fastened to mine. I bit my lip to keep from swearing.

"Do you feel venerated, Tialla?" he asked, his eyes glittering as he looked at me.

"Not quite, Sovereign," I said.

His eyes sparked at the imperious use of his title. His lips twitched in amusement. "Tell me."

"I want you inside me," I whispered, my voice husky and raw. "Venerate me with your cock."

"Such a dirty tongue for a Goddess," he chided, and I laughed, opening my legs as he slid between them. I reached my hand down and stroked his hard length, rubbing my thumb over the liquid beading the tip, swirling it around the head of his cock.

He inhaled sharply, and I slowly guided him inside me. I sighed and moaned at the fullness of him, wrapping my legs around his waist to take him in deeper.

He let out a slow hiss. "Fuck, you are going to make me come with all those pretty little noises you make."

"Surely one of your many abilities can help with that," I murmured innocently.

"I told you—my abilities won't work on a Goddess."

"I beg to differ, Sovereign. As a matter of fact, I would say that you are very gifted at working your magic on Goddesses."

He pulled out completely and then slid inside me again with a low groan, his eyes closed in rapture, his body setting a slow and steady rhythm that I responded to, matching him thrust for thrust. He kissed me slowly as we danced our hedonic dance, and I gripped his shoulders as the placid pool of euphoria inside me rippled to life again.

He intertwined his fingers with mine, lifting my hands above my head as he drove into me. He looked like a God above me, fluid pools of fire swirling in his eyes as he stared at me so hungrily, I wanted to slip out of my skin and into his to get closer to him. I wanted to be completely consumed by his flame, to burn and ignite like a goddamn phoenix setting itself ablaze before taking its last breath, only to be reborn again.

I watched his face as the ecstasy began building for him—eyes swirling, jaw clenched, lips parted. Watching him only excited me more, adding fuel to the fire of my desire, stoking it higher.

"Come for me," I whispered, tangling my hands in his hair.

"Not before you do," he rasped, his breath short and ragged as he grabbed my hips and ground into me. Slipping his hand between our bodies, his thumb found my clit, stroking slowly.

"Oh God, I'm almost there," I cried clenching my inner muscles around him, rocking my hips forward. "Ash . . . Faster. Harder."

"Even your blasphemy is fucking seductive," he said breathlessly, driving into me as he carried me all the way with him over the edge into oblivion.

I threw my head back and moaned as I climaxed, my body shuddering and spasming around him, and he followed a moment later, his cry of pleasure echoing in my ear, his body taut and immovable as he came. For a moment, he went completely slack, and then he rolled and pulled me on top of him, kissing me passionately, his hands trailing down my waist to cup my ass.

My heart hammered against his chest, every nerve in my body hypersensitive to the tactile meridians of his. I tangled my hands in his hair, relishing the feel of his lips against mine, the warm caress of his tongue swirling lazily in my mouth, the tantalizing friction of our bodies moving against each other. There was nowhere else in the universe I wanted to be.

The woman from my dream—did she know that this is what awaited me on the other side? Was this the moment she had intended? Never in a million years would I have guessed this was what I was walking into.

"I trust I met all your celestial expectations?" he asked, stroking my cheek with his knuckles.

"You far exceeded them, Sovereign."

"You have the most divine body I have ever seen," he murmured, his tongue snaking along my collarbone.

"I'm sure you say that to all your late-night conquests."

"Never," he said, flipping me onto my back and moving lazily down my body. "I especially love the wide flare of your hips from your tiny waist. As for the curve of your ass, it's completely out of this world."

I smiled, the irony of his words not lost on me.

As he slid back up my body, he tangled his hand in my hair. Once more, my gaze locked onto the cuff on his wrist. It was crafted with rippling silver, the image of a crescent moon and a bird in flight over a sea of flames adorning the length of it. I hadn't imagined the soft, pulsing light radiating from the cuff. A memory stirred inside my mind.

"I had a dream about a cuff like this when I was a little girl," I said as the details of the recollection flickered to life.

"What kind of dream?" he said, his voice drowsy with contentment.

I traced the edge of his cuff with my fingers. "I was standing in a room with the tallest ceilings I've ever seen. The entire interior was bathed in light streaming in from the windows around me. At the front of the room was an altar, on which two velvet-lined boxes rested, and inside each box was a cuff like this, both radiating this same light. Except they were a mix of gold and silver, and a different image was etched on them."

Ash's eyes flashed with interest as he studied me. "What did they look like?" He shifted his weight, turning us both on our sides to face each other.

"They were identical, with four symbols on them: a crescent moon, a sun, three vertical stars, and what looked like a constellation." I looked away from the cuff to see Ash watching me with a guarded expression.

He sat up, flipping me onto my back and lowering his hand to my hips. He peered at my skin, his thumbs skimming over my hip bones. His body grew rigid. "You do not have a Drukhiu," he said, his eyes boring into mine before shifting to my hand. "And your wrist is bare."

My wrist was bare? "Is that a question or an accusation?" I lifted myself up to rest on my elbows. My gaze flitted down his body to where a red, crescent-shaped birthmark, identical to the one Gwynn had shown me, was visible on his right hip.

"Neither. It's an observation." His eyes narrowed as he studied my face and traced his thumb across my jaw. "From the moment you appeared in this room, the overwhelming need to have you chased all logic and reasoning away. Everything inside me surrendered to your spell—even the caustic darkness that consumes me." His fingers snaked down my shoulder, dipping lower to trace the swell of my breast.

I sucked in a breath, unable to tear my eyes away from his.

His hand moved back up to clasp the side of my neck, his index finger caressing the sensitive spot behind my ear. "My sense of discernment claims you as my eternal soul's shadow," he said, his voice a low rasp. "Something that is more myth than possibility, I know." Slowly, he tilted my chin up. "Despite this intrinsic and primal response to you, I need to know—who are you really, Tialla?"

I swallowed. I didn't know what to say. I was elated that he'd experienced the same overwhelming need I did, but other sobering emotions were flanking me in the aftermath of all that heat and passion. What had he called me? His eternal's soul's shadow? I'd never heard that term before. What did it mean?

I sighed softly. "My name is Eleyse." A cloak of unease settled over me in response to his intense scrutiny, the abrupt shift in the mood between us permeating the air.

"You called me Ash," he said, reaching for my hand. "Only those precious to me call me by that name. How do you know me?"

I looked at him, unable to explain anything about my predicament. Frustrated, my eyes welled with tears. "That's the thing—I don't remember how I know you. I only know that I do, and *my* heart tells me that *you* are precious to me, so maybe that's why I call you Ash?"

"Trust me, Tialla, I would remember if we'd met before," he said softly as he pushed himself back onto his heels. "There is nothing remotely forgettable about you."

"I can't explain," I whispered. "I do know that although I don't remember any of our time together, you feel different to me, as if you're a different version of the you I know."

His face clouded over in confusion just as the realization hit me. The coronation. He'd said earlier that it was the eve of his coronation as Sovereign. Didn't Gwynn say that their parents had died over a century ago?

"Can I ask a question?" I said, sitting up and grabbing a pillow to cover myself.

He yanked the pillow away and tossed it behind him.

My mouth dropped open as I glared at him.

"I like you without any clothes on," he said, his tone dry, his gaze unreadable. "Ask your question."

"You said before that it was the eve of your coronation." I swallowed slowly. "How long have your parents been gone?"

His eyes grew hard and cold. "It's been almost two years."

"Shit," I said, rolling away from him. How the hell was this possible? I'd gone back in time a century? What the fuck had I done?

"What is it?" he asked, his eyes flashing with concern.

"Just give me a moment to think," I said, closing my eyes.

Suddenly, the words of the woman from my dream washed over me once more, and understanding dawned. *Through the eye of this vortex, past, present, and future converge.* His past, my present, our future. That had to be it.

Earlier, in the hot spring, Gwynn had mentioned that losing their parents almost destroyed her brother—that he completely fell apart and was consumed with anger and self-loathing after their death.

That had to be what I sensed, the difference I felt in him. There was such rage and bitterness simmering beneath the surface. I remembered the words of the woman in my dream that night so long ago. *He comes, and on his heels, your future.* And the woman with wings earlier today. *He filled my heart with so much love, but his heart was always meant to be yours.*

I lifted my face and gazed at him, and in an unexplained rush of clarity and conviction, it hit me. Ash was indeed the *he* I'd wondered about earlier. How this was all possible and what it all meant, I didn't have a clue, but my heart proclaimed the truth of it.

In front of the bed, the swirling vortex that brought me here reappeared with a flare, and my heart plummeted. My moment was up. It wasn't nearly enough.

Ash stared at the sphere incredulously as I quickly climbed onto his lap, my legs gripping his hips.

"You really are a fucking Goddess, aren't you?" he said, his lips parted slightly, his brows knitted together. "I know a Senshifter when I see it. Only the Gods can command one."

I shook my head as I ran my hands across his broad chest. "I don't know what that is, and no, I'm not a Goddess. A magical-looking woman with violet hair and music inside her sent me here through that thing." I shifted my weight onto my knees and reached for his face with both my hands. "Did you mean what you said about what your senses told you about me?"

"Every word," he said, confusion etched on his face as his hand reached around me to settle in the small of my back.

"And have your senses ever been wrong?"

"Never," he replied, his eyes holding me captive.

I lowered my head and kissed him, committing him in this moment to my memory.

He tightened his grip on my waist and kissed me back, slow and deep, his mouth slanting over mine as his tongue explored the recesses of my mouth. I tangled my hands in his wavy hair, wanting more, but knowing that it was time to leave.

I broke the kiss, my hands still cradling his handsome face. "I can't explain any of this, but I'm asking you to trust your senses and what they tell you about me."

I closed my eyes, whispers from a time filled with despair ringing through my mind. That voice. Unmistakable.

I stroked Ash's jaw, my gaze locked with his. "I'm going to say to you now what I believe you will one day say to me in my most desperate hours. *Be strong, Ash. Live. Fight the darkness.*"

His eyes flashed with sadness and longing, and he reached for me once more, his hand clasping the side of my face.

"You asked me who I was," I said. "My name is Eleyse, and I am from the human world. I only just got to Ariadna and met your sister, Gwynn, for the first time today. Now, you and I have met before in *my* past, but I only exist in your future. Find me there, Ash. I have no idea how I slipped back in time a century to be with you now. All I know is that just like you say I am meant for you, you are meant for me."

He stared into my eyes for a long moment, a myriad of emotions flitting across his face. "I will, Tialla. I promise."

"Please, call me Elle. All those who are precious to *me* call me that." I brushed my lips against his once more before sliding off the bed toward the swirling, golden sphere. "Goodbye, Ash," I said, looking back at him one last time.

"Only until the next time I see you, Elle," he said softly. "And so you know, when I think of you, you will always be Tialla mata."

My Goddess.

My eyes welled up as I stared at him with longing. Not looking away, I stepped backward into the orb, and in a whirlwind of movement, I was swept back to the present, leaving him and the past that didn't belong to me behind.

Chapter 8

I STUMBLED OUT OF the vortex back into my room. By the time I turned around, the gilded round object was back where it was before—affixed to the wall above the fireplace, the arrow at the top pointing straight up again and the three stars in their neutral position at the center. As if nothing had happened. The woman from my dreams was nowhere in sight.

Senshifter, Ash had called it. Commanded only by the Gods. What the heck did that even mean? There was so much about this world that defied logic.

A myriad of thoughts and emotions surged through me. Was it all a dream? It couldn't be. I was naked, for heaven's sake. In addition, my body tingled and ached lightly from my time spent with Ash. I still smelled his intoxicating scent on me, tasted him in my mouth.

Woodenly, I walked to the bathroom and plopped down in front of the vanity. My violet hair was a tangled mess, and my face and chest were flushed. From one ear, the earring I'd slipped on earlier that morning dangled. The other side was gone. I unhooked the jade earring from my ear and placed it back in the jewelry box. Was the other one stuck back in time in Ash's room? Along with the robe and nightgown he magicked away?

As I walked to the closet to find another nightgown, my mind was rife with questions. How was it possible for what just happened to happen? Was there a reason that I went back in time to that moment? What did it mean? Who was the woman with the violet hair? How did Ash and I know each other in my world? Every fiber of my being told me that we were intimately acquainted, that he was precious to me.

Ash, as he was when I crossed the threshold of the vortex, had never met me before, but he was undeniably drawn to me. Being with him was as natural as breathing. It felt right. His sensing abilities told him that I was meant for him, just like I *knew* the same thing the moment I laid eyes on him.

Climbing into bed, I slid under the covers, lulled by the fire-licked shadows thrown from the hearth as they waltzed on the ceiling above. I was numb. I didn't know what to think. I'd only been in Ariadna for a few days—today being the only lucid one—but it was as if who I was before was fading away; I was slipping on another skin, assuming another identity.

I touched my lips, still swollen from Ash's kisses, and a pang of sadness nestled deep in my heart. Where was *my* Ash? The one who knew me. Clearly, he had found me through time. That, in itself, was difficult to wrap my head around. Somehow, tonight, I'd slipped back in time and encountered him before he even met me—although I'd already met him in his future—and then almost a century later, he'd found me in a time when I had no idea who he was, and we'd developed some kind of relationship, the details of which I couldn't remember. Here, in this moment, everything was full circle—*past, present, and future converge* indeed. It was convoluted and messy, and none of it made any sense.

He had to know I was here. Right? Did he have anything to do with what happened to me and how I ended up here? My mind brimmed with so many questions. And what about the rebounding curse Andreo said was responsible for my memory loss? What did that mean?

My head hurt. It had been a long, exhausting day. In the back of my mind, a question begging to be acknowledged all day finally rose to the surface: *Why wasn't I more concerned about returning home?*

I already knew the answer. There was nothing left for me there that I wanted to return to.

My life as I remembered it had been void of purpose and meaning for a long time. Oh, the terrible lengths I'd taken to drift away into nothingness. For a while, the pursuit of my demise was a quest that consumed me, the pain of my hollow existence too unbearable to endure.

This morning, as soon as my eyes had flown open, before even speaking to Gwynn, an awakening began—something dormant inside me opened its eyes and yawned contentedly. I couldn't deny that. This place called to me in a way I'd never experienced before. There was a feeling of belonging—when I stood on the balcony outside my window, when I was with the woman with wings and with the silver-eyed woman from my dream, and when I was with Ash. I didn't know how or why, but what that voice inside me said earlier this evening was true: *You have only ever belonged here.*

My thoughts strayed to Ash again. I couldn't get him out of my head. What I'd just experienced with him was mind-blowing. Was it like that with him when I knew him? For the life of me, I couldn't imagine it being any other way. He was fantasy, danger, power, sex incarnate. Being with him was thrilling and effortless. He was confident, charismatic, and gentle, with a wicked sense of humor. He affected me in a way no one else ever had.

A wave of longing crested over me and I stirred restlessly, wanting, needing to see him again. I had to believe that I would; he was the Sovereign of Valkyse after all, and I was in his domain, ensconced in one of his Sovereign residences, no less. That, too, couldn't be a coincidence.

My eyes grew heavy, and amid my mind's replay of our wild, hedonistic adventure, sleep claimed me, sweeping me away into dreams of a happier time, where laughter and joy filled my heart, and music was meaningful again. And tangled in my dreams, the caress of fingers brushed against my cheek as I laughed and sang, and a voice whispered softly, "There is nothing more beautiful than your smile, Tialla mata."

Chapter 9

THE NEXT MORNING, GWYNN introduced me to the housekeeper, Ezla. She was an impressive woman—tall and willowy and beautiful, her dark hair twisted into a neat braid at the top of her head. Immediately, I was at ease with her. Her eyes were filled with light and happiness, and I gravitated toward her instantly. It was clear from the way she treated Gwynn that she was a mother figure to her. She insisted that I come to her for anything I needed, and I promised that I would.

Gwynn and I ate on the terrace again, and all through breakfast, I wrestled with telling her what had happened last night after I left her. Shit. Was I frigging nuts? I'd slept with her brother. Who knew how she would react to that? What if she used her crazy banishment magic on me? No. I couldn't take that chance. For now, my lips were sealed.

After we ate and the plates were cleared away, Gwynn mentioned that Andreo had left for Cazara Torannon to look through some texts on curses in the library there. We would see him later that evening.

"Can I ask you something?" I twisted my napkin in my lap.

"Of course," Gwynn replied, taking a sip of her water.

"That object hanging above the fireplace in my room—what is it? I've never seen anything like it before."

Gwynn's forehead wrinkled, but then her eyes sparked with

96

understanding. "Oh, that's a Senshifter," she replied.

My heart skipped a beat. This morning after I'd woken up, I'd lain there disoriented, staring at the still and lifeless object on the wall, wondering if the encounter last night was nothing but a figment of my imagination. But hearing Gwynn so casually identifying the Senshifter, using the same name Ash had, was proof enough that it was real.

"What does it do?" I asked cautiously.

"It's largely ornamental, really. A magical artifact with limited capabilities. It responds only to a Sovereign and a Queen Consort, showing either one what the other is feeling in that moment, regardless of where they are."

Wait, what? It had responded to me twice—once yesterday morning when I first awoke, and then last night before it turned into the vortex. Whose feelings did it show me? Then again, Ash was adamant that only the Gods commanded it.

"Is that all it does?" I asked, not sure how to ask what I really wanted to know.

"Yes and no." Her fingernails clicked against the arm of her chair. "The real power behind the Senshifter lies with the Gods. They can use it to create a pocket in time."

My heart was hammering now. "A pocket in time?" I swallowed the lump stuck in my throat.

"I've only heard stories of it being done, but it's been said that some of the Gods can imbue a Senshifter with power that creates a pocket in time, allowing a person to travel forward or backward to another time dimension for a set amount of time."

I gulped quietly. So Ash was right. Did that mean the woman from my dream was a Goddess? That's what Ash had called me. *Tialla*. Something he'd asked about again when the Senshifter returned to take me back. However it was possible, I had indeed traveled back in time.

"Is that what the arrow at the top of the Senshifter does? Move time backward or forwards?" Last night, the pealing chimes had sounded like they were counting down to something, and the arrows had kept steadily shifting to the left with each chime.

"To be honest, I don't know," Gwynn replied, her head tilted to the side. "Like I said, I've only ever heard stories. And I never really asked questions about it. Why do you ask?"

"Oh, I was just curious. It's a peculiar-looking object, and I wondered about it."

Gwynn nodded. "That's only one of many magical artifacts in existence."

"Right. You did mention magical artifacts yesterday."

There had to be some other way to get answers. Gwynn had mentioned a library earlier. Maybe there?

She raised her right arm, pointing to the thick cuff she wore on her wrist. My pulse raced as my gaze locked onto it. It was similar to the one Ash wore, with a few variations. Hers was silver, like his, but contained intricate engravings all around it, with the image of a crescent moon in the center. Unlike his, hers was not emitting that soft, blue light.

"Since we're going somewhere today, I need to explain a few things." Her fingers circled the cuff on her wrist. "This is a giln. Everyone in Ariadna wears one. I've had mine since a few days after I was born. From the moment it is placed on your wrist, it becomes an extension of you, and it can't be removed, except through death, or in the case of a new Sovereign, through succession."

That's what Ash had meant when he said my wrist was bare. I wasn't wearing one of those.

"What does it do?" I peered closer at her wrist. The silver in the cuff was fluid, moving in dark ripples across the band. Ash's did as well.

"The giln allows you to travel in Ariadna, but each one is unique to the person wearing it. Depending on who you are, the giln determines where you are allowed to go. A person has but to think of where they want to go, and the giln takes them there. Mind you, the range of most gilns is limited, to varying degrees, but there are a few that are limitless, allowing for travel across Ariadna, and to select sacred places in the four dominions and the Sangelis. The ones with limitless power—labrals—belong to the four Sovereigns of Ariadna, and it is through the labral that succession is determined."

Well, color me intrigued. I stared at the giln in amazement. It was strange, but incredible. Being able to get somewhere without having to take a train or plane or car? Saving hours of travel? Unbelievable. How did it even work? Surely by magic. And what of the gilns with limitless power? The labrals. What more could they do?

"Unless you are a Sovereign, the giln cannot be removed once it is bonded to you. It may evolve to allow new access or to restrict previous access, but once it reads you, it is made just for you."

"Once it *reads* you?" I asked, not exactly sure what that meant.

"Yes. In order to obtain a giln, everyone must visit Cazara Colpra, the Giln Keeper's sanctuary. Oletho Colpra is the steward of all gilns in Ariadna and has been the Giln Keeper for over 3,500 years."

I gulped. 3,500 years? Holy crap! He was older than Jesus! Although Gwynn had explained about long lifespans, that someone truly could have such a long lifespan was still unfathomable to me.

"I told you yesterday about the Ethereal Harmonies," Gwynn continued, "the main source of power in this realm. The gilns draw their power from the same source. In the Giln Keeper's sanctuary, there is a place where everyone must stand to be read. After this reading, the Ethereal Harmonies fashion a giln that is unique and bonded to the person being read." She paused and looked at me, her amethyst eyes flashing. "I am taking you to see the Giln Keeper."

"But why?" I blurted out. "I wasn't born in this world." What kind of giln would be fashioned for me if I did stand to be read?

"You are in this world now. And it is my hope that Oletho may be able to provide some insight or guidance on your presence here."

What could this Oletho possibly know about why I was here? Did he have special powers too?

"Where is the Giln Keeper?" I asked. "How do we get there?"

"The Giln Keeper's sanctuary is in Radiac, an island at the center of Ariadna—the point where all four dominions meet. It's an independent territory, a power of its own, outside the jurisdiction of any one dominion. My giln gives me the power to carry someone else. I used it to bring you here after I rescued you in the alleyway, and I'll use it to take you to the Giln Keeper's sanctuary."

I twisted my fingers in my lap. I was both nervous and excited at the prospect of the journey, not sure what to expect. Would the Giln Keeper be able to provide more insight into my predicament as Gwynn believed he might? Would he know more about who I was and my connection to Ash?

I pushed my chair back and got to my feet. "When are we leaving?"

"As soon as we get dressed." Gwynn adjusted her shoe and stood up. "We have a busy day ahead of us. After we're done in Radiac, we are going to Torannon."

"What's in Torannon?" I was disappointed that we would not be returning to this place that I was beginning to see as a safe haven.

"Answers, I hope."

Chapter 10

"**A**RE YOU READY?" G**WYNN** squeezed my hand reassuringly. We were standing in the main foyer of the house, both dressed in comfortable garb—flats, pants, short-sleeved shirts.

Was I ready? Hell no. The rational part of my brain was on overdrive. Was this way of traveling safe? Was there any risk of body parts or internal organs getting left behind in the magical teleportation process? I couldn't get the picture of a leg aimlessly hopping around on its own out of my head.

I shrugged off a shudder and looked at Gwynn. "No. I can't help but feel nervous. I don't know what to expect."

"Don't be," Gwynn assured. "Just hold on to my arm, and we'll be there before you know it."

Making sure my entire body was in one straight line and mentally summoning all the atoms in my body to pay attention and stick together, I took Gwynn's right arm. With her left forefinger, she touched the giln in a clockwise circular movement, causing the air around us to splinter. A loud pop and an intense pressure filled my head. My insides felt like they were being twisted in a corkscrew, but then, just as quickly as it happened, it was over.

Shit! That was . . . something. My head spun and my stomach churned uneasily. I kept my eyes closed and waited for the wave of nausea to subside. It was nothing like when I'd stepped through the Senshifter last night. That had been seamless.

Within a minute, I was back to normal, and my eyes flew open, immediately checking to make sure that all of me had made the trip. Breathing a sigh of relief that I was in one piece, I looked up to find that we were standing in front of a massive, dome-shaped stone building with large marble columns all the way around.

It had really worked! In a matter of seconds, we were somewhere else entirely, all body parts intact and accounted for. Incredible!

The sunlight streamed down upon us, the skies blue and cloudless. A towering crystal arch over twenty feet tall stood some distance away to our right, shimmering in the bright morning sun, and an identical one stood rooted to our left. Above us was a third. It was like nothing I'd ever seen, colorful bands of light rippling through the entire length of each arch.

"This is the gateway entrance from Valkyse," Gwynn explained. "Each of the four dominions has its own entrance and main doors. The dominion you belong to determines which gateway entrance you will come through. That one on the left is the gateway from Solanis and the one on the right is from Tandor. The gateway from Averon is on the opposite side of Cazara Colpra. Now, when we go in, there will be many people around, but as I belong to the ruling family of Valkyse, our presence there will grant us an audience with Oletho himself. Don't be alarmed if no one notices us when we're inside. We are shielded to ensure no one detects our presence."

"Oh," I said, staring at her with what I was sure was a dumb expression. Of course we were shielded. She'd said it so casually, the same way someone would say that circles were round or that chocolate was delicious.

As we walked toward the building, the large crest looming above the wide doors directly in front of the walkway stopped me in my tracks. Blue, silver, and violet, depicting a crescent moon shining above a bird in flight over a sea of silver flames. This was the same design that was on Ash's giln.

"That's the Valkyse crest," Gwynn explained, seeing me studying it. "Each dominion bears their own." She inclined her head toward me. "Come on, let's go inside."

It made sense. Ash was the Sovereign of Valkyse, so it would only follow that his giln reflected that.

I followed Gwynn to the door, my heart pounding nervously in my chest.

We stepped into a large, cavernous atrium where four separate lobbies were cordoned off around the expanse of the interior. At the center of each lobby was a grand circular desk, ornate and wooden, each bearing the crest of one of the four dominions. Four attendants stood at each desk, some talking to people, others with no one in front of them.

In our lobby, several people were talking quietly and milling around. None of them noticed or paid any heed to our presence. Next to us, a young woman was rocking a crying baby back and forth, whispering soothing words as she paced the floor. She looked through us as if we weren't there.

Within a few minutes of us arriving, a short, plump woman with auburn hair and a friendly smile beckoned to us to follow her. She led us to the center of the room and then up a large crystal staircase that reminded me of the one I'd seen in the cavern with the woman with wings. She ushered us into an expansive waiting room with full-length windows and a magnificent panoramic view of the ocean that made my breath catch in my chest.

"That's the Sea of Celestials," Gwynn explained. "And way in the distance, you can faintly see the southern tip of the region of Shanta in the Dominion of Solanis."

I stared in wonder at the view outside. For miles around, there was not a cloud in sight. I'd just made out the shadow of a land mass in the distance when the door behind us opened and a stocky, barrel-chested man with graying, curly hair and a short, trimmed beard walked in. He was wearing a long, green robe, and an oval-shaped, bejeweled amulet hung around his neck. His skin was flawless—not a crease or wrinkle—and in his eyes shone a quiet, ancient wisdom.

I couldn't stop staring. Holy crap. How old did Gwynn say he was? Thirty-something hundred? He didn't look any older than fifty . . . well, maybe sixty. And he definitely looked like some kind of wizard. Very mysterious and magical.

He smiled as he walked toward us. "Gwynnis Valkyse!" He clasped both of Gwynn's hands in his. "It does these old eyes good to see you. It has been a long time." He smiled, his eyes crinkling at the corners. "How can I be of service to you, dear heart?"

"Oletho, so lovely to see you again," Gwynn replied warmly, squeezing his hands in hers. She looked at me and touched my shoulder. "This is Eleyse. I was hoping that you might be able to help us."

Oletho turned his attention to me, and his eyes opened wide for a moment. "A human woman," he said, appraising me slowly. "And yet not entirely a human woman. Interesting."

"What do you mean?" I asked, thrown by his words. "How am I not entirely human?"

Oletho's eyes bore through me. "A shroud obscures you in shadow, Eleyse, making it difficult for me to see you clearly, but I see enough to know you must be read. I know enough not to be surprised at your presence here."

My brows furrowed in confusion. Read how? Gwynn said we were just here for answers. And why was he not surprised by my presence?

Oletho turned to Gwynn, a grim expression on his face. "I take it Asher knows she's here? The presence of a human in the Dominion of Valkyse is something that wouldn't go unnoticed by the Sovereign."

"I don't know," Gwynn replied. "He's been gone for four days and I haven't been able to sense him when I reach out. I'm starting to get worried. It's not like Ash to be unreachable like this."

The concern in Gwynn's voice set me on edge. Had something happened to Ash?

Oletho clasped his hands behind him, rocking back onto his heels. "Very curious, but likely not a coincidence. Follow me." He headed toward a door on the far right.

"You think Eleyse's appearance and Asher's disappearance are linked?" Gwynn's eyes were wide as we followed Oletho through the door and into an airy chamber.

"Asher is nothing if not meticulous," Oletho said. "You know that. You can rest assured he knows Eleyse is here. His absence is by his own design."

"You don't believe Kaliope has something to do with this, do you?"

"Unfortunately, yes."

Kaliope? Why did the name sound familiar? *Right!* Faron had mentioned it yesterday to Gwynn. I couldn't recall what he'd said about her, though. As for Ash, why would he choose to disappear because I was here? My spirits plummeted. All I'd thought of since being with him last night was seeing him again. What did this Kaliope have to do with keeping him away?

I looked away from Oletho and Gwynn, my mouth falling open at what stood in front of me. At the end of the room was a crystal dais, almost identical to the one I'd witnessed in the cave with the woman with wings. But this wasn't a dream. This was real.

One thing was clear to me: this couldn't be a coincidence.

"Are you all right, Eleyse?" Gwynn asked, her eyes flashing with concern. "You look like you've seen a ghost."

Oletho stared at me intently. "You've seen this before."

"I . . . no, I mean . . . maybe?" I didn't know how to explain. "I saw something like it in a dream."

Oletho exchanged glances with Gwynn. "Eleyse, quickly now. Step onto the dais for me." He gestured for me to move onto the crystal podium. "The Ethereal Harmonies clamor for you to be read. This place is a conduit for their power, one of the few sanctums in Ariadna where the Harmonies are channeled in perfect tandem."

I turned to look at Gwynn and she nodded encouragingly at me, urging me to step forward. Cautiously, I made my way onto the dais. Shit. Not again. Instantly, just like in the cave, I was sucked in, convinced I was going to be crushed from the inside out. It went on for at least a minute. I was breathless and gasping by the time I was released. The ground rumbled beneath me, and just like in the cave, a grotto ascended from the floor, covered in all manner of precious stones.

Instead of the strange being I had seen yesterday, in the center of the grotto were two gilns, bathed in soft, warm light. I stumbled backward, my heart racing as I looked at the two cuffs hovering before me. They were both a mix of white and yellow gold, but one of them was identical in design to the cuff Ash wore on his wrist, the only difference being that his had been pure silver.

Behind me, Gwynn gasped, and I turned to see her staring at the grotto with wide eyes. Beside her, Oletho's face shone with surprise and reverence.

I turned my attention back to the grotto, hugging my arms to my chest when I focused my attention on the second giln.

Dear God. How was this even possible?

The cuff was identical to the one I'd described to Ash—the one from my dream when I was a little girl. A mix of white and yellow gold, with four symbols across the top: a crescent moon, a sun, three vertical stars, and a cluster of constellations.

On the outer edge of each giln, an indentation ran along the top length. The silver and gold were fluid on both gilns, sluicing across the length of the cuff as I looked at them.

My heartbeat accelerated. Why did the Ethereal Harmonies return these after reading *me*? What did it even mean?

Oletho stepped forward and took both gilns from the grotto.

"Zidiurrh," Gwynn whispered reverently. "Oletho, it can't be. And why are there *two* of them?"

"The reading is never wrong."

"That one is identical to Ash's," Gwynn said, pointing to the one with the Valkyse crest. She chewed on her lip, her face lined with worry. "Kaliope will hunt her down and kill her if she learns of this."

My head snapped up. Kaliope again. Who was she? Why would she want to kill me? Wait. Was she the one who had tried to kill me? And what was zidiurrh?

"Can someone please tell me what's going on?" I asked, anxiety smothering me at the panic in Gwynn's voice.

Gwynn ran her hands through her hair. "Remember when I said there were gilns of limitless power that only Sovereigns wear?"

I nodded. "Labal—no, labral."

Gwynn lifted her wrist. "Every giln is made of trinzum, the strongest metal on Ariadna. Each Sovereign, on the other hand, wears a labral—crafted entirely out of zidiurrh, the most rare and precious metal on Ariadna. A labral contains magical properties that make it indestructible and receptive to the directives of its owner."

I stared at her blankly. "What exactly are you getting at?"

She pointed to the giln in Oletho's left hand. "That is a labral. It is identical to the one my brother wears as Sovereign of Valkyse. That other one is also a labral, but I have never seen anything like it before. I don't know what it means."

Oletho stepped toward me, his gaze piercing and solemn. "In the recorded history of Ariadna, the Ethereal Harmonies have only ever returned two labrals in the same reading once." He lifted his right hand, his index finger pointed up. "Just once."

"What?" Gwynn exclaimed. "I didn't know such a thing was even possible. When did it happen? And with which Sovereign? Was this something that you were even aware could be a possibility?"

Oletho's face was grave as he studied the labrals. "One of the most ancient texts here at the sanctuary—one that all heirs to the Sovereignty must familiarize themselves with—describes such a scenario, and what it means when two labrals are returned in a reading. It's not something we've ever had to contend with. I think it's important that Eleyse understands how succession to the Sovereignty works if the significance of these labrals is to make sense to her."

"Succession to the Sovereignty?" I blurted out. Okay. Ash was Sovereign of Valkyse—I got that. What did that have to do with me? Why did the Ethereal Harmonies return *me* two labrals? That they returned any at all was unexpected.

Oletho took a step closer. "Succession to the Sovereignty can be a tricky thing, but the Ethereal Harmonies always have the last say. In most instances, succession passes to the next of kin. After a Sovereign passes on, the magic of the Ethereal Harmonies returns his labral here—to Cazara Colpra—where it stays in the Pavilion of Harmonies until the coronation of the new Sovereign. In the meantime, the rightful successor's giln—the one they've worn all their lives—becomes infused with Shinoran light, protective magic found on all artifacts of power that draw their strength from the Ethereal Harmonies. Shinoran light serves as affirmation that the successor has been deemed worthy. Upon their coronation, the incumbent Sovereign must submit to the giln reading process again, and it is then that the giln they have worn all their lives is unbonded from them and replaced with the labral of their predecessor. It remains with them until death."

Understanding dawned on me. I'd encountered Ash on the eve of his coronation, the giln on his wrist pulsing with a soft, blue light—this Shinoran light Oletho referenced. His giln, when I'd seen it, was pure silv—no, trinzum, based on what Gwynn explained earlier. The one I was looking at now was made of zidiurrh, as Gwynn explained—a Sovereign's labral.

"Now this is where it gets interesting." Oletho's eyes were bright with excitement. "At the time, I didn't understand, but it's falling into place now."

"What is it, Oletho?" Gwynn's eyes were wide, her mouth parted.

I was just as curious as Gwynn to hear what he had to say.

"Remember before when I said that only *once* have the Ethereal Harmonies returned two gilns in a reading?"

Gwynn and I looked at each other and nodded.

"Well," he continued. "It was at Asher's coronation that it happened."

Chapter 11

"WHAT?" GWYNN BLURTED OUT, her eyes wide with surprise. "That was almost a century ago. Why am I only now hearing of this?"

I couldn't shake the churning excitement inside me as I waited for Oletho to explain.

He shook his head. "It wouldn't have been common knowledge, Gwynn. Remember, at a Sovereign's coronation, the labral bonding ceremony is a hallowed and private affair, held in the Pavilion of Harmonies, overseen by only myself and the other reigning Sovereigns, and sanctified by the Cloryals."

"Cloryals?" I asked.

Oletho nodded. "Each of the four dominions is home to a celestial being called a Cloryal. They are Keepers of the Ethereal Harmonies and are bound to oversee and carry out the will of the divine power source. When it comes to succession, the Cloryals are the ones to consecrate those who are chosen."

"So they're like Gods?"

"Something like that, but not quite," Oletho said. "They exist solely to serve the Ethereal Harmonies." Oletho passed the labrals in his hands to me and stepped into the middle of the room, the amulet around his neck flat in his palm. He ran his fingers over the green stone in the center, and in a whorl of shadows, an antique-looking wooden cabinet appeared in front of him.

I took a step back. His amulet possessed magical abilities! My gaze flitted to the pulse of warm, blue light encircling it. The Shinoran light. It was a magical artifact.

The door to the cabinet opened with a groan as Oletho pulled on the handle. Gingerly, he lifted something off one of the shelves and closed the door. When he turned around, he held what looked like an inverted pyramid-shaped bowl, held in place by a base in the shape of two clawed feet. Tendrils of blue smoke eddied around and inside the object, shifting and swirling as if it contained a life of its own. The bowl itself looked like it was crafted out of the same material as the labrals in my hands.

Oletho lifted the bowl. "The Pavilion of Harmonies—where every labral bonding ceremony has been held since the beginning of this age—has a living memory. As Giln Keeper, I can conjure any specific one using this magical artifact, a Calife." He let go of the pyramid bowl, and to my surprise, it stayed suspended in midair, turning slowly. "In order for the Pavilion of Harmonies to divulge its secrets, however, I will need a drop of your blood, Eleyse." Oletho shifted his gaze to me.

"My blood?" I asked, my eyes wide as I stared at him. "Why *my* blood?"

"Because of the labrals in your hands. The Ethereal Harmonies returned those specifically for *you*, and although right now you might not understand what that means, those labrals make it so that you, and by extension anyone present with you," he inclined his head toward Gwynn, "can access the memories retained by the Pavilion of Harmonies."

What the—Was anything ever simple here? Every time I was beginning to grasp a certain concept or explanation, everything went to hell with the revelation of something new.

"Do you consent?" Oletho asked, reaching his hand out toward mine.

I nodded, my curiosity overwhelming me.

Oletho guided my hand over the Calife, and retrieving a small dagger from the folds of his robe, he pricked the tip of my index finger. "The labral bonding of Asher Valkyse," he whispered into the Calife.

I watched as a bead of crimson swelled on my skin and dripped into the bowl. Instantly, the smoke inside the bowl writhed and turned a brilliant shade of magenta just as the pungent odor of something tangy but floral blitzed my senses. My heart lurched as a stream of light shot out from the depths of the Calife and projected all around the room.

The light began spinning at breakneck speed, pouring into every crevice it touched until it shrouded every inch of space in its mellow luster. A soft, pealing sound—like many copper wind chimes trilling in the breeze—fractured the silence, and the space around us transformed.

My mouth dropped open. Everything in my line of sight was different. It was as if we had been transported to another place.

"Now we watch," Oletho said quietly.

I gasped when I saw where we were. It was the room from my dream—the one I had told Ash about—with the tall ceilings and long windows, light streaming in from every direction. At the front of the room, a crystal dais stood behind a gilded altar. Around the dais stood four crystal thrones, each of which was occupied. Four beautiful, spectral-looking women sat gracefully, each of them looking out serenely into the room in front of them. In appearance, they were almost identical, except for the color of their hair and eyes—lavender and silver, copper and amber, pale blonde and blue, burgundy and green. They were dressed in matching ivory toga-style gowns, held in place over one shoulder by a gemstone clasp.

I could not tear my eyes away from them. The one on the left shifted her gaze, her silver eyes seeming to burrow into mine. A wave of alarm coursed through me and I shifted uneasily on my feet. This was a memory, right? There was no bloody way she was actually looking at me.

"The Cloryals," Gwynn whispered, and when I turned to look at her, her jaw was slack, her eyes wide with awe.

A soft melody filled the room. Instantly, I recognized it. The one from my dream with the silver-eyed woman, and from last night in the grotto. My heart warmed to the lilting notes swirling around us.

Oletho—the past version of himself—stood against the wall, in the middle of the four thrones. His face was calm but solemn as he stared straight ahead, his robe fanned out around him.

Behind us, the doors opened, and the sound of heralding trumpets broke the silence, making me jump. I turned around to see three male figures striding together down the purple-carpeted aisle. Each one wore a rich velvet cloak trimmed with white, and on their heads, a glittering, bejeweled crown.

"The Sovereigns?" I asked Gwynn, and she nodded.

We stood just off to the side near the front of the room, with a perfect view of everything. I studied each of the Sovereigns as they approached us. The one on the right wore a yellow cloak and looked older than the other two. His eyes were glittering and hard, his lips pursed in a thin line, no hint of softness on his face.

The one in the middle with the green cloak was tall and handsome, his skin a glowing copper complexion, his eyes a startling shade of blue. The trace of a smirk lifted his lips.

As for the one on the left, he was wearing a red cloak, and although not as tall as the one in the middle, he still towered above the Sovereign on the right. His brown eyes were warm and kind, and his skin glowed with the soft hue of a tan. He was older than the Sovereign in the middle, but to my human eyes, he didn't look a day over fifty.

"The Sovereigns of Solanis, Averon, and Tandor," Gwynn whispered, pointing from right to left.

They walked to the front of the room, coming to a stop before the altar, each one facing a Cloryal. Only the Cloryal on the left had no one facing her.

The sound of trumpets rang out again and the doors slowly opened once more. My heart leapt into my throat when I saw the tall, broad figure silhouetted against the light.

Ash.

My knees turned to jelly. He took a step forward and entered the room. Breathtaking. A wave of longing bowled me over as I stared at him, heart pounding.

As he walked slowly down the aisle, his short, dark hair framing his serious face, his emerald eyes so bottomless I could drown in them, I could not tear my gaze away. With his rich sapphire cloak around him and his glittering crown on his head, power and charisma dripped from him. Strangely, like I was able to the night before, I sensed the sorrow and anger simmering inside him.

He reached the front of the altar, and the Cloryal on the left stood gracefully from her throne. "Step onto the dais and be deemed worthy, son of Valkyse."

Deemed worthy. The same thing the woman with wings had said to me.

A low, rumbling sound filled the air and the ground beneath us shook. Just like it did in the cavern with the woman with wings, and earlier with Oletho and Gwynn, a grotto emerged out of the ground, covered with a multitude of twinkling gemstones.

114

Ash stepped forward and crossed the altar onto the crystal dais.

"Place your wrist in the grotto," back-in-time Oletho said, stepping forward from his position between the Cloryals, his robe billowing around him as he moved.

Slowly, Ash placed his wrist as instructed, his giln pulsing with Shinoran light. A soft hum echoed from the grotto and bands of light weaved from inside. When the hum subsided and the light faded, Ash removed his hand to reveal a bare wrist, his giln gone.

"With the unbonding of your giln," Oletho proclaimed, "the Ethereal Harmonies will read you."

My heartbeat quickened.

Standing on the dais, his back facing us, only his rigid posture gave any indication to what he was feeling. Surely, it was the same for him as it was for me—the terrifying feeling of being crushed from the inside out, breathless and torturous.

Finally, his shoulders relaxed and he heaved a big breath. The grotto was bathed in light, and in the center, two gilns hovered, just like it did for me. They were indeed identical to the ones I still held in my hands.

Hearing it from Oletho was one thing—seeing it for myself was entirely different. My heart thudded as I looked at the labrals suspended in the grotto.

One of the Sovereigns—the one wearing the yellow cloak—gasped quietly, his shoulders stiffening. From the profiles of the other two Sovereigns, surprise and shock were visible on their faces.

Ash turned his head toward the grotto, and from what I could see of his face, his brows were furrowed. He stepped closer and turned to the side, the shift in position baring his face to me. I watched as he studied both labrals as if working something out in his mind.

He wasn't surprised. I was certain of it. He would surely have expected to see his father's labral, but as for the second one, we were together the night before his coronation, and I'd told him about the identical cuffs I saw in my dream—described them for him in detail. It would have been fresh in his mind, especially considering his reaction after I'd told him.

With an almost imperceptible head shake, his lips lifted ever so slightly in a smile, and he reached for the labral with the four symbols on it. He rolled it around in his fingers and then looked at Oletho and the Cloryals. His deep voice rang out in the expanse of the room. "Only when my eternal soul's shadow summons the labral that mirrors this one, will this belong to me."

The roar of my pulse pounded in my head and gooseflesh tore across my skin. His eternal soul's shadow! That's what he'd told me his senses claimed about me.

I lifted the matching labral to the one he was holding, my mouth ajar in astonishment. I was holding the one that mirrored it! Me. His eternal soul's shadow. Something inside me sang with contentment. But what the hell did it all mean?

Ash stepped forward once more—so confident and majestic—and returned the labral he was holding. He reached for the other one—his father's labral—and slipped it onto his wrist, and in a swirl of light and haze, it bonded to him.

Without any warning, a blinding flash of light filled the room, and the illusion around us was ripped away. The breath whooshed out of me, and I gasped and sputtered. I looked around to see the Calife hovering in front of us, calm and unassuming, the soft Shinoran light still encircling it.

Gwynn broke the silence, her voice filled with awe and comprehension. "Oletho . . . is it what I think it is? Even so, I still don't understand."

"It is," Oletho replied. "What you're thinking of has only ever occurred twice before in the known history of Ariadna, but never before on this scale."

"What are you talking about?" I asked, looking between Oletho and Gwynn.

Oletho shifted to face me. "I explained earlier about how succession works for a Sovereign. Well, a Sovereign's Consort goes through a similar process, where the giln they wear also becomes infused with Shinoran light. At their consecration ceremony, however, where they are officially anointed as Consort, their existing giln is *not* unbonded from them, but instead undergoes a metamorphosis and is imbued with more power. Strands of zidiurrh interlace with trinzum to show the giln's ranking in the hierarchy of power. Sometimes, the Consort for a Sovereign is evident right away, particularly if that Sovereign already has a spouse, but there are times when it can take much longer for Shinoran light to reveal a choice. In the case of Asher, it has been just over a century since he inherited the rule, and the throne at his side still sits empty." He inclined his head toward the labrals in my hands. "Until now."

I stared at him. "Wait. What?" My heart skipped a beat when I saw the smile playing on Oletho's lips. Did the labrals in my hands tie me to the Sovereignty somehow? Even as the rational part of my brain rebuffed such a notion, somewhere inside me, something preened and crowed.

He reached out and took the labral with the Valkyse crest on it from my hands. "Let's start with this one. This giln is no ordinary giln. It is the twin of the labral that cements the Valkyse Sovereignty." His voice was low and reverent as he turned it over with his fingers, examining it carefully.

The hair on the back of my neck raised. A twin labral?

"Do you understand when I say that this is not just a Consort's giln? It is a labral made of pure zidiurrh, a match for Asher's in every way but one."

My eyes tracked the design of the Valkyse crest at the top. "Do you think I'm a match for Asher?"

"The labral doesn't lie, Eleyse," Oletho replied, stroking his beard absently. "I can tell you with absolute certainty that these two labrals have never before graced the wrist of anyone. They were both made especially for you by the Ethereal Harmonies, the ruling source of all power and magic in the Sangelis. See these markings here?" he said, lifting the labral to the light to reveal a series of glyphs round the circumference of the band.

Gwynn and I peered closer.

"What do they mean?" Gwynn asked.

I looked at the labral in my hand and saw the same symbols flitting in and out incomprehensibly.

"This is Hasheyn, the language of the Gods," Oletho answered, his voice filled with awe. "The language of Arazul, the Great Creator; the language of the Cloryals."

Language of the Gods! Last night, when Ash had called me Tialla, he'd said something about a non-Goddess who understood the language of the Gods. At the time, I didn't have the slightest clue what he was talking about, but I'd also been preoccupied.

Gwynn was staring at me as if I'd sprouted multiple heads. I shifted my feet uneasily, not knowing how to respond.

"Can you read the glyphs?" Gwynn asked Oletho, her voice barely a whisper.

"No," he replied gravely. "I can see that four phrases are engraved around the labral, but the zidiurrh is fluid and keeps shifting quickly, obscuring the glyphs so I can't read them. I can only make out random letters. It's the same with the labral Eleyse is holding.

My instincts tell me that when it's meant to be read, it will become visible, but for now, it remains indiscernible."

Gwynn's jaw dropped open and she looked at me as if seeing me for the first time. "Eleyse!" she exclaimed. "Who in the name of Medra are you?"

"She is Asher's eternal soul's shadow, Gwynn," Oletho said, arching a brow as he looked at me. "His Gloweyen Queen."

His what? I didn't know what to say.

"What is Gloweyen?" I asked. "What does being Ash's eternal soul's shadow mean?"

There was undeniably something powerful between Ash and me, but I couldn't define it. The only thing I innately understood was that we were meant for each other.

"I'll explain," Oletho said, taking the labral from my hand and returning it, along with the one he was holding, to the grotto, where they hovered gently. "But first, you said that you saw a dais like this in a dream. Tell me what you saw."

"I . . . I . . . there was a woman with wings," I said, trying to recall the details. I went on to describe what had happened in the cave with the creature in the grotto and what the woman had said to me.

"That creature was a manifestation of the Cloryals, Eleyse," Oletho said. "It explains why I felt such an urgency for you to be read."

"The Cloryals?" I asked with a frown. "As in the same four women we just saw in Ash's coronation?"

"The very same," Oletho replied, stroking his beard.

"The woman with wings that you saw," Gwynn said, her eyes flashing with curiosity. "What did she look like?"

"She was young and beautiful with silver-blue hair and silver eyes. She was wearing a silver and lavender gown, with a crown of amethysts and sapphires on her head. When she transformed, her wings were a kaleidoscope of color."

Gwynn gasped and covered her mouth with her hand.

"Do you know who she was? It's not the Kaliope you spoke of earlier, is it?"

"No," Gwynn replied, tears slipping down her face. "That woman was my mother."

Chapter 12

HER MOTHER? AS IN her *dead* mother? What the hell?

Gwynn was clearly shaken by what I'd revealed, her eyes still filled with tears. I hated to be the one causing her pain.

"But wasn't your mother killed over a century ago?" I said. "How was I able to see her?"

Crap. *I am a phantom of Ariadna's past.* That's what she had said to me. It made sense now.

"The spirit world is still closely connected with ours," Oletho answered. "They may not be able to directly intervene in our lives, but they can still influence when need be, especially in situations of significant unrest. No one is truly gone when they pass on."

Was that true in my world too? I hoped it was. It made me happy to think of my loved ones still existing somewhere, being able to exert some influence on my life.

"In the cave, did my mother say anything to you?" Gwynn asked, her voice a scratchy whisper.

"Yes," I said, trying to remember the exact words. "She said, 'He filled my heart with so much love, but his heart was always meant to be yours. Don't hold back.' She faded away right after that."

For a long moment, Gwynn was silent, tears slipping down her cheeks. Finally, she wiped them away and smiled wistfully. "This is further proof that it's Gloweyen," she said, looking at Oletho, her eyes filled with wonder. "My mother returned from the dead to confirm it. Eleyse is Ash's eternal soul's shadow and he is hers."

A layer of virulent obscurity sloughed off my mind, flashes of memories playing out in my head. Ash and I walking on a beach, my squeal of laughter echoing as he tossed me over his shoulder; the two of us at a restaurant; us laughing as we walked down the promenade; me sparring in my backyard with him. Just snippets of mundane, normal things I had seemingly shared with him.

In every one of those flashes, I was happy—utterly at peace. I'd had these beautiful moments of true happiness and had completely forgotten all about them. It was frustrating, maddening even. The cruel irony of my life never ceased to amaze me. I didn't know what Gloweyen was or what being his eternal soul's shadow meant, but perhaps it was the same as what I felt inside for him.

"We need to tell Eleyse about Kaliope," Gwynn said to Oletho. "She needs to know who she's up against. We can't risk Kaliope finding out about her."

Oletho sighed. "If Andreo is right and Eleyse's memory loss is as a result of a rebounding curse, I'm afraid Kaliope already knows about her."

"Who is Kaliope?" I asked. "Why would she want me dead? Is she the one who tried to kill me?"

Gwynn clasped her hands together, her lips whittled in a thin line. "Kaliope is a calamitous blight—the one threatening the peace of this realm. This is bigger than any of us, Eleyse. After everything that's happened here today, it's clear that you play a part. The gift of Gloweyen has only ever occurred in times when Ariadna was under the threat of great evil, and Gods know, that's what Kaliope embodies."

The woman from my dreams had said as much years ago, that my life with *a paramount future* awaited, and at the time, the force of her words provided me with the strength to go on, to live. My life after I lost Liam had contained absolutely no meaning or purpose. Fuck, I could barely even call it a life, as barren as it was, with absolutely nothing worth living for. *Everything in your past was always leading you to this moment*, a small, insistent voice inside me whispered. *This is what you were meant to do, who you were meant to be.*

A feeling of indescribable sadness flooded through me, and a lump lodged in my throat. Oh, to have a purpose, a life that was actually worth something. Wouldn't that be incredible? I was so tired of feeling empty and dead inside. My happiness was mowed down so many times by the bullet train of misfortune, mangled and flattened into oblivion. How I longed for a different kind of life.

A tremor of feeling lifted my spirit, the whisper in my heart becoming more persistent, pinpricks of clarity recognizing the ring of truth to it all, urging me—compelling me—to give in. I could not ignore the pull.

"I feel it too, Gwynn," I said. "I can't deny what's happening to me. This feeling of certainty that I can't fight or doubt is overwhelming."

Gwynn squeezed my hand.

"Tell me about her," I said. "Tell me about Kaliope."

Gwynn nodded grimly. "We should sit down for this."

Oletho led us back to the antechamber we'd first entered. As we crossed the room, he ushered us to armchairs positioned in a semi-circle near the window, overlooking the grounds and ocean in the distance. With each second that passed, I felt the heated emotion seeping out of Gwynn. Her body was rigid, her jaw clenched as she sat upright in her chair.

She turned toward me, and my gaze flitted to her closed fists in her lap.

"First of all," she said, her voice tight and laced with distaste, "it irks me that I have to waste even a second of breath on that pile of filth. If it were up to me, she'd be weighted down with rocks at the bottom of Demon's Maw, being ripped apart and devoured by Jiacotie Soulshredders, some of the most terrifying creatures in Ariadna. That, in my opinion, would be the most fitting end for the soulless bitch."

Whoa. I stared at her, trying to process her reaction. I didn't know what Demon's Maw or Jiacotie Soulshredders were, but this raw, unbridled hatred from Gwynn was unexpected. Not even when she had talked about losing her parents had she shown this kind of emotion. Which begged the question—what the hell had Kaliope done to evoke this extreme reaction?

Oletho, seated next to her, leaned over and patted her shoulder gently, his face lined with sympathy.

Gwynn exhaled quietly, her shoulders drooping for a moment, her expression haunted. She shook her head, as if chasing dark memories away, and then sat upright and turned toward me. "I'm sorry for the outburst, but I think you'll understand soon."

I nodded, waiting for her to continue.

"Kaliope is the daughter of Ruskil and Lydia Tandor, Sovereign and Queen Consort of Tandor," she began. "The Dominion of Tandor was Valkyse's closest ally for centuries. Kaliope is a few years older than Ash, but they were childhood friends, along with Faron—whom you met yesterday—and his twin sister, Astrid."

So Kaliope was the daughter of a Sovereign, just like Gwynn. Sovereign of Tandor. My mind flashed back to the memory of Ash's coronation. Ruskil Tandor had been the one wearing the red cloak if I remembered correctly. Kind eyes, gentle face.

Gwynn's eyes clouded over with sadness. "As much as I detest the creya, her origin story is chilling. She . . . she is the result of a brutal rape perpetrated on Lydia Tandor by an enemy prince from another world in the Sangelis—the world of Treth, home to mortal beings known as the Shen."

The memory of my assault in the alleyway swarmed my mind, and immediately, all the frightening and helpless emotions from that experience came roaring in. That this woman—a Queen Consort, no less—had endured a brutal physical attack was terrible.

Gwynn exhaled loudly. "Just over two centuries ago, Dark Shen warriors led by this enemy prince began infiltrating Ariadna's borders with the sole purpose of going to war with us, though at the time, we were unaware."

Yesterday, she had said that there were multiple worlds with civilized life. This Treth had to be one of them. A sickening feeling churned in my gut. "I know I've only been here for a couple days, but I can't imagine this beautiful place being touched by war. It hurts my heart to think of that."

"With beauty and prosperity comes jealousy," Oletho interjected, folding his arms. "And the Dark Shen have always been envious of Ariadna's connection to the Ethereal Harmonies. Long lifespans, magic, peace, prosperity. Wars have been waged for much less."

Indeed they have. The history of humankind was brimming with accounts of just that. Greed, jealousy, lust for power and control. They had terrible ramifications.

"Why would this prince attack the Consort of a Sovereign?" I asked. "Was that how he hoped to incite war?"

Gwynn cocked her head, her face thoughtful. "To be honest, I think Tynor Crivonh's actions with Lydia Tandor had less to do with war and more to do with arrogance and entitlement. You see, the Queen Consort of Tandor is half-Shen, and it's entirely possible that her heritage is what drew his attention."

"Did he get caught?" I asked.

Gwynn shook her head sadly. "No, the bastard disappeared without a trace. The truth is, for a long time, they didn't even know who was responsible. All Lydia could say for certain was that he was Shen."

Shit.

Gwynn's face softened slightly. "Some might say that Kaliope never stood a chance at happiness, but despite the heinous crime that brought about her existence, there was much love in the relationship between Ruskil and Lydia. Ruskil didn't care that Kaliope wasn't his, and he and Lydia decided they would raise her with love, as if she were both theirs. They told no one who her real father was, not even Kaliope herself."

Admiration for the Sovereign of Tandor grew inside me. He was honorable to take on that responsibility. Not many men would have done the same. He must have loved Lydia very much.

"Kaliope was only a week old when her parents brought her here to be read for a giln," Oletho interjected. "I could tell just by looking at her that she was almost fully Shen, with her slitted gray eyes and bone-colored hair. I wasn't sure what reading she would get, and the Ethereal Harmonies returned a giln unlike any I ever saw. A rare form of black trinzum, fused with tiny threads of white and black cadamite, a metal not even found in Ariadna. The other striking thing about the giln was the full moon in the center. The crescent moon is one of the symbols of the Valkyse Sovereignty, and when I saw Kaliope's giln, I wondered if it meant that she would have some connection to the Dominion of Valkyse."

He tapped his amulet absently, his expression thoughtful.

"Sometimes the Ethereal Harmonies can be cryptic, as they were with Kaliope, but at other times, as was the case with Asher, they can be exceedingly clear. Asher's giln was a mirror image of his father's labral, except his was made out of trinzum. It was evident from the outset that he would be the heir to the Valkyse Sovereignty when the time came."

He stroked his beard slowly. "Kaliope's giln was extraordinary—the first I have witnessed that was made of something other than trinzum, and even after extensively researching the annals of giln history in our archives, I still don't understand the full significance of it."

I didn't get it. It made no sense. Why would the Ethereal Harmonies single Kaliope out with a special giln? There had to be a reason. Perhaps something to do with her Shen heritage?

Gwynn snorted. "Just because her giln is unique doesn't mean *she's* extraordinary, Oletho. Unless you'd like to say extraordinarily depraved and heinous." She turned to look at me. "I'm sure you can tell there's no love lost between Kaliope and me." She said her name between gritted teeth, as if it pained her. "The bitch and Ash spent a lot of time together as children. I think my parents, as well as hers, believed they were a good match for each other. Of course, she wanted nothing more—she adored my brother—but Ash always kept her at arm's length. As the years passed by and she grew more aggressive in her pursuit of him, he became more aloof and pulled away from their friendship, spending most of his time with Faron and Astrid. His rejection only made her want him more. She believed that the moon on her giln was a sign that she and Ash were meant to be together."

My Ash? A pang of jealousy gripped me in its clutches, and deep inside me, a low, warning growl rumbled through my body. *Mine*, it seemed to declare. I looked down to see my hands digging into the leather armrests of my chair.

Gwynn stood and walked toward the window, her lips drawn in a thin line. "Kaliope was thirty and Ash twenty-seven when war broke out in Ariadna. After years of scheming and hiding in the shadows, the Dark Shen finally raised their war cries, and Ariadna—well, *we* were caught unawares. Both Kaliope and Ash were thrust into the blood and gore of battle."

Gwynn turned to face Oletho and me, wrinkling her nose as if she had smelled something unpleasant. "The Dark Shen were fierce warriors, and what they lacked in numbers, they made up for in ruthlessness. They decimated many of our forces. Where killing in battle was a distasteful necessity for Ash, Kaliope reveled in it. Even then, she had a thirst for mayhem and bloodshed. She took no prisoners on the battlefield and showed no mercy. Her brutality matched that of the Dark Shen army, and it drew the attention of the dark prince, Tynor, her father, though she didn't know that at the time."

A devastating sadness seeped through me. Yes, the reality of war was still well and alive on Earth, but I was so far removed from it that it felt surreal. It hurt me to think of Ash having to live through that. As for Kaliope—the more I heard about her, the more I could see why Gwynn hated her. I ground my teeth, telling myself that my growing dislike had nothing to do with her belief that Ash was hers, but really, who was I kidding?

Gwynn folded her ams and turned, staring out at the ocean in the distance. "The four dominions banded together, and the Sovereigns of Ariadna unleashed their collective powers to defeat the Dark Shen and put an end to the bloodshed. The surviving Shen warriors were rounded up and banished to Pashket. The Dark Dominion had never seen criminals so violent and unscrupulous."

Gwynn's body tensed where she stood, her back ramrod straight as she continued to look out over the water. "A few years after the war, Kaliope persuaded Ruskil and Lydia to approach my parents with the prospect of a union between Tandor and Valkyse to solidify an alliance between the two Sovereignties. My parents were not opposed to the notion, but Ash would hear nothing of it. They acquiesced to him for the time being—the choice of a spouse wasn't entirely up to him anyway. As the heir to the Valkyse Sovereignty, the Ethereal Harmonies would ultimately decide, but since my parents were both still alive, marriage was not a pressing issue."

For the life of me, I couldn't suppress the feeling of satisfaction that surged within me. Ash had refused Kaliope. He didn't want *her.* Last night, he had told me that his senses had told him that heart, body, and soul I was meant for him. Something inside me gloated at the thought. Even the Ethereal Harmonies had linked us together. But although nothing had ever felt so right to me, I just had to know for sure—for my own peace of mind.

"Is that how it always works with the Sovereignty?" I asked, shifting in my seat. "The Ethereal Harmonies choose a Sovereign's spouse?"

Oletho leaned forward in his chair. "In the history of Ariadna, the consecrated spouse of a Sovereign has never been one the Sovereign didn't ultimately agree with. When the Ethereal Harmonies read someone, they assess everything about a person—personality, moral character, strengths, weaknesses, likes, dislikes. For someone like a Sovereign, this reading is even more critical. The Ethereal Harmonies wouldn't pair a Sovereign with someone they were incompatible with."

I cocked my head. "Has there ever been a situation where at the time of a Sovereign's succession, they already had a spouse who the Ethereal Harmonies didn't agree with?"

Oletho shook his head, adjusting the folds of his robe. "No. Every Sovereign who was already espoused before ascending to the Sovereignty have always had their spouse consecrated as their Queen Consort."

Interesting how this all worked. I mean, it made sense when I thought about it. This was a world filled with magic. Sovereigns were powerful beings, chosen to rule over and protect this realm. It made sense that the source of that power and balance would guide that rule. To ensure peace and stability, it would have to. Which made me all the more curious—how the hell did Kaliope fit into all of this?

Gwynn leaned her back against the window. "Trust me, Eleyse, there is no one happier than me that Ash refused to even consider that union." She let out a small huff. "Just the thought of that possibility makes me sick. Many years after, when I asked him why he'd said no to her back then, he told me it was because he'd always sensed the truth of who she was—that a cold and unsettling darkness lived behind her eyes, waiting for the perfect provocation to burst free."

She let out a forced laugh. "Only Ash could be so eloquent. I would have just said she was a psychotic bitch and been done with it. Ironically, Ash's rejection of Kaliope was the catalyst for her unraveling. After he refused her, she simply . . . disappeared. It's whispered that she found her father, Tynor, when she left; there is also talk that *he* sought her out. Many believed that he had died in combat, but his body was never found among the dead. I should point out that one of the special abilities of the Shen is shape-shifting, and the common belief is that he used this to escape detection and execution. I don't think anyone really knows what he looks like—what his true face is—except perhaps his own people, Kaliope, and possibly Lydia."

"I'm sorry," I blurted out, staring between Gwynn and Oletho. "Did you say shape-shifting? As in the ability to physically take the form of anyone they want?"

"Yes," Oletho piped in from his chair. "It's an extraordinary ability, one that isn't grounded in magic whatsoever—it's just part of their genetic makeup, but it only exists in those descended from the Shen royal bloodline."

My mind reeled. Life in the Sangelis was the stuff of movies and fantasy, of wild imagination given breath. It went beyond the euphoria of getting swept away in a story of fiction and make-believe. Here, concepts and hypotheses that all my life had been limited to my imagination *were* reality.

Gwynn folded her arms, still leaning against the window. "One thing you'll come to learn is that Kaliope loves to hear herself talk, and so we've all heard how the moment Tynor saw her on the battlefield flying the Tandor banner, her ivory hair shining for all to see, he knew she was his. During her self-imposed exile, he acknowledged her as his own and welcomed her into his fold from wherever he had been hiding in Ariadna. There, she learned the truth about who she really was. Ruskil and Lydia never told her the truth of her parentage, hoping to spare her that humiliation, but when she found out, Kaliope embraced her new heritage. Finally, everything made sense to her."

"She turned her back on her own family?" I asked incredulously. "She had parents who loved her, and instead chose the man who brutally raped her mother and waged war against her own people?"

Gwynn lifted her eyebrows and shot her index finger out. "Yes, yes and yes. Like I said, a psychotic bitch. Ruskil and Lydia deserved better."

Absolutely, they deserved better. I was starting to see it—the picture Gwynn was painting. For Kaliope to embrace war and destruction and welcome the man who . . . Something was seriously *wrong* with her. Thank God for Ash's senses, or he might have found himself saddled to her.

Gwynn turned to stare out the window once more. "Ten years Kaliope spent with her father before she returned, and when she did, she was changed—a woman spurned, reeking of dark magic and acrimony. She tried to overthrow Ruskil Tandor, but my father banded with him to defeat her, and together, they banished her to the Dark Dominion. Her powers were still fledgling and evolving, but she was becoming dangerous and powerful and had to be contained. It would have been better if they'd condemned her to die, because there, in that dismal wasteland, she blossomed. In the Dark Dominion, she was surrounded by the most hardened criminals, some of whom were her own people."

I furrowed my brows. Based on what Gwynn had said yesterday, the Sovereigns of Ariadna were powerful. Had Kaliope really thought she had a chance of defeating Ruskil Tandor? Or was she just that disillusioned?

Gwynn turned, sliding her back down the window until she was sitting on the floor. Knees bent in front of her, she stared at a spot on the polished marble, a faraway look in her eyes. Oletho, sitting within arm's reach of her, extended his hand and touched the top of her head gently. She closed her eyes and shuddered. The hair on the back of my neck rose. Something bad was coming. I could sense it.

Gwynn cleared her throat, her voice unsteady. "Being banished to the Dark Dominion carries with it a life sentence, so there was no anticipation of Kaliope returning, but return she did, and in grand fashion. Somehow, she was able to escape after sixty years there. Normally, when someone is banished to Pashket, their giln loses all function. They are not able to travel anywhere ever again. Without a working giln, it is impossible to leave, but she and the Dark Shen found a way, undoubtedly with the aid of powerful dark magic. They were able to establish a portal into Treth, and from there, gain entry back into Ariadna."

"How does that work?" I asked. "What causes a giln to lose all function?"

"The Ethereal Harmonies," Oletho replied, his hand resting now on Gwynn's shoulder. "The inmates of Pashket are cut off from the magic of the Ethereal Harmonies."

"But there is dark magic there?"

Oletho frowned. "There are many deep and unexplored regions in the Dark Dominion—places where the light of the Ethereal Harmonies does not breach. For someone as resourceful and power-hungry as Kaliope, those places are a bounty. To answer your question, yes, there is dark magic there."

My eyes drifted to Gwynn, her body rigid as she sat on the ground. All the blood had drained out of her face, and she looked like she was going to be sick. I opened my mouth to ask if she was okay, but the look of resolve that stole over her face stopped me. I could tell that whatever she was going to say next was big. And not in a good way.

Her voice wavered and her hands shook as she spoke.

"Kaliope timed her return to coincide with Ash's one hundredth birthday. My parents had organized an elaborate gala at Cazara Torannon, and much of the nobility of Ariadna was invited. A few minutes before midnight, all the guests were asked to make their way onto the terrace, and my parents took turns to say a few words about their beloved son. Ash accepted their praise with humility and grace, and after they finished speaking, they raised a toast to my dear brother, and both my parents moved forward to wrap him in their embrace."

She paused, her eyes welling with tears. I stiffened, my heart thudding in my chest.

The muscle in Gwynn's jaw clenched tightly. "You can imagine the utter horror when my father's head slid off his neck and bounced to the floor with an awful thud. Beside him, my mother's stomach was slashed open, her body crumpling in a bloody mass on the floor next to my father. Ash just stood there quietly, two blood-stained scimitars in his hands."

My mouth dropped open, my heart pounding in my ears.

No. No. No. What the actual fuck?

I felt like I'd been punched in the stomach.

In front of me, a solitary tear trailed a slow path down Gwynn's face. Oletho's expression was grim as he leaned forward in his seat, squeezing her shoulder.

Gwynn's voice was abrupt, bitter. "In a matter of seconds, the two people I loved most in this world and who loved me back unconditionally, the two people who instilled in me the importance of kindness, gratitude, and living my life in service of others, were both dead."

I gaped at her in horror. The silence was deafening. My heart ached as I looked at her anguished face, tears silently spilling down her cheeks. How could Ash have done this?

He didn't. He could never.

The thought sprang unbidden into my mind, barreling in with a fierce loyalty and confidence that left my rational brain perturbed.

You know he didn't.

The image of Ash's emerald gaze from the night before materialized in my mind, the compelling words he had spoken—the ones that had crumbled all my defenses like aged, brittle parchment—ringing out in my head.

They tell me that you are a promise and a storm. And that heart, body and soul, you are meant for me.

Ash. The man I knew but couldn't remember, the one who made my heart sing and set my body and soul on fire. He would *never*. And in a flash, it hit me.

Kaliope.

Gwynn quickly retreated out of her thoughts to continue. "I have no words to describe the shock of seeing my parents lying there, butchered at the hands of the brother I loved so dearly," she said, her features schooled into an unreadable mask. "I will never forget the look on Ash's face. He was smiling, his eyes shining with triumph as he raised the two blades forged from black cadamite and imbued with powerful magic, slick with the blood of our parents. I could not believe it. I would have fainted if it wasn't for the roar of absolute anguish and rage that splintered the silence from one of the upper balconies just then. I looked up to see Ash looking down at himself and the devastation he had caused. I was entirely bewildered; I couldn't understand what was happening."

Her eyes were unfocused and hazy, almost as if as she was watching the memory play out in her head. "The real Ash and the Sovereigns of Ariadna sprang into action then and unleashed their power onto the imposter standing next to my dead parents. Everyone watched in shock and disbelief as the murderous Ash transformed into Kaliope. She had inherited her father's ability to shape-shift. It wasn't something anyone had even realized she could do."

My heart clenched at the atrocity of what had happened, at the same time shuddering in relief that it hadn't been Ash. My *senses* were right. He could never have done such a heinous thing. But for the love of God, what Kaliope had done—it was unforgivable. She was pure evil. Completely sick and twisted. I understood now, just like Gwynn had said I would.

Gwynn inhaled sharply, as if stepping out of the past and back to reality. Her sad gaze met mine. "At first, Kaliope was unfazed by the combined powers of all the Sovereigns, but eventually, she was encased in their magic and unable to break free. The Cloryals stripped her of all her powers and she was locked away in Glanag, the most dangerous prison in the Dark Dominion, guarded by the Hagdern, three of the most terrifying and vicious beasts under the Ariadnan sun. She was to be executed for killing my parents—that is the punishment for regicide. It was to be a public execution, to be held in Torannon, in the city square. The other three Sovereigns were present, and Kaliope was brought in, bound and caged, like the monster she was, to await her fate. Even her father could not contain the disgust and disappointment on his face."

I tried to put myself in Ruskil's shoes. To accept and love Kaliope as his child, only to have her turn against everything she had been raised to believe? Devastating. And Ash and Gwynn—I couldn't even imagine how they must have felt enduring this pain.

"The Cloryals shocked everyone when they ruled that she would live. They declared that the Mavigos—the divine will of the universe, or fate, so to speak—had deemed that Kaliope's time was not yet at hand, that she had yet to fulfil the destiny for which she was born, a destiny that was supposedly world-altering and could not be interfered with."

Gwynn's face constricted with pure anguish. "I could have killed her right then. From the look on Ash's face, it was clear he felt the same way, but the word of the Cloryals is law, and the will of the Mavigos surpasses any other judgment, so we were forced to abide by their decision. She was locked away again in Glanag—powerless and outlawed—to await the time when the Cloryals deemed fit to release her to fulfil her so-called destiny." She shook her head. "Ash was inconsolable in his grief, rage, and guilt, and he retreated into himself after that. Kaliope was released from her imprisonment three years ago by the Cloryals. She proclaimed herself Queen of the Dark Dominion, declared her intention to take her rightful place next to my brother as Queen Consort of Valkyse, and eventually, the first female Sovereign of Tandor. She believes her giln is a match to Ash's, and that together, they will be invincible. She also wants to make the Dark Dominion a legitimate and recognized area of rule. And she'll do anything to make it all happen."

I couldn't believe my ears. How could someone get away with such a heinous crime? She was unstable and delusional—the most dangerous kind of crazy. A shiver went down my spine. This was the woman who wanted me dead. That thought alone was terrifying.

"What about the Cloryals?" I asked. "How could they allow this? Why didn't they put an end to it?" Seriously. Is this what equated to justice in this world?

"That's the question everyone is still waiting for an answer to," Gwynn answered bitterly. "Because of what the Mavigos declared, the Cloryals have neither opposed nor supported Kaliope's claims, and she has been left to her own devices. She is untouchable, at least until the Mavigos or Gods deem otherwise."

"So what now?" I asked. "You said she was released three years ago. What has she been doing since?"

"She splits her time between Ariadna and Treth, coming and going freely, even though there are no known portals open between the realms. There have been whispers that she is amassing an army under the guidance of her father, whose seat of power is in Kindrik, the kingdom of the Dark Shen. Dark magic abounds there, and all manner of ferocious beasts—the likes of which we have never seen in Ariadna—roam freely in their lands. For the past three years, Ariadna has been bracing for war. We will not be caught unawares again, despite these ridiculous games the Divine have chosen to play with us."

"Gwynn! To speak against the Divine is blasphemy," Oletho admonished, getting to his feet.

"I don't care, Oletho," Gwynn cried, her nostrils flaring in anger. "She killed my parents in cold blood and went unpunished. She deserves to be gutted in the street like the rabid dog she is. I wish Ash had ripped her apart that day. We both know he was powerful enough to do it."

"Regardless, Gwynn, we have to trust in the will of the Mavigos," Oletho said gently. "She will get her comeuppance."

Mavigos. Gods. Divine. I was out of my depth here. Where I was from, the notion of the divine was more conceptual, faith-based, abstract even. Here, they were more concrete and factual. But even so, Oletho's response was awfully similar to any ardent religious practitioner on Earth who relied on their faith to guide them through every decision in their life.

Gwynn sighed deeply, pushing herself to her feet. "What do we do now? The moment Eleyse puts the Valkyse labral on her wrist and it bonds to her, there will be no hiding who she is. The Shinoran light will proclaim to all that she is the Ethereal Harmonies' chosen spouse of the Sovereign of Valkyse. She will be drawn to Ash, and he to her."

"The choice of accepting the labral is ultimately hers," Oletho answered. "And as for being drawn to him, with or without the labral, they are drawn to each other."

"What about the other labral?" Gwynn asked. "What part does that play in all of this?"

"That one is secondary at the moment. Right now, Asher wears the labral of the Sovereign of Valkyse, and its twin is the one Eleyse must choose first."

Oletho beckoned for us to follow him through the antechamber back into the adjoining room where the labrals rested within the grotto. I followed slowly, pondering his words.

Choose wisely when the moment is at hand, the creature in the grotto had told me. Were they referring to this moment? To Ash? Just hearing his name made me feel peculiar inside. Fiery. Territorial.

And as for what Oletho said about us being drawn to each other—was that true? Yes, when I thought of Ash or when someone said his name, I couldn't deny the pull. When I was with him last night, I was completely consumed by his presence. But I hadn't sensed him here, in the present, since I'd woken up at Cazara Chantilis yesterday.

I closed my eyes and focused on the sound of my own breathing. What did I feel? What did I *believe*?

Your broken spirit holds the fate of this realm in the balance, the being in the grotto had said.

God knew that first part was the truth. I was the most broken person I knew.

In the depths of your dark heart, a grain of hope flutters inside you, floundering to survive. It must thrive.

My dark heart. Did seeking out death make me dark? Or was it my utter loathing of myself? Was this darkness the reason everyone who loved me had died? Or was there some other darkness lurking inside me that I didn't have any memory of?

There was hope, though. The being had said there was hope. The woman from my dream that night had given me hope. But she had also spoken of him. Ash. I heard the whisper of his name in my mind again. My hope. Yes, it rang true. A surge of conviction coursed through me. I knew nothing about anything, but this felt right.

Ash was my path.

Everything else faded into the background—my memory loss, the mystery of this world, Kaliope. My eternal soul's shadow. I chose him. Inside me, a roar of triumph reverberated through my body.

On either side of me, Gwynn and Oletho looked at me expectantly. I stepped onto the dais and picked up the Valkyse labral from the grotto. "I accept," I said to Oletho, extending my wrist to him. "Put it on."

Chapter 13

A<small>S I STOOD ON</small> the dais, Oletho placed the labral on my wrist, and the change overcame me instantly. Like a second skin, my supple flesh absorbed it, welcomed it, and a tingling sensation moved through my entire body, as if the giln was searching, learning me, determining my mettle—it was bonding itself to me.

I looked down at my hands, marveling at the iridescent glow exuding from my skin. My hair whipped in front of me, the glow shining there also. My entire body was bathed in the soft light emanating from the labral.

A soft, radiant glow enveloped the entire cuff, transitioning from silver to blue in gradual waves. From the grotto in front of me, a shimmery blue mist billowed airily, holding my gaze hostage. I watched, enthralled, as it shifted and spiraled, and before my eyes, a hand materialized, reaching out to me. I extended my hand to touch it and brushed against a coalescence of gossamer silkiness. The phantom fingers swirled around mine in a wispy caress, and as I moved closer, there was a sharp tug on my hand, and I was pulled forward in a flash of blinding light.

Slowly, I opened my eyes. I stood at the edge of a glade, surrounded by blue and silver trees rustling around me. Opalescent in the twilight, their branches arched in obeisance to something sacred in their midst. At the center of the clearing was a silver lake, the surface undulating gracefully, shimmering like silken ribbons in the fluttering breeze.

What was this place? Where were Gwynn and Oletho? The atmosphere was different here—entrancing and majestic—my senses telling me that I was no longer in the Giln Keeper's sanctuary. And yet strangely, I felt not a trace of fear or misgiving.

A lilting melody broke the silence of the night, seeping into my thoughts and usurping my attention. It emanated from within the grove of trees. I recognized the melody, but before, where it was the trill of a bird outside my balcony door at Cazara Chantilis, this was a woman's voice, captivating and hypnotic. I followed the music to the other side of the lake, to a circle of trees with silver leaves, laden with violet blossoms.

There, in the center of the grove, stood the woman with wings—Ash's and Gwynn's mother, the former Queen Consort of Ariadna—Harwen Valkyse. Her voice was lifted in song, her wings unfurled, fanning out behind her in a flourish of pageantry. The crystal mask on her face was gone, revealing her ageless beauty. She beckoned me forward, and of their own accord, my feet led me to her.

She took my hand in hers as she stopped singing. "Hello, my sweet Eleyse," she said softly. Her eyes shone with a fierce intensity, but I glimpsed the tenderness in their depths.

I stared at her, captivated by her other-worldly presence. How was it possible that she had been permitted to cross that threshold back into the world of the living?

She lifted her hand and tucked a stray tendril of my hair behind my ear, her eyes glistening with tears as she held my gaze. "You stand on hallowed ground, outside the confines of time and space.

This is Falayen, the sanctum of the Sovereign of Valkyse. It is time for you to learn the truth of *what* I am, the special identity that will also be your legacy."

A mix of curiosity and trepidation inflamed me. What was she talking about? What was my legacy? The trees around us rustled gently in the tranquil glade, a heartening symphony of birdsong erupting from the silver and violet foliage above us. The sky was emblazoned with hues of lavender, pink, and indigo. Outside the confines of time and space. That's where we were. What did that mean? Were we not in Ariadna anymore?

I stared at Harwen Valkyse, seeing traces of both Ash and Gwynn in her face. I couldn't help the pang of sorrow as I recalled Gwynn's description of Kaliope's heinous act. Her life had been cut short.

Her smile turned whimsical as she regarded me. "When I was alive, I was the Songbird of Valkyse, a protector of Ariadna chosen by the Gods. My time in Ariadna was magical and beautiful. It was filled with love, laughter, and music, the threads of which wove a rich tapestry of a life well-lived—a life of happiness." She touched my cheek gently. "Such a life once belonged to you in the human world—carefree and jubilant—alas, too feeble and tenuous to survive as death and loss wreaked havoc on your heart. All that remains now of that life are obscure shadows in a waning mist."

I couldn't remember the last time my life was carefree and jubilant. Happy. When did that change? Was it when Liam died? Or was it long before that? When I lost my parents?

"To understand the future, we must return to where it all began, Eleyse."

I stared at her blankly. "Where *what* all began? What do you mean?"

"Trust me. It will all make sense shortly. We must slip into the past and step into the mind—seeing through the eyes of one who was there. Will you come with me?" She reached her hand out to me.

"Slip into the past?" I asked. "Time travel?" Like I did with Ash?

"We are sliding into a memory. Silent observers to an event as it unfolds. All we can do is watch."

Whose mind were we stepping into anyway? Where did it all begin? As much as I was skeptical, I was even more curious.

I took her hand, and she led me to the center of the grove where silver leaves on the ground lifted slowly before whipping into a swirling mass. My heart lurched when a scene formed from within the swirl of silver—a scene of another time and place.

A woman stood there, dressed in hospital scrubs, her back to us as she gazed out a window.

"Shall we, Eleyse?" Harwen said.

I looked at her tentatively and slowly reached my hand out, and together, we stepped forward.

Chapter 14

J ACKIE STEPPS FROWNED AS she peered into the shapeless gloom. Raindrops hammered the windows of Gladeview General Hospital, the incessant battering reverberating off the double-paned glass in a frenetic racket. At the nurses' station on the fifth floor of the east wing, she was just beginning her shift. The skies were a macabre shade of gray, shrouding any glimpse of sunrise behind a veil of shadow and mist. A bone-chilling dampness lingered in the air, and she shivered reflexively, rubbing her arms for warmth.

She picked up her clipboard and examined the list of patients on the maternity ward. As she made her way down the hall, she adjusted the stethoscope around her neck and snapped on a pair of sterile disposable gloves.

Grabbing the chart in front of the first room, she read through it quickly and started on her rounds. She made it through the first two rooms without incident, and headed to the third.

Baby Satler, the chart notes read—a girl, seven pounds, three ounces; mother, Kylie Satler. Pushing open the door, she was greeted with a zephyr of cool air on her face. The scent of mint and evergreen invaded her nostrils, and she swore she heard someone whisper her name as she stepped inside. "Jaacckkiieee . . ."

Standing still, she forced herself to listen, her heartbeat a jackhammer pounding away in her chest. After a few seconds elapsed and nothing happened, she convinced herself it was her imagination playing tricks on her. She never did like storms; they made her mind work overtime, seeing ghosts and bogeymen in every corner.

Shrugging her cowardly thoughts off, she refocused her attention on her patients. As in the room before, mother and infant were asleep, and so she quietly made her way to the incubator. The baby was still, which in itself was not unusual, but Jackie's senses instantly shifted to high alert that something was amiss.

A slice of lightning arced through the gray skies, illuminating the room and incubator, causing Jackie to freeze. The infant's face and lips were blue.

Her heart careened. She hit the alarm on the opposite wall to alert the nurses' station. Hurriedly slipping on the fresh pair of gloves in her pocket, she switched on the overhead lamp for the incubator and reached down to examine the infant.

A loud clap of thunder cut through the silence of the room, startling the hell out of her, but she refused to let it rattle her from the task at hand. She looked down at the baby and paused abruptly, her heart leaping into her throat as she let out a strangled yelp of surprise. A pair of startling blue eyes peered out from the swaddling blanket, regarding her curiously.

Out of the periphery of her vision, she caught a quick movement near the window, but when she turned her head to look, there was nothing there. The hairs on her arms stood on end, her senses acknowledging a presence she couldn't explain.

Grace, the other nurse on duty from the night shift, came bolting into the room, waking the baby's mother in the process, and they both turned to look at Jackie. She stood there, dumbfounded, holding the stirring infant in her arms. The baby gurgled quietly, her cheeks pink with warmth, squirming to be free of her swaddle, and Jackie rocked her on her shoulder, trying to settle her.

"What happened?" Grace asked, concern flashing in her eyes.

"Umm . . . nothing . . . everything's okay," Jackie replied, desperately trying to keep the panic out of her voice. "I, uh . . . that bright flash of lightning startled me and I hit the alarm by mistake. Sorry if I woke you," she said, placing the baby into Kylie Satler's arms. "I think she might be hungry."

The exhaustion on Kylie's face was evident as she cradled her daughter gently. Even so, her eyes filled with adoration as she slipped the strap of her nightgown down over her shoulder and cooed soothingly to her daughter, guiding the infant's head to her breast. The baby's mouth opened, the rooting reflex kicking in as she impatiently searched for her mother's waiting nipple.

Jackie watched for a moment, needing to reassure herself that everything was indeed okay with the newborn.

The mother looked up and smiled a tired smile. "Thanks for checking in on her," she said quietly. "I had such a hard time settling her down after her last feeding."

"That's what we're here for," Jackie replied woodenly, everything inside her screaming to get the hell out of the room. With a nod of her head, she turned to leave, absently noting that the smell of mint and evergreen was gone.

Grace followed her back to the nurses' station. "Are you all right, Jackie?" she said, touching Jackie's hand gently. "Your face was as white as a sheet when I walked in."

"Yeah, I'm fine," Jackie assured her, squeezing Grace's hand. "That flash of lightning and the loud crash of thunder that followed scared the shit out of me. This storm just has me on edge."

She retreated to the break room to make herself a cup of tea, and then returned to the nurses' station to check her clipboard again. After skimming through the remaining names on the list, she headed back down the hall to complete her rounds. She happened to glance out the window as she walked by, surprise surging that not only had it stopped raining, but the sun was breaking through the receding dark clouds. An involuntary shudder ran down her spine.

She hesitated for a moment at Room 311—Kylie and baby Satler's door—unable to dispel the unsettling suspicion churning in her stomach that she hadn't imagined any of it—the perplexing chill and smell in the room; the voice whispering her name; the blue, lifeless child wrapped in the swaddling blanket; and the presence of something ancient and unearthly standing in the shadows, watching.

Chapter 15

A S WE SLIPPED OUT of Jackie Stepps's head and back into the grove, my mind staggered with the realization of one thing. This was my past! Kylie Satler was my mother. My heart had raced when I saw her. She looked the same as she did in my memories—her beautiful dark hair, steel-gray eyes, and that lilting, melodic voice. A pang of longing snaked through me. It had felt so real. Looking at her through Jackie's eyes, I'd yearned to throw myself into her arms, to feel her hands in my hair and on my face again, to tell her how much I missed her, to beg for forgiveness for being the reason she was gone.

Baby Satler was me. This was my birth. Why had Harwen Valkyse taken me back to that moment? Because of the things Jackie saw and heard? There was clearly a strange presence in the room when she entered, and I saw what she had seen—the lifeless, blue baby one moment and then the bright-eyed, alert child the next. I sensed the thing in the shadows watching. It felt and smelled like death.

Harwen Valkyse turned to face me. "What we just saw was the earthly beginnings of your origin story," she said. "Seen through the eyes of someone who was there. The trepidation and foreboding Jackie felt were real and serve as validation that there is more to you than meets the eye and that you have been marked by the Mavigos. Keep that in mind as you embark on this new path."

"What are you saying? Who am I really?"

"The Giln Keeper's proclamation holds true, Eleyse: human, but not entirely human. A veil of mystery shrouds your identity, one that I cannot see past to glean the full truth. What I do know is this: here begins your future, if you would have it. Love, laughter, and music—your destiny written in the stars, ordained by the Gods. You were born to save this realm."

My heart pounded in my ears. How could that be?

Born to save this realm.

That was no simple declaration. The weight of those five words clamped down on my chest, making it hard to breathe. Why me? Destiny, the Gods. I didn't think much of either. And how could I be human but not entirely human? What did that even mean? As for music—once, music was my entire world, but I had turned my back on it a long time ago. What she said about a new beginning sounded eerily similar to what the woman from my dreams told me years ago.

Everything that had been revealed since I got to Ariadna only highlighted what a miserable life I'd led since I lost Liam. I was a morose, depressing person. It was sickening, but it was my normal.

There is nothing left for you there, that soft, still voice in my head whispered. In my heart, I knew that was the truth.

"Lift your voice with me, Songbird," Harwen Valkyse said. "From the ashes of your sorrow, the flames of rebirth flicker."

A trill of excitement echoed through me as she clasped both my hands in hers and began singing. The words were foreign to me, each phrase and enunciation unfamiliar, and yet the song ripped through me—my soul embracing it lovingly, like a long-lost companion. The words spilled out from some unknown place inside me—as if it was always there—and I opened my mouth. Together, we sang "The Song of Sorrow," the song to end a dying age and usher in another.

The dark days of mourning are at an end
The dying heart beats once more
The long nights of misery are settled and spent
As hope banishes fear out the door
The time for living is at hand,
The past scattered to the mighty winds
The promise of a new age sweeps across the land
As the season of redemption begins

We sang, our voices blending in perfect harmony, and as "The Song of Sorrow" transitioned into "The Song of Rebirth," a slow heat consumed me, swallowing me in its luster.

From the darkness comes the light
To break the curse of the dismal night
From the ashes and the pain
New life blossoms on a healing, warm rain
From a charred and ruined heart
An ember sparks, heralding a new start
From the silence, the spirits call my name
As the magic renews me in its mighty flame

Our melody swelled to a glorious crescendo until a projectile of power exploded from within me, illuminating the grove in breathtaking effulgence. I felt it before I saw it—the new weight on my body, the fusing of magic and flesh. Wings unfurled across my back in a blaze of splendor, and the former Queen Consort of Valkyse smiled at me in my metamorphosis.

She cupped my face with both hands. "Here, amid this ancient grove of angorns, in this most hallowed sanctum, you have been reborn. From this moment on, you must be wary. With your rebirth, the power to deduce truth from lie, and illusion from reality has fully awakened. You alone hold the title of *truth diviner*; it will serve you well. Wife, lover, friend, mother, queen, Songbird—the many faces of Harwen Valkyse—I wore them well. The mantle passes to you now, but *you* have more faces to wear: Gloweyen Queen, conqueror, savior. In the history of Ariadna, no one has worn as many. In the heavens, the constellations of Sorin and Eolith are almost at their zenith. The board is set, the pieces are in place, and the next move belongs to Valkyse."

There was that term again—Gloweyen. And what did constellations have to do with anything?

I shook my head. "What do I do now?" I asked softly, my heart racing at the magnitude of all she'd said. "I don't know what any of that means. How do I save this realm?"

"War is coming, Eleyse. It is written in the stars, and you are instrumental to Ariadna's success. Across each dominion, the Sovereigns of Ariadna guard what, when united, only you can wield. You must maintain the balance, or Ariadna as we know it will collapse into darkness."

War. The magnitude of that word blasted through me, yanking me back to reality, laying my fears and insecurities bare. What was I doing? What the hell could I do to prevent a war? What was it that I alone could wield? I wasn't even able to save myself in the alley from two attackers! Furthermore, I wasn't even able to save myself from myself!

"This is all happening too quickly," I said, my eyes wide with panic. The air was suddenly hot and stifling around me. "I'm not capable of what you're asking. I am no savior; I'm no one. What do the Sovereigns guard that I can wield? What does that even mean?"

Harwen reached out a hand and cupped my face, her eyes

shining with compassion and tenderness. "You do not understand yet, Eleyse, but you will. You are the key to preserving the balance in the Sangelis. The Sovereigns each protect a powerful artifact that only you can unite to ensure harmony is preserved. As for your doubts and fears—your past doesn't define you, Eleyse. Your experiences shape who you are, but alas, yours have skewed and mangled the way you see yourself. You cannot tell me that you have never looked up at the stars and longed for something more, for your life to have purpose and meaning, to love and to be loved, to feel at peace with yourself. I am telling you that all of that is possible, that you are worthy, but you need to want that, to believe in yourself."

I swallowed the lump in my throat as the image of her face blurred in front of me. Of course I wanted that. I wanted that more than anything, but at what cost? Loss? Grief? Guilt? Insurmountable heartbreak? That was the true price of happiness. Of love.

I exhaled slowly and lifted my gaze to find her looking at me with sorrow, her eyes filled with tears as she reached out to embrace me.

"You stand on the threshold of something monumental, Eleyse. But only you can take the first step to cross that line. The power of the Songbird of Valkyse and the truth diviner are yours, already awakened inside you, but you must make the choice to use them. From across the realms, my son was drawn to you. Two broken souls, guarded hearts, and kindred spirits—you were always meant to find each other, to save each other. As for my darling daughter, she will love you as fiercely as she loves her brother and will fight for you as relentlessly as she would for him."

With each word she uttered, the certainty in my heart grew, drowning out the voices of self-doubt and fear in my head. It was all real—my peculiar connection to this world, the destiny I was chosen for. Somehow, I, an insignificant speck in the grand scheme of things, was chosen for something this consequential.

But what about Ash? We had a past; what about a future? Was I truly meant to be his queen? As much as my heart told me to embrace this new world, I was scared to venture out of the walled-up tower I'd constructed around myself. I was safe there. Protected. What Harwen said was true—my life on Earth was a hollow existence. There was nothing left for me there, and even the thought of going back filled me with dread.

"Life is all about choices, Eleyse," she said, squeezing my fingers. "And you have choices. You can return to your life on Earth, or you can stay here and start over, unencumbered by the burden of greatness hanging over you. Or you can lean into that future of greatness and embrace the unknown with an open heart and mind. Search yourself, Eleyse, weigh your options, and listen to your heart. That is the best counsel I can give you, which, if you follow, will guide you to the right decision. Valkyse's Falayen belongs to both you and Ash," Harwen said, gesturing to the space around us, her eyes shining with affection. "It will always be a place of safe haven, comfort, and rejuvenation, even in the darkest of moments. Remember that." She touched my wings, tucked in close to my shoulders. "I would love nothing more than to see you spread your wings and fly, Eleyse, both figuratively and literally, but both those choices rest with you, and you must be ready to accept them."

"How do I switch back to my normal form?" I asked, casting a furtive glance at the fusion of color behind me.

"I will transform you back. But as the Songbird of Valkyse, a wellspring of power resides within you. You have only to search inward to find it. Let your intuition guide you. When you're finally ready to embrace your power, tap into that wellspring, find the melodies, and sing the songs to unleash your magic." She lifted her hand, and a stream of light issued forth, taking the weight on my back with it.

I turned my head to find the wings gone. I felt awkward—uncoordinated, pained, like a vital part of me had been taken away. Why? They were only mine for mere minutes, for heaven's sake.

Harwen Valkyse took me in her arms and embraced me, and when she pulled away, her eyes were sad. "This is where I leave you, sweet Eleyse," she said, gently stroking my cheek. "Use your labral to return to the Giln Keeper's sanctuary. Please tell my son and daughter that I love them with all my heart and that I am so proud of the man and woman they've become." Tears slipped down her cheeks as she placed her hands on my shoulders. "Fare thee well, Eleyse, and choose wisely." She smiled once more, and just like in my encounter with her in the cave, she faded away slowly, and I was left standing alone.

Chapter 16

MY MIND RACED AS I stood on trembling legs in the twilight. Above me, the leaves rustled in the trees, whisper-soft scintillas of wind lifting my hair and swirling it around my face. In the silence of the glade, a strange calm settled over me. Even as the place resonated and pulsed with power, something else trilled—a welcoming call, an insistence that I, too, belonged here.

Drawn to the lake in the center of the clearing like a moth to a warm flame, I ambled resolutely in that direction, a staggering reverence slowing my steps. I had no words. The crescent moon shining overhead was imposing and brilliant—a luminous juxtaposition against the backdrop of the sable sky—bathing the glade in radiant light. My entire body tingled as I approached the edge, and as I drew closer, I sensed the torrent of power emanating from its depths. *Come closer*, it beckoned, a whisper in my mind, spoken softly, like a lover's caress.

Abruptly, my thoughts shifted to Gwynn and Oletho, yanking me out of my dreamlike state. Crap! I had to get back. Surely, they would be wondering where I'd gone? Harwen Valkyse had said that this place existed outside of time and space, though, so did they even know I was gone? But even as I fretted, a sense of calm pushed past my worry, urging me to let go, to sink into the moment and just be. I acquiesced, slipping into the thrall of my surroundings.

This was a hallowed place, that much was clear. Every fiber

in my being cried out to be immersed in the silvery waters. I kicked my shoes off, rolled up the legs of my pants, and moved to the edge. Sitting on the bank, I tentatively dipped my feet in. The moment my toes touched the water, the silver changed to a glittering sapphire. I trailed an arc with my feet and watched the color shift with it.

It took me a moment to realize that it was not water at all. On the surface, it looked like it was, but it was not *wet*. It was satiny and smooth—like liquid silver—beading off my skin the moment I retracted my feet from its depths. I lowered my legs and submerged them beneath the surface.

Time slipped away as I sat there in silence, the wind whistling through the trees and the cool breeze grazing my skin. Tendrils of my violet hair drifted around my face softly. The moonlight cast a warm glow on the lake, and my body grew slack, peace and contentment settling like a silken cloak around me.

As I sank into the comforting embrace of the glade, I recognized the signature essence that permeated the entire space. *Ash.* I sensed him here, in this place—vestiges of his presence everywhere. The wind-kissed lapping of the lake, the rustling of leaves on the evening breeze, the soft trill of birdsong flitting through the blue and silver trees, the quavering of the mossy undergrowth all around me—they all proclaimed that this place belonged to him.

I shivered, flooded with a yearning I couldn't make sense of. My heart leapt in excitement and anticipation, and I looked out toward the middle of the lake where the surface stirred gently, bobbing and rippling. Suddenly, the movement intensified, and the water began sloshing and swirling in a frenzy of activity. A loud, cracking sound tore through the air, and the sky lit up in an arcing wave of blue and purple light. I looked down at the water, now a bright sapphire shade, bioluminescent in its brilliance.

It was subtle—the shift in the air then—but I felt it. My heartbeat quickened, gooseflesh tearing across my skin. The entire glade crackled with energy, the night heavy with the essence of unadulterated power. I watched as a trailing arc of glittering sapphire moved steadily from the center of the lake toward me. A spark of excitement radiated through my body as it grew closer, coming to a stop in front of me.

I held my breath, waiting, my body tense and upright.

"Elle . . ." a voice whispered, not near me or in my head, but around me, above me, everywhere.

My skin tingled with awareness.

"Ash," I said breathlessly, my hands reaching for him.

The caress of phantom fingers skimmed the arches of my feet, trailing slowly up my legs. My heart thudded as I grasped the air, searching for him. Fingers tangled in my hair, drifting down across my jaw, moving up to trace my lips. Wisps of silver mist and flickering shards of lightning flared in front of me.

"Please, let me see you," I begged.

"Make me, Tialla," he whispered, his voice close against my ear, sending a shiver down the side of my body. "Use your power to command me."

"I . . . I don't know how to."

"Elle, apart from the Gods, you're the only one in this world with the power to compel me."

"Why do you say that?"

"The labral on your wrist says so. Show me what you can do, Tialla mata."

My Goddess. A shiver tingled against my skin as his fingers wrapped around the cuff, before snaking up my arm to cup my face.

"What do I do?" I asked.

"Delve inside yourself. Feel your breath as you inhale and follow it to the source of your strength, just below your navel. See it in your mind's eye and summon your power to you. It will answer."

I had a source of power inside me! That notion was mind-blowing, but as hesitant as I was, the ease and certainty with which he spoke about what I was capable of filled me with a fledgling confidence. If there was anyone who knew what they were talking about, it was him.

I closed my eyes and burrowed inside myself, searching for my source of strength. Harwen Valkyse had said there was a wellspring inside of me, that all I needed to do was tap into that source to access my power. I reached deeper inside myself, silencing the doubts and self-ridicule in my head—searching, calling, cajoling. And then I *heard* it—faint but undeniable—an assonant hum that answered in reverent welcome from the depths of my soul. I couldn't help the laugh that escaped my lips.

In my mind's eye, the surface of a lake emerged, just like the one in front of me—depthless and placid. I stood at the edge, reaching out my finger to touch the glassy veneer. It rippled softly, spreading out slowly in undulating circles.

"That's it, Elle," Ash said. "I can feel the draw of your power calling to mine. Summon it to you. It is yours to command."

I dipped my finger into that wellspring, speaking the words with intention in my mind as I communed with that lake of power. "Let me see him."

I opened my eyes and watched in wonder as the swirls of lightning and mist dissipated, and Ash materialized in front of me. For the longest moment, I just stared at him, my eyes drinking in every detail: the deep emerald of his eyes, the sharp planes of his jaw, the softened expression on his face, the curve of his smile.

He stood fully clothed in the depths of the lake, the sleeves of his black shirt rolled up to his elbows, the first button undone at his neck. I didn't even realize I was holding my breath until I let out a long exhale.

My heart sang with happiness. This was *my* Ash—the version of him that I knew, the one who knew me in my world. I felt it in my bones—there was nothing strange or unusual about the magnificent God standing in front of me. I reached out my hand and traced his cheek with my fingers, my skin on fire where it touched his.

I tried summoning my memories to me, just like I did with my power, but my mind remained shuttered, sheer curtains blocking the stage behind which scenes were playing out and moving, making it so that I couldn't see clearly through the veil to make sense of what was happening. Every now and then, the edge of the veil would lift and I would catch a vivid glimpse—a smile, a flash of laughter, emerald eyes looking at me with sheer intensity—but only for a moment, and then it would blur and the veil would flutter closed again.

My heart, though—it had no such impairment. It exultingly proclaimed its feelings for the beautiful creation in front of me. As a surging spate of emotion tumbled me, I gasped and burst into tears.

Ash, standing between my legs in the lake as I sat on the edge of the bank, moved closer toward me, pulling me into his arms. I buried my face in his neck as he held me to him, uncontrollable sobs wracking my body.

"I didn't know if I'd ever see you again," I cried, and even as the words left my mouth, I wasn't sure if I meant after last night or whenever the last time was that I saw him before ending up in Ariadna.

"I promised you the last time we saw each other that it wasn't goodbye," he whispered in my hair.

I wrapped my arms around his neck, turning my face to trail kisses across his jaw.

"I'm sorry, Elle," he said, his voice heavy with emotion as he pulled away to look at me. "This is not how I wanted things to go. I've waited for almost a century for the day that past and present would come full circle for us, when there would be no more hiding or secrets, when all our prior encounters were caught up to us, but fate has made it so that at least one of us still remains in the dark."

I shook my head. "I might not remember our time together, Ash, but my heart hasn't forgotten. I know what you are to me."

"What's that, Tialla?" he asked, his fingers brushing my tears away.

"Mine," I said, fisting my fingers in his shirt and pulling him toward me.

I lifted my face to his and kissed him, my lips slanting slowly over his as he kissed me back. My mouth parted as his tongue slid past my lips and found mine, swirling slowly. I buried my hands in his hair, pulling him closer as I slipped my tongue into his mouth, brushing the tip against his teeth. I wrapped my legs around his waist as his mouth left mine to move down my jaw, snaking lower toward my collarbone.

"Fuck, I've missed you, Elle." He moved back up to kiss me again, his hands cupping my face.

His words cut through my haze of desire, and I opened my eyes to look at him. "When was the last time we saw each other?" I asked.

"The last time we were together was a little more than five months ago."

Five months! He was gone that long from my life and I didn't remember any of that time, or the time before with him in it? How much time had I lost?

"How long have we known each other?" I asked, clutching his hands against my chest.

He brushed his lips against my forehead. "The first time I met you was almost a century ago when you came to me through the Senshifter. The first time you met me was almost two years ago in the human world."

Almost two years. And I didn't remember any of it.

My body stilled. "Was it at Crusoe's that I met you?"

"Yes, it was," he said with a smile.

That was the last clear memory I had. Going into Crusoe's for a drink after work. Everything after that was gone. Was it a coincidence that my memory loss was limited to the time directly after I'd met him? It couldn't be.

"Andreo and Gwynn said that you have the power to restore my memories," I said, hope flaring that at last, I would remember him.

My heart plummeted at the look of anguish on his face.

"I do, Elle," he said, stroking my cheek. "And if I could, I would in a heartbeat, but after answering a summons from the Cloryals this morning, they cautioned me against restoring your memories."

"The Cloryals?" I blurted out. "Why would they not want my memories restored?" Panic seeped in. That part of my past couldn't remain lost to me.

Ash's jaw clenched. "It's because of the rebounding curse, particularly the source of the power that ignited it—ancient, unstable. I need the help of someone who understands that kind of magic to properly heal your mind. It's too dangerous to risk doing it on my own."

"I don't understand," I said, shaking my head.

A loud roar of thunder cracked through the air, making me jump, and I looked up to see the skies bathed in a shock of crimson.

Ash turned to me, his eyes filled with remorse. "Elle, I know everything must be so confusing for you right now. More than anything, I want to stay with you, but I'll have to go soon."

A bolt of hysteria sliced through me. "What? Where are you going?"

He squeezed my fingers in his. "To attend to something the Cloryals have commanded of me."

"Take me with you," I cried, my desperation mounting.

He cupped my face and touched his forehead against mine. "This is something that as Sovereign, I must do alone. Trust me, I don't want to leave you like this."

"Did you know that last night would be the night that I came to you in your past?" I asked.

He placed his hands on my waist and pulled me closer to the edge of the bank. "Yes. When you came to me on the eve of my coronation, you told me that you only just arrived in Ariadna, meeting Gwynn for the first time that day. You basically told me what to look for. That's why I stayed away, why I blocked you from sensing me. I couldn't risk changing anything that would jeopardize that encounter."

He had blocked me. Earlier, Oletho said that we would be drawn to each other, even without the labral.

He brushed his lips against my temple. "The first time I met you might have only been last night to you, but for me, it was almost a century ago. I waited ninety-seven years before I saw you in the flesh again. I'm not going to let you go now, Tialla." His long fingers encircled my waist gently. "The day of my coronation, when the Ethereal Harmonies returned that second labral, it all fell into place for me—the dream you told me about, who you said you were, the Senshifter bringing you to me, what I sensed about you."

"Oletho showed us that memory," I said, sliding my arms around his neck. "I saw the moment you put it all together."

He brought my hand to his lips and brushed a kiss against my knuckles, his eyes shining with pride. "I knew then that you were a gift from the Gods—that what my senses said about you being my eternal soul's shadow was true. You would be my Gloweyen Queen."

My breath caught in my throat, my heart bursting with emotion. "Oletho said as much." I pulled away to look at his face. "But what does that mean? What is Gloweyen?"

Ash reached down and lifted my hand, lining up my labral with his. "Gloweyen happens when the Mavigos conspire to bring a Sovereign and a Consort together—despite all odds or obstacles—because their souls and destinies are intertwined and meant for greatness."

"Mavigos, as in fate?"

"In a manner of speaking. They are not unique to any one realm or domain. The Mavigos are the supreme deities in the vastness of the entire cosmos."

The entire concept of deities and fate was something I'd always scoffed at as a result of how my life unfolded, and I wasn't sure I was ready to let go of my cynicism yet. Not without proof.

"Your labral is the twin of mine," Ash said. "That, in itself, is incredibly rare. Only twice before in the recorded history of Ariadna have the Ethereal Harmonies returned a labral for a Sovereign's Consort."

A Sovereign's Consort. My heart fluttered excitedly. I still couldn't believe it. The Ethereal Harmonies had chosen me to be his Consort.

"With Gloweyen, one soul calls to another across space and time, each one binding to the other in an unbreakable and symbiotic union. The term *eternal soul's shadow* refers to that connection. Each soul becomes the other's shadow. No matter what happens, both souls can always reach and recognize each other."

I couldn't help the jolt of electricity that ripped through my body at his words. I wanted to stake my claim, to let the world know that this magnificent creature was mine.

He intertwined his fingers with mine. "Gloweyen in a Sovereign couple means invincibility. It means immeasurable power and strength."

"So why is Gloweyen such a rare thing?" I asked. "What does it mean for me?"

Ash smiled, tracing his thumb across my jaw. "Well, it means you are my equal, Elle. Not just my Queen Consort. This labral," he said, tracing the cuff on my wrist, "it pulses with Shinoran light, a sign to everyone that the Ethereal Harmonies have chosen you to be the Sovereign Queen of Valkyse."

I stared at him, my mouth parted, my brain reeling as I processed his words. Bleary heat spread to my face, and I bit my lip to stop the tears from rushing out. "Fuck, Ash," I whispered, squeezing his fingers tight, a lump forming in my throat. His equal? A Sovereign Queen? "I'm not worthy."

I wasn't. I'd wasted my life away. How could I be worthy of him? Of this great destiny? I felt like a fraud.

Hell, my emotions were all over the place, the past couple of days a turbulent roller-coaster ride. One minute, I was confident, the next, a sopping mess. Happy one second, and then a pitiful wreck the next.

"You are the only one who is worthy, Tialla," Ash whispered, lowering his head to brush his lips against mine. "The one who chased my darkness away, the one who slaked my thirst for bitter vengeance, the only one my heart soars for. I knew it the first moment I saw you—that heart, body, and soul, I belonged to you. I told you then—my senses are never wrong. And the Ethereal Harmonies—they certainly don't lie."

A flood of warring emotions coursed through me. From the moment the woman with violet hair had come to me in my dreams that night years ago, she had planted the seed. *Your entire life with a paramount future awaits. All will be revealed in due time.* I couldn't deny it; certainty bubbled deep in my soul. This was that time. *When everything is laid bare, accept the truth of who you are. Claim it as your birthright.* Was this the truth of who I was? Ash's Gloweyen Queen? The Songbird of Valkyse? Savior of this realm?

The being in the grotto—the manifestation of the Cloryals—had told me that I was deemed worthy. It, too, saw the truth of my identity. All these proclamations were made about me, but the crux of my turmoil—hitting me like a ton of bricks as I stared at the beautiful male in front of me who claimed me as his—was that I didn't know who I was. Even that night in my dream, when the woman with silver eyes asked me if I knew who I was, I didn't know how to answer her.

Ash moved from between my legs, and, bracing with his arms, pulled himself out of the lake and sat next to me. The water, or whatever substance was in the lake, beaded off his skin and clothes, leaving him completely dry. He turned and grabbed my waist with his hands, lifting me onto his lap so that my legs straddled him. "I know that look, Elle," he said, tilting my chin up. "Tell me what's going on in that head of yours."

I looked up at him, his green eyes filled with so much strength and warmth, I wanted to get lost in them. "Who am I, Ash?" I asked, clutching his shirt in my hands. "Where did I really come from? Oletho said I was a human woman, but not entirely human. What did he mean?"

He brushed his fingers through my hair, his face thoughtful, as if he was considering how to answer me. "I want you to close your eyes for me, Elle," he said. "Delve down to that place inside you—the source of your power—and ask yourself that question. And then tell me the answer it gives you."

I stared at him for a moment, and he smiled, his eyes urging me to do as he asked.

Reluctantly, I broke his gaze and closed my eyes, traveling to that place inside me. In a heartbeat, I was standing at my lake of power, rippling the surface gently, releasing my question into its depths. In a flood, it answered my call, whispers of affirmation pouring out, dancing all around me.

My eyes flew open, meeting Ash's. My voice rang out in excitement. "The first thing it tells me is that I am yours."

His green orbs flashed, possessiveness and desire flickering at the same time. "What else?" he asked, his fingers trailing across my collarbone.

I arched into his touch, my body seeking the heat of his, even as the words kept on coming, ringing out in my head. "It tells me that I belong here in this world, with you. That the Sangelis is where I have always belonged and was always meant to be." I closed my eyes, focusing on the words that were getting louder in my mind. "It tells me that together, you and I are unstoppable and can defeat any foe threatening the peace of the Sangelis."

Ash cradled his hand around my head, pulling my face closer. "You are powerful, Elle," he said, "even more powerful than me."

"What do you mean?" I asked. "You are a Sovereign. Apart from the Cloryals and the Gods, aren't the Sovereigns the most powerful beings in Ariadna?"

Ash's lips lifted in a soft smile as he wrapped his arms around my waist. "I am a Sovereign, yes," he said, "but you, Tialla, are much more than that. You are the Secret of the Gods."

Chapter 17

SECRET OF THE GODS. Did he really just say that? For so long, I'd wanted to know what the woman in my dream had meant by that. It had to mean the same thing. How many secrets of the Gods could there be, especially when it came to me?

I furrowed my brows as I looked at Ash. "Do you know what that means?" I asked, my voice brimming with curiosity.

He nodded. "I've known for a long time."

"How long?" I asked, narrowing my eyes. "Did you know when you met me in my world?"

"I have known since shortly after my coronation," he said, his face serious as he regarded me.

"How?" I asked. "What does it mean?"

Ash cocked his head to the side. "Before you left me that night, you told me that a woman with curly, violet hair and music inside her had sent you through the Senshifter. Like I told you then—only the Gods can command a Senshifter. And so, I sought out the God—in this case, Goddess—who had."

My eyes widened as I looked at him. "You know who she is?" I asked, my voice ringing with incredulity.

"I do."

"Well? Who is she? And what does 'Secret of the Gods' mean?"

"You're not going to be happy with my answer," Ash said, a contrite look on his face. "You are *their* secret, and so only they can reveal the full truth of it to you—again."

I frowned. "Wait. What do you mean *again*?"

"It means you already know, but it's one of the things that got erased from your memory. Who the Goddess is, the secret—it was already revealed to you before you got to Ariadna."

"Well, that's just perfect," I blurted loudly, my frustration flaring in a rush. "Another huge revelation that I don't remember." A blur of tears stung my eyes and I swiped them away. "How am I supposed to navigate this new world without all my memories? Without the full knowledge of who you are to me." My breath hitched as a sob slipped out. "I lost you, Ash. You said we've known each other for almost two years, and all I have are glimpses and flashes. I want it back. Every look, laugh, touch, kiss—every first, second, third of everything I shared with you. I want it *all* back. There's so much I just don't know about our relationship. Big things. Little things. Like, did you call me Tialla when you knew me? And if you did, did I ask you what it meant? Did we fight? And if so, did we have wild make-up sex? When I was with you, how was I? Was I happy, timid, sad? The list of all the things I want to know is endless."

Ash touched his forehead to mine, his arms still wrapped around my waist. Finally, he let out a deep breath and pulled his head back to look at me, sadness and grief shining in his eyes. "If I could give all those memories back to you, Elle, I would in a heartbeat." He cupped my cheek gently. "For starters, I did call you Tialla, and yes, you asked me what it meant. You accepted when I said it was 'Goddess' in another language. You also liked every other endearment I lavished on you: beautiful, sexy, baby. Honestly, I don't think it would have mattered what I called you. You loved feeling cherished, and I was more than happy to oblige."

Tears spilled freely down my cheeks, and I wound my arms around his neck, aching to be closer to him.

Slowly, he trailed feather-light kisses down the side of my face. "As for the sex," he whispered against my ear, "it was *always* wild."

Desire roared to life inside me, and I arched my hips into the hard length of him I could feel growing against the inside of my thigh.

He grabbed my backside and pulled me closer, his hands sliding up to skim my torso. "As for how you were when you were with me?" He tilted his head to the side, his fingers absently brushing against my ribcage. "Outside the bedroom—you were bold, blunt, funny, irreverent, fearless. Inside the bedroom—well, pretty much the same," he said with a grin. "But also, so uninhibited and insatiable." His eyes glazed over with hunger, and the heat flared between us—palpable and coiled tight, ready to burst free.

I was achingly aware of his erection so close to where I wanted him the most.

"You always kept me at arm's length, though," he said, kissing my forehead. "Too afraid to get closer, to bring emotion into it, to endure any more hurt. Too wrapped up in your belief that you were cursed and didn't deserve to be loved."

His words snuffed out the desire inside me, leaving an acrid taste in my mouth.

"Elle, across space and time, you and I found each other." He tilted my chin up, his eyes boring intimately into mine. "I knew long before I found you again in the human world who you were to me. And because I knew the Secret of the Gods, I wasn't afraid of getting close to you, attached to you. But in doing so, I inadvertently put you in harm's way, and you did get hurt."

"Was it Kaliope?" I wrapped my fingers around his labral.

His eyes flashed at the mention of her name. "I take it Gwynn and Oletho have brought you up to speed?"

I nodded. "They told me about your history with her and about the threat she poses."

"To put you in danger was the last thing I ever wanted, Elle," he said, his eyes swirling with pain. "Sometimes I tell myself that if I could go back in time and change things so she never found out about you, and you never got hurt, even if it meant I never found you again, I would do it, just to keep you safe."

A surge of anger coursed through me. "Stop! Don't even think that. Do you know how many times I tried to end my life before you came along? I desperately wanted to die because I had absolutely *nothing* worth living for. The life I had before I met you was torture—a living, walking death sentence." A bitter laugh escaped my lips. "It seems I'm not easy to kill." I cupped his jaw with my hand. "Don't wish me away to keep me *safe*. I might not remember our time together, but the songs my heart sings tell me it was beautiful, and that you and I were always going to be inevitable."

"I would never wish you away, Elle," he replied softly. "I thought of you every single day after that night, waiting for the time when the Gods would bring you back to me again. But that feeling of helplessness at not being able to protect you—I never want to feel that again."

"Well, maybe that's why I have powers of my own." I cocked my head to the side. "So I can save myself when you're not there to do it."

He smiled. "You always have a blunt way of putting things into perspective."

"One of us has to be the brains of the operation," I said, wrapping my arms around his neck.

"I need to tell you about the second labral." he said.

The second labral. "Gwynn said she didn't even know such a thing existed."

"It's knowledge that only the Sovereigns and Keepers of magic have. The ancient text in the Giln Keeper's sanctuary tells of a time when two labrals will be returned, bearing the symbols of each dominion of Ariadna: the crescent moon for Valkyse, the sun for Solanis, three vertical stars for Averon, and a cluster of constellations for Tandor."

My heart thudded in my chest. "Just like the ones from the dream I told you about. What does it mean? Why did it return those for *us*?"

"Well," he said, gesturing to our labrals, "just like these are a proclamation of Gloweyen between us, so too are the labrals from your dream. But they take Gloweyen to an entirely different level."

"What level is that?" My pulse thrummed in my ears.

"They elevate us to High Sovereigns of all of Ariadna," he said quietly.

I blinked, my mind reeling at his words.

"Holy shit, Ash! I haven't even wrapped my head around the whole Sovereign Queen of Valkyse proclamation, and now you're telling me that this thing between us is even bigger than that?"

"I know it's overwhelming, but you're not alone in this. We have each other. I'm right here with you."

Another peal of thunder splintered the air, causing us to both look up. The crimson clouds writhed restlessly as shards of lightning lit up the ominous sky.

Ash pulled me to him once more, wrapping me in his arms. "My time's up, Elle. I have to go. As soon as I finish what I have to do, I'll come back to you, I promise."

"Wait," I said in a rush, suddenly remembering my earlier encounter. "I saw your mother."

He blinked, confusion and then wonder visible on his face. "How? When?"

"I don't know how," I said, "but she came to me twice. Once

yesterday, and then before you got here, over there, in the grove of angorns. She passed her Songbird mantle to me." I laced my fingers through his and delivered the message Harwen Valkyse asked me to relay.

Ash's eyes filled with tears. "I knew of her Songbird mantle being passed to you, but I didn't know she came to you." He looked off toward the grove of angorns, his face lined with pain and sadness. "Fuck, I miss her."

I wrapped my arms around his neck, brushing my lips against his cheek.

"Thank you for telling me," he whispered, locking our gazes together. Swirling emotions flickered on his face—sadness, fear, resolve. He lowered his head, his lips gently skimming mine. He pulled away and traced my lips with his thumb, staring at me long and hard, as if debating something with himself. Slowly, he rested his forehead against mine. "In case you weren't sure how I feel, in case you don't remember me saying it," he whispered, tilting my head back to look at him, his eyes shining with heated emotion, "I love you, Elle. Heart, body, and soul."

I blinked, thrown by his admission. My heart hammered wildly in my chest.

"You don't have to say it back," he said. "I know you don't remember what we had, but I want you to know that every moment of that time was beautiful for me too."

"Ash . . ." I whispered, my throat clogging with the weight of my emotions.

"You'll say it to me again, Tialla," he said with a wink. He lifted me off him and placed me down next to him before lowering himself into the lake.

I'd say it *again*. So I had told him I loved him before. The way my heart was rejoicing made me believe I did.

Sidling himself between my legs, he rested his hands on my thighs. "I'll only be gone a day or two, but I need you to stay close to Gwynn, Andreo, and Faron in the meantime. Until your coronation and your powers are fully realized, you are still vulnerable."

"Please don't block me from finding you."

"I have to shield my labral from yours," he said. "That connection can be intercepted, and we can't afford attracting Kaliope's attention." He squeezed my fingers gently. "When I get back, we'll start honing your use of your powers. Everything hinges on the Convergence, a little more than a month away. There is a lot to do until then. I know none of this makes sense to you, but I will explain everything. I promise."

"What's the Convergence?" I asked.

"It occurs once every century when the constellations of Sorin and Eolith align in the heavens. I'll explain it all when I return."

Ash's mother had mentioned the same constellations when I was with her earlier. A surge of panic washed over me. With Ash next to me, all my fears and insecurities had evaporated, and the magnitude of all that had been revealed about me was manageable and less daunting somehow. But he was leaving—abandoning me—and my heart twisted in a vise at the thought of facing whatever came next without him.

For God's sake! What was wrong with me? I needed to get my shit together. Ash wasn't abandoning me; that was clear. I'd never allowed anyone to have this kind of power over me. Never allowed myself to need someone like this. But I couldn't let my fear of loss sabotage me anymore. I needed to give myself permission to trust, to believe in living again.

As if sensing the downward shift in my thoughts, he reached for my hands and pulled me to him. "I'm only a thought away, Elle. You can use the source of your power to find me in your mind if you need me. Just follow that path that leads to me. Catraia will show you how if it comes to that."

"Who's Catraia?"

"It'll all make sense when you reach out to find me. Trust me." He brushed his lips against my forehead. "I'll be back as soon as I can." He cupped my face in his hands and kissed me once more, and then slowly pulled away, taking a few steps backward into the lake. His green eyes didn't leave mine as he moved away, and then a few seconds later, he shifted to mist and lightning, and in a crack of thunder, he was gone.

Chapter 18

I SWORE PART OF my soul left with him. It was oddly similar to when Harwen Valkyse transformed me back from having wings and the loss of them rocked me.

The angry crimson of the sky quickly changed back to inky night, stars twinkling from afar, a constellation surrounding the crescent moon.

I lifted my feet out of the lake and slipped my shoes on, rolling my pant legs down. My body hummed with restless energy. I was still numb from his declaration of love for me. He loved me. He fucking loved me!

I didn't want to linger here any longer. I needed to get back to Gwynn and Oletho.

I looked down at the labral on my wrist. The white and yellow zidiurrh eddied and rippled lazily across the length of the band. I couldn't move it or take it off—it was as much a part of me as my fingers were. '*Til death do us part*, I whispered, remembering my conversation with Gwynn about gilns. It was hard to believe that that was only this morning; so much had happened since then.

I watched the molten meandering of the zidiurrh on my giln. I traced its path with my fingers and conjured a mental picture in my mind of the chamber in Cazara Colpra. Could I do this? Harwen Valkyse had said that my labral would return me to Oletho and Gwynn. There was only one way to find out.

I swirled the giln in a clockwise pattern just as Gwynn had done, and like before, there was a loud pop, gut-wrenching pressure, and the splintering of air around me, and I was whisked away.

I gasped loudly.

"Eleyse!" Gwynn cried out, reaching for me.

I opened my eyes to find myself standing on the dais in Oletho's chamber again. Oletho was standing behind her, his face mirroring the concern reflected on Gwynn's.

"Where did you go?" she asked, her eyes flashing with curiosity.

"How long was I gone?" I stared at the grotto in front of me, the second labral hovering there.

She glanced at Oletho, who had moved to stand beside her. "Not long. You vanished through the grotto, and a few seconds later, reappeared."

Bloody hell, this was incredible. It had felt like I was gone for hours. But Harwen Valkyse had said that Falayen existed outside the confines of space and time. That had to be why time had barely moved here.

"What happened?" Gwynn asked.

"I was with your mother," I answered. "And then with Ash. In a place called Falayen."

"Falayen?" Oletho asked. "Are you sure?"

"Yes. That's what she called it."

"You saw my mother?" Gwynn asked, her eyes wide as she looked at me. "And Ash? They were there together?"

"No," I said. "Your mother was with me first, and a little while after she left me, Ash appeared."

Gwynn stared at me, dumbfounded, her lips quivering as she studied me. "I don't even know where to begin," she said, lifting her hands. "My mother herself never entered Falayen when she was alive. My father was the only one who could go there, and then Ash after him."

"This confirms it, Gwynn," Oletho said. "Eleyse and Asher *are* Gloweyen. Falayen is a place of consecration, a hallowed sanctuary where the powers of Sovereigns are replenished and renewed. Each Sovereign has their own sanctuary. With Gloweyen, the power of the Queen Consort matches that of the Sovereign's, and Falayen is a place where both powers can be fused—where the two become one."

"Tell me everything," Gwynn said, gripping my hands.

I proceeded to recount all that had happened in the grove with Harwen Valkyse. Tears streamed down Gwynn's face when I gave her the message her mother had asked me to deliver.

"I wish I could have seen her and spoken to her just one last time," she said.

A deluge of guilt washed over me. I could understand how unfair it might seem to her that I was able to spend time with her beloved mother, not one, but two times, and she, who yearned to have just one glimpse, was not. I'd experienced that same feeling of longing when I saw my own mother through Jackie Stepps's eyes.

She must have seen the look on my face because she grabbed my hands tightly. "I don't resent you, Eleyse," she assured me. "Please don't think that. She came to you for a reason."

She was right. The dead didn't just come back to visit on a whim. Again, the magnitude of everything that Harwen Valkyse had revealed hit me, fear coursing through me once more.

"What happened with Ash?" Gwynn asked, her words prying me away from my thoughts. "Did you remember him when you saw him?" Her eyes were bright with curiosity.

"Not exactly," I said. "I mean, on some deeper level, I knew him and felt the powerful connection between us, but my actual memories of the two of us remain lost." I went on to explain what transpired between me and Ash—how long we knew each other, what the Cloryals said about the rebounding curse, why he had to leave. I glossed over the emotional details, completely omitting him saying that he loved me. I hadn't had time to process that on my own yet.

"You said he shielded his labral?" Oletho asked.

I nodded. "He said that connection could be compromised, and he didn't want to take the chance that Kaliope could use it against us."

Oletho stroked his chin gently. "Normally, you would be tethered to each other through your gilns. Yours began calling to his the moment you put it on. The Shinoran light will remain, but if he shielded his labral, you won't be able to use it to communicate with him."

"He did tell me that I could use my source of power to find him in my mind if I needed him."

"Yes," Oletho said. "You are Asher's soul's shadow and he is yours—that Gloweyen connection allows you to sense each other on an innate level through the source of your combined powers."

"He didn't say what the Cloryals asked him to do?' Gwynn asked, rubbing her shoulders with her hands, her face lined with worry.

I shook my head. "No, only that it was something that as Sovereign he needed to do alone." I searched my mind for anything I might have forgotten. "He also explained what the second labral meant."

Gwynn's brows furrowed in a frown. "What does it mean?"

I glanced at Oletho, who nodded for me to continue, and I

proceeded to tell her what Ash had revealed.

"High Sovereigns of all of Ariadna?" Gwynn said, her eyes wide, chest heaving. "I . . . I don't know what to say." She chewed on her lip, clearly lost in her thoughts, and then she looked at Oletho, her head tilted to the side. "There's something that keeps nagging at me, Oletho. At his coronation, Ash didn't seem surprised when he saw the second labral. How could he have known? And he's known all these years that he would have a Gloweyen Queen and never said anything? I feel there is something missing that I'm not seeing."

Oletho flicked his gaze toward me, and I stared at him uneasily. How could I explain what had happened with the Senshifter?

"That is a question only Asher or someone with insight into his mind can answer, Gwynn," Oletho replied. "He never shared that with me." He glanced at me pointedly, and what looked like a knowing smile hovered on his lips for a moment.

I looked away. It was clear he suspected something.

"I will say this. Eleyse and Asher being High Sovereigns of Ariadna only lends credence to them being the ones the well-guarded Hasheyn star etching speaks of."

"What star etching is this?" Gwynn asked, her brows furrowed in confusion.

"Wait. What's a star etching?" I asked.

Oletho shifted his gaze in my direction. "Star etchings are proclamations of the future—they are how the Mavigos transcribe signs and news of great significance. They are made up of Hasheyn glyphs that are literally written across the heavens in the stars. The one I speak of is the oldest to have ever been recorded, older than even the Gods of the New Age of the Sangelis themselves, imprinted in the stars long before the Great Creator, Arazul, ascended to the heavens."

I didn't know any of these Gods he spoke of, but it was enough to get the gist. Whatever he was talking about was really old. Which begged the question—how could it possibly have anything to do with me?

"I say it's a well-guarded star etching because the Great Creator, Arazul, was the only God of the Sangelis aware of its existence, as far as I know. It was only revealed to Keepers of the Old, Arcane Magic and the Ethereal Harmonies a few centuries ago."

"So as Giln Keeper, you would know," Gwynn chewed on her lip. "Why is there so much secrecy around it?"

I stared at them blankly. Old, Arcane Magic? Was that different from the Ethereal Harmonies?

"The predictions it contained were too . . . controversial, I suppose," Oletho said. "Other Gods would not take to it lightly."

What the hell did this thing say if other Gods would be riled by it?

"And you think Ash and I are a part of this?" I said, nettles of unease trailing down my spine.

"I believe so, yes. If what I believe is true, then Kaliope, too, has a part to play." He touched the top of his giln, and to my amazement, the trinzum parted and stretched open. He slipped his fingers inside and retrieved a small scroll, about six inches long, enclosed in an intricate filigree casing. My eyes were wide as I beheld it. How did that fit in there?

His giln rippled and knitted back together seamlessly as he handed the scroll to me. "When you get to Torannon, this is for you and Asher." He looked at me pointedly, a peculiar smile on his face. "If what I believe is true, you should be able to decipher its contents. I strongly suspect that Asher already knows, but it is up to him and you if you want to share that knowledge with anyone else." He gestured to my labral. "Close your eyes and picture stretching your labral open like I did with my giln."

I frowned, staring at my labral intently. Tentatively, I touched the crest at the top, and in my mind, pictured it yawning open. Amazingly, it slid back on itself, leaving a narrow gap. Slowly, I inserted the scroll, and it slipped inside and kept on going as I pushed until it was completely covered. It was incredible to watch.

"Now, picture your labral melting back into place."

As I conjured the image in my mind, the labral rippled and fused back together smoothly.

Oletho clasped his hands together. "As long as it's secure in your labral, no one will be able to take it from you." He reached out and clasped Gwynn's shoulder. "You and Eleyse should head back to Torannon now. Because of this monumental Gloweyen proclamation, there are others who might see Eleyse as a threat, not just Kaliope. Be extra cautious and mindful of who you trust."

A feeling of foreboding unsettled me. Who else was there that would see me as a threat?

Gwynn nodded. "We will, Oletho." Her eyes were serious, but filled with uncertainty. "Thank you for everything." She embraced him tightly.

He cupped her face gently. "There is hope, Gwynn. Even if war is an inevitability."

She nodded and clasped his hands. "What happens to that labral now?" She inclined her head to the labral with the four symbols hovering in the light-filled grotto.

"It will join its twin in the Pavilion of Harmonies, and there they both will stay until Asher's and Eleyse's Ariadnan coronation."

The hair on the back of my neck stood on end. In my mind, I pictured it—the two labrals resting on velvet-lined boxes in the Pavilion of Harmonies. I had seen this future in my dreams long ago and hadn't even known the significance of what it meant.

"Be courageous and safe, Eleyse," Oletho said, reaching out and squeezing my shoulder. "Don't be afraid to heed the wisdom of your heart. It will not steer you wrong."

The same words the woman with violet hair had said last night.

I nodded. "Thanks for everything, Oletho."

I turned toward Gwynn and took her hand. She smiled encouragingly and touched her giln, hurtling us through space to Torannon.

Chapter 19

GWYNN'S GILN DEPOSITED US on a rooftop terrace with breathtaking views of a bustling city. Like Cazara Chantilis, this residence, too, was situated at the top of a mountain. Behind us, a stone pergola stood proudly—colossal and stately—its graceful arches yawning across the expanse of a shimmering pool.

"Welcome to Cazara Torannon," Gwynn said, striding across the terrace. "This is the capital city of Valkyse."

The view was gorgeous. In the late afternoon sun, everything around us was vibrant and crisp. A harbor sprawled in the distance beneath us, and inland, the city fanned out as far as I could see to the left and right.

We almost collided with Faron as we turned the corner into a large, open sunroom with floor-to-ceiling glass windows and a domed glass roof.

"Gwynn! Eleyse!" He wrapped his arms around Gwynn, enfolding her in an embrace. In the bright sunlight, the jagged scar above his lip stood out even more. Strange that in a world with miraculous healing magic, he carried a wound like that.

"We came here from Oletho's," Gwynn explained as she hugged him back. "Have you seen or heard from Ash?"

Faron shook his head as he reached for my hands in greeting. "He's not here. He returned this morning, in a hurry. He and Andreo were locked away in his quarters for a short time, and then he talked to me for a couple minutes before he left."

"What did he say to you?" Gwynn asked, her voice wavering.

He squeezed my fingers gently. "That we must protect Eleyse at all costs and keep her hidden from Kaliope until he returns."

Kaliope. Did she know I was here? And if so, what specifically did she know? She hardly sounded like the rational type—more like the kind who would kill first and not even bother asking questions after. And given that she was obsessed with Ash, I had no doubts that she would take me out in a heartbeat.

"Did he give you any indication of where he might be going?"

"No, he wasn't here long enough for me to ask questions."

Gwynn chewed on her lip thoughtfully.

Faron's face was solemn. "I feel helpless, Gwynn. Something is in motion, but I have no idea what, and I don't know how to help him."

"Stop your bellyaching, Faron!" a voice growled from behind me. "He gave us his orders. Protect the *human* woman."

I detected a hint of disdain in those last words. I turned around to see a tall, imposing warrior woman striding toward us, dressed in head-to-toe black leather, her pale blonde hair braided in a single plait down her back. Her eyes were the same piercing silver-blue as Faron's. Holy frig, she was fierce. I couldn't help the shiver of admiration that snaked through me at her confidence.

She stopped next to Faron and studied me appraisingly, her eyes sweeping over me in barely concealed disapproval. "I take it this is *she*?" Her lips curled slightly in derision.

I blinked in surprise. Not only was she confident, she was also excellent at throwing shade.

"Tone it down, Astrid." Gwynn's eyes flashed in warning. "And yes, this is Eleyse. From this moment on, we do as Ash said. Apart from us and Andreo, we tell no one who she is. We protect her with our lives. Oletho is the only other person who knows the truth."

"And what exactly *is* the truth, Gwynn?" Astrid asked, her eyes narrow and tone gruff. "What are we risking our lives to protect?"

"Enough with the attitude." The warning in Gwynn's voice was unmistakable. "Eleyse and Ash are Gloweyen. It's as simple as that."

Astrid said nothing, but her eyes grew wide as she looked at me, a mixture of surprise and something else—disappointment, hurt—flitting across her features. Hmm . . . Interesting.

"Gloweyen?" Faron stared at me, a look of incredulity and reverence on his face, his eyes shifting to my light-infused labral shining its intent for all to see. "Does Ash know?"

"Yes." Gwynn took my hand, touching my labral. "From now on, Eleyse, this stays hidden. This proclaims to everyone who you are, and we can't let anyone see it. Once we speak to my uncle, we'll have a better sense of what our next move is."

"I would like to speak with Andreo as well," I said.

"Our *queen* speaks," Astrid said, her face void of emotion.

I turned, studying her carefully. She didn't know me from Eve, but right out of the gate, had come charging at me. She was hiding something, something that was responsible for her bitterness toward me, but what?

She is in love with Asher, a calm, confident voice—unmistakably female—whispered in my mind, audible and distinct. What the— Where did that come from?

I shook my head and rubbed my forehead. "Did you say something?" I said, turning to Gwynn.

She shook her head as she looked at me, brows furrowed.

She has been in love with him for over a century, and yet she understands and accepts that he will never be hers. She is loyal and will protect him with her life, would protect his family with her life.

Whose voice was whispering in my head? This was different from the small, still voice that was always with me—the voice that had been awfully vocal since I arrived in Ariadna—but in the same breath, it was strangely similar, except it was louder, more distinct, independent of my own thoughts.

It was happening. I was losing my goddamn mind. Hearing *real* voices in my head was a sign of that, right?

I am real, the voice uttered again. *There will be time to explain, Eleyse.*

For a moment, I stood there, with what I was sure was a dumb look plastered on my face. Something fluttered in the back of my mind, crying out for notice, but I couldn't quite grasp it. It was important, though. Something that gave credence to this voice in my head.

You are her queen, Eleyse. Whether she likes it or not. You must be prepared to act like it. Address her. As for the questions you might have for me, we can talk when you're alone.

Astrid just stared at me, a spark of defiance in her eye.

I touched the labral on my wrist, the zidiurrh warm against my skin. In making the choice to wear it, I'd willingly accepted my place at Ash's side. The voice was right. This might all still be entirely new to me, but the reality—as incredulous as it was—was that I was going to be a queen. I needed to decide what persona I was going to project, who I was going to be.

I will never steer you wrong, Eleyse. Trust your senses.

As many questions as I had, those senses of mine were telling me that I wasn't crazy. The calming hum echoing through my body agreed. What the voice relayed about Astrid was very specific information, and if it was true that she was in love with Ash? Then it was no wonder she hated me. She had known him all her life. I was the usurper here.

Another one in love with Ash. How many more were there that I didn't know about? What was it about him that inspired such territorial feelings? Gosh, I was one to talk. The part of me that claimed him as mine was ready to spit venom and claw eyes out, thinking of him with someone else.

I took in Astrid's rigid posture and stepped closer to her. "Listen, I know we don't know each other, and trust is a fragile thing that must be earned. I will try my best to earn yours."

She said nothing, but her eyes flashed sardonically.

Okay . . . she was taking the surly bitch route. Noted. I didn't miss the frowns on both Faron's and Gwynn's faces.

"Is Andreo here?" I asked, shifting the attention away from Astrid.

"No," Faron replied. "He has been with the Council of Governors since Ash left. He was concerned that we needed to fortify our defenses immediately. Astrid and I will meet with the Valkyse Guard tomorrow in Clearkinin."

Gwynn raised her hand. "I'd like to be there for that. In the meantime, Eleyse and I have not had anything to eat since breakfast, so we'll have an early dinner, after which, hopefully, Uncle Andreo will be back, and we can decide together what our plan of action is."

Faron and Astrid nodded and left the room, leaving Gwynn and me alone.

"I'm sorry about Astrid," Gwynn apologized. "She is . . . she's very protective of Ash."

"That's a nice way of putting it," I replied with a laugh. "I get it. I'm a stranger to her; she's known him all her life. She's bound to be protective."

"That doesn't excuse her rudeness." She turned toward the door. "Why don't we get something to eat? I don't know about you, but I'm starving."

I nodded even though I was too worked up to be hungry, my

appetite abandoning me as it always did when I felt overwhelmed.

Gwynn headed out the door toward the kitchen and I followed, my mind a sweeping vortex of information that still needed to be processed and catalogued. Maybe a good meal and a glass of wine would clear my head and bring some clarity.

"Oh my goodness, Gwynn. This is breathtaking!" I stared at the room in front of me, my eyes open in wonder as I looked around.

Gwynn and I had quickly eaten, and afterward, she led me through a maze of corridors—rich and luxurious in décor—to the other end of the cazara.

We were standing in a massive, circular-shaped room with ceilings over twenty feet high. All around the room, except for a large window straight ahead, the walls were covered from floor to ceiling in bookshelves. A narrow wooden staircase stood to my left, leading to a landing about ten feet up that wrapped around the circumference of the room.

"The library at Cazara Torannon is the biggest one in Valkyse," Gwynn said.

I eyed the two plush armchairs on either side of the floor-to-ceiling window, imagining how lovely it would be to curl up with a good book there, that incredible view of the city spread out majestically before me.

Gwynn walked toward a shelf on her right and skimmed through the titles, finally settling on a large, thick tome. She brought it over to a long, wooden table in the center of the room, around which red, velvet-covered chairs were tucked in.

All through dinner, I was plagued with the conviction that

I should tell Gwynn about what had happened with the Senshifter—how it had taken me back in time to Ash. Oletho had told me to trust the wisdom of my heart, and my heart was urging me to come clean with Gwynn.

She beckoned for me to sit, placing the book on the table. "I know this is all new to you, and for some of this to make sense, I need to tell you about the Gods."

Right! The Gods. What did Oletho call them? Gods of the New Age or something like that. Perhaps this was a good segue into telling Gwynn about the Senshifter. It had to do with the Gods, too, based on what Ash and Gwynn both said.

"Where I'm from," I said, "people have diverse beliefs, and the gods vary based on those beliefs. I couldn't tell you the names of all of the gods if you asked me. In some belief systems, or religions, as we call them, there are hundreds of deities."

"Here, the Gods of the New Age of the Sangelis reign supreme," Gwynn said. She ran her fingers across the book on the table.

I leaned forward to get a closer look. The cover was thick, hard, and weathered, dark brown with gold lettering. "A *History of the Gods*."

"Eleyse!" Gwynn's eyes were wide as she looked at me.

My head shot up at her outburst, and I sprang back in my seat.

"This is truly incredible. Not only can you speak and understand Valkyn, but you can read it as well. I have an idea!" She snapped her fingers and rushed over to the bookshelves behind her. She picked out three books and brought them over to the table. "Read the title on this one." She pushed a thick, blue volume in front of me.

I looked at the white lettering for a moment before the words came to me. "*What Lies Beneath the Casponis?*"

"Now this one." She handed me a small, thin, black leather book.

191

"*The Case for Ariadnan Sovereignty.*"

Gwynn placed the last book she was holding on top of the others in front of me. The lettering was a deep burgundy with an illustration of multiple strange creatures beneath it.

"*Beasts of Pashket: Truth or Myth?*" I read.

Gwynn studied me with a strange smile on her face.

"Well?" I asked, waiting for her to say something.

"Each of these books is written in a different Ariadnan language. The first was Solani, the second Averonian, and the third Tandorin, and you read them all with no hesitation, as if they were as familiar to you as breathing. I have never seen anything like this! I don't even think there is a name to describe this ability. You never studied or learned these languages; you simply know them!"

How was this even possible? Where were all these strange abilities coming from? On Earth, I considered myself smart and educated, but by no means would I have considered myself a genius.

"Well, let's just add this to the list of things that make absolutely no sense to me," I said, the frustration of all the things I couldn't explain setting in again.

"This will all make sense eventually." Gwynn's voice was low and reassuring. "We have to believe that. Let's hope that it all starts falling into place soon." She pushed the three books aside and opened the book on the Gods.

"You called them the Gods of the New Age of the Sangelis," I peered closer at the pages as she was flipping through them. "Does that mean there was an old age?"

"From what I've been taught, this is the Second Age of the Sangelis, also known as the New Age. The First Age of the Sangelis was before that, but I know next to nothing about it. All the records we have only go as far back as the New Age."

"How long are we talking here? Thousands of years?"

"Not thousands, millions."

My eyebrows shot up. "*Millions*? And in all that time, Ariadnans have existed here?" Thoughts of dinosaurs walking on Earth millions of years ago flashed across my mind. Surely, the evolution of species would work the same way across worlds?

"It's believed that a cataclysmic event in the cosmos caused the end of the First Age of the Sangelis and brought about the Second Age," Gwynn said. "Now, I can only speak for Ariadna, but the first records of Ariadnans we have date back to over fifteen million years ago."

This was incredible. Ever since I was a little girl, the vastness of the universe had always fascinated me. I mean, what was the likelihood that there *wasn't* other life out there, in the great expanse of time and space? Earth was just a minuscule speck, after all.

Gwynn turned to a page with a stunning portrait of a male figure—breathtaking, with light-brown hair, piercing silver eyes, a haze of light around him. As I focused on the page, I froze, my heart lurching in my chest, a sickening dread churning in my gut. I *knew* him. I knew this twisted son of a bitch well. The face staring back at me had haunted my nightmares since I was five.

It was the face of the Reaper himself. Death.

Chapter 20

"ARE YOU ALL RIGHT, Eleyse?" Gwynn asked, touching my arm. "You look like you've seen a ghost."

"I . . . wh . . .who is this?" I stuttered, panic washing over me in waves, my head dizzy and hot as I stared at the image on the page.

"This is Arazul, the Great Creator," Gwynn said, her forehead crinkling as she studied me. "At least, the most common form he is known to take. The Gods are shape-shifters and can assume any form they choose, be it a person, creature, or even elements in nature—wind, water, fire. Arazul was the first of the Gods of the New Age, the most powerful one as well."

What the hell was happening? My mind raced, trying to make sense of everything, but for the life of me, I didn't understand. I'd seen this face many times before—fifteen, to be precise. His image was burned into my mind. He was Death—there was no other way to explain it.

When I lost my parents, Mags, Liam—he had appeared to me in the moments after they died, and then again at their funerals. I saw him all of the times I'd tried to take my life, with the exception of the last. Not once in all fifteen times did he ever say a word to me, but he had made his presence known to me, shown his face, as if taunting me. I'd even written a goddamn song about him.

"I've seen him before," I said quietly.

"What?" Gwynn exclaimed, her eyes wide. "When? How?"

"He's visited me many times," I said, my voice tinged with bitterness. "When I lost each of my loved ones, and then after, when . . ." I couldn't continue, couldn't tell her how low I had sunk in my despair. "I always thought of him as Death," I whispered. "He took everyone I loved, but not me. Never me."

"Oh, Eleyse," Gwynn said, pushing her chair back and rushing to me, throwing her arms around me. "There has to be an explanation," she said softly. "I have no idea what it is, but there has to be a reason. Are you certain this is who you saw?"

"Completely certain. How many Gods are there?" I asked, unable to tear my eyes away from those silver eyes leaping off the page at me. I didn't understand what was happening. I felt numb. Like my dream about the twin labrals, here was yet another startling revelation from my past tying me to this world.

Earlier, when Harwen Valkyse and I had slipped into Jackie Stepps's mind moments after my birth, that presence Jackie sensed in the room had felt and smelled like death to me—the same as it did each of the times I saw the figure on the page in front of me. Mint and evergreen. An aura of invincibility. Unbidden, my memory conjured the smell and the feel of him, and it toppled my senses as I stared at the God on the page.

"There are six Gods of the New Age," Gwynn said, flipping through the pages as she knelt next to me. The portrait of another male figure took up the entire page she stopped at. His hair was black and wavy, his features angular and chiseled, and his eyes shone with fire. Although I'd never seen him before, something inside me sparked with excitement and curiosity at the sight of him.

"This is Sorin, Summoner of Light and Darkness. He is the second most powerful of the Gods."

Like Arazul, he, too, was captivating, his eyes ablaze with a scalding intensity and a sad seriousness.

Gwynn combed through some more pages and stopped at the portrait of a female figure with silver hair, silver-white eyes, and a diadem of stars on her head. A fierceness shone in her eyes, her lips drawn in a thin line. A feeling of wariness came over me at the sight of her.

"This is Jaraya, Goddess of the Night." Gwynn traced the portrait with her index finger. "She is espoused to Sorin."

"She's his wife?" I asked. I guess it was no different than Zeus and Hera in Greek mythology.

Gwynn nodded, flipping through pages again. "This is Eolith, Goddess of the Ethereal Harmonies." Her fingers brushed over the portrait of a woman with curly violet hair, her eyes bright silver. She wore a crown of violet flowers around her head. Her cheekbones were high, her lips parted in a smile.

My mouth dropped open. No fucking way! I couldn't tear my eyes away from her face. It was her! The woman from my dream all those years ago. The woman who, just last night, had guided me through the Senshifter to Ash! The one who had called me the Secret of the Gods.

"On Ariadna, we refer to her as the Goddess Mother," Gwynn was saying, "as she is the Supreme Guardian of the Ethereal Harmonies."

Gwynn must have seen the look on my face because she turned and touched my arm. "Eleyse. What is it? You're as white as a sheet."

"I . . . I've seen her before as well," I said, my head spinning as I stared at the image of the Goddess.

Gwynn pulled a chair closer to her and sat, facing me. "Where? When?" she said, taking my hands in hers.

I told her about my dream all those years ago and what the

woman had said to me—her strange comments about how long she'd slept and waited to meet me, her calling me the Secret of the Gods, her proclamation about what my future held.

Gwynn stared at me blankly, a look of pure shock on her face.

"That's not all, Gwynn." I shifted in my chair as she arched a brow quizzically. "She came to me last night . . . through the Senshifter in my room."

Gwynn's mouth fell open. "That's why you were asking about it this morning."

I nodded. "She . . . she sent me through the Senshifter to him . . . to Ash. Back in time to the night before his coronation."

Gwynn's throat bobbed as she swallowed. Her eyes opened wide, and a soft squeak escaped her lips. "Medra, Eleyse," she whispered. "What happened?"

And so I told her everything that had happened, providing as little information as possible about sleeping with her brother, but explaining everything that had happened afterward.

Gwynn's eyes widened, and her lips moved, but no words came out.

My face heated as I looked at her, wondering what was going through her mind. This was her beloved brother, after all.

"So at his coronation, that's how he knew that he would have a Gloweyen Queen," Gwynn whispered.

I nodded, not knowing what else to say.

Gwynn swallowed and clutched my hand. "Last night, when I steadied you from falling outside, I saw a vision of you and Ash together . . . in the throes of passion. From what I was able to see, it looked like you were in your world, though."

That's why her face had turned white and she'd run off.

"I'm at a complete loss, Eleyse," she said softly. "I am in shock and awe. I feel it in my bones, though, the connection you share with each other. It is powerful."

"There's something else," I said.

"Gods, I don't know if my heart can take any more," Gwynn said, biting a fingernail.

I leaned forward, my voice a hushed whisper. "When I was with him in Falayen, he told me that he loved me."

"Holy shit, Eleyse," Gwynn exclaimed, her hand flying to her mouth. "My brother has never spoken of love with anyone. Never. Trust me, many have tried to capture his heart, but none have ever succeeded." She leaned closer to me. "What did you say?"

I ran my hand through my hair. "I didn't know how to respond, but he was quick to assure me that he didn't expect me to say it back. He did give me the impression that I'd said it to him before, though. I must just not remember."

"Do you think that's true?"

I nodded without hesitation. "I feel it with every fiber of my being—this intense devotion and all-consuming fire for him. I've never experienced that with anyone before. Not even Liam, whom I loved very much."

"Gloweyen is forged in deep love," Gwynn said. She reached out and took both my hands. "I know we only just met yesterday, Eleyse, but from the very beginning, I knew there was something special about you. There is no one's judgment I trust more than my brother, and if Ash loves you, it speaks volumes." She shook her head, surprise and wonder on her face. "If everything we've heard today is true, as Ash's queen, you and I are fated to be sisters."

My heart skipped a beat. Ash's queen. I still couldn't believe it. Being his *anything* made me happy. I just wanted to be his. And to have a sister—well, that was just icing on the cake.

Having a sister, a family—it made my heart hurt. Old habits died hard. It was difficult to hope for a happy ending. My life had been bereft of those.

I smiled, squeezing her fingers. "There's more, Gwynn," I said. I told her what Ash had said about seeking out the Goddess who sent me through the Senshifter.

"He sought out the Goddess Mother?" Her voice was a high shriek.

"Yes, and she told him about the Secret of the Gods." I explained what he'd said about not being able to tell me what it meant. "Why would she call me her treasure? I don't understand."

"Gods, Eleyse, I'm completely clueless. I don't even know where we start looking for answers," Gwynn said. "I'm not disputing that the Great Creator has appeared to you before, but my gut feeling is that there is more to his presence than you think. He is the God of Gods. That he has appeared to you so many times tells me that you must be exceedingly important and special. As for the Goddess Mother, perhaps the Cloryals might know what her connection is to you."

"The Cloryals?" I asked, furrowing my brows.

Gwynn nodded. "Yes. The Cloryals are the daughters of the Goddess Mother."

Her daughters? The Gods had children?

She flipped through some more pages, stopping at one with a portrait of the four female figures we'd seen at Ash's coronation in the Pavilion of Harmonies. "This is Medra, patroness Cloryal of Valkyse," she said, pointing at the one with lavender hair and silver eyes.

"She's the one who stood and talked today," I said. "Would she have been the one from my vision in the cave?" I asked, my gaze sweeping over the stunning being.

Gwynn cocked her head to the side. "Probably. As you are in Valkyse and were with my mother, she might have been the one."

"Her form was different, though," I said, remembering my encounter with the being in the grotto. "Plus, when she spoke, more than one voice came out of her."

"It might have been all four of them, then," Gwynn said, tapping her lip with her finger. "They usually only appear together when it has something to do with Ariadna as a whole. Which would make sense, as you are tied to the fate of Ariadna. The other three Cloryal sisters are Caladra, Avaia, and Zarra." Gwynn pointed to the other three female figures in the portrait. "Patroness Cloryals of the Dominions of Tandor, Solanis, and Averon."

Hallowed one, you are known to us, the creature in the grotto had said. What exactly did they know about me? I remembered the flicker of emotion when the creature had studied me. What did it mean? Was the Secret of the Gods known to them too?

"What is the role of the Cloryals as opposed to their mother?"

Gwynn pursed her lips. "Well, Eolith is more of a figurehead. Except with the Sovereigns, the Gods and Goddesses rarely interact directly with the people of Ariadna or other realms in the Sangelis. When it comes to the Dominions of Ariadna, the Cloryals are the bigger presence. They're considered lesser Goddesses, and don't have the full powers of the Gods. You can think of them as the voice and arbiters of the Ethereal Harmonies. They are the gatekeepers of the great power."

Gatekeepers. That's what Eolith had called herself when I asked who she was. She'd said she guarded the secrets of my identity. I needed to know who I was. What I was. Something sentient and *other* was now awake inside of me, and without hesitation, it welcomed this place, welcomed every revelation that was brought to light. The pull to accept and embrace and *become* was overwhelming.

The old me was disappearing—the broken, cynical, empty

person that tragedy had turned me into. I could feel the change—like a serpent shedding its stunted skin, something inside me was shifting, evolving, breaking free of the confines my crippled life had encased me in.

"The remaining two Gods of the Sangelis are Twylos, Goddess of the Elements," Gwynn said, flipping through the pages in the book until she stopped at the portrait of a female figure with green and blue curly hair, her eyes a brilliant shade of copper, "and Cazril, God of Chaos." She flipped through the pages again, landing on one with a portrait of a male figure. Even at a glance, it was clear he was trouble. His green eyes danced with mischief, and his smile curled upwards in a self-assured smirk.

"Where I'm from," I said, "the realm of the divine is more faith-based than anything. You can't see the wind, but you know it exists—that sort of thing."

"Ah," Gwynn said. "From my understanding, other deities and supreme powers exist in the universe, but I'm only familiar with the Gods as they exist within the spectrum of the Sangelis."

A soft knock on the door stirred me out of my thoughts.

"Come in," Gwynn called.

The door opened, and Astrid's head popped in. "Thought you'd want to know. Andreo's back."

"Perfect," Gwynn replied. "We'll be right out."

Astrid nodded and stepped out, closing the door as she left.

Gwynn turned toward me. "Now that Uncle Andreo's here, we can find out what's going on. He might also be able help us look for answers."

An exquisite tremor of feeling rocked me, my pulse quickening in anticipation. The intrigue was drawing me in. The notion of being a part of something consequential called to me like a siren's song. And that wasn't a bad thing. There was hope for me after all.

Chapter 21

G WYNN AND I CROSSED the foyer of the main hall on our way to meet with Andreo. I skidded to a stop at the sight of a massive portrait of a couple hanging on the wall. I recognized the woman right away.

"My parents," Gwynn said, staring at the portrait wistfully.

Harwen Valkyse looked exactly the same as when I had seen her in Falayen: wavy, silver-blue hair, delicate features on a beautiful face. Her eyes, surprisingly, were different. When I had seen her, they had shone silver, but in the portrait, they were the color of amethysts, like Gwynn's.

Arlon Valkyse was a tall, handsome man. Dark hair, chiseled face, silver-blue eyes. His resemblance to Andreo and Ash was remarkable. He and Harwen were a striking couple. Even from the portrait, an air of charisma and authority seeped through.

I stared at the image of Harwen, completely mesmerized by her face. "Gwynn," I said, "can you tell me about the Songbird of Valkyse?"

"Of course." She turned away from the portrait. "What do you want to know?"

"What does it mean to be the Songbird of Valkyse? How does that fit into everything else that's been revealed about me?"

"Walk with me," Gwynn said, leading the way to two double doors at the end of the hall.

As we stepped onto a large balcony, the view of the city below us made my breath catch in my throat. The skyline in the violet twilight was magnificent. Towering buildings loomed against the backdrop of the harbor, lit up by a multitude of lights as far as my eyes could see. From where I stood, it looked similar to urban landscapes on Earth. All around, different roadways—straight, meandering, circular—divided the city into sections, with the tallest buildings situated in the distance to the left of the harbor, in what looked like the heart of Torannon.

The smell of the air was vibrant . . . alive. There was no other way to describe it. The sights, sounds, and smells were crackling with energy and fervor.

Gwynn leaned forward, resting her elbows on the balcony railing. "In the history of Ariadna, there have only been a handful of Songbirds, or Sviyens—the Hasheyn word for Songbird—and they weren't all from Valkyse. There have been four in total: the Sunrise Songbird, followed by the Sunlight Songbird, then the Twilight Songbird, and finally my mother, the Starlight Songbird. Two of them were Gloweyen Queens—Verah Valkyse and Symia Solanis. Although they weren't all Valkyse Gloweyen Queens or Queen Consorts, they all had ties to Valkyse. Symia Solanis and Clorynn Tandor were both daughters of different Sovereigns of Valkyse."

"How did they get chosen?" I asked.

"Same way you did. By the Ethereal Harmonies. But they were chosen at their consecration ceremonies when they were ordained as either Gloweyen Queens or Queen Consorts. That's when they were given their Songbird titles—Sunrise, Sunlight, Twilight, and Starlight."

"I take it there's a purpose to being a Songbird?"

"Yes. The main purpose is to serve Ariadna. Like my mother told you—guardians. Each Songbird's power lies mainly in the melodies they are gifted with. My mother was gifted with five melodies: 'The Song of Sorrow,' 'The Song of Rebirth,' 'The Song of Transformation,' 'The Song of Healing,' and 'The Song of Unification.' The other Songbirds had access to different melodies."

Melodies. Harwen Valkyse and I had sung "The Song of Sorrow" and "The Song of Rebirth." She had told me that other melodies dwelled inside me, waiting to be summoned.

"'The Song of Sorrow' is the first song a Songbird sings," Gwynn was saying. "With that melody, the past is put to rest and the future begins anew. Leaving the past behind is never an easy thing, and 'The Song of Sorrow' is a song to mourn what was. It also ignites an awakening."

Was it bad that I was happy in leaving my past behind? Not the memories I carried with me of my loved ones—they would never leave me—but my life itself. My only regret was that I could not remember those two years with Ash that I had lost. I didn't care what I had to do to get those back; one way or the other, I would reclaim them.

"'The Song of Rebirth' summons the first change," Gwynn said. "With that melody, the Songbird emerges from the death of your old life, and your Songbird powers come to life. From that moment on, you have but to summon 'The Song of Transformation' when you want to change into your Songbird form. The songs of Sorrow, Rebirth, and Transformation are common melodies that all Songbirds have, but others like the songs of Healing and Unification are specific to certain Songbirds. For instance, Verah Valkyse did not have access to 'The Song of Unification,' but she had access to the songs of Healing, Enchantment, and Scourge. Symia Solanis had access to the songs of Healing, Unification, and Prowess."

"So each song holds a different power?" I asked.

Gwynn nodded. "That's right. The two Gloweyen Queens had access to six melodies each. Both Clorynn Tandor and my mother only had five. Each melody is powerful and capable of great things. As an example, 'The Song of Unification' is capable of healing divides and bringing people together in accord."

"The songs were the sole source of their power?" I asked, trying to process and compartmentalize everything she had said.

"I would say it was their biggest source," Gwynn replied. "They had other abilities as well, outside their Songbird powers. For instance, banishment, protective shields—both physical and mental—and perception, to name a few."

Gwynn shifted and leaned her hip against the balcony wall. "This is my take on the Songbirds, and on Gloweyen. The Songbirds' melodies were directly tied to the state of Ariadna at the time. Verah Valkyse and Symia Solanis were Songbirds at a time when Ariadna was in great upheaval: the Shacquiri Rebellion 39,000 years ago and the Pirthenon Wars 14,000 years after that."

She folded her arms in front of her chest. "Their melodies as Songbirds played a huge role in the outcome of those wars. Rywin and Verah Valkyse used a Valkyse artifact of great power *and* 'The Song of Enchantment' together to win the Shacquiri Rebellion. Symia Solanis used the songs of Unification and Prowess to help end the Pirthenon Wars."

I shifted my stance as I leaned on the balcony. "So in the entire history of Ariadna, there have only been two great wars?"

"As far as magnitude goes, that's right," Gwynn added, her eyes shining. "This theory would explain why Verah and Symia were Gloweyen queens, if Gloweyen only presents itself in a Sovereign couple in a time of great unrest. The Dark Shen Invasion was not even close in terms of scale, but my mother's healing abilities were important on the battlefield." She turned, looking off toward the harbor. "I wasn't born yet, but I've heard so many stories of her using 'The Song of Healing' to restore the wounded. With her abilities, she was able to heal multiple people at once, allowing them to rejoin the battle."

A look of pride shone on her face as she splayed her hands on the railing. "My father always said that the part she played was crucial in Ariadna defeating the Dark Shen. Without her using the songs of Healing and Unification, many more Ariadnan lives would have been lost. It was the same with Clorynn Tandor, who was Songbird during the Malika Uprising 7,700 years ago. In addition to her using 'The Song of Healing,' she also had access to 'The Song of Shadows,' which allowed her to shroud enemy minds in confusion."

This was fascinating. Questions whipped around my mind in a frenzy. What other songs dwelled inside *me*? What would my Songbird title be? What special melodies would I have access to as a Gloweyen Queen?

In Falayen, Harwen Valkyse had told me that I had more faces to wear than she did. Was that because of the Gloweyen proclamation between Ash and me? What had she called me? Truth diviner. With the power to tell lie from truth and illusion from reality. It gave me shivers just thinking of it.

I couldn't deny the uneasiness twisting my insides at the prospect of the future. If, as Gwynn believed, Gloweyen only presented itself in times of great upheaval, then so much would rest on my shoulders as Ash's Gloweyen queen and Songbird of Valkyse. Was I ready for that?

I had to admit, though. I felt a strange sense of kinship with the musical component of the Songbird legacy. Music was in my blood—once upon a time, that dream had been my everything, the life force that kept me going after my parents died. But after Mags died, I'd closed the door on music. When Liam died, I'd sealed it shut.

Maybe, just maybe, it wasn't a coincidence that in this new world I had ties to, music was a part of my calling. Perhaps it would reignite that passion once more.

The biggest, most beautiful cat I had ever seen was lying in the center of Andreo's study when we entered. A fire was blazing in the hearth, and the feline lay prostrate on the plush, luxurious area rug, limbs splayed and relaxed, savoring the warmth. I was struck by the magnificence of the animal.

I'd always been a cat person—well, except for that mangy, cross-eyed hell cat from years ago. That flea-infested terror had been a vicious, hissing, piece of work. Thank God it had slunk off and disappeared, never to be seen again.

This cat was the antithesis of that one. Unusual white and blue markings—an intense shade of royal blue—covered its entire body, concentric spirals all across its fur. The markings on its face were remarkable: a blue, swirling spiral on white fur over one half of its face and a white-on-blue half-masquerade mask pattern across the other, covering the top half of its face. Slitted, emerald-green eyes regarded me curiously, the shade of green so similar to another pair of eyes that I was enamored with.

"Tryxie," Gwynn cried, falling to her knees and throwing her arms around the cat. It was as big as she was, its paws almost covering her entire face as it touched her cheeks. It let out a guttural cry in greeting, sniffing and licking her face as it wrapped its front legs around her shoulders.

"This is Tryx," Gwynn said to me, scratching the cat's head. "She is Ash's baby."

"What kind of cat is she?" I asked. "I've never laid eyes on a creature like her before. She's so beautiful."

"She is a beyngyle feline," Gwynn replied. "Ash rescued her six years ago when she was just a kitten."

"Rescued her?" I asked, unable to tear my eyes away.

"He found her when he was out inspecting a forest border with Faron and a few others. She was tangled in a cluster of bushes, curled up next to her dead mother, who had been killed by what looked like a wild banguar, the most vicious predator found in that region. The chances of surviving on her own without her mother were slim to none, so Ash took her with him. She's been with him ever since."

The cat stared at me steadily before getting to her feet and padding over to where I stood against the wall. She sniffed the air in my direction, moved closer to me, stood on her hind legs, and licked my cheek. Then she got back down on four legs, lowered her front paws and head to the floor at my feet in a low bow. She stayed in that position until I reached down and touched her head with my hand. She purred loudly before sprawling on her side at my feet, her gaze still glued to my face.

"Well, that's different," Gwynn said, wonder in her voice. "She knows you are . . . special. She doesn't warm to strangers easily. She usually keeps people she doesn't know at arm's length."

I wasn't sure what to feel. That brief encounter was peculiar and unnerving. Those emerald eyes stared at me intently, as if boring into my soul. What did she see there? Did she smell Ash on me from earlier?

The door opened and Andreo stepped inside. "I'm sorry to have kept you waiting," he said as he walked toward us. He kissed Gwynn on the cheek and turned to me. "Come, Eleyse. Sit." He gestured to the leather armchair closest to the fire.

I walked the short distance to the chair and sat, sinking into the thick cushioning, and not two seconds later, Tryx padded over and curled up at my feet.

"That's incredible, Eleyse," Andreo commented, looking at Tryx's head resting on my feet. "Beyngyle felines are cautious creatures, fiercely protective and loyal. Tryx would kill for Ash, and it's clear that she is drawn to you."

I gazed at the cat, her dark emerald eyes glued to mine. I smothered a smile. Another female to add to the list. Just as long as she didn't challenge me for top rights to her master's affection or attention, we'd be fine.

"She just bowed to Eleyse before you came in," Gwynn said. "Fully prostrate."

Andreo's gaze met mine, his eyes flashing with amazement.

"Would you like a drink, Eleyse?" Gwynn asked as she lowered herself onto the sofa next to my chair and reached for the crystal decanter on the side table.

"No, I'm fine, thanks," I replied, smiling as Tryx rolled onto her back for me to scratch her belly.

"Have you learned anything, Uncle?" Gwynn asked, pouring herself a drink. "So much has happened with Eleyse; I don't even know where to start."

"Well, Ash was here briefly to see me," Andreo said leaning against his desk.

"Eleyse saw Ash today also," Gwynn said, taking a sip of her drink.

Andreo's eyes widened. "When? Where?"

"In Falayen," Gwynn replied. "Just before we came here."

"That must have been after he left here because he didn't mention it." He looked at me eagerly. "Were you able to talk?"

"A bit," I said. "He didn't stay with me long. He was summoned away and had to leave."

"Falayen," Andreo murmured. He looked down at my wrist where my labral rested, radiating Shinoran light.

"Did he tell you where he was going?" Gwynn asked. "Do you know what's going on? Is he in danger? I haven't been able to sense him when I reach out in my mind."

"He couldn't risk coming to you, Gwynn," Andreo said, his handsome face etched with concern. "Especially because Eleyse is with you. He doesn't want Kaliope getting wind of Eleyse's presence here. As for where he is, he's meeting with his Dulogrien. Treye sent word that they needed him."

Gwynn's face paled.

"What is it, Gwynn?" I asked. "Who is Treye?"

"Treye is the commander of the Dulogrien," Gwynn replied. "They're Ash's cabal of elite spies. They're so deep underground that even their cover identities have cover identities."

Dulogrien. *Phantoms.* A Hasheyn word, perhaps? Gwynn's reaction was worrying. It could only mean one thing. Danger.

Gwynn turned her attention back to Andreo. "Ash told Eleyse he had to do something the Cloryals directed him to."

"Yes," Andreo replied, "but he needs to plan his approach with Treye, Gilham, and Ovix for that mission, so two birds, one stone."

Gwynn pressed her hands together. "Please don't tell me he's in Kindrik."

Kindrik. Why did that name sound familiar?

Gwynn turned to me. "Kindrik is in the world of Treth. It's the kingdom Kaliope's Shen father rules over."

"So he's in the same place as Kaliope?" A ripple of fear spread through me.

Gwynn's face twisted in a scowl. "In all likelihood."

Andreo sat in the other armchair next to the sofa, a slight frown on his face. "Gwynn, he wouldn't go there unless he absolutely had to, and even so, Ash knows how to take care of himself."

Gwynn bolted upright in her seat, her eyes blazing. "He's off-world, Uncle. The same rules don't apply there. This is the Dark Shen we're talking about. It's fucking *Kaliope* we're talking about!"

Andreo reached out and touched her knee reassuringly. "I'm well aware, Gwynn, but Asher is a powerful Sovereign, capable of weighing the risks and making his own decisions. He doesn't need your or my permission."

I heard the fear in Gwynn's voice, and conflict tore through me. On the one hand, I wanted to trust Andreo's belief that Ash could take care of himself, but on the other hand, Kaliope was a psychopath and totally unpredictable from everything I'd heard about her.

I couldn't shake the feeling of unease inside me. It twisted in my gut, settling like a sack of rocks, weighing me down. I hated feeling helpless—in over my head, not knowing what to do.

Just as I knew and accepted that Ash was mine and believed that there was something unbreakable and mighty between us, I knew that everything revealed to me about my place in this world was true. But that knowledge didn't make me *feel* any more powerful, didn't fill me with confidence that I would be able to live up to all that was expected of me.

Shit. I was in over my head. When I was with Ash, as he had guided me to the source of my magic, I sensed how vast and deep that lake of power inside me was. I'd only rippled the surface—a feather-light touch with my finger—and it had responded to me, obeyed me. The thought of going in any further terrified me. Something fearsome and untamed lived in the fathomless bedrock of that lake—even now its languid stirring in the deep unnerved me. Even though there was something soothing about its presence within me, I didn't want to think about what would happen if it were unleashed.

I closed my eyes and dove into myself, in record time arriving at my lake of power. A surge of triumph filled me. It was getting easier.

My thoughts drifted to Ash, hoping that wherever he was and whatever he was doing, he was all right. Maybe I didn't have to reach him to know the answer. Maybe if I used my magic to ask a question, I would get an answer through our Gloweyen connection. Similar to when I had asked it who I was when I was with Ash.

Completely wrapped up in my own mind—Gwynn and Andreo somewhere on the fringes of my awareness—I rippled the lake gently. "Just tell me he's okay," I whispered.

I opened my consciousness, and immediately in my mind, I was swept away, standing in front a wall of crystal spread out as far as my eyes could see all around me, trapping me in the middle. I stood facing a tall, impenetrable gate.

Uh-oh. What the hell did I do? Whatever it was, I didn't mean to do it.

"Take me back," I said in desperation, rippling the lake once more, but nothing happened. I called to my power again, fighting the panic as it seeped in, but the wall in front of me stood firm.

Shit! How the frig did I get out of here?

More importantly, where *was* here?

Chapter 22

GEEZ. HOW STUPID COULD I be? Why did I access my power on my own? Ash had told me that my magic needed to be trained. I should have waited for him before I used it again.

I turned in a slow circle, taking in the crystal wall around me. It reminded me of the tall crystal archways outside the Giln Keeper's sanctuary. Like those archways, the crystal in front of me contained strands of light pulsing through them—like shards of lightning crackling throughout.

At intervals around the perimeter, gateways with golden slats were embedded. I counted six in total. I was standing directly in front of one, which looked out onto a pathway of light of some kind. Beneath me, the ground in the circle was a moving mass of silver—similar to the surface of the lake in Falayen, but solid. Wisps of mist clung low to the ground, sashaying in and around my legs.

Crap. Now what? My mind was a complete blank as a hysterical laugh escaped my lips. What a joke I was. Here I stood, with supposedly enough power to save this world, and I had absolutely no clue how to use any of it.

Hold, Eleyse, a voice commanded in my mind, halting me in my tracks, preventing me from going into full-blown despair spiral mode. It was the same voice from before—the one that had told me the truth about Astrid's feelings for Ash.

When your emotions are heated, you lose your grip on your power.

Heed what I have to say.

Who are you? I asked silently. Why are you in my head?

I am a part of you, the voice answered back, the source of your truth and steward of your power; the tether to your conscience and your moral guide. I am the anchor staked in the light to keep you grounded.

Wow. That was a mouthful. I wasn't sure which part to focus on. You say you're a part of me? Since when?

Always, the voice replied at once. Upon your transformation into the Songbird of Valkyse, I was awakened, but I have always been a part of you.

Wait. Was this what Ash's mother had referred to? Harwen Valkyse told me that the power to deduce truth from lie, and illusion from reality was fully awakened inside me with my transformation. Is that what you are? Who you are?

In part. I am Catraia.

Catraia. The same name Ash mentioned before he left me.

What is this place? I asked.

You are sequestered within your mind, looped into the deepest levels of your consciousness. This is the entrance to the Void. Multiple planes of consciousness exist here.

I frowned. The Void? What does that mean? What is the point of being here? I don't even know how I got here.

The Void is how you travel in your mind.

Like astral projection? An out of body sort of thing?

Not exactly. You do not travel through physical space when you move through the Void. You journey through the realm of consciousness. Your mind remains in your body, but is inaccessible to your physical form. Your consciousness connects with your shadow self and enters the Void.

I cocked my head. Like when I flew with Harwen Valkyse to the *cavern in the valley?*

Similar to that, yes. There is much you have to learn about traveling between the planes of consciousness. Many dangers lurk in the Void. The last thing you want is for your mind to become trapped or waylaid.

Whoa. Rewind. Did she say trapped or waylaid? What did that even mean?

The first thing you must know is that time works differently there. It slows down. A second in the realm of Ariadna or another world might be an hour in the Void. There are some planes here where time doesn't exist at all. As for your body—it slumbers when you travel through the Void, but because of how slowly times moves there, unless you're stuck for a long period of time, it is barely noticeable. In the Void, you retain a semblance of a body—your shadow self—but it is not fully corporeal.

What happens to my physical body if I get stuck?

It becomes vulnerable and can be stolen, possessed by another, or destroyed, leaving your consciousness trapped in the Void.

I swallowed. I was sorry I asked.

It is always wise to have someone watch over you when you travel to the Void.

How much time has passed with Gwynn and Andreo since I've been here?

Fractions of a second. As of yet, they would not have even noticed a difference.

Okay. This was starting to freak me out. I wasn't sure I wanted to linger in the Void. What if I did find myself trapped in here? How would I get out?

With the proper wards and shields in place, traveling through the Void is safe.

Am I not in the Void now?

You are at the gateway to the Void. You're already tapped into your consciousness, but you haven't ventured into any given plane yet. That lies beyond the gateway.

Is the Void how I connect with Ash in my mind? I asked.

Yes. Outside the gate is a plane of consciousness that connects you to Asher through your Gloweyen bond. This plane cannot be accessed by any living being with less power than a Sovereign. You must learn how to use your power before you can travel through the Void. Your magic is vast and will require training. You must learn to cast wards and construct shields to protect your mind.

So different planes of consciousness lie beyond the gate? I moved closer to the tall barriers, peering through the slats into the vast expanse of the Void.

Yes. A great many planes can be accessed if you know what you are looking for. The lit-up path in front of you is the path of your Gloweyen bond that leads to Asher.

I looked ahead of me to the path she was referring to, lit up in a stream of blue and silver light. A hum of energy radiated from it, beckoning me forward. The pulse of Ash's power called to mine.

Of its own accord, my hand slipped through the barrier, my fingers tingling the moment they came in contact with the Void. A different hum sounded in the Void as a path of shadowy, gray light suddenly appeared to the left.

Get your hand back inside, Catraia commanded abruptly.

Before I could pull my hand back in, something gripped my fingers and yanked savagely. My heart lurched in fear as I was sucked through the barrier, my body hurtling toward the shadowy path that had appeared. I screamed, my arms and legs flailing as I plunged through the air.

"Pretty Songbird," a voice whispered near my ear, and my head snapped in that direction.

Hold on, Eleyse! Catraia cried out in my mind.

But there was nothing I could do. I tumbled and tumbled, head over heels, catapulting to some unknown corner of the Void.

When I stopped moving, I looked around slowly to get my bearings. I'd stumbled into a bathing chamber of some sort. The ceilings were tall, and the rushing of water reverberated loudly throughout the space. Thick marble columns flanked a massive bathing pool where the water churned and bubbled. The floor beneath me was white marble, gleaming from the natural light filtering down from the seamless glass ceiling above.

Where in blazes was this place? Was this a part of the Void?

Catraia? I called out in my mind.

Nothing. Wait. Wasn't she supposed to be a part of me?

"My, my, my, what have we here?" an overtly seductive voice chimed from the corner of the pool.

My eyes flew toward the voice, and my mouth dropped open. Elbows propped casually against the edges of the pool, a man sat there, watching me with wry amusement. And hungry focus.

He stood up and leisurely made his way out of the water toward me. "Divine shitballs, aren't you a hot terror."

Shit. He was naked. Instinctively, I turned away, causing him to chuckle.

"What's the matter, doll? Don't think you can handle seeing a God in all his glory?"

My eyes leapt to his, and I stared, trying to place him. In a matter of seconds, it came to me—Gwynn's book. *History of the Gods.* Yes. He was one of the Gods. The smirking one. He had the same stupid smirk on his face now, everything about him screaming that he believed he was hot shit. But which God was he? I wracked my brain. Chaos, I think it was. I couldn't remember his name.

Weird. I would have expected being face to face with a God to be more intimidating. That I'd feel some holy fear or burning compulsion urging me to my knees in a show of reverence, but instead I felt . . . nonchalant?

He was handsome, I'd give him that. Bad-boy handsome. His ash-blond hair was short and mussed—in a messy bedroom sort of way—and his bright green eyes twinkled with devilry. It was clear he was trouble—fuck-you-senseless trouble. It rolled off him in soft, billowing waves. He towered above me, standing his ground, taunting me with his eyes, water dripping onto the marble floor beneath him as he faced me.

An asinine need to irk him consumed me, and that in itself unnerved me. What the hell was wrong with me? This was a God, for heaven's sake. He could probably burn me to a crisp just by looking at me.

My insides twisted as that terrible thing at the bottom of my lake of power lifted its head and chuffed, egging me on, filling me with courage and an arrogance I didn't know I possessed. I'd show this God just what I could handle.

I plastered on my sweetest smile and deliberately let my eyes do a slow perusal of him. I paused when I was eye-level with his chest. Holy crap, he was sculpted. Maybe I should abort. Then again, that probably came with the God territory. Right? At the mere snap of a finger or the wink of an eye, he could probably carve himself ripped abs. My eyes dipped lower. Yep. Carve himself ripped abs *and* a huge cock. Both of which he proudly sported.

Being a God certainly had its advantages.

I boldly met his gaze again. "Not too bad, God of Chaos."

He laughed, his voice melodic and deep, and although I sensed the threat he posed, his laugh made my skin tingle. "You know who I am. My reputation must precede me. Call me Caz." He grabbed a towel off a marble bench, drying himself off before wrapping it around his waist.

"I think I'll stick with Your Godliness." My eyes scoured the room for an escape. "Where am I? How do I get out of here?"

"Leaving so soon, Terror?" He turned toward me and instantly squinted, his face twisted in distaste. "Gods. How can that Sovereign of yours stand to look at you? You're eye-gougingly blinding. He must have to close his eyes when he's fucking you."

A surge of anger flared inside me, and I poked my finger at his chest. "Can any arrogant cocksucker be a God, or did they make an exception for you?"

"Hey," he said, peeling my finger off his chest. "I like sucking cock as well as anyone else, but that's no reason to sling insults."

"Wait, what?" I said, confused and dismayed at the turn our conversation was taking.

"Don't you worry, Terror. I'm just as skilled at eating pu—"

"Okay, that's enough," I cried. "And why do you keep calling me that? I have a name. I'd like to get out of here and be on my way, please."

"I think the name suits you. It's the promise of what you are. I can sense it with every fiber of my godly being."

The promise of what I was? A shiver went down my spine. His words were eerily similar to what Ash had said his senses told him about me. But where Ash's words had filled me with desire and excitement, this God's words made me feel afraid.

"Don't pretend you don't like this little mating ritual we've got going on here," he said with a wink.

"Mating ritual?" I shook my head in disbelief. "*Really*? Can your ego be any bigger?"

He cocked his head. "The ruling's still out on that one." He continued to study me, his eyes assessing me like prey.

I refused to let him cow me, staring back defiantly.

"Divine be damned, Terror. You really are green, huh?"

"What are you talking about?"

"Can you not *see* your essence?" he said, circling me. "Can you not see mine?"

I stared at him blankly, no idea what he was going on about.

"You can't hide your darkness from me," he said, his expression suddenly wolfish. "You might be blinding, but it just makes your darkness stand out. These two tendrils here have been angling for my attention ever since I got out of that pool."

Tendrils? What the hell?

He lowered his hand and stroked the air in front of him lazily, and a tantalizing tremor of pleasure coursed through me.

He laughed wickedly when I gasped.

Gripping the back of my head, he brought his face closer to mine. His pupils dilated just before his eyes blazed with green fire. "Where is your Sovereign?" he asked, his voice cold and hard like steel. "What does Arazul want with you?"

I yanked his hand away from my head and took a step back, that thing inside me sauntering closer to the surface, fueling my anger. "Screw you, God of Chaos. I'm not telling you shit."

He blinked, and I didn't miss the shock in his eyes as he stared at me.

"Green, but powerful," he said quietly. "You're living up to the name, Terror. There are very few who can shrug off a God's compulsion."

I hid my surprise as best as I could, even though his casual observation threw me. He might be a prick, but he was right. I was green. Horribly so.

He smiled, his eyes burning into me. "Kal believed Gargie had taken you out—that you were just a harmless bug to be splattered."

Kal. He had to be talking about Kaliope. But who the hell was Gargie?

He looked at me appraisingly. "She was wrong, though. But let me warn you, doll. That bitch is lawless. And fucking devious. And that's saying something, coming from *me*. Don't say I never gave you anything. She's coming for you, Terror. Coming for you hard."

The ground suddenly shook beneath our feet, toppling me off balance just as a pulse of power vibrated inside me.

Ash.

The God of Chaos looked at me and grinned. "Uh-oh. Time's up, Terror. Your Sovereign's coming for you. And he is *pissed*. But on the bright side, maybe he'll rage-fuck you hard tonight. Don't forget his blindfold, though. He's going to need it."

Anger exploded inside me and I lunged at him, but he spun me around, holding me around my waist as I flailed my arms and legs to get free.

He brought his head closer to my neck. "And for the love of all six of us Gods, make a fucking effort. It's pathetic how little you know about your power. At least make it a fair fight. We Gods like our entertainment."

"Let me go!" I screamed, ramming my elbow into his chest.

He laughed and trailed the tip of his tongue down the side of my face. "Sometimes the only way to fight darkness is with darkness. I'll see you soon, Terror. Ta ta." And with those words, he pushed me away from him and I went sailing through the air, back into nothingness, hurtling into the Void.

Chapter 23

I TOPPLED INTO THE Void, powerless to stop myself from careening forward. I screamed, fighting against the feeling of being sucked into the vacuous expanse around me. As a jolt of rage—tinged with fear—invaded my senses, vibrations rippled through the space, a loud, rumbling clamor getting closer. It wasn't *my* rage or fear—it was Ash's.

All my senses—sight, taste, touch, sound, smell—acutely bore witness. The Void was flooded with bright light, and I squinted against the harsh glare. The taste of ash—bitter and chalky—filled my mouth, just as gooseflesh tore across my skin. Twin bolts of lightning sliced through the air, followed by a roar of thunder that shook me to my core. I breathed in the pungent smell of chlorine—the release of ozone after the lightning discharge.

Suddenly, I collided with something hard and hot, two hands gripping my waist before darting away with me in another direction. *Trapped or waylaid*, Catraia had said. I couldn't let that happen. I had no idea what else was out here with me. Where was Ash? I pushed against the force, fighting to break free, but I made no headway.

Abruptly, we came to a stop, and the grip on me loosened. "Elle," Ash said, wrapping his arms around me.

My body instantly went slack, relief washing over me at the sound of his voice. I opened my eyes, my hands clinging to his chest, fighting the churning nausea that roiled in my gut.

Breathe, Eleyse, Catraia whispered in my mind.

What the— Where the hell had she buggered off to? Wasn't she supposed to be my tether or whatever? She'd deserted me at the first sign of trouble, leaving me alone with that cocky shit of a God.

You were in the presence of the God of Chaos, a deity who cannot know about my existence. I had to submerge myself so he wouldn't detect me.

I had no idea what she meant.

"Are you all right?" Ash asked, tipping my head up toward his. His face was lined with worry, his green eyes flickering with traces of anger. "Did he hurt you?"

"I'm sorry, Ash," I said, tears pricking my eyes. "I don't know what I did. I shouldn't have used my power without you there to show me how. It was just a small question, and then the next moment, I was at the Void, Catraia started speaking in my mind, and one thing led to the next and . . ." I trailed off, thinking of his rage echoing through the Void. I desperately did not want to be on the receiving end of it.

He brushed his knuckles against my cheek. "I'm not angry with you, Elle. Never you."

A surge of relief washed over me, and I looked up at him questioningly. "How did you know where to find me?"

"Catraia told me."

My eyes widened. "Catraia? But isn't she a part of *me*? Can she talk to you too?"

"She is a part of you, and that means she can use the Gloweyen bond between us to communicate with me if she has to. Which is what she did."

"She reached you through the Void?" I asked, remembering the stream of blue and silver light shining through the gateway. She had said it was the path of our Gloweyen bond.

"Yes. This plane of consciousness in the Void is called Naori, and the only ones who can directly tap into this space are the other Sovereigns and the Gods. Each Sovereign has their own stream within Naori that no other Sovereign can access. He gestured to the space around us. "This stream we're standing in now has a unique signature—yours and mine. It is our Gloweyen connection. We are enclosed within it."

I lifted my head and took notice of where we stood. The blue and silver stream of light pulsed brightly beneath our feet, humming with vibrant energy. Around us, there was nothing but space—space lit up in a profusion of ambling color, similar to the Northern Lights on Earth that I had seen so many images and videos of. It was both beautiful and surreal at the same time, the colors swirling and coupling around us, suffusing us in its warm glow. The bands of our combined power—that's what I sensed they were. Awe, so staggering and ardent, toppled me as I reveled in the power of our bond surrounding us. I welcomed the reverence seeping into my soul.

Unable to stop myself, I stood on tiptoes and brushed my lips against Ash's. If ever I doubted what existed between us, this moment succinctly put everything into perspective, connecting me to him more intimately than we already were.

He traced my jaw with his fingers, his eyes mirroring the wonder in mine.

For a moment, we just stood there, wrapped up in each other, exulting in the feeling of being suspended in time and space together like this.

Finally, I let my thoughts drift back to our conversation. "Can the Gods reach us here?"

He shook his head. "Unless condoned by the Great Creator

himself, they cannot enter Naori. And even if they did, they would not be able to breach our bond. That is sacred and cannot be touched."

"So how did—"

"Either the Great Creator allowed it, or the God who intercepted you is defying the God of Gods."

Caz. He definitely seemed like the type who marched to the beat of his own drum and gave zero shits about following the rules.

"What did the God of Chaos want with you?" Ash asked, the muscle in his jaw clenching.

"I . . . I don't know, to be honest. He was more curious than anything about me. About you, about Arazul."

"Did he touch you?" Ash asked, his eyes blazing, his voice clipped. I sensed the anger building in him, even as he tried to tamp it down in front of me.

How did I answer without fanning his rage? I pictured Caz strutting around naked in front of me, of him stroking my *tendrils*, as he called them, of him gripping my head as he tried to compel me, of his arms clasped around my waist as he licked the side of my face. Oh dear. None of it was good.

"He didn't hurt me, Ash," I answered quickly.

And he hadn't. He had taunted me, insulted me, warned me, sort of complimented me, challenged me, threatened me, but he didn't hurt me.

Ash's eyes narrowed as he studied my face. "That's not what I asked, Tialla." His voice was a low growl, his body entirely still as his eyes bore into mine.

Shit.

I swallowed slowly, composing my words carefully in my mind. "He was a little handsy with me, but nothing I couldn't handle."

The fire in his eyes flared to life and I flinched as his anger built.

"Please, Ash," I said, laying my palm against his chest. "I don't know what he wanted with me, but it was clear he was digging for information. He knew who I was, knew about Kaliope trying to kill me. Even warned me that she was coming after me. The moment he sensed you coming, he let me go."

"He is a slippery God," Ash said, his tone hard and strained. "He's not called the God of Chaos for nothing. He's unpredictable and dangerous and revels in making trouble."

"Plus, he's a God," I said. "You should probably just let it go."

Ash smiled, a predatory sort of grimace, and I balked. "I don't give a shit that he's a God. You are my Gloweyen Queen, and he took you against your will. I will make him pay for that, and not even the Great Creator himself will stand in my way."

Shit. It was one thing going to war against Kaliope, but going toe to toe with a God?

As if sensing my fear, Ash's features softened as he tilted my chin, coaxing my gaze to his. "Trust me, Tialla. There's a reason he let you go when he sensed me coming, and it has everything to do with him knowing who I am."

I wouldn't worry about Asher, Catraia whispered in my mind. *Your Gloweyen bond binds him to protect you at all costs from any who may mean you harm, especially the Gods of the Sangelis. There is much you have to learn about who you truly are and what you are capable of. These are all lessons you must learn about your Sovereign as well.*

Her words skated like ice across my skin, flooding me with a curious excitement.

Ash wrapped his arms around my waist. "Time to go back, Elle. We shouldn't linger here any longer. Catraia will lead you out of the Void. I'll be right behind you."

He brushed his lips against my forehead, and before I had a

chance to respond, he was gone.

Come, Eleyse, Catraia commanded, and still disoriented over Ash's exit, I yelped as a tug at my center jerked me, and the Void rippled, then faded away.

Chapter 24

I GASPED AS MY awareness slammed back into my physical form.

Tryx lifted her head at my feet and Gwynn stared at me, her faced furrowed with concern.

"Are you all right, Eleyse?" she asked.

A second later, Ash appeared in the center of the room, and all hell broke loose.

Gwynn let out a scream, clutching her chest, Andreo jumped to his feet, and Tryx roared, pouncing on Ash, almost knocking him over.

"Fuck, Ash!" Gwynn yelled, standing up. "Are you trying to kill me? Where the hell did you come from?"

With Tryx standing on her hind legs, her front paws on his shoulders, Ash moved toward his sister and kissed her on the head. "Sorry for startling you, Wynn."

"That's a nice way of putting it. I almost wet myself." She sprang toward him. "My turn, Tryxie." She bowled Tryx out of the way and flung herself into Ash's arms. "You stupid idiot," she chided, her voice cracking as tears filled her eyes. "I was so worried about you. Don't ever lock me out like that again."

He wrapped his arms around her, and for a moment just held her. My heart ached as I watched them, for the second time today seeing the indomitable force that was Gwynn crumble and lose all control.

As she disentangled herself from his embrace, she inhaled deeply and punched him on the shoulder for good measure. "I'll kick your ass if you leave again without telling me."

"Noted, baby sister," Ash said with a smile.

Andreo nodded and clasped Ash on the shoulder. "I assume we have a lot to talk about?"

"Yes, there's a lot to debrief on," Ash said, turning his head to meet my gaze.

I floated out of my seat and went to him, my heart sighing in contentment as he pulled me into his arms, his lips crashing against mine. God, I loved the feel of his mouth on mine.

I lost track of everything and everyone, until behind us, Gwynn cleared her throat. I reluctantly pulled away, my eyes still fastened to Ash's.

"I feel like I'm missing something," Gwynn said. "You don't look surprised to see each other. What's going on?"

"I, uh . . . I don't even know how to explain," I said sheepishly.

Ash's lips curved in a smile as he touched my earlobe. "She accidentally used her power to stumble into her consciousness, where she got taken by the God of Chaos in the Void, and I had to go find her."

Gwynn's mouth hung open as she stared at me, a confused look on her face. "Wait, what? When?"

"Just before I got here," Ash replied.

"Holy shit, Eleyse. I had no idea your mind even left."

"It would have only been a second or two at the most here, Wynn."

"What did the God of Chaos want?" Andreo asked. "I take it he knows who Eleyse is to you."

"He knows who she is, yes, but not *what* she is."

My head snapped up. "Well, that would make two of us." *What*

229

was I? Secret of the Gods? If so, was the God of Chaos not in on the secret? He certainly knew a lot of other things about me.

"Who is Gargie?" I blurted out.

"Gargie?" Ash asked, arching a brow.

"The God of Chaos said something about Kaliope thinking that Gargie had taken me out."

Andreo and Ash exchanged glances.

"I know those looks," Gwynn said. "Spill."

"It's not that simple, Wynn," Ash said.

"Actually, it is, Ash. You just open your mouth and words come out." She glared at him, crossing her arms against her chest.

"Before you tell them," Andreo said, "what news of Kindrik?"

Ash sighed. "It's as we feared. Tynor has summoned his war council. By Ovix's account, they won't make a move before the Convergence. Kaliope won't risk it."

Convergence. This was the second time Ash had mentioned that. He'd said it was more than a month away.

"What exactly is the Convergence?" I asked.

Ash lowered his head to look at me. "It's a celestial event—when the constellations of Sorin and Eolith converge in the heavens. It happens once every century. Over the course of three days, the Convergence creates a mighty vortex of power throughout Ariadna, one that Kaliope undoubtedly wants to leverage to her advantage."

"Your mother mentioned the Convergence when I was with her," I said, looking at their surprised faces.

"You saw Harwen?" Andreo asked, his eyes wide.

I nodded. "In Falayen. She passed the Songbird of Valkyse mantle to me."

"Two back-to-back Songbirds," Andreo said, his face radiating awe. "This is truly remarkable, Ash."

"I know," he said, and my heart skipped a beat at the pride in his eyes as he looked at me. Lowering himself onto the chair I'd recently vacated, he pulled me sideways onto his lap. "What did my mother say about the Convergence, Elle?"

I gripped his shirt at his shoulder. "She said something about the board being set and pieces in place, with the next move belonging to Valkyse."

Andreo sat on the sofa, leaning forward slightly. "Do you think she's talking about the Gloweyen proclamation between you and Eleyse?"

Ash nodded slowly. "I can't think of what else she could mean. Everything now hinges on Eleyse completing her transformation."

"My transformation?" I asked, pushing against his chest to look at him.

"Yes," he said stroking my wrist. "As Songbird of Valkyse, there are phases to your transformation, plus there is the matter of your coronation. Valkyse is the hub of importance right now."

As much as the thought of being crowned Ash's Gloweyen Queen excited me, I couldn't help but feel terrified about the magnitude of *everything*.

The moment my body tensed, Ash lifted my hand and pressed a kiss against my palm. "I'm right here with you, Tialla. We do this together. Every step of the way."

A flood of emotion surged through me. Fuck. How could I forget loving this man? Every molecule in my body sang for him. I was completely cocooned in the intense emotions I felt radiating off him.

I looked up to catch Gwynn's gaze, and she smiled at me wistfully, her eyes welling with unshed tears.

"So what now?" Gwynn asked, swiping at her eyes. Did you discuss next steps with Treye and the others?"

Ash shook his head. "Didn't have time. Treye, Ovix, and Gilham will be here tomorrow to do just that."

Wait. Did he not have time because of me? Did I get in the way by getting myself into trouble? Planning his next move—was that what he should be doing this very moment?

"Ash," I said, feeling like more of a liability than anything. "I'm sorry if I was a nuisance and took you away from your duty. The last thing I want to be is a distraction, something else you have to worry about."

His eyes grew serious as he looked at me. "I just want to make one thing clear, Elle. And I want you to listen carefully." He cupped my face with his hands, his thumb tracing my lips. "There is nothing I wouldn't do for you. And when it comes to keeping you safe, I will do whatever it takes, become whomever I need to, adapt however I have to, so long as you are protected. I'm here right now because you need me, and frankly, I *want* to be with you. Your entire world and your reality has been turned on its head. I *need* to be here for you. Everything else can wait until tomorrow."

I swallowed and leaned into the warmth of his body. I had to admit—I liked a man who was so generous with his assurances.

I met Gwynn's gaze, and she lifted her brows, a small smile playing on her lips as she nodded at me. Approval shone in her eyes.

For a moment, I couldn't quite place the feeling that settled into my heart, and then it hit me—I felt loved. Accepted. Valued. That I could feel that in spite of the tumultuous upheaval in my life was mind-blowing. If only I could bottle this moment, I would fill as many cases as I could and hoard them in droves.

I slid my arms around Ash's neck, hiding the blur of my tears in the curve of his shoulder.

His arms locked around me as he kissed the top of my head. "No more tears, Tialla," he whispered, his fingers stroking my hair.

"They're happy tears," I said, lifting my head to look at him.

He tilted his head sideways, the question clear in his eyes.

"It's just that there are certain things I feared would never be a possibility for me again." I looked from him to Gwynn and Andreo, and even Tryx sprawled lazily at our feet.

"Like what?" he asked.

Tears rushed to the surface again. "Love. Life. Family. Contentment. I see the possibility, and well, it fills me with hope that it could be a lasting reality."

His eyes swirled with emotion. "It most definitely can, Elle. But what about music? Does that feel like a possibility again?"

I choked on a sob. Blast it all to pieces. The man really did know me. "Yes. How could I forget music? I would die without music."

"I know," he said softly. "And I would die before I let that happen. Music is synonymous with life for you." His fingers snaked along my jaw as he looked at me, eyes filled with so much tenderness and warmth. "The mantle of Songbird of Valkyse might have only passed to you today, but the truth is, that's what you've been your entire life, Elle. A songbird. At your core, it's who you are."

Chapter 25

I TOOK A SIP of Ash's drink, savoring the subtle hints of honey and vanilla on my tongue just before the sweet burn of alcohol seeped down my throat and spread into my chest. He'd poured it just before stepping out of the room with Andreo to talk to Faron and Astrid.

I placed a hand on my heart, cocooned in a comforting blossom of warmth. With the power of his words, Ash had reached inside my soul and reattached my severed connection to my music, circulating the flow again.

"How are you feeling?" Gwynn asked, squeezing my arm from where she sat next to me on the sofa.

I turned toward her. "Honestly? Like I can do anything. But I think that has more to do with Ash than with me. Every time I'm with him, I feel invincible. He makes me see the best version of myself."

Gwynn smiled. "You know, it's one thing knowing what the two of you are to each other; it's another thing entirely watching the two of you together. I have to say—all that raw emotion and energy pulsing off the both of you—lust, love, power—it's fucking intense. I've never seen anything like it before."

My face grew warm at her words. "Oh God, Gwynn, I hope it doesn't make you uncomfortable."

"Not at all. I've never seen Ash so alive. *You* did that, Eleyse."

"Please, call me Elle."

She squeezed my hand. "Soon enough, I'll call you sister."

I looked up as the door opened and Ash and Andreo stepped inside. Ash's gaze found mine right away. My heart thudded excitedly as contentment pulsed through me. I handed him his drink as he sank into the sofa between me and Gwynn.

"So," Gwynn said, her voice suddenly no-nonsense, "now that we know what's what, big brother, are you going to tell us who Gargie is?"

I sensed the tension in him immediately, as if whatever it was, it wasn't something he was happy to talk about. He let out a slow exhale and shifted his body forward. "Right. Where do I start?" He placed his drink on the coffee table and reached for my hand. "Gargie, as the God of Chaos called him, is the reason you're here, Elle. Hindsight is an incredible thing, and I say that because I'm starting to see that how things unfolded was always how they were meant to."

He brushed his fingers against my knuckles absently, his touch soothing the unease I felt inside about what he might say.

"I know you don't remember, but up until five months ago, I had been visiting you regularly for almost a year and a half. Always for a day or two at a time, but never longer. It wasn't enough for me, but it was all I could manage, especially with Kaliope being free. You were the blind spot I couldn't afford to have, but I couldn't stay away."

I touched his thigh. "How did you find me?"

A faint smile appeared. "The Great Creator, Arazul, and the Goddess Mother, Eolith, led me to you, years before I was able to go to you physically. I told you I sought out the Goddess Mother after you came to me. At the time, you weren't born yet in the human world."

God. That really was something. This phenomenal thing between us—it transcended space, time, and even possibility, really. It was enough to make even the biggest skeptic believe in the existence of destiny. And I sure as shit considered myself a skeptic.

"Eolith, with the Great Creator's blessing, told me the truth of who you were, but Arazul made it clear that he would only reveal you to me when the time was right. And even so, I wouldn't be able to go to you until, as he said, 'the Mavigos lifted the veil.'"

"The veil? What does that mean?" I asked.

"I'll explain," he said. "I promise. One of the things binding us together was grief—my grief over my parents, and your grief over your loved ones. The first time you came to me, I was drowning in my grief, filled with so much anger and despair that it was eating me alive. Everything changed for me after that night. You happened, and the entire trajectory of my life shifted. Trust me, my life would have turned out a lot differently if the Senshifter hadn't brought you to me."

I stared at him, speechless that I held that kind of sway over someone. It was even more crazy that for me, that defining moment was just last night.

"Five years ago, the Goddess Mother came to me. She was panicked, desperate, and it disturbed me that a Goddess would feel so much distress. I will never forget her words to me. 'The Secret of the Gods is shattered,' she said. 'Darkness has spread its inky wings over her soul. The light must not go out.' Then she showed you to me. It was the moment I'd been waiting for since you left me the night before my coronation, and what I saw devastated me. The weight of your loss—the death of Liam—had completely destroyed your will to live."

I closed my eyes, my throat constricting as the memories and emotions punched their way to the surface.

Ash pulled me closer, his fingers trailing soothing circles on the back of my hand. "After you lost him, your life spiraled out of control the way mine did after I lost my parents. I wasn't able to find you in the human world, but I was able to see glimpses of you, especially in your darkest moments. For almost two years, I watched helplessly as you lost yourself, completely fell apart and actively sought out death. I tried to feed you hope, to encourage you to fight, always relaying the words you spoke to me the night you came to me, but you were in a terribly dark place."

Fight the darkness, Elle. Live . . .

"At times, I was so entangled in your pain that I didn't know where mine began and yours ended."

"I remember your voice, you know," I whispered, tears blurring my eyes. "I always thought of you as the hope in my head. After a while, when the pain became so unbearable, I just wanted you to be quiet so I could wither away in peace. I'm glad you never stopped."

He kissed the top of my head, his fingers brushing my tears away.

Gwynn and Andreo sat silently, simply listening, as if they didn't want to intrude, both their eyes filled with sympathy for me.

I nodded for Ash to continue.

He intertwined his fingers with mine. "The day Kaliope was released from Glanag, I was able to see you—really see you. Everything around you became vibrant and sharp, filled with color, and I just had to summon you to mind and my labral would show you to me. The Mavigos had lifted the veil. You see, it's all connected. You, me, Kaliope."

On the other side of Ash, Gwynn gasped, her eyes growing wide. "The celestial star etching, Eley—Elle," she whispered.

Ash's eyes flicked to hers. "You know about the celestial star etching?"

"Oletho mentioned it," she explained. "He said that he believed it spoke of you, Elle, and Kaliope. He gave his Hasheyn scroll to Elle."

I touched my labral, stretching the zidiurrh open to reveal the scroll. I slipped my fingers inside and retrieved it, pulling it out just as my labral shifted closed. "Have you seen it before?" I asked.

He nodded. "I know what it says."

I handed the scroll to him, and he clutched it in his palm.

"The celestial star etching is tied to everything I'm saying," he said. "Everything. You'll see what I mean. Once the veil lifted, and I was able to determine where you were in the human world, I was anxious to go to you, but Uncle Andreo urged me to create a plan first."

"Wait," Gwynn interrupted, turning to look at Andreo in the armchair next to her. "You knew? This whole time, you knew who Eleyse was and didn't say anything?" Her eyes flashed with anger and her body grew rigid as she glared at Andreo.

"Gwynn," Andreo said, reaching for her hand, but she pulled away.

"No," she cried, staring between her uncle and Ash. "I know the two of you think I'm a child. Ash might have half a century on me, but I am a grown woman. Why would you—"

"Wynn," Ash said softly, but firmly.

She stared at him, her eyes welling with tears.

He rested his hand on her shoulder. "I swore him to secrecy. He wanted to tell you, but I forbade it. He may be our uncle, but I am his Sovereign, and I asked him not to say anything."

I cringed at the look of hurt and betrayal on Gwynn's face at his words. I didn't blame her for being upset. I didn't understand what Ash's motivations were for keeping her in the dark, but it was clear Gwynn was on the edge. If he didn't start explaining, I had a suspicion that she was going to lose it.

"Why, Ash?" she asked, her eyes flaring with anger.

"For a number of reasons," he said, blowing out a breath as he ran his hand through his hair. "I know you're a grown woman, Wynn, but you will always be my baby sister. My first instinct will always be to protect you, at all costs, even if that means keeping you in the dark. Father and Mother died because of Kaliope's unhealthy obsession with me, and I was powerless to do anything about it. I will not lose you too."

Shit. I couldn't argue with that. I sensed the fear beneath his words driving his regimented control. If I had even the sliver of a chance to save any of my loved ones from death, I would have done anything—even selling my soul—if it meant they would be safe.

Gwynn frowned. "Ash—"

"Please, let me finish. I never told anyone about Elle because the Great Creator Arazul and the Goddess Mother demanded my silence when they revealed their secret to me. Until the veil was lifted, I could not say anything to another soul. But afterward, when I made up my mind to go to her, I needed allies—people I trusted if I were to move back and forth between worlds unseen."

"And you didn't think you could trust *me*?" Gwynn cried.

"I just didn't want to drag you into this, Wynn. I thought it would be safer if you didn't know. If Kaliope ever captured you or threatened you, at least you wouldn't know anything." He leaned forward, angling his body toward her. "I don't blame you for being upset, Wynn."

"Oh, how kind of you to give me your blessing to feel upset," she retorted.

"You can be mad at me 'til you're blue in the face, but I did what I believed was best." He reached for her hand. "Listen, I know you love me. You are compassionate and fierce and loyal, but you are also impetuous, especially in highly charged emotional situations. And your rage and hatred for Kaliope makes you unpredictable. And this entire situation with Elle was one that I needed to manage very carefully."

"You know what your problem is, Ash?" she said, pulling her hand away. "You shut everyone else out because of your need to protect them, to control all the variables, to make sure everything goes the way you want. Well, you know what? Life isn't controlled. It is messy and unpredictable, and you can't control everything. Things are going to go to shit no matter how much you try to control and manage. Me, Astrid, Faron—the three people who love you the most—you push us to the side instead of trusting us, leaning on us, working together with us. And I get that you think you're protecting us, but that's not your responsibility."

"It *is* my responsibility!" Ash roared, tendrils of his power flaring to life in his eyes. "I am not just brother, friend, nephew. I am also Sovereign, and the very definition of my duty is to be the protector of all those under my rule."

Sprawled on the rug at Ash's and my feet, Tryx lifted her head and mewled loudly, her emerald eyes alert as she looked at Ash with concern. He lowered his hand and scratched her chin in reassurance, and she stared at him intently before slowly lowering her head to the floor.

This was intense. I didn't know what to think. Ash was caught between a rock and a hard place. I understood his motivation—I truly did—but I also sympathized with Gwynn. I'd be angry too if someone took away my choice by deciding for me. I had no clue how to diffuse the situation.

"Enough, you two," Andreo interjected, his tone firm. His pale blue eyes darted between Ash and Gwynn. For a moment the room was silent, the crackling of the fire in the massive hearth the only sound filling the room. "I have seen many centuries go by—nineteen, to be exact—and if it's one thing I've learned, it's that family makes life worth living. Not just the ones we're born with, but also the ones we find along the way." He turned to look at his nephew and Sovereign. "Ash, you are like a son to me. Words can't even express how proud I am of the man and ruler you've become. Your parents would be incredibly so. I have done my best to fill the hole their deaths have left in your and Gwynn's lives, but I can never compensate for their loss. It's a thin line I balance between being mentor and subject, and I believe it's my duty to your parents and to you to voice my concern and offer my advice. I acknowledge, though, that you are my Sovereign, and I must abide by your decisions, even when you choose a different path than one I advocated for. I shared my concerns with you when you asked for my help with Eleyse—I didn't feel that it was right to leave Gwynn, Faron, and Astrid in the dark—but I understood you not wanting to put them in harm's way, especially when you wouldn't be here to protect them if you were off world, and I did as you asked."

Ash's body was rigid next to me, heated energy emanating off him. As I stared at his profile, I didn't miss the muscle clenching in his jaw. Next to him, Gwynn was equally stiff, her arms crossed, a scowl plastered on her face.

"I need you to listen to me Ash," Andreo said. "For your own good, listen. You are *not* alone. You have a tribe of people who love you and would lay down their lives for you. Why should they not be allowed to have a say in making that sacrifice? Why do you feel that *you're* the only one who can do that? You're so focused on defeating Kaliope, but consider this—isn't she winning if it means you live your life closed off from the ones you love? Dooming yourself to single-handedly shoulder the burden of saving everyone?"

241

I had to admit—Andreo definitely made some good points. Undoubtedly, leadership came with challenges and difficult choices. I didn't fault or envy Ash any of the choices he was forced to make.

Andreo looked at me and smiled warmly, and it was a smile that seeped into my soul, spreading light into my dark and tormented places.

"In the two years you have been with Eleyse," he said, looking at Ash again, "I have never seen you so happy, so free. And I know it's a testament to what the power of love can do when it's allowed to breathe and blossom. But my boy, the moment Kaliope found out about your earthly visits, your fear took over, strangling you where you stood. And now, Eleyse is here—a Sovereign queen to rule alongside you, capable of phenomenal things we don't yet understand—and you are at a crucial crossroads." He leaned over and reached for Ash's hand. "Don't let your fear of loss drive you to stifle that love, to prevent you from enjoying each moment of happiness you're given. Life is meaningless without love and family, Ash. You have both, in abundance. Trust in your family, lean on them. You don't have to carry the weight of this world on your shoulders."

This was the kind of wisdom that living 1,900 years—still mind-blowing—brought with it. I swallowed the lump in my throat as I looked at Gwynn. Tears ran down her face as she looked at Ash. Her love for him shone freely.

Ash was still, his face unreadable. Finally, he turned to Gwynn. "Wynn," he said, pulling her into his arms. "It was never my intention to ostracize you or to shut you out of my life. Ever since Mother and Father, the need to ensure that no one I love gets hurt has driven every decision I make. That is how I justify my actions. As Sovereign, I have to make hard calls every day, calls that sometimes do not factor in others' feelings on the issue. I can't promise that I won't still be evasive in communicating certain things, but I'll do better. I promise."

She hugged him tightly, her head resting on his shoulder. "Ash. We need to be united in everything that's coming. Father and Mother wouldn't want it any other way. When it comes to Kaliope, together is how we defeat her. Do you not consider us as part of your inner circle?"

"Of course I do," Ash said, eyes flashing. "Trust was never the issue. You need to see that. Perhaps I justified my actions by believing that it was better if you were safe and hated me rather than ending up hurt or dead. I couldn't live with the latter."

"You are not an island, Ash," Gwynn said. "If you really think about it, the only feelings you were thinking about were your own. As selfless as you are in sacrificing yourself for others, that kind of thinking is selfish because you make your decisions unilaterally."

A look of shock, mixed with hurt, flickered in Ash's eyes. He opened his mouth to say something, but closed it, his face deep in thought.

I had to admit—what Gwynn said blew my mind. She was absolutely right. Noble intentions, but noble in whose eyes? And man, I still felt caught in the middle. They were both justified in their reasoning.

"You're right," Ash said softly. "The last thing I want is a dictatorship. And I especially don't want to be seen that way by the people I love. I promise to do better, and I will welcome your reminders if I stray back to my old ways." He turned to Andreo, clasping his arm. "Thank you, Uncle. I might not have wanted to hear everything you said, but I needed to. A good Sovereign knows when to make himself heard and when to listen, when to heed advice and when to be decisive, when to lead and when to delegate. A good Sovereign recognizes the worth of his people. Father taught me that. I am grateful to both you and Gwynn for reminding me."

Chapter 26

I<small>N THAT MOMENT,</small> I didn't doubt that I loved Ash. Not for one second. I didn't expect him to be perfect; perfection didn't exist. Fuck, I was as far away from perfect as could be. What I'd just witnessed—a powerful man acknowledging his own shortcomings and vowing to be better, to be more mindful of his decisions and how they impacted the people around him—well, it blew me away. My heart was bursting with the weight of my feelings for him.

I leaned over and pressed a kiss against his temple.

He looked over, the question reflected in his eyes, but I couldn't bring myself to say the words, trying instead to communicate it with my touch, with my eyes. Until I remembered my time with him, I didn't think I could tell him I loved him. Not anytime soon anyway. I wanted to remember how he'd earned that place in my heart I *knew* he possessed completely.

"I know, Elle." He brushed a kiss against my palm.

My throat clogged, and I swallowed. "When did you change your mind?" I asked, changing the subject. "You said before that when you found out where I was in the human world, Andreo urged you to wait until you had a plan."

"Well," he said, "for a while, observing you from afar—from Ariadna—was enough, and I began putting safeguards in place to come to you. The pull to know you—the desire to see you in person—kept getting stronger, until finally, I couldn't stay away.

The Goddess Mother and the Great Creator opened the path for me to go to you."

Goddamn it. I wanted to remember him. From the first moment I laid eyes on him to the last time I saw him. I hated not having that knowledge of him.

His brows furrowed and his expression grew dark. "About five months ago, two of my most trusted spies reported that Kaliope had learned of my visits to the human world. That was my absolute worst nightmare." Ash closed his eyes, his fingers gripping mine tightly. "At that point in our relationship, you didn't know everything about who I was, but you knew I was different, that you were different, and that we were tied together. You'd already learned about the Secret of the Gods, and I'd warned you that a time might come when I would have to leave suddenly. I prepared you as best as I could, did my very best to enjoy the time we did spend together, told you and showed you I loved you every chance I got. I promised you that even if that time did come, I would find my way back to you. Whatever the cost. All I could do was hope like hell that you would believe me."

I stared at him, my eyes wide. This went against everything I knew about myself, was entirely contradictory to the way I protected myself from getting hurt. The old me would have bolted for the hills at the first sign of danger, would have invoked my mantra—*Can't lose someone if you have no one.*

There was only one explanation, and I already felt the truth of it in my bones. What I had with Ash was powerful, soul binding. It would have had to be to convince me that being with him was worth the very real possibility of losing him when loss was the one thing I feared more than anything else in the world.

Ash frowned, and his eyes took on a faraway look. "When I found out about Kaliope, I was here, in Torannon, and I knew that I couldn't go back to you. Not if I wanted to keep her from finding you. Although I had prepared you, it didn't make it any easier for me. I knew you would be heartbroken, and I hated myself for that. I just held on to the hope that you would believe that we'd find our way back to each other."

My heart ached. Although those memories were lost to me, knowing myself—particularly the me I remembered—I could certainly imagine how I would have reacted to Ash's disappearance, especially if I was in love with him. I didn't know what frame of mind I was in at the time, but the old me would have felt abandoned, destroyed, with my inner demons taunting me ceaselessly for betraying my mantra. Even if he did prepare me. I was very, very good at being unkind to myself. I didn't have to have my memory back to know the torture I would have inflicted on myself. I hoped that wasn't the case.

He lifted my hand to his mouth, his lips brushing gently against my knuckles. "These last five months have been unbearable, Elle. I couldn't even use my labral to see you; that's the connection Kaliope was able to intercept in the first place, and that's how she learned of my visits to the human world. To not be able to talk to you, to know you needed me and I couldn't come to you—it made me sick to stay away, but in order to keep you from Kaliope, I had to do it. The only thing I could do was try to connect to our Gloweyen connection and hope that somehow, even though it wasn't yet awake inside you, that you would feel me. I don't know if you ever heard me, though."

I couldn't say either. My chest was heavy with grief. For a brief moment, I was glad I couldn't remember. I didn't want to think about me slithering back down into that abyss of despair I'd been trapped in after Liam died. I hoped I hadn't gone that route. I hoped I'd been stronger.

"For a while," Ash continued, "I believed you were safe. I had stopped my visits to the human world, and I'd heard no further reports coming in about Kaliope prying there. I was completely devastated at letting you go, but I kept reminding myself that it was the only way to protect you."

Tears pricked my eyes as a lump clogged my throat. I didn't doubt that I'd been in pain, but I couldn't bear to think of Ash hurting.

"This explains so much," Gwynn said, understanding shining in her eyes. "For the life of me, I couldn't understand what was wrong with you these past few months. You were so distant and agitated, Ash, and just . . . adrift. I was never able to get a good read on your emotions, and I suspected you were blocking me."

Ash was lost in his thoughts for a moment, but then cleared his throat and continued. "I'm sorry for shutting you out, Wynn. I didn't want to burden or worry you. Especially because Kaliope was involved. I didn't want you reliving any of the pain she caused us." He unclasped his fingers from mine to run his hand through his hair. "About a week ago, things suddenly escalated. I don't know how Kaliope found out and managed to locate you, Elle, but she sent some of her ghastly Manatocht beasts after you. The Great Creator's power prevents her from leaving the Sangelis or she would have dealt with you on her own. Thankfully, I got there in time to destroy her beasts and save you."

Ghastly beasts? I shook my head rapidly as an image of me tearing through the forest behind my house skittered through my head. Tall, terrifying creatures. Long tusks and sharp teeth. Red eyes. And then a voice! Ash's voice in the darkness calling my name, guiding me to safety, assuring me that everything would be all right. Shrill screeches splintering the silence. The beasts roaring in agony and terror, the smell of fear everywhere.

"After that incident," Ash continued, "I asked Andreo to create wards of protection for you, and he did, with the Goddess Mother weaving into the spells a . . . trapdoor mechanism, you might call it, in case you were ever in danger again." He paused for a moment, a pained expression on his face. "Elle, I had no way of knowing what would happen next, but what did occur is the reason you're here, and why you lost your memory."

My body tensed at his words, but I nodded for him to continue.

"After Kaliope's first attempt failed, she was furious that she had lost her Manatocht warriors, but she was also consumed with jealousy that there was a woman in my life. And so, she sent the creature, Gargmoin, to finish the job."

Gargmoin? Was this the Gargie the God of Chaos had mentioned?

"Wait!" Gwynn interrupted, her eyes as wide as saucers. "Gargmoin is *real*?" Her last word was a high-pitched shriek. "I thought he was just a monster of myth meant to scare children into being good."

Monster. The memory of something quietly watching me lit up my mind. Tall, wide, terrifying. Dead, black eyes. I prodded deeper, but couldn't see past that glimpse.

"Oh, he's very real," Ash replied. "And he does Kaliope's bidding. They managed to find each other in Glanag, and when she was set free, she found a way to release him."

Oh, God. This sounded bad—really bad. As much as I was loath to admit, Kaliope was bloody resourceful, finding loopholes and ways out of even the darkest predicaments.

"But how could the Cloryals allow that?" Gwynn blurted out, incensed. "It's as if no rules apply to her and she is allowed to have her way, unchecked."

"There are some things the Cloryals are blind to," Andreo said quietly from his seat next to Gwynn.

"More like some things they turn a blind eye to," Gwynn said derisively.

"Gwynn," Andreo said, a warning tone in his voice.

"No!" she retorted. "I said it. What's the worst that can happen, Uncle? She murders a Sovereign and his Queen Consort, walks away unscathed, and is then allowed to leave Glanag with the most ruthless, fearsome, and despicable creature in the annals of Ariadnan folklore, and I should worry about what I said? This is ridiculous!"

I shifted uneasily in my seat. Gwynn's anger was visceral, and it hung in the air like a sodden, weighted blanket. And who could blame her? Kaliope did seem to have gotten a free pass despite all the heinous acts she committed.

"I understand you're upset," Andreo said.

"I am *beyond* upset!" Gwynn yelled, her voice shrill with rage. "I am livid. I hate her so much!" The room was silent for a moment, and then finally, Gwynn sighed deeply. "I'm sorry," she said, her tone soft, although her voice still wavered precariously. "I'm just angry and so tired. I don't know how much more of this I can take before I completely lose it."

Ash's face was somber as he looked at his sister. "If anyone understands how you feel, Wynn, it's me."

"I know, Ash," she said, reaching for his hand.

I sat there frozen, staring at the two of them. I couldn't imagine what that felt like—to witness your parents being murdered in front of your eyes, and then having to watch the person responsible for the act walking free and assuming an air of victory, arrogance, and even worse, entitlement.

"Please," Gwynn said, "tell us what happened with Elle and Gargmoin."

"I think Uncle Andreo can explain better, as he was actually a witness to what happened. Again, I am sorry that I made him keep this from you."

I turned to look at Andreo, confused as to what kind of witness he had been.

Andreo ran his hand through his hair as he stood and walked over to the window. He paced for a moment, his forehead creased in a frown. "Ash was called away by the Cloryals when Kaliope sent Gargmoin. It was a couple days after the incident with the Manatocht warriors. Eleyse, you were at the hospital near your house recovering from a wound you sustained when they chased you, and Gargmoin tracked you there."

I gripped Ash's fingers, my body tense as I waited to hear what happened.

"Treye, Gilham, and Ovix—three of Ash's most trusted spies—were the only ones apart from me who knew about you. They provided an extra layer of protection and kept a watchful eye over Kaliope when Ash was away visiting you. They were the ones who alerted us when Kaliope sent her Manatocht warriors after you, and then when she dispatched Gargmoin."

It was surreal listening to Andreo as he recounted something monumental that had happened to me and have it feel like something that had happened to someone else. I had been chased, hurt, hospitalized, almost murdered. Ash's presence in my life was a highly planned, top-secret operation that he had run like a stealth mission across two worlds to keep me safe, and Kaliope had still found me.

Andreo turned and leaned against the window. "At the hospital, Gargmoin tracked you to your room. One of his abilities is mind mincing—shattering someone's mind and rendering them useless. That is what he tried to do with you. The moment he entered your room, he blasted you with his power, but it rebounded off the wards I'd placed on you. The moment the wards were activated, I was able to see what was happening in that room. The wards caused a ripple in time for a few moments, but it was enough to whisk you away to Ariadna, thanks to the magic the Goddess Eolith had woven into the protection spell. Unfortunately, the wards weren't strong enough to withstand all the power Gargmoin hit you with. Some of that power rebounding off the wards snapped back inwards, managing to hit you, which I believe resulted in your memory loss."

My body stiffened as I absorbed Andreo's words. It was chilling. A powerful, ancient creature had simply stepped into my hospital room and attacked me, no questions asked, intent on ending my life. My mind went numb. Next to me, Ash squeezed my hand gently, intertwining his fingers with mine.

"Now, this is where it gets strange," Andreo continued. "In that short ripple in time, when you were snatched away, I saw something—another presence—in the shadows, and it came to hover over the other patient in the room with you. I think it transferred your scent to that person, because Gargmoin didn't seem to notice that you were gone. He continued his onslaught, but on that unfortunate soul, and he did not stop until he ground her to dust."

Gwynn and I both gasped, and Ash tightened his grip around me as my body went rigid. A flash of fractured images lit up my mind. A wide smile. An empty food tray. A woman fast asleep in the bed next to mine. Someone was killed because of *me*. I felt sick to my stomach. An innocent person had lost their life, but it should have been me.

Gwynn must have seen the emotions on my face because she started shaking her head. "No, Elle. This wasn't your fault. Don't do that. I know what you're doing."

"I feel terrible," I said, lowering my head into my hands. "It should have been me."

"You are not responsible for this, Elle," Ash said, wrapping his arms around me. "This is all Kaliope. And unfortunately, there will be many more senseless deaths at her hands before this is over. Unless we can stop her."

Of course, he was right, but it still didn't bring me any comfort. I may not have killed that woman, but she died because of me. Death followed me wherever I went. That innocent lives were lost as a result of me made me sick. It just wasn't right.

"Listen, Elle," Ash said, tilting my chin so I looked at him. "We can't live in the past. Obsessing about what was or could have been will get us nowhere. I know that, and you know that. It's our actions in the moment that count. And I'm telling you, my beautiful love, that you are capable of incredible things and are meant for greatness." His thumb grazed my cheek. "Remember what I said about hindsight earlier?"

I nodded, furrowing my brows in confusion.

He lifted the scroll I'd given him. "It's all in here, Elle. Carved into the heavens by the Mavigos millions of years ago. The celestial star etching is a story of greatness, of good prevailing over evil, of the courage to face the darkness within. But more importantly, what it is for the most part . . .well, it's your story, Tialla mata."

Chapter 27

"MY STORY?" I LOOKED at Ash, my eyes wide. Oletho was certain that the star etching spoke of me, Ash, and Kaliope, so what did Ash mean?

Slowly, he removed the clasp from the scroll and began unfurling the parchment. He handed it to me, smiling encouragingly. "Read it, Elle. It's written in Hasheyn, but I'm confident that you know the language of the Gods."

That's what Oletho had said as well.

"You can understand and read all the other Ariadnan languages," Gwynn said. "It would only make sense that you can do the same with Hasheyn."

I took the scroll from Ash, my hands shaking. He placed his hands over mine, steadying me, his touch grounding me.

I looked down at the elegant, sweeping words on the parchment, each one registering as my eyes drank them in. Clearing my throat, I read them out loud.

When the Celusian Moon is no more and the light of Selayne disappears from the heavens, the Cradle of the In-Between will birth the child of celestial love, who will grow and dwell in obscurity until Selayne rises in the Sangelis again, lifting the veil to dissolve the season of celestial mourning.

By a shard of the Old, Arcane Magic, she will be summoned—her rebirth ushering in a new age to the Sangelis. Born of light and darkness, born of love and music, born to rule . . . she will rise. All-consuming love and power she will command with the High King of the Light Age, and war they will wage against the daughter of the Laureal Moon and dark Gods of the ages.

The truth of her nature is two-fold: the High Queen of the Light Age and the Celestial Songbird, guided by the Anchor—Catraia. Without Catraia, darkness will prevail and will swathe the Sangelis in doom. Catraia is the guardian; Catraia is the bridge.

If she, whose name is lost, can claim the Ankhira and harness the power of the Ethereal Harmonies, she will have dominion over Shadow and Light and will take her rightful place in the Sangelis.

I dropped the scroll onto my lap, my fingers shaking. I looked up at Ash, unable to hide my fear and confusion. A swamp of emotion doused me, slowing my heartbeat. I closed my eyes and sank into myself.

Catraia, I called, filled with an inexplicable need to hear her voice.

I am here, Eleyse. You are not alone.

Ash squeezed my fingers gently. The combination of his touch and Catraia's voice in my head calmed me and my body relaxed.

"What does it all mean?" I asked, confusion battering my senses.

He picked up the scroll from my lap, and his fingers traced the words. "The Celusian Moon was the smallest of seven moons that lit up the Sangelis. It exploded just over thirty years ago, and about a year after that, Selayne, once known as the evening star of the Sangelis, faded from the heavens completely. Three years ago, Selayne reappeared again."

"The veil lifted," Andreo said in wonder.

Ash nodded. "That coincides with Kaliope being released from Glanag, with me being able to see Elle and go to her." He squeezed my thigh gently. "The part about the Cradle of the In-Between birthing the child of celestial love has to do with your identity as it pertains to the Secret of the Gods. All I can say is that the obscurity it speaks of is your life on Earth."

"Secret of the Gods being what the Goddess Mother called Elle?" Gwynn asked.

Ash nodded.

The secret that I apparently knew but didn't remember. The secret that Ash couldn't tell me because the Gods swore him to secrecy. If it were that important, would they reveal it to me again? The Goddess Eolith had visited me last night. Why didn't she tell me before she sent me through the Senshifter? Or did she, and I just wasn't smart enough to see it? Leida mata, she'd called me. My *treasure*. She'd said she was the gatekeeper to the secrets of my identity.

My mind summoned a memory, and I quickly turned to Ash. "When the Goddess Eolith visited me in my dreams that night years ago, she said to me, 'You are back where it all began—in the In-Between.' Do you think she was talking about the same In-Between as in the scroll?"

"There is only one Cradle of the In-Between that I know of," Ash replied, "so it would have to be, although why she would come to you from there, I'm not sure."

I nodded. "You said that the evening star, Selayne, disappeared almost thirty years ago. I'm almost thirty years old."

"Right," Ash replied. "It just lends more credence to this being about you, especially when you learn about the Secret of the Gods."

I flashed back to the scene of my birth that I'd witnessed with Harwen Valkyse. I was convinced it was the presence of the Great Creator Arazul I'd sensed in that room. For the life of me, I couldn't get the image of the blue, lifeless baby out of my head. That was me. What did it all mean? All of it had to be connected with the star etching. I sensed it.

I peered at the scroll. ". . . will grow and dwell in obscurity until Selayne rises in the Sangelis again, lifting the veil to dissolve the season of celestial mourning."

"What is the season of celestial mourning?" I asked.

Ash glanced at the section I was pointing at. "I'm not entirely sure what that refers to, but my suspicion is that it is almost as ancient as the star etching itself, since I haven't been able to find any records or accounts of a period of celestial mourning. The Great Creator, Arazul, and the Goddess Mother were both tight-lipped on the origins of the veil as well."

"I've not heard of such a thing either," Andreo said. "Have you asked Lorien? He may have some idea."

Ash nodded. "Yes. He was just as tight-lipped." Seeing the question in my eye, Ash explained. "Lorien Reo is one of the Keepers of the Old, Arcane Magic, an ancient source of magic that is also found here in Ariadna."

"Do you think they know and just didn't want to say?" Gwynn asked.

"That's my gut feel," Ash said. "That they either couldn't or wouldn't say."

"What does the Old, Arcane Magic have to do with this?" Gwynn asked.

"'By a shard of the Old, Arcane Magic, she will be summoned,'" Ash said, reading from the scroll. "I am positive this has to do with how Elle ended up in Ariadna. Gargmoin is an ancient creature, as old or older than Ariadna by accounts, and his power is steeped in the dark sway of the Old, Arcane Magic. A shard of his power—however inadvertent it might have been—is what triggered Eleyse's arrival in Ariadna."

"That actually makes a lot of sense, Ash," Andreo agreed, sinking into the armchair next to Gwynn. "And it goes back to what you said earlier about everything happening the way it did for a reason. It was all inevitable."

My heart thudded. Inevitable. I had mixed feelings about that. What this Gargmoin enacted had resulted in the death of an innocent person, while the wards Andreo and the Goddess Eolith placed around me had saved my life and transported me here. Without the wards, I would have been the one ground to dust.

Events had unfolded in such a way that the celestial star etching was fulfilled, but the reality of it all was a glaring reminder that everything came with a cost. I needed to be mindful of that. This journey I was embarking on would not be easy. All life was precious. Perhaps it would be wise if I made that my new mantra.

I turned to Ash. "So the shard of Gargmoin's power that hit me erased my memory, and then Andreo's wards brought me here. Do you think my memory loss was always inevitable?"

Ash frowned. "I can't really answer that question, Elle. Do the Mavigos work entirely in absolutes or is there an element of fluidity in their predictions? I have to believe that while certain outcomes may be absolute, there are multiple paths to arrive there. That being said, just as there are absolute outcomes, I also believe there are those that are not concrete. The majority of the celestial etching is a proclamation of absolutes until it shifts to something else—when it focuses on who *you* are and what you are capable of. At that point, it's almost as if the Mavigos are saying, 'This is the situation; these are the stakes. The power in determining what happens from here lies with you.'"

Shit. No pressure at all. But even as I was overwhelmed with the magnitude of that responsibility, the notion that the final outcome wasn't predetermined, that I might have some level of control over my actions and the path I chose soothed me.

I looked at the scroll. "Do you think this part—'her rebirth ushering in a new age to the Sangelis'—is the same as what happened in Falayen with your mother? When we sang 'The Song of Rebirth,' her Songbird mantle passed on to me."

Ash nodded, running his hand across his jaw. "Yes, that brought about your transformation. That has to be the rebirth referenced in the star etching." He glanced at the scroll again. "The next part—'born of light and darkness, born of love and music'—that is tied up in the Secret of the Gods, and although you don't remember now, it will make sense when you learn of it."

"And you're sure that I know what the secret is?"

"Yes. And I am convinced that you will learn the details of it again. It's too important for them to keep it from you."

I nodded absently. "Born of light and darkness, of love and music." It was part of the secret. What could it mean? Was this about my life on earth and the family I was born into? My parents had loved each other very much, and music was the foundation of our family. Perhaps the light and darkness referred to the path my life had traveled: from light into darkness?

Ash squeezed my hand gently. "In the history of Ariadna, only four Songbirds have existed, and the Ethereal Harmonies bestowed on each of them a title—Sunrise, Sunlight, Twilight, Starlight. Yours Elle, is written in the star etching. You are the Celestial Songbird."

Pride shone in his eyes as he smiled at me. I didn't know what to say. *Celestial Songbird.* As far as titles went, it was incredible, but how was I supposed to go from who I was yesterday to being the person who accepted this powerful new identity and path? It all felt so insurmountable.

"Tell me, Elle," Ash said, sensing my distress.

I wrung my hands in my lap. "How can I explain this?" I said looking between him, Gwynn and Andreo. "Take you for instance, Ash. From the time you were born, you were groomed for your role as Sovereign of Valkyse. It was instilled in you, was all you ever knew. Me, on the other hand, I'm coming in *completely* blind. I mean, up until yesterday, I didn't even know the Sangelis even existed. There's just so much to absorb and I can't help but feel overwhelmed."

"Listen, Elle," Gwynn said, leaning forward to look at me, her expression empathetic. "None of us expect you to be okay with any of this. This is all so colossal. It's perfectly all right to be overwhelmed. I can't even imagine what must be going through your mind right now."

"Gwynn is right," Ash said, reaching for my hands and urging me to face him. "I wish you had the luxury of time to ease your way into all of this. If there was a way for me to give that to you, I would. I can't tell you how to feel or take your fear and misgivings away, but I meant what I said before. I'm with you every step of the way. Gwynn, Andreo, as well as everyone loyal to me, will be loyal to you." He tilted my chin up. "Trust me, Tialla. You are not alone. Far from it."

I closed my eyes as his palm slid against my cheek, sending frissons of warmth through me.

"Even the star etching makes that clear," Ash said softly. "With the twin labrals that declare us High Sovereigns over Ariadna, it's apparent that you and I are the High King and Queen of the Light Age referenced." He squeezed my fingers gently. "I'm right here, baby, by your side, just as the star etching tells it. And not only do you have me, but you have Catraia. The star etching calls her out by name, emphasizing what a huge part of you she truly is."

He was right. The star etching was glaringly specific. "...Guided by the Anchor—Catraia. Without Catraia, darkness will prevail and will swathe the Sangelis in doom. Catraia is the guardian; Catraia is the bridge."

"Wait," Gwynn said. "Who is Catraia?" She looked at Andreo. "Do you know?"

He shook his head.

"Catraia is a part of Elle—an entity—that has awakened with her transformation," Ash explained.

"What the star etching says about Catraia is pretty ominous," Andreo said, rubbing his chin. "She . . . it . . . seems to play a consequential role in all of this."

"Elle still has a lot to learn about her, as do I," Ash said, intertwining his fingers with mine.

You are the one with the power, Eleyse, not me; I exist to serve you, Catraia whispered in my mind.

Did it make it any easier hearing that? It did make me feel relieved, knowing that I wasn't alone.

Andreo leaned forward in his chair, a grim expression on his face. "As for the daughter of the Laureal Moon, Kaliope is almost fully Shen. The Laureal Moon is one of the two moons of Treth. It cannot be a coincidence. Her giln also has the image of a moon on it."

"Oletho said her giln is different from any other he's ever seen," Gwynn said. "It makes sense, Ash."

My heart thudded in my chest. Yes, too much sense. And this was written millions of years ago? Wintry tingles slinked down my spine.

"And this part," Ash said. "'If she, whose name is lost, can claim the Ankhira and harness the power of the Ethereal Harmonies, she will have dominion over Shadow and Light and will take her rightful place in the Sangelis.' I don't know what the Ankhira is, but I suspect it's some kind of magic or a weapon."

I cocked my head. "When I was with your mother, she said that the Sovereigns each guard a powerful artifact that only I could unite and wield to preserve harmony. Could this be related to that?"

Ash looked at me, wide-eyed, his mouth open. "Of course! It didn't even occur to me that they could be united."

"What?" Gwynn asked, leaning forward in her seat.

"The Phanteras," he replied. "Earlier today, the Cloryals commanded the Sovereigns to unearth the Phanteras from their burial places."

Weapons. Magical Weapons. More powerful than anyone could imagine. That's what Ash had explained they were. Four Phanteras existed, each one belonging to a Dominion and protected by a Sovereign. The Cerulean Embers was Valkyse's; the Viridian Tide, Averon's; the Sandstone Shadows, Solanis's; and the Sable Tempest, Tandor's.

In the northwestern Territories of Brus-Winnd, still within the Dominion of Valkyse, Valkyse's Phantera—the Cerulean Embers—lay buried. As Sovereign, Ash was the guardian of this great weapon; only he had the power to retrieve it.

He explained that in the history of Ariadna, the Cerulean Embers had only been wielded once—during the Shacquiri Rebellion, 39,000 years ago, when Rywin and Verah Valkyse were Gloweyen Sovereigns of Valkyse. None of the other Phanteras belonging to the other dominions had ever been actively used.

God. I was exhausted. Ash, Gwynn, and Andreo were still engrossed in conversation around me, but I had tuned out. The past two days had been the longest of my life. I didn't think there was even a single crumb of additional information I could cram into my brain. I was done. I just wanted to be with Ash.

As if sensing my thoughts and my exhaustion, he stood and pulled me to my feet. "Want to call it a night?" he asked, tucking my hair behind my ear.

I nodded.

"See you both in the morning," Gwynn said as her lips curved in a smile. "Try to at least get a little sleep."

Ash's brows furrowed, a small smile on his lips as he shook his head at his sister. He turned to me. "Walk or labral?"

"Labral."

"Labral it is, then." He wrapped his arm around my waist and touched his cuff, splintering the air around us.

Chapter 28

W E WERE STANDING IN a bathing chamber, if it could even be called that. The room was massive. I slowly looked around. Jutting out from the wall behind us was a long marble countertop with dark, built-in cabinets and a wide, deep sink. Above that, an ornate gilded mirror occupied the length of the wall.

In front of us was an open concept floor-to-ceiling shower—no enclosures. Dark gray slate tiles were set in a pattern along the back wall with jets embedded every foot or two. The showerhead was built into the ceiling, taking up the entire length of the shower. I gaped at it in awe. Where did the water drain to? There were no drain holes in the floor. Then it hit me. Of course—magic.

Similar to my bathroom at Cazara Chantilis, a bathing pool sparkled in the corner of the room. The ceiling above it was completely open, the night sky ablaze with stars, moonlight streaming down softly onto the water. The room was neither hot nor cold, and a soft breeze drifted in from outside, the air alive with energy and something else I couldn't place. It made my heart race; it smelled like . . . life, magic—like home.

Even as my blood pulsed with fervor, confusion tugged at me. At Cazara Chantilis, I'd experienced the same deep sense of belonging and contentment, but the essence of the place was completely different. Chantilis and Torannon were night and day, but they both felt entirely *right*.

Ash stood quietly, his lips curved in a smile as he watched me take everything in.

I met his gaze, my mouth parted in wonder. "This is heavenly, Ash."

He chuckled quietly. "I know how you enjoy a luxury bathroom."

He was right. My bathroom at home was one of the two places I had really splurged when I bought my house. That, and my kitchen.

"You've had a long day, and I figured you'd enjoy a good soak in the bath."

I watched in wonder as the floor shifted beneath us and an enormous clawfoot tub emerged in the space below the shower. As the tub rose, it began filling with water. My mouth almost hit the floor when hovering candles appeared around the back edge of the tub, casting flickering shadows along the wall.

I squealed in delight. "Oh my God. I love this."

"I knew you would," Ash said, pulling me into his arms.

"Join me?" I said, splaying my palms against his chest.

He stroked my cheek gently, his green eyes dark and turbulent. "Trust me when I say that I would love nothing more, but I don't think that's a good idea."

"What? Why?" I asked, disappointment and rejection burrowing into my chest like voracious cicada nymphs.

"Consequences . . ." His voice trailed off as his fingers slowly trailed down my collarbone, his thumb brushing against my pulse at the base of my neck. "Elle, the last time you were with me—well, a version of me—was last night. For me, it's been five months, and trust me, those five months have felt so much longer than the ninety-seven years I waited for you after our first night together. The moment you're in my arms, with no clothes on, I will want to fuck you, and we can't do that, Tialla."

I stared at him. What. The. Fuck. Was he kidding? My body was strung as tight as a bowstring—because of him—and I wanted—no, *needed*—him to release it.

"Why can't we?" I asked, a spark of frustration bubbling up inside me. "Am I missing something? Did I do something?"

"You didn't do anything," he said, running his hand through his hair. "Fuck. I'm not explaining this very well."

"No, you're not."

"To consecrate our Gloweyen bond, and to ensure our powers are fully merged and bonded, we must physically consummate our union right after your coronation, in Falayen."

Physically consummate. Oletho's voice rang out in my head. *Falayen is a place where both powers can be fused—where the two become one*, he had said. I didn't really pay it much heed when he said it, dismissing it as a figurative statement.

"As long as your labral shines with Shinoran light—which it will until the coronation—we cannot have sex. The Gloweyen bond has to be consecrated with a physical union, which must happen in Falayen, specifically in Alonai, the lake of rejuvenation."

The lake. The one I'd sat at when I was there—the one he'd emerged from when he appeared in Falayen. I had felt the thrum of power in its depths, responded to its call when I was there.

"When you put your labral on your wrist, you accepted the Gloweyen bond between us, and in order to amass the full strength of the powers the bond provides, we must wait. But—and this makes things more difficult—our Gloweyen bond heightens our physical need for each other. It's all-consuming. Gloweyen is a very primitive and hedonistic connection; that's why things feel very out of control when we're together."

"Oh, the irony," I said, acutely aware of my skin tingling with the need to be close to him, to be consumed by him. "Well, are *other* things allowed, or is everything off the table?" I asked, tilting my head up to look at him.

His eyes blazed as he traced my lips with his thumb. "Allowing *other* things is playing with fire."

"I like playing with fire," I said, wrapping my arms around his neck.

He smiled. "I know."

"What happens if we can't control ourselves and give in?"

"We don't get the full power of the bond."

"Hmm . . ." I mulled over what he said. Of course, I didn't want to risk that. I didn't even know how grave the consequences of not having that full power would be. But at the same time . . .

"Ash," I said, cupping his handsome face in my palms. "You waited ninety-seven years for me, so I'm going to go out on a limb and say you have superior control, which you've probably spent decades and decades honing. I mean, you are a powerful Sovereign after all, right?"

His eyes danced with amusement. "I love the way you rationalize things."

I gave him a bright smile. "Perfect. Then, I'd like to raise my hand for playing with fire and trusting you to keep us from getting burned."

He threw his head back and laughed, and I laughed along with him.

"I'm happy you think I'm funny, but I was dead serious."

He pressed his lips against mine quickly. "I know you're serious. I laughed because you're just as impatient here as you were when I met you back in your world."

"I was impatient?"

"Very."

"Well, you're fucking hot, and you do tantalizing things to my insides that defy explanation. What you said about the Gloweyen bond heightening our need for each other makes sense. Whenever I'm with you, I want to jump out of my skin to get as close to you as I can."

His eyes crinkled as he laughed. "Trust me, that was the case two years ago as well. You were very vocal about wanting the physical connection with none of the emotional parts."

Even as he said, it, I knew he was right. That had absolutely been my MO. Zero attachment. I didn't often seek out physical connection, but when I had, I'd selfishly taken what I wanted and moved on. No goodbyes. No remorse. No heartstrings involved.

"God, how did you respond to that?"

Ash smiled, flicking the tip of my nose. "With a tremendous amount of restraint. It wasn't easy, but I resisted your advances to get me in your bed for a long time. I always had the end game in mind, and from day one, my goal was to bring you back to life, to make you feel something real again, believe in love once more."

His words were a punch to the gut, filling me with sadness, shame, and gratitude all at once. Sadness and shame for how low I had sunk in my despair, and gratitude at the lengths he had gone to pull me out. My eyes burned, and I looked away.

"Elle, I didn't say that to make you upset." He pulled me closer.

"I know," I said, swiping at my eyes. "Trust me, Ash, I remember exactly who I was before I met you. I was barely a person."

"But you're not that person anymore, Tialla." He brushed his lips against my forehead. "How about this?" he said, as his hand curled around my neck, then slowly moved across my collarbone and down to the swell of my breast. "Whenever we have the chance to seize the moment, we can *play*, and I'll call on my superior control, as you called it, to keep us grounded."

A rush of heat pooled in my core. The way he said *play*—he knew exactly what he was doing to me.

"*But*," he said, moving his hand back up around my neck, "no waking up to you on top of me."

My knees went weak. "Did I do that a lot?"

He nodded, his eyes dark with desire. "It was one of your favorite ways to wake me up."

I closed my eyes as a twinge of sadness tugged at my insides. It wasn't fair that he remembered and I didn't. All I had were the dark memories of my shitty life. I wanted to share in the happy memories of him in it.

Goddamn it. I needed to focus on now. Not the past. I needed to enjoy the moment as it was happening.

"Deal," I said, standing up on tiptoes to kiss him. "Going to reconsider joining me?"

He kissed the top of my head. "You take a long, relaxing bath, process all your thoughts, and when you're done, I'll be waiting for you on the balcony."

And therein lay the rub. I wasn't sure I wanted to process everything yet. To feel the magnitude of everything that had happened today truly settle into me. I wanted him to make me forget, wanted to get lost in the feel of his skin against mine, to escape into the rapture that swept me away when he was buried deep inside me.

As much as I tried to ignore it, something else weighed heavily on me. My encounter with the God of Chaos had unsettled me deeply, and now, after hearing the celestial star etching proclamations about me, I was even more uneasy in my own skin.

Unworthy. Not enough, the demons of my past taunted, and I pushed the voices aside. No, I didn't want to be alone with my thoughts just yet.

Let Asher go, Eleyse, Catraia said calmly in my mind. *You're not alone. We need to talk.*

Great. Instead of Ash wrapped around me in the bath, I was going to have a heart-to-heart, reciprocal conversation with myself.

That's right, Catraia said, and I swore I detected a hint of snark in her tone.

"I almost forgot," Ash said. "Don't be surprised if you get a visit from Tora while you're in here. She runs things at the cazara, and she's anxious to meet you."

"Wait," I said. "The person who runs things at Cazara Torannon—her name is Tora?"

He nodded.

"I must say that you Ariadnans are quite . . . original when it comes to names."

Ash chuckled. "It'll make sense when you meet her."

"And she may visit me in the bath?"

He smiled. "I'm just warning you up front so you're not surprised if she does pop in." He brushed his lips against my forehead. "Enjoy your bath, Tialla mata."

My Goddess. I was never going to get tired of hearing him call me that.

Chapter 29

"CATRAIA, ARE YOU A separate being from me?" I asked aloud before ducking my head under the water.

We exist together or not at all. I preserve the balance, keep the darkness you wield from encroaching into your heart.

Darkness? What did that mean? What exactly am I? I asked tentatively, unsure if I really wanted to know the answer.

A vessel . . . conduit . . . pure power. You are light and darkness, curator of death and bringer of life.

She was doing it again. Talking in riddles. How could I be any of those things? I didn't even recognize myself in any of what she declared.

Your entire existence thus far has been grounded in your human life. That life was a means to an end—you were in limbo, hidden away in the human world until the time came for the veil to be lifted, ushering in your entry to Ariadna.

A means to an end? Is that what my life was? I had a family. Love. Happiness. Purpose.

Until you didn't, and then all you longed for was death.

The fuck? What a cold, bitch-faced thing to say.

I don't say that to be cruel, Eleyse. The truth is that your life on Earth was always meant to be temporary. And until you set aside your preconceived notions, your misgivings, fears, insecurities—all things that defined your earthly existence—you will not be able to embrace the truth of who you really are.

Who I really was.

Tell me what you've learned.

About what? I asked.

Who you really are. Tell me.

I closed my eyes. What had I learned? So much that it was overwhelming. The Goddess Eolith had called me the Secret of the Gods; leida mata—my treasure; Renala Cielta—Celestial Queen. The Cloryals had referred to me as hallowed one, with fire in my veins. They'd said I had a broken spirit and a dark heart. Harwen Valkyse had said I was bound by fate to her and that I was always meant to hold her son's heart. She had called me conqueror, savior; passed her Songbird of Valkyse mantle to me. She'd declared that only I could wield the artifacts that the Sovereigns guarded. Ash's senses had told him I was a promise and a storm, his eternal soul's shadow. The Ethereal Harmonies had chosen me as Gloweyen Queen—of both Valkyse and Ariadna. The celestial star etching had referred to me as the child of celestial love, the Celestial Songbird, High Queen of the Light Age.

All of that holds true. It is who you are meant to be. It is your identity.

The Goddess Eolith's words came rushing back to me—*When everything is laid bare, accept the truth of who you are. Claim it as your birthright. You will be many things to many living beings, but to yourself, you are whomever you choose to be. Never forget that. That omnipotence lies within you.*

My heart warmed and expanded as the words sank into my bones.

You have been reborn, Eleyse, Catraia said. *You must embrace the truth of who you are. Stop seeing this world and yourself through the lens of your human eyes. That version of you belongs to the past.*

Here lies your future.

She was right. I was seeing everything through my human eyes. I didn't know any other way. Only when I was with Ash did I feel like anything was possible.

That's because he already sees you for who you are: the woman he loves, his powerful Gloweyen Queen, the future of Ariadna.

And Ash, what is he to me? I asked.

Life ... love ... everything.

My heart ached at her words, and a flood of emotion surged through me. I wanted to go for it—to rush in guns blazing, shouting "Yes, I've got this," but I couldn't. In the back of my mind, playing on repeat since I left him, were the God of Chaos's jeering words—*It's pathetic how little you know about your power.* Those words made me feel sick and useless. He was right. I knew jack shit about my power. Hell, I'd gotten myself into trouble just trying to ask a question, and ended up having to rely on Ash to save me. I was a joke.

Enough, Eleyse. That is what Asher and I are here for. We will train you to use your power. Together, we will ensure you're ready. There is much that I have to impart to you. Because I have only just awakened inside you, I am still assessing and absorbing who you are as a person—your strengths, weaknesses, motivations, moral character, personality. You are indeed the one spoken of in the ancient celestial star etching, but the entirety of who you are is not yet a reality, but rather, a tiered metamorphosis. There are levels to your identity and the power entrenched therein.

Okay. She was going off on a tangent again. Tiered metamorphosis? Levels? I was going to have to teach her the simplicity of plain language.

I swore I heard an exasperated sigh, but it was so hushed, I might have imagined it.

You won't come into all of your power at once. It is gradual. As of this moment, you are the Songbird of Valkyse, chosen Gloweyen Queen to the Sovereign of Valkyse. You have amassed only a portion of the power associated with that title. Once you have amassed all of the power that title has to offer, you will transition to the next level.

Do I get to know what all the levels are?

Let's just take it one at a time. It will make things less overwhelming.

Do you really think I can handle all of this? I asked.

I know you can.

I was silent as I absorbed her words. Catraia's presence in my mind gave off its own unique signature—it exuded confidence, calm, wisdom, authority. I felt—well, relieved. I wasn't alone. The sound of her voice was lulling—it smothered my anxiety and put me at ease. I was grateful to have her with me.

A sudden knock on the door caused me to jump.

"Coming in, coming in," a cheery, melodic voice called from outside, and before I had a chance to answer or slide down into the tub, a figure slipped *through* the door.

I stared at the woman in front of me because—well, I didn't know what else to do. Her hair was a mass of green and silver, coiled elegantly in a loose knot at the top of her head. Her eyes—frig, I couldn't stop staring. Cat-eye shaped, they were a glowing, golden color. I had never seen anything like them before. Her lips were full and sensuous, and her body—all curves. The woman dripped sex appeal as she glided—yes, glided—across the room, not walked.

She was wearing a fitted silver gown—a strappy number, showing off an extraordinary amount of cleavage. Around her neck, a green gemstone necklace hung. She had to be, by far, the most fascinating and colorful creature I'd ever seen, and that was saying something, given that in just the past two days, I had come face to face with a God, a Goddess, Cloryals, a Giln Keeper, and a Songbird.

"Renala mata!" she cried, clasping her hands as she sank into a low bow in front of the tub. "Long have I waited for your return."

My queen. What did she mean she had waited for my return?

She must have seen the confusion on my face because she rose and moved toward me, sitting on the edge of the tub. "Anyone who enters Cazara Torannon must go through me," she said. "Even if it is through a Senshifter." She winked, her lips curving into a sly grin.

She had known I had visited Ash that night? "Are you Tora?" I asked.

"Oh, Arazul's balls, how rude of me," she said, clasping my hair and wringing the water out of it. "Yes, baby queen, I am she."

Baby queen? That was a new one. I couldn't stop the high-pitched titter that slid past my lips.

She conjured a jeweled hair clasp out of the air and fastened my hair at the top of my head. "Smolders told me it was all right for me to introduce myself."

Smolders? What the— "Are you talking about Ash?"

"Of course. Who else walks around this place with all that smoldering intensity? It's enough to make any woman drip puddles from her slit."

"Oh, dear God," I said, bursting out laughing, my eyes wide with disbelief.

"Hold that thought, love," she said, humming as she glided toward the sink and slipped into the walls. I watched, mouth agape as the walls became translucent and she moved from one end of the bathing chamber to the next, all within the wall! She stooped for a moment near what I assumed was the dressing room, then disappeared briefly before returning, holding a robe and a short, silky nightgown.

"If I were you, I'd just wear the robe, dear. This poor thing would just end up in shreds when he rips it off you." She shook her head, laying the nightgown on the counter next to the sink.

"What?" I asked, my mouth still open.

"Smolders is wound pre-tty tight." She sighed, leaning against the counter, her head cocked to the side. "I tell you, being the guardian spirit of this place can be rough sometimes. As much as I try to plug my ears, it is hard to drown out the sound of a Sovereign when he's fisting himself and thinking about the woman he loves."

I sputtered, taking air in the wrong way and spasming into a coughing fit. I had no words. None. Nothing in the world could have prepared me for this creature.

"I didn't take you for a prude, love," she said, her melodic laughter bouncing off the walls. "The last time you were here, you were pretty eager to get on that cock of his."

Holy shit! I was going to kill Ash.

She patted my hand gently. "I can only assume that's what happened, love. Rest easy. I wasn't actively listening, but I did have to plug my ears. But don't worry. I already took measures to block out sounds from these rooms tonight, so you're all set." She winked again, reaching for the soft, fluffy towel at the side of the tub. "Come on, out with you. You don't want your skin to prune before you go to him." She held the towel open, and I stepped out of the tub carefully. She gave me an appraising look. "Gorgeous," she said. "Tight and supple. Great tits."

My face flamed as she wrapped the towel around me. I reached down and grabbed the ends, holding them in a death grip.

She turned to face me. Her expression softened as she looked at me with warmth and affection. "Nice to have you where you belong, Agaia. See you in the morning."

Before I could even acknowledge her, she was gone. I stood there, clutching my towel around me.

Agaia, she had called me. *Storm*.

Chapter 30

THE MOMENT I STEPPED out of the bathing chamber, my senses were assaulted by his presence. His smell, aura, magnetism—they permeated the bedroom completely and hung heavily in the air. I breathed in the scent of him—clean, crisp, and mind-swirlingly intoxicating—a blend of sandalwood and citrus, with a soft hint of vanilla.

I looked around the room slowly. It was the same room the Senshifter had taken me to. I'd been too distracted then to pay attention to the details. The bedroom was dimly lit, the space open and expansive, with high ceilings and dark hardwood floors. A massive four-poster bed—the same one we'd claimed each other in—was positioned against a wall in the middle of the room, and a striking painting of rolling hills at dusk hung above it. Rugged bedside tables stood imposingly on each side, and a rich, plush rug blanketed the floor, splayed wide on the sides.

Moonlight streamed in from the magnificent floor-to-ceiling windows on the adjacent wall. Two long panels of charcoal-colored drapes were drawn on either side of the thick window casings, hanging regally from a dark, wooden rod, the craftsmanship on the carved finials elegant in its design.

A colossal stone fireplace nestled in impressively against the wall facing the bed. The colors throughout the room were a combination of light and dark: soft grays, creams, and charcoals, blending together effortlessly.

Outside the window, the arresting view of the city and harbor stole my breath away. The sky was as black as ink, a stark contrast against the plethora of stars adorning its tapestry. The ocean stretched on for miles in the distance, the horizon line invisible in the darkness as it blurred and blended with the sky.

Inland, the twinkling lights of the city below shivered and pulsed as I gazed at them. Nothing moved on the ground, and for a moment, that surprised me, as I expected to see the bustle of vehicular traffic in a city setting. But there were no vehicles here, which would make sense, given that gilns were used for travel.

A cool breeze drifted through the balcony doors in the corner of the room as I made my way in that direction. My feet skidded to a stop. Ash was lounging on a wide, long chaise, one leg bent, looking out at the harbor, a drink in his hand. A soft, dark robe was draped around him, open at the waist, revealing his sculpted, bare chest and stomach. Low-slung drawstring pants rested loosely on his hips.

He turned toward me and smiled. My heart fluttered as I basked in his attention. For a moment, every thought in my head evaporated. God help me. My reaction to him was crazy, to say the least. The man completely consumed me with his presence. It was safe to say I had never experienced this level of attraction to anyone before.

He stretched his hand out to me and I walked toward him, my skin aching to be closer to his. He took my hand and pulled me down onto the chaise with him, tucking me into his side as he kissed the top of my head.

His hair was damp, and he smelled utterly divine. To my horror and simultaneous delight, I turned my face and sniffed him—yes, sniffed him, like a ravenous dog in heat, unable to flood my senses enough. Goddamn it, I was a mess.

"Did you enjoy your bath?" he asked, shaking me out of my stupor.

"I did. I didn't realize you were also going to have one. Alone." I couldn't help the accusatory tone that tinged my voice.

He wrapped a tendril of my damp hair around his fingers. "I took a shower," he said, his eyes dark as his gaze slid to my mouth. "You said you wanted to play, so I had to . . . well, take the edge off before I came out here."

Oh God. A rush of heat sluiced through me as I pictured him in the shower, head thrown back, hand wrapped around his cock. But then, Tora's voice in my head jarred me back to the present, sending the sinful image scuttling into the shadows.

"So I met Tora," I said, turning to look at him. "Thanks for preparing me for that. And I hope you realize I'm being sarcastic, because I was so not prepared for that."

He laughed—a deep, hearty sound—and I couldn't help the smile that curved my lips. I fucking loved hearing him laugh.

"I don't think anyone in the history of this place has ever been prepared for Tora. She is an unbridled firestorm of magnificent proportions, the epitome of blunt and crude wonder." He chuckled quietly. "I wish I'd been there to see your face."

I laughed. "Jaw, meet floor. That pretty much describes my reaction." I cocked my head to the side. "What is she? She mentioned something about being the spirit guardian of this place."

"You heard us talk about the Old, Arcane Magic earlier, right?"

I nodded. "Yes, you said it's another source of magic that exists here in Ariadna."

"There are those who believe that the Old, Arcane Magic is the magic of the old Gods—Gods of the First Age of the Sangelis."

I frowned. "When Gwynn was explaining to me about the Gods and ages, she said that nothing was known about the First Age."

"She's right. It's believed that something catastrophic happened to wipe the old Gods from the Sangelis, but there are no records to say what. That being said, strains of the Old, Arcane Magic survived, and can be found here and in other places in the Sangelis. Just like there is light and dark magic, the Old, Arcane Magic has its dark elements. We call it the dark sway. Ancient beings like Gargmoin summon this type of magic. Tora, on the other hand, wields the light strain."

"So she is an ancient being like Gargmoin?"

"She is what she said—a spirit. She's what is known as a prime elemental spirit. Cazara Torannon has been in existence for over 50,000 years, and Tora has been here all that time, and long, long before that. The magic of both the Ethereal Harmonies and the Old, Arcane Magic runs through the walls of the house, and Tora bonded herself to the cazara when it was built. She is the heart of the house. Everything here is infused with her magic and the magic of the ruling Sovereign. As a result, Cazara Torannon is one of the most impenetrable places in all of Ariadna."

"She is definitely something. I've never met anyone like her."

He intertwined his fingers with mine. "I trust Tora with my life. And I trust her with yours. She might be raunchy and outspoken, but rest assured, you have nothing to fear from her."

"Is she someone who can help with getting my memories back?" I asked. In Falayen, he had told me that he needed the help of someone who understood the kind of magic Gargmoin wielded to properly heal my mind, that it was too dangerous to risk doing it on his own.

Ash's brows furrowed. "The only one with the power to destroy a rebounding curse this powerful is Lorien Reo, Lord of Dramhelm,"

Ash explained. "He is an ancient being like Tora, who also wields the light strain of the Old, Arcane Magic. He is the only one strong enough to trap and destroy Gargmoin's magic. His residence, Dramhelm Manor, is located in the Territories of Brus-Winnd."

My eyes flicked to his. "Isn't that where you're going to retrieve the Phantera?"

He nodded. "It was my intention to ask for his help."

"Can I come with you?"

His gaze drifted off toward the harbor. "The Territories are dangerous and volatile. The magic there is . . . temperamental. Did Catraia explain the phases of your transformation to you?"

I nodded. "Somewhat. She said that once I amass all the power that the Songbird of Valkyse has to offer, I will transition to the next level."

"Absorbing the power of the Old, Arcane Magic is the next phase," Ash explained. "That source of power runs rampant in the Territories. Its core is there. But you must complete this phase before you can move to the next."

"So I can't go to the Territories until I've completed this level of my transformation?"

"That's right. But there is a chance that we can make that happen before I leave to go there. Let me think on it and talk to Tora tomorrow. I don't want to delay getting your memories restored."

My heart soared at the prospect. To have my memories back? To remember my life with Ash in it? I wanted that more than anything. What else did I have to do to complete this phase of my transformation? And realistically, could that be done by tomorrow?

A warm crackle of heat flickered from the other side of me, and for the first time, the delicate wall of languid fire at the other end of the balcony drew my attention. "Is that Tora's magic?" I asked, studying the soft, flickering flames that climbed the right side of the balcony in a translucent trellis, throwing warmth in our direction.

He smiled. "Yes, that's hers. Probably her idea of setting the mood."

I laughed, and my mind replayed her comment about soundproofing the room.

He offered me his glass, and when I took it from him to take a sip, he reached out and grabbed a fistful of my hair. "I like your hair this color," he said, nuzzling his face against my head.

Right. My violet hair! "How did that happen? And my eyes—I never had flecks of silver in my eyes before."

"It's part of your transformation," he said. "Your human body is adapting to the magic of Ariadna. Physical changes are part of the first phase of your metamorphosis."

I placed the glass on the side table next to the chaise. "So does that mean my lifespan will change and I will start aging slower?"

He traced the outline of my eyebrow with his thumb. "Thirty is the age when everything slows down for Ariadnans aging-wise. It's considered full adulthood, and at that time, we enter the period of life longevity that we call caltisos. I don't think it's a coincidence that you're here right at that age. Over the coming weeks and months, you will start noticing a difference physically. More energy, stronger, more mentally alert. As well, because of our Gloweyen bond, our attraction to each other takes on a life of its own."

My eyes flitted to his and immediately, the roaring in my core surged, setting my blood on fire. I closed my eyes and tried to tamp it down. "Does our bond have a life of its own?" I asked, turning my attention to our entwined fingers.

He trailed his other hand over my robe to my waist, just

below my navel. "The source of your power resides deep in your core, here. When you're connected to that source, do you feel something stirring deep inside?"

My eyes went wide as I looked at him. Yes. The thing! The fearsome and untamed beast at the bottom of my lake of power.

His fingers traced small circles on my stomach. "I take it you know what I'm referring to. That thing is our Gloweyen bond. It resides within the depths of our power source. Remember when I first met you and I told you that my sense of discernment told me that you were my eternal soul's shadow?"

I nodded, looking at him in wonder.

"That was the first time I felt the stirring inside me. The second time was at my coronation when the Ethereal Harmonies returned the two labrals. It has been awake since then, even when I came to you in the human world. Acceptance of the labral is acceptance of the Gloweyen bond. It is what gives the bond life."

"So our bond is a living thing," I whispered, placing my hand over his on my stomach.

"Yes, and just like your magic, it needs to be honed and trained. If left unchecked, the power of that beast could overwhelm you. The only time we can set it loose is in Alonai."

"The lake?" I asked. "Why there?"

"The waters of the lake of rejuvenation are steeped in power—the raw essence of the Ethereal Harmonies, to be exact. When we consummate our union there, we set the beasts of our bond loose. In that moment, they are given free rein; that is how we amass our joint Gloweyen powers."

"You said we needed to wait until after the coronation, and that we had to be in Alonai. But we've had sex before. Why do we have to wait now?"

Ash's gaze met mine. "Our Gloweyen bond only clicked into

place when you put your labral on today, so we could have sex before today because you had not accepted the bond yet. Although the beast of my bond has been awake for a long time, without its other half, it was, for the most part, powerless. As for why we have to wait until your coronation, it's because that is when your powers as Sovereign queen are consecrated by the Ethereal Harmonies. I don't know if Oletho explained this, but at a Sovereign's coronation, after the labral bonding ceremony in the Pavilion of Harmonies, the Sovereign visits Falayen, where his powers are fully imbued upon him in Alonai. I told you before that Gloweyen is a very primitive and hedonistic connection, and as Gloweyen Sovereigns, not only do we claim each other physically in Alonai, but so do the beasts of our bond."

A ripple of anticipation sluiced deep inside me, as if my creature was responding to his words, clucking in contentment. My mind flashed back to my encounter with the God of Chaos, when I'd felt the presence of the beast. It was angry, had tried to incite and provoke Caz.

"Does the bond have the power to protect us?"

"The beasts of our Gloweyen bond exist for one purpose—to honor and preserve our union. They will lash out at anything threatening that."

I grew quiet, letting his words sink in.

"Did something happen with the God of Chaos?" he asked softly, his eyes watching me intently.

"Yes," I said, as his body grew still beside me. "What's my essence, Ash?"

His eyes narrowed. "What did he tell you?"

I chewed on my lip. "He said that my essence was blinding, and that he could see my tendrils, particularly my darkness. And then he called me pathetic because I didn't know how to use my power."

I choked on the last few words, my eyes welling with tears.

"Don't you dare, Elle," Ash said softly, his fingers brushing against my cheek. "Don't you shed a single tear because of that sack of shit's cruel words."

"But he's right, Ash. I don't know anything about my power." My voice was a whisper, my vulnerability raw and exposed.

Ash clasped my head, lowering his face against my cheek, kissing my tears away. "Do you know what I see when I look at you?"

I didn't answer, unable even to conjure something humorous to say.

His emerald eyes gazed into mine, so full of heated emotion, I couldn't look away.

"I see what I've always seen—raw, untamed power, fierce and wild. He's right—you *are* blinding, but you are *glorious* to behold. You are many things, Tialla, but pathetic isn't one of them."

His lips trailed a path to my mouth, and then slanted over mine. I opened for him, and his tongue swept into my mouth as he kissed me, his hand cupping my cheek. I wrapped my arms around his neck, burying my hands in his dark hair, savoring the spicy-sweet taste of him. His tongue tangled with mine, and I groaned against his lips, tugging on his bottom lip with my teeth.

Slowly, he pulled away and looked at me. His thumb traced my lips as he shifted me, pulling me closer to his chest. "Every living being possesses an aura," he explained. "That aura can be seen and felt by beings of power. Essence is different from auras. In beings of great power, their essence is a physical manifestation of their magic that is visible around their body," he explained. "Each being of power has an essence, whether they can see it or not. The more powerful the being, the bigger and brighter the essence, and it manifests around them in cloud-like tendrils."

I frowned, looking at him for signs of his essence. "Why can I not see mine? Or yours, for that matter? I can feel yours, but I can't see it."

"Until you receive the blessing of the elemental spirits of Ariadna, which is the remaining step in this phase of your transformation, you won't be able to."

"Elemental spirits? Is that what you said Tora was?"

"She is a prime elemental spirit—the only one of her kind. Five elemental spirits exist. They act as protectors of Ariadna. Land, air, water, fire, and ether are their domains, one spirit for each element."

"Did you have to get their blessing?"

"I was born a son of Ariadna—their blessing was given at my birth."

"So how do I receive their blessing?" I asked. "Is there some type of formal ceremony like the coronation?"

"They will come to you of their own accord when they are ready," he said. "Although, if Tora has any say, that will be sooner rather than later. That's what I want to talk to her about tomorrow."

I frowned. "Why is that?"

He ran his fingers gently through my hair. "Tora is the *only* prime elemental spirit. She has dominion over all five elements, although she chose Cazara Torannon as her abode. She can commune with the other spirits; they revere her. If she summons them, they will come."

It was amazing how many layers there were to everything. The magnitude of all the things I had to learn was overwhelming.

"Ash," I said, turning my head to look at him. "Did I have an essence when you came to me in the human world?"

His fingers grazed the base of my neck. "Yes. It was very faint, but it had the same signature it does now."

"So you could see it?"

"Yes, and feel it. Your essence changes subtly with your moods; the signature of it is the same, but it changes color, and your feelings are amplified."

My eyes grew wide. "Wait. So you can tell any kind of mood I'm in? Can other beings with power do that?"

He chuckled softly. "Fortunately, it's just me, because of the Gloweyen bond. The very first time you came to me before my coronation, your essence was bright, but that's probably because you were already in Ariadna, even though we were years apart. When I came to you on Earth, your essence was fainter, but at that point, I'd already accepted my labral. The beast of my bond was awakened inside me, and it knew you as my eternal soul's shadow."

"So I've always been an open book to you?"

He cocked his head to the side. "Does that upset you?"

Did it? In one way, it felt like a violation of my private emotions that my moods were always on display for him, but was that any different than two people who were in tune with each other so deeply that they *knew* each other's moods? Or someone who wore their feelings on their sleeve? Innately, I knew Ash wasn't the type who would take advantage of me that way.

I curled my feet under me and moved closer to him. "No, it doesn't upset me."

He tilted my chin to look at him. "You know I'd never—"

"I know," I said, lifting my head to kiss his chin. "I do have one more question I want to ask."

He studied me for a long moment. "You're afraid," he said softly, taking my hand in his. "What do you want to know?"

I looked at him, my skin clammy and warm, a lump forming in my throat. I was scared, yes, but I needed to know. "What is the darkness that lives inside me?"

Chapter 31

MY HEART THUDDED IN my chest as I waited for Ash to answer. I felt sick, my stomach roiling nervously. I was no stranger to darkness; I'd meant that last night when I said it to Ash. After Liam died, all the light in my life had winked out. Until the night the Goddess Eolith visited me in my dreams, I'd been drowning in sorrow and darkness.

She planted a seed of hope in my heart, but I'd still lived in a state of depression and sadness afterward. The only thing that kept me going was the hope that a better future awaited me. The state of my life was marginally better at the time I walked into Crusoe's that night after work. Everything after that, I had no recollection of.

Since I'd been in Ariadna, mention of my darkness was made several times. The Cloryals had said that within my dark heart, a grain of hope fluttered inside me, floundering to survive. Earlier, Ash said the Goddess Eolith told him that darkness had spread its inky wings over my soul after Liam died, something that troubled her greatly. The celestial star etching spoke of me being born of light and darkness, and said that without Catraia, darkness would prevail in the Sangelis. Catraia herself told me that she was responsible for keeping the darkness I wielded from encroaching into my heart. She, too, called me light and darkness, curator of death. And then there was the God of Chaos, who told me that

I couldn't hide my darkness from him, that it stood out against the light of my essence. He'd even offered his advice of fighting darkness with darkness.

I stared at Ash, my eyes wide with trepidation.

He reached for me, his hand cupping the back of my head. "Listen to me, Elle. As long as Catraia is a part of you, you have nothing to worry about. She is called the Anchor for a reason."

I gripped the edges of his robe with my fists. "What if it's too much? The darkness inside me. Ash, all I remember is darkness. I can barely recall my life before Liam. Life with my aunt Mags and with my parents. They feel like a dream. Isn't that fucked up? Happiness feels like a dream to me. Even you and me—whatever happiness we had is lost to me." I choked on a sob, my breath hitching in my throat.

He pulled me into his arms, his lips pressed against my temple. "We'll face whatever comes together, Tialla. You're not alone anymore."

His hands tangled in my hair, pulling me closer. I held on for dear life, needing his closeness, his warm touch, his calming presence, his love for me that pulsed out of him like a beacon, calling me home.

"I want to explain something to you that hopefully will make you feel better." He trailed his hand down my back, his fingers gliding up and down in a soothing rhythm.

I lay my head on his chest, listening to the steady thumping of his heart against my ear. I buried my face against his warm skin, my body relaxing in the safety of his embrace.

"Inside every living being, there is light and darkness. An ordinary person with a strong moral compass and firm grasp of right and wrong walks easily in the light. Even so, for that person, a small slip in the darkness may not have crippling ramifications.

Someone like me, on the other hand, who wields considerable power, needs to exert more control to keep the darkness in check. Especially in situations where emotions are high. An entity such as Catraia is that part of a being with extreme power that keeps them in check. Hence, the term, 'the Anchor.' She is your conscience, your moral compass, the inner voice that guides you. And when you use your power, she is the part that reins you in, keeps your power grounded in the light. Power is dangerous, especially the world-altering kind. Wielding extreme power can be exhilarating, and if someone is not careful, they can easily cross that line into the darkness. You, however, have Catraia, and you have me. You do not shoulder the burden of greatness alone." He tipped my head up, his eyes glittering with strength and determination. "Do not let your fear keep you in its rusted cage, my love. You were meant to fly."

I shivered at his words, leaning into his steadying warmth.

Asher is right, Eleyse, Catraia said reassuringly in my mind. *Do not be afraid. You are a child of the light, and even a sliver of light chases the darkness away. As well, there is a big distinction between darkness and evil, and evil is something that is not a part of your core nature. In almost all living creatures, even if they are mired in consuming darkness, there is always a path back to the light. Remember that.*

A ragged breath escaped my lips as a fledgling peace seeped into my heart. It felt as if a heavy weight was lifted, and I sank into myself, a sense of calm settling over me.

"The truth of who you are, Tialla, is in here." Ash's hand came to rest over my heart. "You get to decide who that is."

The Goddess Eolith had said something similar. *You will be many things to many living beings, but to yourself, you are whomever you choose to be. Never forget that. That omnipotence lies within you.*

Shifting my weight, I turned to face Ash. His handsome face shone with love and acceptance, and a surge of wonder tumbled me in its wake. This beautiful creature was mine. What had I done to deserve him?

"Thank you, Ash," I whispered.

"For what?" he asked, stroking my jaw with his knuckles.

"For finding me, saving me, loving me."

"I can say the same thing to you."

He pulled me onto his lap, and I placed my legs on either side of him, holding his face in my hands. He wrapped his arms around me, burying his face in my neck. I tangled my hands in his hair, savoring the feel of his body against mine, the contentment that came from being with him.

I had spent all my life believing certain truths about myself. Truths that I now needed to unlearn, and do so quickly. I understood why I felt safe and invincible with Ash. He had known the truth of who I was for close to a century; it was all he believed about me. I was drawn to that—his unshakeable faith and trust in who I was and what I was capable of. He made me see past my insecurities and fears, made me want to be the woman he saw.

I slowly pushed him against the backrest of the chaise, running my hands up around his neck. Leaning forward, I pressed my lips against his chest, moving up to his collarbone, his neck, his jaw. I pulled back and looked at him, and I swore I heard the beast inside me cry out as a rush of heat coursed through me.

"There it is," he said with a smile, meeting my gaze. "Your desire has a color, you know. Fiery orange."

I ran my hands over his chest, his voice fanning the slow flame consuming me. "I don't have to see your essence to see your desire." I trailed my lips across his cheekbones. "It's all in your eyes. Your power flares to life when you want me." I nipped his earlobe with my teeth. "Plus, your cock is a dead giveaway." I ground my hips against his to prove my point, the rigid length of his erection digging into my thigh.

He laughed quietly, his hands gripping my hips and holding me in place, letting me take the lead.

I pushed his open robe off his shoulders, and he shrugged his arms out of it, his upper body bare to me.

"God, Ash, you are so gorgeous," I whispered reverently, running my hands over his chest and down his stomach. As my fingers moved over his skin, the throbbing between my legs grew more intense, heated waves of wetness pooling there.

His eyes blazed as he looked at me. His hands trailed down my thighs, and I watched them as they moved, mesmerized by the sight of his long fingers and the prominent veins along his hands and forearms.

"What do you want, Elle?" he whispered, his voice low and tantalizing, inciting the beast inside me. My eyes flew to his lips, soft and pillowy against his golden skin, and I bit the inside of my cheek, thinking about his mouth on every inch of my body.

"I can't have what I want," I said with a shiver, my chest barely grazing his.

His lips twitched. "Tell me anyway. I do so enjoy your sexual commentary."

My face grew serious as I stared at him. "I want your cock buried to the hilt inside me, slamming into me over and over, until my pussy is numb and my voice is hoarse from screaming your name, and I pass out from coming."

He groaned, his body growing still as he trailed his hands up my torso. "That's definitely the beast inside you coloring your thoughts."

"Well, I think she's very articulate and descriptive."

"She certainly nailed it."

I shifted my hips and dragged my throbbing core over his erection, a jolt of pleasure ripping through me. Fuck. There was no way I was going to be able to control myself.

"How long do we have to wait for a coronation?" I asked, my voice low and raspy. "Please don't tell me two years."

"Fuck, no," he said, his voice tight with restraint. "It has to be as soon as possible, so we can amass all the power we can before the Convergence. A week, max. We can make it happen."

"Thank fuck," I said.

I immediately shut out all other fears of threats and wars and Gods. I just wanted to be here in the moment with Ash, reveling in him.

I ran my hands through his short, dark hair, trailing the tip of my tongue down his neck. His hands moved up my thighs, caressing lightly and then flitting back down, avoiding the heat between my legs.

My frustration mounted, and it must have shown on my face because a flutter of laughter escaped his lips.

"Something wrong?" he asked innocently.

I grabbed his hand and lifted it to my lips, kissing his palm.

He arched a brow as he looked at me.

"Can I borrow these fingers real quick?" I asked, closing my hand around his index and middle fingers and pressing my lips against the tips of them.

His eyes swirled with heat, and his expression grew turbulent. "My fingers or tongue?" he asked, his lips curving suggestively.

A blast of pleasure tore through me at his words and I grimaced, trying to squeeze my legs together, but failing because they were spread wide across him. Shit. The way my body was reacting, it would get to its destination without any contact at all.

With my fingers still wrapped around his, I unbelted my robe with my other hand, pulling it open. I had taken Tora's advice and chosen not to wear the nightgown—or anything else, for that matter.

He groaned, his eyes liquid fire as they devoured my flesh, lust blazing in his stare.

I lowered my face to his. "I'm borrowing your fingers. I want your tongue in my mouth."

I kissed him, gripping his fingers and dragging them down my body to my throbbing wetness. Another tremor of pleasure rocked me as his fingers pressed against me, and I moaned at the same time Ash growled against my mouth.

Desperate for release, I lost myself to the feel of his fingers on my clit, quickly thrusting my hips forward. One . . . two . . . I barely made it to three before my climax ripped through me, rushing like the waters of a demolished dam through my body. I spasmed and shuddered, gripping his fingers with my hands as I rolled my hips and ground against his hand, riding out the waves of my release.

I collapsed against his chest, my body limp. His heartbeat hammered against mine, and for a moment, we were both still.

His breath stirred the tendrils of hair near my forehead. "I feel used. I barely played a hand that round."

I laughed, the fine hair on his chest tickling my nose. "Trust me, baby. You were the catalyst for that orgasm. My sexual muse, so to speak. At any given time, all you have to do is just *be*, and my body goes wild for you."

He chuckled, his voice low as he growled, "Enjoy your rest. I'm counting to sixty, and then I get to have my way with you."

A ripple of excitement snaked through me. "Why sixty?"

"Because that's how long you need to recover before having your clit touched again."

I groaned. Clearly, he knew my body very well.

He brushed his mouth against mine, his tongue grazing my lips. "Be warned. Forty-five more seconds, and that pussy is mine."

Holy hell, I loved his dirty talk; it made my body sing for him. I could feel how slick and wet I was.

He slipped his fingers under the fabric of my robe and slid it off my shoulders. A swirl of cool air caressed my skin, and I lifted myself onto my knees, my hands caressing his jaw as his tongue tangled with mine.

He pulled away, his gaze heated and breath shallow as his eyes snaked over my skin. Every part of me tingled from his thorough scrutiny. "Gods, I've missed your body. You are perfection, Tialla." His fingers cupped my breasts, and I moaned at the contact, almost jumping out of my skin when he rolled his thumbs over my aching nipples.

I threw my head back, the friction of his fingers sending pulses of pleasure skittering straight to my core. I gripped his face, angling him to my breast.

"Always so impatient," he whispered, pinching my nipple, causing me to cry out.

"Ash," I rasped, my nails gripping the back of his shoulders.

"Don't worry, baby. I know what you like."

"Then give it to me," I cried.

"Demanding too," he said as he pulled my body closer, lowering his mouth to my nipple. I could not tear my eyes away as he slowly rolled his tongue over the hardened flesh, licking, flicking, before taking it into his mouth and sucking gently. I moaned loudly, and he smiled, moving his mouth to my other breast.

His hand trailed down my stomach, and I almost jumped out of my skin when his fingers slipped between my legs, parting my lips and sliding over my clit.

"Oh, dear God," I cried, my hips moving of their own accord against his fingers. All the while, his mouth lavished attention on my breasts, kissing, licking, sucking.

He flipped me onto my back abruptly, his eyes glazed over with desire. "Sorry, Tialla," he said, his voice deep and raspy. "I'll go mad if I don't taste you."

He parted my legs and moved down my body, burying his head between my thighs, his mouth licking up and down my slit before clamping down in a tight suction, settling on me like a man stumbling upon an oasis after wandering the desert for days. His tongue slid inside me in slow and languid pulses, and I gripped his hair in my hands, shamelessly grinding myself against his face.

"Oh, God," I groaned, lifting onto my elbows to watch him.

His eyes locked onto mine, and he smiled wickedly as he spread me with his fingers, swirling his tongue over my swollen, aching flesh. Slipping two fingers inside me, he plunged into my slick heat, filling me, sliding in and out as his tongue sucked and swirled over my clit.

My blood pounded in my ears, my entire body spellbound by the delectable havoc his mouth and fingers were wreaking on me.

He lifted his head. "See. Fingers *and* tongue work well together."

Damn straight, they did. His long fingers were magic as they pumped into me with ruthless ferocity. And as for that tongue of his—it was a well-oiled machine, glorious and masterful in both efficiency and technique.

"Come for me, Elle," he said, lifting his head, his eyes flashing with barely restrained hunger.

I arched my hips off the chaise, moaning as his fingers curled inside me. My body was restless and hot, my head flailing from side to side as my release built inside me.

"Ash!" I cried frantically, wrapping my legs around his shoulders as I rode his face and fingers, my orgasm erupting in a sea of light and color as it stampeded through me. Uncontrollable spasms gripped me and I pushed his face away, fighting for control as I ground my fingers against the throbbing part of me, the aftershocks of my release slashing through me in relentless fury.

He slowly inched his way up my body, the hard length of his arousal brushing against my thigh. Unable to stop myself, I pushed at the waistband of his pants, causing his cock to spring free. As my eyes drank in the thick, rigid length of him, a rush of wild need hit me full blast, and the beast of my bond—that sexual banshee—roared to life inside me, letting out a keening wail. Demanding to be set free.

I lost all control, the need to have Ash inside me overruling everything. Of its own accord, my hips lifted as my body fought to be joined with his.

Raging heat coursed through me and the blood pounded in my ears, pummeling me into submission. "Ash," I cried, my eyes wide and desperate as I fought to regain control.

"Fuck," he said, pressing me into the chaise, angling his body away from mine.

The pounding in my head was relentless, my body flooded with searing heat. My vision blurred and nothing but single-minded, manic *want* consumed me.

"Catraia," I called, clutching my head frantically.

"It's okay, Elle," Ash whispered. He pressed his fingers to my temple, and immediately, a rush of warmth seeped into my mind, calming me, grounding me.

Just relax, Eleyse, Catraia whispered inside me.

"Catraia, send her beast back to the deep," Ash said.

The heated whirlwind of chaos left me instantly, and a welcome stillness washed over me.

Ash moved on his side next to me, his brows furrowed as he brushed my hair away from my face.

"What the hell was that?" I asked, my voice a terrified whisper.

He brushed his lips against my forehead. "That, Tialla, was a close call. That is why we shouldn't play with fire." His fingers drifted to my temple, rubbing gently. "Sleep now, Elle."

Chapter 32

THE SOFT, GAUZY CURTAIN of dawn was descending when I opened my eyes, and I squinted in the muted darkness. Immediately, I felt it—the cool splash of tingly mint swirling in my mouth. How crazy and clever was that? The magic here was truly . . . thoughtful? Practical?

I was in Ash's bedroom, in his bed, with him. His warmth next to me was delectable, inviting, luring me in like a siren's song. I shifted closer, and he murmured softly in his sleep, pulling me to him. I wrapped my arm around his waist, resting my head on his chest.

Soaking in the clean, crisp smell of him, I listened to the calming rhythm of his heartbeat as it thudded against my ear, felt the steady rise and fall of his chest as he breathed. I loved being in his arms. Here, in the stillness of the fracturable solitude, a peace like I'd never known radiated through me. I felt safe. Cherished. Happy.

Ever so slowly, I tilted my head to look at him, his face shrouded in pale light. A lock of hair grazed his forehead, and I fought the urge to brush it aside with my fingers. His long lashes framed his high cheekbones, the early morning shadows accentuating the sharp planes and angles of his handsome face. His mouth was full and sensual even in sleep, and I was tempted to trace his lips in repose. He looked completely relaxed.

My mind flitted back to last night. Being with Ash was magical, intoxicating, and thrilling. It was everything I'd hoped for—well, up until the madness ensued. I'd come really close to screwing things up. Again, because I had no control over my power. It's *pathetic how little you know of your power.* The God of Chaos wasn't wrong. On the contrary, I kept proving him right.

Enough with the self-hate, Eleyse, Catraia whispered in my mind.

Wait. Wasn't she supposed to prevent that sort of thing from happening? Keeping my powers in check or something?

Let's be clear on a few things. As far as last night goes, Asher explained the situation and the risks to you, cautioned against physical intimacy, but you insisted. You made the choice to tempt fate, placing your trust in him to prevent anything unfortunate from happening. I had the utmost faith in Asher's ability to protect you in this matter, and if I'd felt that he wasn't capable, I would have said something.

As much as I hated to admit it, she was right. My all-consuming need to be with Ash physically had overruled any reason. I should have listened to him and repressed my urges.

That is not what I'm saying, Eleyse. When it comes to your intimate relationship with your Gloweyen king, that is between the two of you. I will not get involved or meddle, unless there is a situation that threatens your safety.

So . . . what exactly are you getting at? I asked her. Clearly, things like this needed to be spelled out for me.

That I trust Asher not to put you both in a precarious situation he couldn't handle. That being said, recklessness cannot define your choices. There are many situations when Asher will not be there to save you, and as part of honing your abilities, you must get in the habit of weighing your choices carefully before acting. All actions have consequences, and you cannot take that lightly, especially when you wield the kind of power you do.

She was right. I had taken reckless chances with my life for as long as I could remember, placing little to no value on myself. But my actions didn't just impact me anymore; I needed to be mindful of that.

Two things will keep you grounded, Eleyse. Me, and Asher. When it comes to the beast of your bond, you must learn to control it. It exists to preserve your Gloweyen union, and is as much a part of you as I am.

Shit. At this rate, I would have a menagerie of living creatures taking up residence inside me in no time!

This is a delicate time right now, so learning to master the beast is crucial.

How do I do that?

Acknowledge it. Communicate with it. Respect it. Assert your control. Show no fear. It bows to you, not the other way around. I'll leave you in peace now to determine how you do that.

I considered what she'd said. Yes, I'd sensed the beast inside me, but I *was* afraid, not just of the beast, but of the wellspring of power inside me. And yet, with Catraia, fear was never a factor. Alarm, curiosity, skepticism, but not fear. Okay. First thing—I needed to give the beast a name. I couldn't keep calling it a beast, for cripes' sake.

But what was a good beast name, though? It was also a sexual beast, so maybe a good stripper name, like Cinnamon or Jade or Sparkle. No. I had it! Vixen. Yes. Vixen. Vix. I liked it. Feisty and Powerful. Right. So now that I had a name, I needed to communicate with it.

I carefully rolled away from Ash and lay on my back, closing my eyes as I delved inside myself. I took a deep breath, arriving at my lake of power. My breathing slowed as I looked out over the surface of the lake, visualizing myself peering into that dark bedrock near the bottom. My heart skipped a beat when a crimson eye cracked open. *There you are.*

The eye stared back, still and unblinking, waiting.

You almost got us in big trouble last night, I whispered.

A soft chuff filled my mind.

Vix. That's what I'm calling you. It suits you, don't you think?

A moment of silence passed and then the lake rippled as a feeling like approval filled me. A quiet chuckle escaped me as the lunacy of what I was doing hit me. God. If I was back home, they'd throw me in a straitjacket and lock me away. Talking to voices and creatures in my head.

I felt Vix's attention on me, waiting, assessing. I inhaled deeply.

Right . . . Now, I know you want to get it on with . . .

Crap. Now I had to come up with a name for Ash's beast. Did he already have a name for it? He didn't say. Hmmm . . .

Well, what about Magnus, or Rider or— Oh, *what about Zeus, Vix? Zeus is the God of Gods where I'm from.*

A quiet huff reached me—dissatisfaction? Okay. So she didn't like Zeus.

Yeah, you're right. Bad choice. Zeus was a piece of shit philanderer. We don't need that namesake tainting our boys. What about the other two, though? Rider? Could be a great pun! I giggled at my own joke. *You know—because he's killer at riding.*

Nothing. I guess she didn't get it. Either that, or she didn't care for my sense of humor.

What about Magnus, then? I like that one.

A slow moment passed, and then like before, a gentle ripple shook the surface of the lake and approval seeped in. Great! This was incredible. Now we had names. Vix and Magnus it was.

In my mind, connected to the source of my power, Vix opened

both her slitted crimson eyes and stared at me. I couldn't visualize anything other than her eyes. She was shapeless, formless, without solid substance. She just *was*. And yet those eyes told me everything I needed to know. She was great and beautiful and terrible all at once. The pulse of her power rippled through my lake, filling me with awe.

Okay. Time to put the big girl pants on, as per Catraia's advice. Assert control. I could be in control. I had this.

I gazed into those crimson eyes still watching me warily. *Now, Vix, what happened last night can't happen again. Not until I set you free in Alonai. Then you can unleash yourself on Magnus to your heart's content. At least, I think so. I'm not really sure how it works or what actually happens, to be honest.*

Desire, like erupting blossoms, spread like wildfire through me, sending shivers of heat skating across my skin. What the hell? I crossed my legs as the throbbing in my center pounded and waves of heat tumbled me. Heavens. The bitch had it bad. Maybe I didn't have this.

Stop, Vix, I commanded, visualizing myself plunging both hands into my lake of power and freezing the plummeting depths.

Vix roared in protest, her discontent flooding my senses, pushing back against me, testing how far she could go.

Direct more of your power and will at her, Eleyse, Catraia said in my mind. *You need to see and believe what you want to happen to make it so. Embody the powerful creature that you are. Sink into your skin, Celestial Songbird, High Queen of the Light Age.*

I absorbed Catraia's words as I stood at the edge of my lake of power. *Sink into my skin.* She was right. I couldn't be tentative or afraid. Rippling my power with my finger or my hands was not going to do it. I was going to have to get wet.

Without a moment of hesitation, I dove in, immersing myself in my lake. A blast of energy enveloped me, eddies of power whipping around me, seeping into every pore, and I closed my eyes and soaked in every drop. My body hummed and vibrated with power, my skin tingly and weightless.

That's it, Eleyse, Catraia said, approval in her voice. *Now command her to do your will.*

In my mind, I found Vix, her crimson eyes alert as she studied me with curiosity. I reached out my hand. *Listen, Vix. Your time will come. I promise. And when it does, I will set you free to go to Magnus, but until then, when I'm with Ash, I'm in control.*

She stared at me for the longest while, and finally, the slits of her eyes contracted as she let out a soft huff. I tasted her reluctant submission, and a surge of triumph coursed through me. I'd done it.

Not quite, Catraia said. *You've acknowledged her, communicated with her with respect, given her an identity, defined boundaries. That doesn't mean she will obey. Until your Gloweyen powers have been consecrated, things will remain volatile and unpredictable. You will have to test the waters to know for sure that you can make her yield. I will say this now, Eleyse, and it applies not just to your interaction with the beast of your bond, but with every situation. Yes, Asher is bound to protect you—he will fight to the death for you—but you shouldn't sit back and rely on him to do so—you have the power within you to protect yourself. Learning to use your powers will be a trial by fire. We do not have the luxury of time. The first step is for you to believe in yourself. Believe that your life has meaning and that this is the truth of who you are. Everything else will come.*

She was right. Knowing and believing were two different things, and I needed a mindset shift to take me from the first to the second.

I released my connection to my power and opened my eyes. I

jumped, my heart lurching in surprise.

Ash lay propped up on his elbow next to me, watching me with keen interest. "I'm entirely fascinated and curious to know what's going on here," he said, a smile curving his lips. He wrapped a fistful of my hair around his hand.

My eyes flew to the muscles in his shoulders and chest flexing as he moved, my body heating. Frigging hell. How could I think I could control Vix when I had no control over myself when it came to him?

"What do you mean?" I asked, captivated by the intense shade of his eyes in the soft light of morning.

He stroked my cheek. "I felt a strong surge of your power, and for a moment, I thought you were in trouble, but as I watched you, you looked . . . serene, in control."

"Oh, that," I said nonchalantly, as if it was something mundane he'd witnessed. "I was just talking to Catraia and getting on a first name basis with Vix." My fingers hightailed it across his broad chest, luxuriating in his satiny smooth skin.

He arched a brow. "Vix?"

I nodded. "That's what I called her. The beast of my bond. Catraia told me that I needed to talk to her and show her I was boss, so that's what I was doing."

He chuckled, lifting his hand to stroke my fingers against his chest. "You're serious?"

"You haven't done that with yours?" I asked, shifting onto my side.

"Well, no. I don't have full-on conversations with it. I acknowledge it's a part of me, I sense its desires and motivations; it responds to mine. There's just an unspoken connection between it and me, just like there is with all my power."

"Huh," I said, nodding gently. "Well, I had to give yours a name because mine has a name, so Vix and I both settled on Magnus. She approves, by the way. She didn't like my other choices."

Ash's eyes twinkled with disbelief and mirth as a throaty, rumbling laugh boomed out of him. "Gods, Elle, not for one second do I want to forget how delightful and entertaining you are."

"Are you making fun of me?" I cried, smacking his chest.

"Never, Tialla," he said kissing my fingers. "I just never communicated with my power that way. But I can understand why you would. Catraia is a very real presence inside you, so it would make sense that you would use the same approach with the beast of your bond."

"First of all, I'd like to remind you that her name is Vix," I said, tilting my head up. "And you know what—I was talking to the voices in my head long before I ever met Catraia, so this all feels pretty natural. You watch and see, Ash, you'll take back laughing at me when you see the method to my madness." I moved my hand down his stomach. "I bet I can even get Magnus to respond to me. Isn't that right, Magnus?" I swirled my fingers on Ash's lower stomach.

Ash shook his head, a soft chuckle breezing past his lips. "What else did Catraia say?"

"Oh, the usual type of wise and insightful stuff Catraia says. She did tell me that I would need to test out my powers of commanding Vix. She basically gave us permission to play with fire is what I took away."

"Is that so?" Ash said, grabbing me by the waist and pulling me on top of him. "How can I refuse a beautiful, naked Goddess such a proposition? I have twenty-five minutes before I need to meet my uncle. Ten of them are yours."

I brushed my lips against his, excitement building inside me. "I'll only need five. But this time, it's *my* turn to play."

His gaze heated as he looked at me and pushed himself into an upright position against his pillows, hands behind his head. My eyes were still fastened on his as I trailed a path with my mouth down his body.

Oh God, Catraia, please stand by to shut things down if they go horribly wrong, I whispered in my mind. *And Vix, you better behave.*

I could feel the beast's excitement spiking as I slid my body against Ash's, and as I kissed my way down his stomach, I closed my eyes and delved into myself, arriving at my lake of power. Only after I dove in and was securely connected did I allow myself to open my eyes.

My hands rubbed against Ash's erection through the soft fabric of his pants. I watched as his eyes grew dark and stormy, a flash of power flaring in its depths.

"I see you, Magnus," I whispered with a smile, blowing Ash a kiss.

He groaned. "Did you ever think that talking to my beast might incite him more than soothe him?"

"You know, I did not think things through that far," I said, moving my hands down to fondle his balls. "How about I concentrate on my beast and you wrangle yours?"

He levelled me with a glare even as he groaned in contentment. I tugged at the drawstring of his pants, sliding my hands beneath his waistband to pull them down. His cock sprang free—rock hard and glorious—and for a moment, I stared in wonder, captivated by what a perfect balance between magnificence and practicality he was. I didn't care what anyone said, there was such a thing as being *too big.* Stupid God of Chaos with his ginormous dick. Seriously, who enjoyed getting split open like a coconut? To each his own, I guess. As for me, staring down at the sleek, wondrous specimen in front of me, I felt like Goldilocks digging into that bowl of porridge that was just right.

"Every part of you is so incredibly sexy," I whispered.

Vix surged inside me, and I turned my attention inward. *Don't you fucking dare, Vix,* I commanded. *I told you, I'm in charge.*

She jerked wildly, heating my blood and causing my heart to palpitate.

Stand down, I growled, immersed in my lake, directing my power at her, demanding her submission.

She chuffed loudly, making her discontent known, but I held firm, forcing my will onto her. Slowly, I felt her relent.

I curled my hand around Ash, gliding my fist up and down the hot length of him. His skin was smooth and soft, and I paused at the head, running my thumb across the ridge of sensitive skin.

"Elle," he groaned.

I replaced my fingers with my tongue, licking off the drizzle of liquid leaking from the tip. He fisted his hands in my hair as I licked him from tip to base and then took him into my mouth, sucking as I moved my lips down over him, my hand gripping the base.

Up and down I moved, hollowing my cheeks as I took him in deeper, sucking, swirling my tongue over him, even as he fought for control beneath me.

"Let go, Ash," I said, kneading his balls gently. "Fuck my mouth."

He hissed. "Fucking Gods, I love that dirty tongue of yours." Gripping my head, he thrust his hips forward, spearing his cock deep into my mouth.

My gag reflex kicked in as he hit the back of my throat, but I relaxed my jaw and muscles, determined to take all of him.

He pumped into my mouth three more times before exploding, his groan of pleasure shattering the room. His warm release pulsed out of him into my throat, and still I kept sucking, swallowing all of it down.

His breathing was ragged and shallow as he pulled me into his arms. "I take it back, Elle," he said kissing me. "You didn't lose control once. You are as wise as you are beautiful, Gloweyen Queen. There is absolutely a method to your madness."

Chapter 33

I HESITATED AT THE entrance to the informal dining room. Sunlight poured in from the open window, arcs of light slanting onto the rectangular dining table in the middle of the room. Faron, Gwynn, and Astrid conversed quietly as they ate, and Tora glided toward Faron's chair, her fingers reaching out to muss his blond hair.

She was wearing a simple sapphire-blue gown, fitted to her curves like a glove and trailing around her feet. Her silver-green hair flowed in soft waves around her shoulders. How someone could be so sophisticated and sinful at the same time confounded me. Her attire was a stark contrast from Gwynn, Astrid, and Faron—all three of them decked out in soft, dark leathers.

"Faron, my love, I had the most decadent dream last night," Tora said, her voice a seductive croon, her lips curling in a wicked smile. "I fell asleep at my chair with my head back, and when I opened my eyes, you were standing over me with not a stitch of clothing on, those comely balls of yours swinging in my face like a pendulum."

Faron spewed out a mouthful of water, erupting into a coughing fit, his strangled breaths tangling with Gwynn and Astrid's snickering. "Good Gods, Tora," he said in between a heave-riddled sputter of laughter. "You could have at least waited for me to finish drinking before you opened that lewd mouth of yours."

"Oh, trust me," she purred. "I opened my mouth, all right."

"You're such a fucking tease," Faron said, dabbing at his face with his napkin. "One of these days, that mouth is going to get you in trouble."

"I look forward to it, my beautiful stallion." She stroked his hair gently, brushing her lips against his cheek.

I couldn't help the chuckle that escaped me. She definitely was entertaining, I had to give her that.

"You ass!" Astrid exclaimed, glaring at Faron as she held up a soggy piece of toast between her thumb and forefinger. "You sprayed water in my food."

"Astrid, sweetheart," Tora said, making her way to the other side of the table. "You really have to stop being such a cunt. And I say that in the nicest way, darling. That cutting tone of yours, combined with your perpetual scowl, is enough to send anyone who comes in contact with you running for the hills. I wouldn't be surprised if the entrance to your pussy is woven shut with barbed Viperis spiderwebs."

"Suck it, Tora," Astrid retorted, her eyes flashing.

Tora crossed her arms. "Not with that attitude, I won't." Before I could even blink, she disappeared.

Faron's ensuing chuckle was short-lived, quickly transitioning into an outraged yelp as Astrid kicked him under the table. "Gods' balls, Ari."

"Come on, Astrid," Gwynn piped in. "Tora does have a point. Your default mode seems to be, 'Even look at me and I'll bite your head off.' You're wound way too tight."

"Oh, please. Look in a mirror, Gwynn."

I involuntarily took a step back, overcome with a feeling to leave. That had gotten dark and heated fast. Or maybe it just seemed that way. I wasn't used to familial bickering, so I really couldn't say.

"I wouldn't want to go in either if I were you," a deep voice whispered behind me as two strong arms snaked around my waist.

I turned my head to look at Ash, relaxing instantly at the small smile curving his lips. I sank into his warmth, his scent and presence flooding me with ease.

"Just another day in the life at Cazara Torannon." He spun me around to face him, lowered his head, and pressed his lips to mine quickly.

After we'd gotten out of bed earlier, he'd dressed quickly and gone down to meet with Andreo. Tryx had sauntered into the room to keep me company while I got ready, and I'd left her sprawled on the bed when I came down.

Ash took my hand and led me into the dining room. "I see we're off to a productive start this morning," he said dryly as he pulled out a chair for me next to his at the head of the table near the window. He pushed my chair in and then took his seat, looking at Gwynn, Astrid, and Faron with wry amusement.

"Tora started it, Ash," Astrid grumbled.

"She totally did," Faron added with a chuckle.

"And then she conveniently disappeared before you got here." Gwynn turned to look at me, a warm smile on her face. "You look well rested, Elle." Her eyes sparkled mischievously as she looked me up and down.

"I am. Slept like a baby." I nonchalantly scooped some eggs onto my plate.

Ash winked at me, and my heart immediately barreled into a somersault. God, I had it bad.

His face grew serious as he looked at the others. "We have a pretty intense few days ahead of us, but before getting into that, there are a couple things I want to say. First of all, I want to apologize. I'm sorry for keeping the three of you in the dark, particularly these past five months. I've been doing a lot of reflecting since yesterday, and Gwynn is right. We need to lean on each other; I need to trust in our ability to work as a team. We're stronger together. Including Andreo, the three of you are my family, and I need to put my fear aside and let you in."

"Ash, you know that there is nothing we wouldn't do for you," Faron said, leaning forward in his chair. "And now that includes Eleyse. I still can't get over that she is your fucking Gloweyen Queen!" He looked at me, his eyes shining with wonder and admiration. "Gwynn filled us in on everything last night. It's completely mind-blowing. Whatever you need from us, we are on board."

I could feel the acceptance and warmth radiating from Faron, but a bitter tang of disappointment hung in the air, and it was radiating from Astrid. She was toying with the food on her plate, refusing to make eye contact with anyone.

Ash exchanged looks with Faron and Gwynn before turning to her. "Ari," he said quietly, his tone softening as he looked at her.

She stiffened slightly before lifting her head. "You don't have to say a word, Ash. I agree with everything Faron said. That's all there is to say."

I watched the exchange between them, feeling a bit awkward by the intense emotions suffusing the room. From Ash, I sensed sorrow and regret, the feelings evident in his eyes. From Astrid, heartbreak and sadness, coupled with bitter resolve.

She has loved him for most of her life, Catraia whispered in my mind. *It will take her some time to accept what she has always known to be inevitable. I sense some indecision in her words. She doesn't agree with everything her brother said. She is completely loyal to Ash, but as far as that extending to you, there is some uncertainty.*

But you said yesterday that she could be trusted, I said in my mind.

That was yesterday; today, her heartbreak casts a shroud over everything else.

What does that mean?

Be wary and patient, but also compassionate.

"What else did you want to tell us?" Astrid said, her desperation to shift the attention away from herself evident.

Ash studied her for a moment before letting out a deep exhale. "Treye, Gilham, and Ovix will be here later today. Together, we'll discuss what our next course of action is. As Gwynn most likely filled you in last night, the Cloryals have commanded the Sovereigns to retrieve the Phanteras from their burial places." He grew silent, turning the food around his plate with his fork. "War is an inevitability. I saw it with my own eyes yesterday when I was in Kindrik. The Dark Shen are on the move. This time, there will be no secret infiltration. They have already gathered by the hundreds of thousands, even the dark beasts—all manner of them—coaxed out of their fetid marshes and sweltering crevasses and led by none other than Kaliope's new *ally*, Gargmoin. We must be ready."

I sensed the turmoil emanating from him. It rolled off him in waves, coating my tongue in the acidic tang of despair. I felt it—his worry and fear for the innocent lives that would be lost. I sensed it—the weight of that blood-soaked future on his shoulders.

"What about a Sovereign alliance?" Faron asked, his eyes thoughtful. "Have Solanis and Averon come around?"

Ash shook his head. "I'm still working on that," he said. "First and foremost, we have an emergency meeting with the Valkyse Council of Governors. Uncle Andreo is at Torannon Lyceum setting that up for this morning. After we're done there, I want to meet with all the generals of the Valkyse army. Faron, Astrid, I trust you to arrange that." His eyes flicked to his sister. "Wynn, I'll leave it with you whether you want to join us or stay with Elle." His eyes met mine, a deep intensity shining in those green orbs. "I don't want you to feel that you are being excluded, but right now, the fewer people that know about you, the better. We can't keep you a secret forever, but right now, you need to stay hidden."

I nodded, biting back a surge of fear. Things were moving forward. Ash had said war was an inevitability. Would I be ready? I knew nothing about war. Could I do this?

Ash must have sensed my trepidation because his leg brushed against mine under the table. I wrapped mine around his, siphoning off the safety and reassurance he communicated with his touch. In that moment, I understood one thing—Ash was my lifeline, and until I got to the point where I possessed some sense of comfort and confidence in my own abilities, I was going to hold on to him for dear life. I had no choice.

Chapter 34

ASHER

I STEPPED INTO MY study, the entrance magically sealing shut behind me. My mind, as always, drifted to Elle. A surge of possessiveness simmered to the surface, threatening to engulf me. Everything had been a whirlwind since she arrived in Ariadna. It was always a matter of time before she ended up here, but when and where was always an unknown.

I couldn't let her get hurt. There was so much she needed to learn about *everything*, and the fear that we wouldn't have enough time had burrowed into my gut like a carnivorous parasite. I would give my life to protect her from danger; that much was a foregone conclusion.

I sat behind my desk, the light from the Pisatine glowing red, drawing my attention at once. I touched the magical artifact, a feeling of unease flooding me. My Dulogrien only used red in their missives to convey grave news. Swallowing the lump in my throat, I placed my palm against the round crystal tablet, waiting for it to verify my identity.

A whorl of silver smoke encased my hand and quickly dissipated as the Pisatine recognized me. My blood ran cold at the three words etched on the magical sheaf in front of me.

Averon is compromised.

Fuck. I had hoped against hope that my fears would turn out to be unfounded, but Treye wouldn't have sent this message if he wasn't certain. Gods be damned. Madio Averon was a piece of shit.

Two months ago, all four Sovereigns had met in Torannon to discuss our plans to fortify our strongholds and borders, and to discuss combining our armies to fight as one united force. Ruskil Tandor allied with me; more than anyone else, he knew how dangerous Kaliope was. But would he face her in open war? I certainly hoped so.

My hope was that all four dominions would unite and fight under one banner. I left that meeting unsure if that could be a reality. Madio Averon was undecided; he felt that each Sovereign was capable and powerful enough of protecting his own borders. As for Dimas Solanis, he had the gall to propose that I make Kaliope my queen, voicing his belief that such a solution would put an end to any talk or threat of war.

Dimas was the oldest of all four Sovereigns. The enigmatic curmudgeon was over 2,100 years old and showed no signs of slowing down. He was conservative and reticent, and shied away from being in the public eye when it came to his private life. He took his official duties seriously, and that was the face he showed to all of Ariadna, resulting in no one being able to say that they really knew the surly bastard. Not even his fellow Sovereigns. In demeanor, he was guarded, reserved, and devoid of emotion.

Madio Averon, on the other hand, was entirely different. He was loud, outspoken, and considered the most controversial, yet progressive Sovereign of the four. He was still relatively young at 365, inheriting the rule about fifty years before I did. Openly friendly and outgoing, he had developed a reputation for being manipulative and self-serving. He made decisions based solely on whether it was in the best interest of Averon, and as a result, the three other Sovereigns kept him at arm's length. Of my fellow Sovereigns, he was the one I worried about the most. He was a wild card, and for the longest while, I feared him forming an alliance with Kaliope if it proved to be advantageous to the Dominion of Averon. Now, those fears were coming true.

Just as I was sure that full-scale war would not be unleashed until the Convergence, I was also certain that Kaliope had something planned for before that. She was well-versed in the art of distraction and would use it in her favor where she could. The element of surprise was a sharp-edged weapon in the creya's arsenal of horrors, and she would use it fully to her advantage. I didn't even want to think about what she'd done to seduce the Sovereign of Averon to her side.

Catching movement out of the periphery of my eye, I looked up to see Tora appearing in the corner of the room from where she glided through the walls. Her face, as always, was warm and playful, but there was a seriousness in her eyes I didn't miss.

"I trust Sovereign playtime went well last night, my ravishing king?" she said, coming to a stop in front of my desk.

I smiled, shaking my head at her. "I trust you kept your ears and eyes to yourself?"

She frowned. "I told you, Smolders. I only peeked in and listened for a few moments the last time because I wanted to make sure none of those Gods were up to no good. They can be cocky dicks and cunts like that. It was pretty brazen activating a Senshifter, and in here of all places. Eolith is the last one I would have expected to be responsible."

"Yes, I'm well aware of the games the Gods can play," I said, leaning back in my chair. "What's on your mind, Tora? I can tell something is troubling you. Let me have it."

Her nose twitched as she pursed her lips. "It's her, love—the source of all your filthy wet dreams and aching blue balls the past century. Let me just say as an aside, though, I can definitely see why. She is built for carnal delight, that one."

I arched a brow, suppressing the laugh that started to bubble up. "You have a point, Tora?"

She sighed, her face growing suddenly grave. "I am worried by what I see, Ash."

My eyes flicked to her, a shiver of unease prickling my skin. Tora very rarely called me Ash. The last time she had done so was after my parents' deaths, when I'd begun to unravel. For her to call me by my name meant that something was very wrong.

She was no simple spirit. She was *the* prime elemental spirit. Her magic was old, steeped in the ages. Although she'd never confirmed it, I always suspected that she was as ancient as the First Age. If so, she would be able to see what not even the Gods of the Sangelis could see.

"Tell me," I said quietly.

"I think I need to show you." She twirled her hands, conjuring an image of Elle, outlined in light. "This is Elle's soul," she said, tracing a light-filled circle around Elle's torso area. "See all that beautiful light and radiance?" She pointed to the swirls of light inside the circle.

I nodded, waiting for her to continue.

"That is her soul *after* you came into it, love. When Eolith came to you five years ago, she pretty much told you that that the light in Elle's soul had faded to an ember. You stoked that back to life again."

"That's a good thing, isn't it?" I said, unsure of what she was getting at.

"Absolutely, it is, but that's not what worries me." Her eyes flitted to mine, her lips a thin line. "Elle lost her memories," she said. "She doesn't remember her life with you in it. Yes, she has flashes and glimpses, and while her heart and soul still remembers, her mind doesn't. Look, my love," she said, her fingers tracing a thick, dark shadow around Elle's soul. "This is the power of the rebounding curse. Infused with Gargmoin's magic, it has attracted all the darkness inside her that has accumulated throughout her life, and has made it so that her light is trapped inside."

A sickening feeling twisted my gut. Reversing the rebounding curse was always the plan, but I just didn't have an intricate enough understanding of the Old, Arcane Magic to be able to do it myself. I needed Lorien's help. And he was in the Brus-Winnd Territories—next stop on my itinerary to retrieve Valkyse's Phantera.

Last night, as I'd lain next to Elle watching her sleep, I'd made up my mind that if Tora could summon the elemental spirits of Ariadna to give their blessing to Elle, I would take her with me to Brus-Winnd. She would be safe with Lorien at Dramhelm Manor, and my hope was that while he did what was needed to destroy the power of the rebounding curse and restore her memories, I would venture on to do as the Cloryals commanded.

I drummed my fingers on the desk, my mind swirling with a plethora of anxious thoughts. "Can Catraia fight it? She must be aware, at the very least."

Tora frowned, leaning her hip against my desk. "Catraia has only just awakened inside Elle. She is still assessing all there is to know about her."

"What are you trying to tell me?" I asked, my heartbeat thudding a warning in my chest.

She pushed off the desk, her eyes flashing with urgency. "Elle is a child of the light, Ash. Her power needs to be grounded in the light. You have seen the dark tendrils in her essence. That they are so prominent worries me."

"Spit it out, Tora," I said, my frustration mounting.

Her body stiffened as she lifted serious eyes to mine. "Elle cannot use the light in her soul the way she should because she is not in possession of the memories that caused that light to blossom. Her metamorphosis hinges on her being a child of the light. With a being like Elle who wields an enormous amount of power, an entity like Catraia ensures that when they use their magic in any significant way to fight darkness, they stay grounded in the light and do not give in to the dark pull of their power. The situation with Elle is unique because of the rebounding curse. She is cut off from the light that will ground her use of her power."

I stared at her in disbelief, at a loss for words.

"But Catraia *will* be able to rein her in?"

Tora sat on the edge of my desk. "Ash, Catraia is not the problem. Catraia can and will handle anything that Elle throws at her. Elle knows right from wrong, yes, but I believe the moment she tries to use her magic in a defensive or offensive manner, the darkness will take over, influencing her decisions. That cannot happen."

I stared at Tora in horror.

Tora's face was grim. "We need to act as soon as possible. I can assure you that if we don't, when the time comes for her to absorb the Old, Arcane Magic, as she must, it will be infinitely more difficult to destroy the rebounding curse. It will cost us time that we do not have."

I narrowed my eyes. "Why would the Old, Arcane Magic make it *more* difficult to destroy the rebounding curse?"

Tora leaned against the side of my desk. "We both know that the core concentration of the light strain of the Old, Arcane Magic is found in Brus-Winnd, within the boundaries of Dramhelm Manor. If we do nothing, I believe the moment she steps foot in the Territories, the darkness inside her—encased in Gargmoin's magic—will be drawn to the dark sway of the Old, Arcane Magic that runs wild throughout the Territories, and that is what she will absorb."

Dammit. I hadn't even considered that. I'd assumed that as part of her transformation, the light strain of the Old, Arcane Magic of the Territories would assimilate itself into her the moment it became aware of her presence. But if the darkness was trapping her light inside? Fuck!

If Tora was right about Gargmoin's darkness around Elle's soul, we were in deep shit. It would mean keeping Elle away from Brus-Winnd, which meant that not only would I not be able to take her with me to Lorien's, but she would also not be able to complete that phase of her transformation.

And just like that, destroying the rebounding curse had now moved to the top of my world-altering things to-do list. Even ahead of retrieving Valkyse's Phantera. Blast it all to Pashket!

Was it too much to ask for even a minuscule reprieve? Gods, I was wound tight. The news about Madio Averon complicated things even more. That disloyal bastard had also been summoned to retrieve Averon's Phantera. If he had indeed formed an alliance with Kaliope, then the Phantera was as good as hers; it was probably what she was after to begin with.

That would mean that if the Ankhira spoken of in the celestial star etching required all four Phanteras in order for Elle to wield it, then we were royally screwed.

Fuck, fuck, and fuck!

I sank into my chair. I felt sick to my stomach. I had to tell Elle what Tora had seen—be open and honest with her about it. I was tired of keeping secrets. My entire relationship with Elle had been clouded in secrecy. For most of it, I hadn't been able to tell her who I really was. I wasn't going to do that anymore. Keeping things from the ones you loved took a toll; it slowly ate away at your soul.

I got to my feet and turned to face Tora. "I'm late for the meeting with the Valkyse Council of Governors. I need to make sure we're ready to handle anything should Kaliope make any kind of move. As soon as I get back from meeting with the Valkyse generals, I'll sit Elle down and tell her. Treye, Gilham, and Ovix should be here by then. We can all meet as a group and come up with a plan. Until then, keep her safe."

Tora nodded. "I know the stakes, love. She'll be safe with me."

Chapter 35

ELEYSE

I COULDN'T SHAKE THE uneasiness that settled over me like a gloom-drenched storm cloud. Before Ash left with the others, he pulled me into the library, and right away, I sensed the dark shift in his mood.

"I'll be back later this afternoon," he said, cupping my face in his hands. "Tryx and Tora will keep you company while we're gone."

I closed the distance between us, wrapping my arms around his neck. "Is everything all right? I feel a lot of heavy emotions rolling off you."

He grazed his thumb against my jaw. "I'm just a bit anxious for these meetings. I don't think anyone can really get into the right headspace when it comes to war."

That was an understatement.

I looked into his eyes, and it was hard to miss the worry and fear reflected there. He lowered his head and brushed his lips against mine. "I love you, Tialla," he whispered against my hair. "When I get back, we need to talk about getting your memories back. It's important that we reverse the magic of the rebounding curse."

My eyes flicked to his. "What's really wrong, Ash?" There was something he wasn't saying. I could see it in his face, feel it seeping out of him.

"We'll talk when I get back," he said, stroking my cheek. "I don't want you to worry. Everything will be all right." He pulled me to him once more, the tension inside him as tight as a drum. Releasing me slowly, he kissed the bridge of my nose and headed toward the door.

That had been about half an hour ago. I'd stayed in the library after he left, looking through the titles of books on the shelves, wondering what the hell had him so worked up. Last night, he had said that he would talk to Tora today about completing this phase of my transformation before he left for the Brus-Winnd Territories. Did something happen? I sensed a deeper concern about reversing the rebounding curse now that I didn't feel last night.

Shit. I needed to do something to distract myself or my thoughts would drive me mad. I picked up A *History of the Gods* from the table where Gwynn had left it yesterday and took it with me over to the chair by the window.

I turned the pages back and forth between the Great Creator Arazul and the Goddess Mother Eolith, and went scurrying down another rabbit hole of mystery. What did they know about me? Ash said that I was their secret. The God of Gods and the Goddess of the Ethereal Harmonies. What was the connection?

Catraia, do you know what the Secret of the Gods is? I asked silently in my mind.

I do not, she replied. *I know nothing of the Gods of the New Age of the Sangelis.*

I frowned. *How does that work? The things you do and do not know?*

Her voice was steady and matter-of-fact in my mind. *When you encounter any living being, I can read them to determine the truth in their words and in their hearts. I can also determine illusion from reality.*

Is that how you knew about Astrid?

Yes. As for what I relay to you, if I sense that there is a need for you to know something, or if you ask me, I will tell you. Apart from that, there is no need for me to bombard you with all the truths I learn.

Right. I didn't want to know random things about others that weren't any of my business anyway.

Does the fact that you can determine illusion from reality mean that something like Kaliope masquerading as Ash and murdering his parents could not get past you?

That's right. Everything that is not grounded in reality is visible to me. My ability to discern truth from lie and illusion from reality is grounded in the present moment, though. Not in the past or the future.

Is that why you don't know anything about the Gods of the Sangelis?

I was asleep when the Gods of the Sangelis came into being, and I slumbered until I awoke in you.

Wait, what? Did that mean she was awake before the Gods of the Sangelis? And who was she in before? Ash said that an entity like Catraia was the part of a being with extreme power that kept them in check.

I awoke with your power when you arrived in Ariadna. Although the knowledge of all I have seen is vast and spans many ages, in this awakening, I am a part of you. I have been a part of you your entire existence.

Even during my life on Earth?

Even then. And I will be with you until the end.

Those words filled me with indescribable calm, settling the turmoil that had been slowly building inside me with every revelation I'd been faced with. To know that I didn't walk this path alone, that I had a guiding presence inside me, brought me immeasurable peace.

I flipped the page and my eyes danced across the image of Sorin, Summoner of Light and Darkness. Like all the Gods, he was beautiful, but there was a soft sorrow that was captured in this portrait. It made me feel sad looking at it. On the next page was the image of Jaraya, Goddess of the Night, Sorin's wife. Her aura leapt off the page at me—vicious and cunning. I had to be imagining all of this, inventing these perceived senses. These were just portraits. How could they possibly invoke such feeling in me?

I turned to the image of Twylos, Goddess of the Elements. Her tawny skin and copper eyes were a stark contrast against her blue and green hair. Was she tied to Tora somehow? Surely the Goddess of the Elements would be associated with the prime elemental spirit of Ariadna. Right?

My fingers traced over the image of Cazril, God of Chaos. Caz. As I stared at his portrait, I heard his mocking voice in my head, his laughter, his irreverent teasing. Danger—that's what lurked in between the shadows of his handsome face. And yet there was something thrilling about him that called to a shuttered part of me.

I slammed the book shut, pushing my misgivings away. What the hell was wrong with me?

A low growl rumbled inside me, and I immediately recognized it as Vix.

Don't worry, girl, I soothed. *There is not one damn thing about that God I need in my life.*

Even as I iterated my reassurance, Caz's voice in my head drawled, *These two tendrils have been angling for my attention ever since I got out of that pool.* What the fuck did he mean?

"There you are, sweet thing," Tora said cheerily, disrupting my thoughts as she stepped through the bookshelf on the opposite wall.

My mouth dropped open as I stared at Tryx trailing behind her. "Wait. Tryx can move through walls too?"

"The little cuntling sure can," Tora said, scratching Tryx's head affectionately. "The collar around her neck is infused with Smolders's and my magic, so she can go anywhere she pleases here."

Tora had changed her outfit. Gone was the blue-sapphire gown from breakfast, and in its place was . . . well, a skin-tight body suit—leather and lime green. A pair of high-heeled, peacock-feathered slippers adorned her feet. Her hair was pulled high into a ponytail at the top of her head.

My eyes opened wide as I studied her. What kind of statement was she trying to make with this getup?

"It's window cleaning day," she said, as if reading the question on my face. "I've found that it's always best to dress how you feel and channel that energy into the task at hand."

I nodded in agreement, smothering my smile. What the hell kind of energy was she channeling here for window cleaning day? I was entirely curious to know.

"I'm sorry for missing you at breakfast," she said, sitting on the armrest of my chair. "I trust that you and Smolders were able to curl each other's toes to your hearts' content last night? Hopefully you were able to work that kink out of his dick that's had him in a Gods-awful mood these past five months."

I laughed out loud. "Oh my God. Are you always so scandalous?"

"What you see is what you get with me, Agaia. Life is boring any other way."

I cocked my head and studied her. There was that name again. Agaia. *Storm.*

"Why do you call me that?" I asked. "You did last night as well."

A puzzled look flitted across her face. "Because that is who you are. At your very core, the sum of all your parts, the consolidation of all your power."

They tell me that you are a promise and a storm. That's what Ash had said his senses told him about me when I visited him through the Senshifter. It couldn't be a coincidence.

Tora got to her feet. "Before I get on with my window cleaning duties, I wanted to see if you'd like to come to the Torannon market with me. With everyone gone, I didn't want to leave you alone. I have to pick up a manuscript from one of the vendors there."

"But Ash said I needed to stay hidden for the time being," I said.

I had to admit, though. A part of me longed to get out of the house, even just to feel like I wasn't sitting still.

"You'll still be hidden," she said. "My cloaking magic will keep you safe. No harm will befall you while you're under my care, love. Smolders would spike both my ass cheeks to the front gate if it did."

You can trust her to keep you safe, Eleyse, Catraia whispered in my mind.

I shifted to face her. "Forgive my ignorance, but how does it work with you being a spirit? You can still come and go as you please, like everyone else?"

"The only thing that sets me apart from everyone else is my magic and what I am capable of doing with it," she said. "I can still do anything that a mortal can. Now, I don't need to in order to survive, but it makes things immensely more enjoyable to indulge in the simple pleasures of mortality." She leaned closer to me, clasping her hands together. "I'm sure you can guess which kind of pleasure I enjoy the most."

I giggled. "Oh yes, I sure can."

"Well, that's all settled," she said, gliding to her feet. "Is there anything you need to do before you leave, or are you ready now?"

"I don't need to do anything," I said, placing the book on my lap on the small table in front of me.

"All right, let's go then," she said, taking my arm.

In the blink of an eye, the air dissolved around us and we were swept away in a loud rush of swirling wind and mist.

The market was a distance away from Cazara Torannon, on the opposite end of the city, as Tora explained to me. We appeared in the center of the market square, beside a magnificent marble fountain shooting jets of water into the air.

For the second time since I arrived in Ariadna, I was outside, amongst people who couldn't actually see me. Like yesterday, when none of the people we'd encountered at Cazara Colpra were able to see us thanks to Gwynn's shielding abilities, Tora was shielding us here.

The Torannon market was located in the artisan district of the city, and Tora was meeting with one of the vendors whose specialty was ancient texts and manuscripts. Unlike before, where Tora glided when she moved, she was actually walking, and making it look incredibly easy in those high-heeled peacock slippers of hers.

The market was a bustling hub of activity, the wide cobblestone paths crowded with people walking, talking, and enjoying the warm, sunny day. For the first time, I was able to really observe the people around me, and I noted that physically, there were no visible features that set them apart from me as different.

We weaved our way through the crowd, Tora leading the way, no one paying us any attention as we walked. The pathways of the market were lined with tents; each vendor had their own—some of them sprawling, some of them small and modest—and the splash of bright colors all around, coupled with the buzz of life everywhere, made my heart light.

As we walked, my head swung on a swivel at the sheer variety of goods for sale: fresh fruit, vegetables, meat, linens, herbs, spices, jewelry, clothing, strange devices and items that were unfamiliar to me, books, tattoos, piercings. My eyes were wide with wonder as I drank it all in.

At the front table outside one of the tents we walked by—a purveyor of fine chocolates, by the signage—a shimmering copper snake twisted around a crystal tree branch that was affixed to a pedestal. Every time its tongue forked out of its mouth, a chocolate truffle slid from its jaws into a silver bowl at the base of the pedestal.

Outside another tent, a young woman sat at a chair with her hand outstretched as a golden quill moved on its own, tattooing an intricate, mandala-like design onto the back of her hand in gold ink.

We breezed by another tent filled with beautiful, illustrated books, and my head snapped around to look at the glittering, eye-catching designs on the covers.

Everywhere we walked, invisible webs of magic thrummed around us—my own power humming in my chest in acknowledgment.

Before I could even ask the question, Tora turned to me. "Although most of these people have no magical abilities, magical artifacts make it so they can harness magic to a specific extent. The majority of magical artifacts you find here draw their power from the Ethereal Harmonies, although there might be the very rare and obscure one that might be grounded in the Old, Arcane

Magic. You never know."

We kept walking until finally, Tora came to a stop at a teal-blue tent. *Scada Rare Books and Manuscripts*, it read. She stepped into the tent and a tall, brown-haired man with a neatly trimmed beard and green eyes approached her. She must have made herself visible to him. Herself. Not me.

"I'll be out shortly, love," she said to me. "My shields are up over the entire market so you'll be safe right here. For your own safety, don't touch anything or go anywhere."

I nodded. I could do that. Keep my hands to myself. Easy.

She stepped into the tent, and I stood at the entrance, off to the side, while she talked with the man.

The air around me crackled with life and energy. The fragrant smell of spices and food being cooked over open flames wafted toward me, causing my mouth to water involuntarily. All around me, people were sauntering by leisurely, chatting, going about their lives, and it was revitalizing to simply stand back and watch.

On a rack in front of the tent, three books were on display on different shelves. I reached out my hand to touch one of them, but remembered Tora's command just in time and jerked away. My gaze flitted to the book on the middle shelf. The tome was old and leather bound, the lettering a faded shade of copper. *The Merits of Chaos*, it read. Huh. What kind of chaos was it referring to?

An oval blue stone—cloudy and swirling—was set in the middle of the cover. As I stood there, peering at the book, a shiver went down my spine as the buzz of the market faded into the background and a myriad of fervent, indiscernible whispers pierced the air, whirling around in my mind. The stone in the book began to glow as the whispers grew louder and more urgent. An overwhelming desire to reach out and touch it gripped me, and my hand lifted slowly.

No, *Eleyse,* Catraia warned.

I yanked my hand back.

Move away from the book, she commanded, and just as I shifted my weight to take a step back, a gust of wind blasted through the space where I was standing, tipping the rack over. The book flew off the shelf, slamming with a thud against my chest.

Abruptly, the air shifted, and before I could make sense of what the change was, a soft voice drawled behind me, "Well, well, well. I told you I'd see you again soon, Terror."

Fuck!

I spun around, heart thudding in my chest. There stood the God of Chaos, leaning against a display table, his arms folded haughtily across his chest. He was wearing a loose white shirt, tucked into form-hugging black pants. His ash-blond hair shone like strands of gold in the sunlight and his bright green eyes sparkled with mischief and the barest hint of menace.

Before I could run into the tent after Tora, he reached out and grabbed my arm. "Let's go for a walk, doll."

And just like that, the tent in front of us disappeared, and I hurtled off into God-knows-where with him.

Chapter 36

WE REAPPEARED IN ANOTHER part of the market. Quieter. Less people. Only two tents stood on opposing sides of us, and they were both empty of shoppers. I had no idea where we were or how far away from Tora I was. Shit. What about Catraia? Would she even answer? I called her name in my mind, but there was only silence. Yesterday, she had said that she needed to stay hidden from Caz when he grabbed me in the Void. I didn't understand. Earlier in the library, she'd claimed ignorance about the Gods of the Sangelis. Was that why she didn't want them knowing about her? Or was it Caz specifically?

Caz stood facing me, looking me up and down slowly. "I almost didn't recognize you shielded by Tora's magic, with your blinding essence muted."

My temper flared. "I almost didn't recognize you with your clothes on."

His eyes danced with laughter. "Been fantasizing about me, Terror? That Sovereign of yours not hitting your spot the way you like?" He stared at me, as if peering deep into my soul, studying me, peeling me back to see what lay underneath my skin. "She's clever, that Tora," he said, gazing out into the market. "She shielded you from everyone and made it so that you cannot be taken from this place. But I am no mere mortal, and she can't shield you from me. Trace magic is a wondrous thing, doll. Who would have

335

thought that you would be standing at the very spot where a book containing traces of *my* magic just happened to be? The book called to me the moment it sensed you."

The book. *The Merits of Chaos*. Of course it was about him. Was that what the whispers were?

I took a slow step backward.

He chuckled softly. "All you had to do was touch the stone, but you were too smart for that, so I had to improvise and bring the stone to you."

Asshole. He had caused the gust that threw the book at me.

He rocked back on his heels with his hands clasped behind his back. "Yes, Tora is clever, but not clever enough to outsmart me."

"Arrogant much?" I said, my eyes darting around me for somewhere to go. What was even the point? He was a frigging God. Where would I even run?

He stalked closer toward me. "I might not be able to take you away from this place, Terror, but there's nowhere here you can hide from me. Plus, I put up a shield of my own. It'll take her a while to get past it."

Fuck. Where the hell was she? Surely, she would have already noticed I was gone. Wouldn't she?

"Why, hello there," Caz crooned seductively, his attention fixed on a spot near my hips. He reached out his fingers and stroked the air, and like before in the Void, a sharp jolt of pleasure flooded my core. His voice was low and seductive as his fingers continued to caress the air next to me. "Oh, Terror, I could have you on your knees, coming harder than you've ever come in your life and begging for more, just by doing this."

Vix's angry roar vibrated inside me, a burst of rage flooding my senses.

I pushed at his chest and stepped backward. "Stay the fuck away from me."

"Tell that to your tendrils, darling," he smirked, reaching his hand out again.

"Back the hell up," I seethed, my hands out in front of me.

"Make me," he whispered, stepping forward once more.

Vix's terrifying keen tore through me as I pushed against his chest with my hands, channeling the surge of power that blasted through me, sending the God of Chaos flying into the tent closest to me.

In a second, he was standing in front of me again, rubbing his jaw. "Eo's tits. She has it bad for your Sovereign, that Gloweyen bitch of yours. You need to find a way to ditch that bond so we can have some fun. On the plus side, though, you've learned a few things since the last time. Glad to see you took my advice."

"You don't get to touch me," I warned, my eyes narrowed.

"The darkness inside you says otherwise, doll. Those velvety tendrils practically moaned as they wrapped themselves around my cock."

What the fuck? Those blasted tendrils again. Something was off here. No part of me wanted him.

"Shut up," I spat.

I shivered as something alien and sinister cackled quietly inside me, intent on proving me a liar.

"I get it," he said, nodding placatingly. "You're one of those women who like to suppress their urges. Hide that they're secretly into dark, kinky shit."

"Trust me," I said, lifting my head a notch. "I proudly own the kinky shit I'm into; it just won't be with the likes of you."

"I think," he said, taking another step toward me, "all we need is a little time before you stop fighting your true nature."

"You don't know anything about my true nature," I seethed.

"I already know everything I need to know about you. Powerful, mysterious, short temper, drowning in angst and bitterness. Life of woe and sorrow. Sound about right? But, then there's the conundrum—the extraordinary developments. Chosen by the Ethereal Harmonies to be Gloweyen Queen of Ariadna, something that's never before happened. You've also inherited the Songbird of Valkyse mantle. All very impressive things for an outsider, but are you really an outsider? What I still want to know, though, is why you? Why does Arazul care so much about *you*? What am I missing?"

I smirked. "If you still have questions, then you clearly don't know everything about me, you dipshit."

His eyes flared with anger, and I stepped back, feeling Vix brace for action inside me. She was Team Ash/Magnus all the way. I had no doubts she could knock the God of Chaos on his ass again.

"I'm going to make your darkness sing for me," he whispered, advancing on me. "It'll tell me all your secrets, everything I want to know."

A loud, clattering crash from the tent I'd sent Caz flying through drew our attention, followed by a pitiful wail.

A young girl, who couldn't be any more than six, came running out of the tent, followed by a tall, barrel-chested man, his face contorted with rage. Neither of them could see us where we stood, a stone's throw away.

"This is interesting," Caz said quietly, stroking his chin.

"Look what you did!" the man bellowed at the child, who stumbled and fell onto the cobblestone path, her eyes wide with terror. "You good-for-nothing creya!" He rushed toward her, his booted foot striking out to kick her in the stomach.

"No, Papa," the girl pleaded as she cried out in pain, curling up on the ground in the fetal position.

Papa? This piece of shit was that sweet child's father? I looked at the terrified girl, barely older than I was when I lost my own father, and I saw red as rage flared inside me. A father was supposed to protect and cherish his child, was supposed to love and shower her with hugs and kisses, not beat the shit out of her.

A faded memory arose unbidden—my own father throwing me into the air and catching me while my squeals of laughter rang out, my tiny little arms wrapping tightly around his neck. My father was loving and kind. A decent man who was ripped from the child who adored him much, much too soon. Now, here stood another bearing the title of father who showed zero reverence and respect for the precious gift he had been given. Angry tears blurred my vision.

Next to me, Caz stood quietly, casually observing the scene with wry amusement. Disgust roiled in my stomach.

The man kicked the girl again in the ribs, and my heart lurched—fear, despair, anger whipping through me in a frenzy. Without hesitation, I delved inside myself and dove headfirst into my lake of power. I gathered a wisp of my power to me, flicking it toward the piece of shit who saw nothing wrong with taking his rage out on his innocent child.

That tiny flick slammed into him with infinitely more force than I had hit Caz with, sending him flying through the back of his tent and into another one behind it.

Caz cocked his head at me, arching a brow. "Gods be damned, Terror. You're fucking killing it."

I ignored him, immersing myself in my lake of power again.

The commotion brought a few people running in our direction, and seeing the child curled up on the ground, two women dropped to their knees to tend to her. Caz and I were still hidden to them.

A sense of calm settled over me as I walked through the ruined tent and into the one next to it, where the man had smashed through a painting, his flabby ass dangling in the air. That's when I heard it. A delighted giggle reverberating from somewhere inside me. That same sinister presence I'd felt earlier. Not Catraia, not Vix. Something *other*. It whispered to me, cajoling me to tap into my power once more.

I shook my head, trying to clear my thoughts, but the whispers grew louder, seeping into my mind.

That sack of shit likes to abuse children? Well, let's see how he enjoys being on the receiving end. Pun intended—send a blast of power right up his ass.

No, this wasn't me. I grabbed my head, massaging, squeezing, trying to subdue the whispers, only to be greeted with taunting laughter.

Do it, do it.

Unable to stop myself, I flicked another shard of power at the man—just a grain this time—and the whispers rose merrily when he cried out in pain, clutching his backside.

Another shard of power shot out from me, and he wailed.

What the hell was happening to me? I was losing control. A part of me was aware of Caz standing quietly beside me. I shifted my gaze to him and was startled to see him watching me intently, approval and raw, hungry desire flashing in his eyes. Oh God. This couldn't be happening.

Unable to control myself, I sent another flicker of my magic toward the man, increasing the potency, and he screamed in horror.

Enough, Eleyse, Catraia commanded in my mind. *This is not the way.*

She had surfaced. Here. In front of the God of Chaos. She was supposed to stay hidden from him.

This is absolutely the way, the whispers inside me spat scathingly. *Men like him are the worst sort. They deserve to pay. What good is having this power if we can't use it to stamp out evil?*

Listen to me, Eleyse, Catraia said calmly. *That is the darkness talking. Fight it. You are not judge, jury, and executioner*, she said firmly. *That is not the purpose of your powers.*

My head felt like it was going to explode as I fought for control.

Leave us be, Anchor, the whispers riled. *We know what we're doing.*

Fight it, Eleyse. Search inside yourself for the light.

A wave of panic washed over me as I retreated deeper inside myself, searching for an opening, a foothold, anything to dig into to take back control.

Caz moved closer to me, his eyes filled with curiosity and wonder. "My, my, what have we here? Something ancient and powerful stirs inside you. Let me in that head of yours. I want to see."

He prodded at the entrance to my mind, and Vix surged. I lashed out at him, sending him reeling backward.

In front of me, the man managed to pull his body through the painting. A crowd had gathered around us, and people were looking around in terror, clearly sensing something in their midst but unable to see what was going on.

My mind was betraying me. My thoughts were not my own. It was as if I was locked away in a soundproof room as something else ran amok in my mind, controlling my emotions and my body.

A surge of irritation flared inside me, not my own. *Too many people*, the whispers cried. *We need them to go away. We're not done yet. Can't let him get away.*

I mindlessly reached for more of my power, preparing to send it scattering around me to clear a path.

Stop right there, Eleyse, Catraia's voice boomed inside me. *These people are innocent. Release your power. Now.*

"That's it, Terror," Caz cajoled. "Let go. Mortals can be so meddlesome and taxing. You are fucking beautiful and glorious when you are angry. Set that darkness free. Aren't you tired of holding back?"

Yes, yes, yes, the whispers cried gleefully. *Set us free.*

I looked at him, the pounding in my head dulling as a wave of euphoria overcame me. A twisted clarity surged in my mind. Yes! He was right. I was tired. So tired. I had spent so much of my life fighting the darkness. What if I just let go? Then I wouldn't have to feel like I was fighting against the tide, swimming upstream, racing into the wind. Is this what he meant about giving in to my true nature? What if I just closed my eyes and simply let go? Would it carry me away in a sublime rush? Would it be like falling into a lover's embrace?

You have a lover, Catraia's stoic voice boomed. *One who loves you more than life itself. And this is not what he would want.*

Her words were a blast of frigid air to my face, clearing my head of the malevolent fog that had taken hold. Ash. My love. My lifeline.

The menacing whispers immediately relinquished their grip on me, as if the very thought of my Gloweyen King unsettled them. The heaviness inside me dissipated, and I inhaled deeply. Instinctively, I reached for Ash in my mind, needing him with every fiber of my being, and I gasped as a faint pulse of emotions rolled over me. Surprise. Concern. Love. Fear.

You can do this, Eleyse, Catraia soothed. *Stand down of your own accord. We haven't even started this journey yet. Remember what I said about not letting your recklessness lead you. Your choices have consequences. You must weigh your actions carefully.*

She was right. But that wasn't all I knew. *Something is wrong,*

Catraia. Terribly wrong. A mangled sob ripped free from my throat.

I know, Eleyse. I know.

A blast of hot air permeated the space, and the tent around me shimmered in a haze of magic as Tora appeared, her brilliant, golden eyes shining as she walked toward me, her face a mask of rage.

Behind me, I heard Caz's quiet laughter, his voice soft and insolent as he said, "This isn't over by a long shot, Terror. Gods—what to do, what to do? Delicious knowledge. Who do I tell first?"

Tora flicked her hand, and the three of us—Tora, Caz, and I—were transported outside the tent and encased in some sort of translucent sphere, where time itself seemed to stand still around us. The people outside the sphere stood frozen and inanimate.

The sky above suddenly darkened, malevolent purple and gray clouds swooping in to blot out the sun. An icy chill rained down from above, pebbling my skin, numbing my tongue with the taste of bitter fury. I felt it—the calm before the storm as the clouds above churned in anticipation, and then a roaring, angry clap of thunder rent the air. In a mass of rolling mist and flaming lightning, Ash appeared in front of me, in the center of the protective sphere Tora had cast around us, his eyes blazing fire, his magic crackling as it dripped from his powerful form.

"Well, if it isn't your Sovereign, doll, here to save the day." Caz was breezy and nonchalant, but even so, he took a small step back. Something flashed in his eyes quickly, but not too fast for me to miss. Fear.

Shit! The God of Chaos was scared of Ash. A perverse trill of satisfaction shot through me at the realization, and my heart swelled with wonder as I stared at the vengeful creature in front of me. *Mine*, my heart declared, staking its claim.

"Godslayer," Caz said, tipping his head at Ash.

Godslayer? What the—

Ash lifted his head, a muscle clenching in his jaw as he fisted his hands at his side. He kept me behind him and moved forward, a surge of power flaring from him. He was blinding. I hadn't seen him like this before. This had to be his essence—brilliant and so incredibly commanding. He was pure power. Even the God of Chaos squinted as he looked at him.

The ground shook beneath my feet as Ash stood toe to toe with Caz. Mist and lightning seeped from his skin and encased them both in a shadowy cocoon that promised retribution. Tora stood beside me, a look of smug anticipation on her face.

Ash's voice was hard as steel and cold as ice. "You know what I am, you duplicitous fuck, and still you're reckless enough—not once, but twice—to abscond with what is mine? Mine to protect, mine to love, mine to serve."

As much as I was confused about what was happening, I couldn't help the soaring in my heart as Ash claimed me. Vix cooed in contentment as she stirred inside me, reveling in his declaration.

A glare of arrogance flashed in Caz's eyes, but despite his puffed out chest and outward bravado, I was able to sense it—his growing trepidation. I imagined this was how an apex predator felt when they realized an even bigger, badder threat was staring them down. Good. He might be a God, but I hoped he shit himself.

Hundreds of needle-like shards of lightning shot out from Ash and into Caz, the latter grimacing as they pierced his skin. "Your reckoning begins now, God of Chaos." Ash's voice was flat and cold. "This is your first and only warning. Stay away from my Gloweyen Queen."

Caz threw his head back and laughed. "You think I'm afraid of you? I am a God of the Sangelis, pup. Just because the Mavigos bestowed the title of Godslayer on you, it doesn't mean you can go around ending Gods as it suits you. Even I know that. There are checks and balances. Rules you must follow. And we both know you're a good little rule follower." He said the last part with a sneer, his tone taunting as he stared at Ash.

I was so frigging confused as I tried to play catch up. The Mavigos had given Ash the ability to kill Gods? Why?

Caz pointed his finger at Ash's chest, and with his back facing me, all I could see was Ash's head dip to look down. "If you weren't concerned with following the rules," Caz continued, his eyes blazing silver, "you would have put that crazy bitch in the ground years ago when she chopped your father's head off and gutted your beautiful mother like a pig."

A roar of rage echoed in my head at the callousness of Caz's words. How dare he use Kaliope's gruesome slaying of Arlon and Harwen Valkyse to taunt Ash.

While my blood boiled, stoking my anger, Ash didn't even move or react. His body was rigid and still. How he possessed that level of control, I didn't understand. I would have already clawed Caz's eyes out and shoved them down his throat if it were me. In fact, only Ash's inaction and Tora's sudden grip on my arm prevented me from lashing out at the God of Chaos for what he had said.

Slowly, Ash gripped Caz's shirt in his fist and pulled him closer. "You might talk a big talk, but I can taste your fear. And I might be a pup, but I delight that it twists in your gut that I have the power to slay the bad, behemoth wolf, as you most likely think of yourself." Ash let go of Caz, his hands fisting as they dropped to his sides. "Let me be clear about this. I will not hesitate to end your sorry existence if you do not heed me. I can only be pushed so far, and she—my Gloweyen Queen—is my limit. Not even the Great Creator or the Mavigos will deny me my rage if you touch her again."

I jumped as Ash quickly lifted his arm and shoved his fist straight through the God of Chaos's stomach. Caz's eyes bulged in horror and shock as he looked down at where he was impaled upon Ash's arm. Silver blood dripped from his mouth, and a sickening, gurgling sound bubbled from his lips.

Ash lifted him off the ground, his arm still planted firmly through Caz's midsection. "Just a little higher and it would be your heart I hold in my hands. Mine to crush. Mine to destroy. Remember that." And with those words, he lifted his arm back a fraction, and before I could even grasp how it happened, the God of Chaos was catapulted into the heavens in the blink of an eye, not even a speck of him visible.

What the—

My heart thudded in my ears. He . . . how . . . Caz . . .

Shit. I couldn't even string two coherent thoughts together.

Ash turned to face me and Tora then, all traces of that powerful ire gone. His face was a mixture of worry and relief as he pulled me to him. "Elle," he whispered, his voice raw with emotion.

At the sheer safety and solace I felt at being in his arms, I lost it. The reality of what I had done at the market came flooding back to me, filling me with a brimming dose of scorching shame and helplessness. I burst into tears, holding on to Ash as he lifted me in his arms and touched his labral, whisking us away from the stifling confines of the market, back to the stalwart safety of Cazara Torannon.

Chapter 37

ASHER

"WHAT THE FUCK HAPPENED, Tora? How did that piece of shit get to her?" I clenched my fists, struggling to rein in my anger. I needed to know. I had felt it. In that brief ripple in our Gloweyen bond, everything had come rushing through. Elle's loss of control. Her rage. Her bloodlust. Her helplessness. Her complete devastation. Her shame.

I'd used my sedating power to make her sleep, and that's how I left her—lost to the world in my bed, tear tracks staining her cheeks, her sorrow and despair clouding her essence, her brows knitted and pulled tight.

"The market was shielded with my power, Ash. He used trace magic to get to her. She was standing next to a book that alerted him of her presence."

My eyes narrowed. "What are the odds? That she would be right there in front of the one book that contained his magic?"

"It can't be a coincidence, Ash. This reeks of the Mavigos' influence. I think they made this happen."

I paced the length of my study like a caged beyngyle feline. "Why would you even think that? Why in blazes would the Mavigos let Elle slip into the God of Chaos's hands?"

Tora leaned against my desk. "Because of what it revealed, Ash. The moment he took her, he cast a shield so I couldn't get to her, but I was able to see everything that was happening. He was pushing her, taunting her, so much so that she did use her power against him, and she would have again, but then the child ran out in front of her. The father assaulting his daughter triggered her, and Elle's need to protect and dole out justice got away from her once she invoked her magic. That shit God didn't help things either, egging her on, encouraging her to give in to the darkness inside her."

My blood boiled. I should have killed the sick asshole.

"It's worse than I feared, Ash," Tora said gravely. "Her tendrils of darkness respond to him, are excited by him."

I stopped in my tracks, my gut twisting in a sickening knot as I tried to smother the jealousy and hurt that flared to life inside me. No. Gods, no. This couldn't be happening.

Tora touched my arm. "Don't go there. Elle loves you. And only you. Listen to me. I know this will be difficult for you to understand, but I need you to wrap your head around what I'm going to say." She tilted my face, forcing me to meet her gaze. "No one else's magic but Gargmoin's could have created this monstrosity in her. That fuck is as ancient and corrupted as sin. Trust me on that. The darkness around Elle's soul is sentient. It responds to other sources of magic like it. There is no way she can set foot in Brus-Winnd. The dark sway of the Old, Arcane Magic will overwhelm her. And when she comes in contact with Gargmoin—and it will be *when*, Ash, not if—her darkness will practically leap into his arms."

"Fuck!" I roared, my mind numb with fear and despair.

"And now, the God of Chaos knows that Eleyse is more powerful than he believed. He sensed Catraia inside her. You can rest assured that lump of shit won't keep that to himself. Arazul kept the celestial star etching hidden from all the other Gods of the Sangelis except Eolith, but there are other ancient beings older than the Gods of the New Age who remember. Word will spread. We always knew that once she got to Ariadna, it was only a matter of time before the truth of who she is got out."

"So what do we do, Tora?" I asked, unable to keep the desperation out of my voice. "Can Arazul or Eolith intervene? Lorien is the only one who can destroy the rebounding curse. How do we make that happen? We need to save her."

"Ash, my love," Tora said, her cool fingers brushing against my cheek. "When it comes to Elle, you and Catraia are her lifelines. Without either of you, her light will go out and she will be lost. First and foremost, we need to preserve that connection. As for the rebounding curse, taking Elle to Dramhelm Manor might be out of the question, but there is another way."

I looked at her, unshakeable resolve coursing through my veins. "Tell me what we have to do."

ELEYSE

My eyes were heavy. Groggily, I tried to open them, but my vision was blurry and uncentered. After a couple more tries, everything came into focus around me, and I looked up to see two emerald eyes—swirling with worry and fear—gazing at me. Ash. A deluge of emotion overwhelmed me as the events from the market came rushing back, and I burst into tears, covering my face with my hands.

I had lost control. Was unable to control my own power, seduced by something twisted and wrong inside me. I'd felt pleasure from hurting someone and almost unleashed my power on innocents who'd done nothing at all except be in the wrong place at the wrong time.

The bed moved as Ash leaned back against the headboard and pulled me into the warmth of his arms. I didn't deserve this. His understanding. His empathy. His love.

"Ash," I said, my voice a ragged plea, my emotions a twisted mess.

"It's all right, Elle," he whispered, pressing his lips to my head.

"No, it's not all right," I said, pushing him away, frustration flaring inside me. "Something is wrong with me."

He was quiet, the indecision and resolve I glimpsed in his eyes sending a foreboding shudder down my spine.

I gasped. "It's true." I slumped forward, despair gripping me in its chilly embrace.

"I need you to listen to me, Elle," he said, taking my limp hand. "I didn't know how grave things were last night when you asked me about the darkness inside you. Everything I told you about Catraia and her ability to keep you grounded when you use your power is true."

My eyes flew to his. "So what has changed since then? What do you know? Does it have to do with the rebounding curse? Is that what you wanted to talk to me about before you left?"

"I won't keep secrets from you," he said, his face solemn and guarded.

"Tell me, Ash," I pleaded, tears slipping down my face. "I deserve to know."

"Yes, you do," he said, brushing my tears away with his thumbs. "I just want you to know that we *can* fix this."

So there was something to be fixed.

My heart thudded in my chest. *Catraia,* I called out in my mind. *Do you know?*

After what happened today, yes. Let Asher tell you.

I turned to Ash and held my breath, my stomach a churning

vortex, weighted with lead.

I was numb, my mind reeling as he explained everything. The darkness inside me. The corrupting power of the rebounding curse. My trapped light. My inability to use my power the way I was meant to. I was a walking time bomb. That's what it sounded like. Using my magic had made me lose control of who I was, gave the darkness a foothold, made me want to surrender to it completely. I couldn't let that happen.

That's not true, Eleyse, Catraia whispered. *I was there. It's not at that stage yet. Your first instinct was to protect that child, even as the God of Chaos sat idly by. I felt your disgust at his apathy. I was not wrong when I said you are a child of the light. We just need to remove that darkness around your soul.*

Ash ran a hand through his hair. "Up until this morning, I had no idea how dire things were for you with the rebounding curse. Because Tora has an intimate knowledge of the Old, Arcane Magic, and has the ability to see things that I can't, she was able to detect Gargmoin's darkness around your soul, cutting off access to the light inside you when you wield your power. Even so, it's not until after the incident at the market that the full ramifications of that darkness made itself known—that it is sentient, and responds to like-minded darkness."

"I feel sick." I squeezed my eyes shut. "He said my tendrils . . ." I stopped short, not even able to get the words out, guilt rushing over me like a wave. "He made me . . . *feel* things against my will—things I freely give to you alone—and I hated it. And as for the drunken power, that sick part of me liked it, wanted to give in, to hurt that man, swat away the people in my way, just because I could."

"It wasn't you, Elle," Ash said, his voice soft and pleading. "The darkness inside you is alive."

"That's fucking awesome," I said, a bitter laugh escaping my lips. "What's one more sentient thing inside me? Aren't I lucky to be the ultimate host."

"Elle—"

"At least tell me that the little girl is all right."

Ash nodded. "Yes. Tora made sure she was taken care of. She is safe with her mother. That man will never hurt her again."

"How could a father hurt his own child like that?"

Ash shook his head. "I promise you, Elle. He will pay for what he did."

I stared at him, anger whipping to a frenzy in my mind. Why couldn't he just have told me before he left? If he had, I would have known, and none of this would have happened. He chose to keep it from me, to lie to me.

He did not, Eleyse, Catraia said firmly. *I can see the truth of that as plain as day. It was always his intention to tell you. He could not have known what would happen at the market while he was gone. Neither could Tora. And what about the child? If today didn't happen, you wouldn't have been there to protect her.*

I swatted her voice away, a spate of rage and frustration pumping into my veins. Why was I at the mercy of all these things outside my control? Destiny, my power, this wretched darkness. Even Catraia was here to control me.

That is not true, Eleyse, and you know it.

Ash was supposed to have my back, to protect me, but instead, he had left me, and senseless lamb that I was, I'd fallen prey to and tangled with a wolf.

Listen to yourself, Eleyse, Catraia chided. *You are being irrational. Your thoughts are spiraling into hysteria. I would say that what your Sovereign did to the God of Chaos is a pretty good indicator of the lengths he would go to protect you.*

I shoved her voice aside, the need to release my pent-up rage overwhelming. I felt helpless, afraid. I wanted to scream, to cause pain like I was in pain, to inflict hurt, like I was hurting.

Don't, Eleyse, Catraia warned. *Don't give in to the anger inside you. Don't let the darkness pull you under.*

I could taste the vitriol settling like bile in my throat, and the vicious words dripped like acid off my tongue as I turned to Ash and spoke. "Shame on you for allowing such hateful atrocities to happen in *your* city."

A muscle clenched in his jaw as a flash of pain flickered in his eyes. For a second, a twinge of regret throbbed, but I hardened my heart and turned away. Screw him. Let him be upset for all I cared.

"I get that you're upset and afraid, Elle," he said quietly. "I know that right now, you're just lashing out to hurt me. It doesn't change that I love you, and that I would never do anything to hurt you."

I saw red.

Stop, Eleyse, Catraia commanded.

I plowed forward anyway. "Well you know what? If this is love, then perhaps I need to reconsider if I have any use for it." I turned away from him and lay on my side, facing the window. "Just leave me alone."

His hand grasped my shoulder and I slapped it away. "Don't fucking touch me," I said, my voice shrill. "Just go."

For a long moment, he was silent, and then he exhaled softly, and the bed moved as he left me. Only after I was certain he was gone did I dissolve into tears.

Chapter 38

ELEYSE

"WELL, LOOKEE HERE!" TORA'S voice chimed from the corner of the room, not even a minute after Ash had left. "Is this a private pity party or can anyone join?"

I sat up to find her standing at the end of the bed, still decked out in her lime-green outfit, hands on her hips. Shit. She must have been listening through the walls. "Go away, Tora," I said angrily, swiping at my tears.

"I will do no such thing, dove," she said, her voice bristling with defiance. She pointed her index finger at me. "*You*," she paused, "were a cruel bitch to him. Actually, *bitch* is putting it nicely. You were more like an acrimonious cunt, really. He doesn't deserve that. Especially from you. Do you think he would ever let anything happen to you? You think he *wanted* that vile shit stain, Cazril, anywhere near you? Ash came dangerously close to killing a God today, in case you didn't notice. But he, unlike you, knows how to keep a handle on his emotions, even when everything inside him might be screaming to simply let go." Her eyes flashed with golden ire as she sat on the side of the bed. "It's funny. What are you even angry with him about? What did he do to deserve that display of venom?"

I stared at her. Did I even know? He had withheld information from me. Goddamn it. Even I knew it; I was a shit. I was reaching. He was up front with me before he left about talking to me about getting my memories back. But in the moment just now, all I'd felt was righteous indignation, and it had consumed me in its flame until I had no choice but to explode.

You had a choice, Catraia said bluntly. *You chose bitterness. You chose to hurt him.*

Great. She and Tora were tag-teaming me with the guilt trips and reprimands.

You deserve it.

"Fear is no excuse to turn on the ones who love you," Tora said, and I flinched at her harsh tone. "I have known Ash his entire life, and the depth of love and devotion he feels for you is something to be revered." She closed her eyes. "In my head, I see a vision of you, Agaia. A powerful queen, kind and just, who is as fearless as she is humble, as compassionate and merciful as she is terrifying. That can be a reality. Be that queen to match the king at your side." She tilted my chin and looked me straight in the eye. "The path of leadership is not easy, love. It's littered with tough choices and good intentions. You'll learn that. Today, I watched Ash war and wrestle with his love for you and make that tough choice to not rip the heart out of a God for taking you against your will. And then, with a few cruel words, you stuck a blade in *his* heart and gutted him. And why? Because it was an easy outlet for your rage and frustration."

It would have hurt less if she'd slapped me. Recklessness. Isn't that what Catraia said about me? That I let my recklessness lead me? My default was to push people away who got too close. To run away when I felt vulnerable. To lash out to protect myself.

Tora crossed her legs and sat up. "Go to him," she said, squeezing my hand. "Time and stubborn pride is not a luxury we have in the waking world. Now that we know what we're dealing with, we *need* to get that darkness out of you."

"Where is he?" I asked.

"On the rooftop terrace," she said. "True love is never hurtful, Agaia. It's always kind, slow to anger, nurturing. Remember that." She opened my palm and placed a little box into it, and with a rueful smile, she disappeared.

I looked down at what she had given me. The box was small, lightweight, and gilded, with an intricate, hammered bronze leaf set at the top.

I opened the lid slowly and was hit with a jolt of recognition. Suspended in the middle of the box was a small, jade-colored stone in the shape of a crescent moon. It was the other side of the earring I'd lost in Ash's bed the night I'd gone to him through the Senshifter—only this was just the stone, not the ear clasp. He'd kept it all those years!

I touched it with my index finger, and the moment I did, the stone melted away, liquefying into a thin film of a peculiar silver substance, which swirled and spun in the box for a few seconds before shooting upwards in a spray of droplets. I watched as the droplets began knitting together to form one moving mass, undulating and rippling in front of me, and then, the mass began transforming into something extraordinary. It was weaving together a scene.

Slowly, everything came into focus. It was *me*, and I was moving and talking. Like a film, the scene was playing out for me to see.

"You want to hear it?" I asked, my eyes in the scene staring straight into mine as I watched it.

"Do I have to?" a voice said teasingly, causing the me in the scene to squeal and throw a pillow at the person speaking. He laughed, a rich, deep laugh, and my heart soared as I recognized Ash's voice. I was watching one of his memories, the scene playing from his point of view.

"Of course I want to hear it," he said tenderly. "I will never get tired of listening to you."

In the scene, I smiled radiantly and turned away. I was wearing a T-shirt and jeans and grabbed an acoustic guitar off the floor and pulled it onto my lap. I recognized it as one Mags had bought for me on my sixteenth birthday. I strummed the strings gently and began playing. The melody was slow and soft, and as it began building, goosebumps snaked a path across my skin. The me in the scene started singing, and my heart skipped a beat. This song! I . . . I had written this. It was mine!

Watching myself singing it was the most surreal feeling. I found myself immersed in the melody and the words.

Lost in the stillness, shrouded in mystery, yet carved in my mind.
I see you before me, the one face that haunts me, and my senses unwind.
I'm so lost and confused, is it only a dream?
An illusion, a ruse, tell me what can it mean?
I've been here before, it all seems so real.
My heart can't ignore, but do I trust what I feel?

I sang you a lullaby each night before I closed my eyes and prayed that you would come
This make-believe reality, a lonely heart's sweet fantasy, now it's all come undone
You're no longer a dream, a ghost in my head
Tell me how must I seem? I feel so misled
I wish you could know what I'm feeling inside
I wish I could show what I'm trying to hide.

I long to touch your heart the way you're touching mine

I feel so torn apart, this emotion I can't define.

Maybe forever, or then maybe never, I wish that I could tell
You're everything I've searched for. Of that, I'm quite sure, but is
this heaven or hell?
Wanting you so much, my heart screams your name.
How I crave your touch, tell me it's not a game.
I've got so much to lose for I've waited so long.
Tell me, how should I choose? Which is right? Which is wrong?
Are you only a dream? Only a dream?

As the song ended and the music faded away, the me in the scene turned back to face Ash, whom I still could not see, and smiled.

"Elle, that was so . . . wow! I have no words," he said softly. "You're a work of art, you know that?" he added, the affection apparent in his voice, and I smiled at him again before the scene slowly faded away.

As the vestiges of the droplets disintegrated and spiraled back into the crescent-shaped piece of glass, one solitary thing lingered and haunted me. I looked so *happy*. I radiated pure joy in that moment, and it had come from doing what I loved most and being with Ash. This song was about him. I'd written it for him; I had no doubt.

Happiness was not an emotion I was used to feeling in my life. Even as I acknowledged that little truth, a deep, gaping emptiness and sorrow gnawed at my insides like a cancer, eating away at who I was. That was in direct conflict with what the scene I'd just witnessed.

He brought you back to life, Catraia whispered in my mind. *That was always what he, and only he, was meant to do. That light in your soul? He fanned the flames, taught you what it was to love again.*

A surge of heated emotion engulfed me, and I looked at the box in my hand in wonder, the jade stone hovering slowly in the center. I was such a fool. How could I have said such cruel things? Attacked his character? Questioned his love? Hurt him?

Tora was right. Catraia was right. He didn't deserve that from me.

Chapter 39

I GOT LOST ON the way to the rooftop. I couldn't remember the way and made several wrong turns, until out of nowhere, Tora appeared and snapped her fingers, sending me where I needed to go. The sun was still high in the cloudless sky, its rays beginning to weaken in the early onset of evening.

Ash sat under the stone pergola near the pool, his back to me. Tryx was sprawled at his feet, her face in his lap. She lifted her head in my direction and chuffed in greeting before leaving him and padding over to me.

Ash turned to look at me, and my heart lurched nervously in my chest. I stood frozen where I was, unable to do anything but look at him. Tryx bumped her head against my hand, demanding my attention, and I stooped down to scratch her face, my eyes never leaving Ash's as he got to his feet and walked toward me.

He was still wearing his dark leathers from earlier, and the breeze stirred his wavy hair as he moved. My throat burned, clogged with the weight of my regret. My skin was hot and clammy, and I wiped my hands on my pants to get the moisture off.

He came to a stop in front of me, his hands in the pockets of his pants. He didn't say anything, just stood there, his face unreadable, waiting for me to make the first move.

I got to my feet, my knees almost buckling from the trembling tumult of my nerves. Slowly, I took two steps forward, coming to stand in front of him.

True love is never hurtful, Tora had said.

Tears blurred my vision as I reached for him. "I'm so sorry, Ash," I choked out. My ensuing sobs were muffled in his chest as he pulled me to him. His hands tangled in my hair, and I buried my face in his warmth, his heartbeat strong and steady against my ear.

Slowly, I pulled away to look at him. "I said terrible things I had no right saying," I said, my mouth quivering with the force of my remorse.

"It's all right, Elle," he soothed.

"No, it's not," I cried. "I was cruel, and you don't deserve that. I have felt nothing but love and devotion from you, and despite having lost my memories of us, heart and soul, I know your love is no illusion. You are not a stranger to me. When I'm with you, I know what peace is. Please forgive me."

"There's nothing to forgive, Tialla," he said, his hand clasping the back of my head. "I understand why you were angry. I'm sorry that I hurt you. I never meant to keep this from you. The moment Tora told me what she saw, I knew you needed to know, and I fully intended to tell you everything after my meetings today."

His frustration was evident, and a pang of guilt twisted in my heart.

He rested his forehead against mine. "I sense the fear that shrouds you, Elle. And by now, I know you well enough to know how you react when you're afraid. You retreat inside those impenetrable walls you built around your heart over the years, shooting flaming arrows and pouring hot tar over anyone who comes close. But that won't keep me out. I see you, and I'm not afraid of you, my love. You are not alone. You never have to fight the darkness by yourself again. I led you out of it before; let me do it once more."

Clutching the front of his vest, I stood on tiptoes and kissed him, tears streaming down my face. I had tried to die so many times, and although I didn't know it then, it was his voice that had urged me to fight, to live. In the scene from the past I'd just witnessed, the light he'd brought to my life was unmistakable; so too was the happiness I felt from being with him.

I was ready to take the next step—to let go of my fear and face the unknown with him. Whatever that ended up being. No reservations, no holding back.

I clung to him as he parted my mouth with his tongue and lazily slid the tip of it along my teeth. His hands moved down to grip my waist, and I trailed my fingers against his jaw. His tongue swept into my mouth to tangle with mine. I lost myself in the feel and taste of him and the heady rush that came from being in his arms.

For so long, I had been a ghost, wandering the realm of the living as if I didn't belong there. Not anymore. I knew where I belonged.

I slid my hand down over his heart, feeling the steady thumping against my fingers. I trailed my lips across his jaw, sending kisses skittering against his skin.

There was an abrupt shift in the air then, and Ash's body stiffened against mine. Radiant power caused the air around us to shiver and spark, and a melodic voice rang out around us.

"Forgive me for the intrusion, my dears, but it could not be avoided. Time is not our friend."

I turned around to see the curly-haired woman from my dream, the one who had sent me through the Senshifter to Ash. The Goddess Eolith.

"I received Tora's summons for help," she said, her silver eyes flashing as she looked at Ash. "And it comes not a minute too soon. We must act, Asher. Something moves stealthily in the shadows—uncharted by the Mavigos—a flash of indeterminate fate with no absolute outcome. We cannot fail."

Ash's body tensed against mine, and he pulled me tighter, his hand firmly planted in the small of my back.

The Goddess's expression softened as she turned her gaze to me. "But before that, leida mata, you and I must get reacquainted."

I stared at the Goddess of the Ethereal Harmonies, my heart beating a wild staccato in my chest. I clutched Ash's hand tightly, needing his strength to bolster me.

"Would you like some privacy to talk with Elle?" he asked her, his thumb tracing a soothing circle against my knuckles.

She shook her head. "You have more than proven yourself worthy of my trust, my son." She took a step toward us, her eyes filled with emotion as she looked at me. "Again, fate has robbed us, you and I. I once told you the Secret of the Gods, but with your memories lost to you, I must tell you again. The truth of it will change your life forever, in even more ways than it has already been changed. Are you ready?"

Hell, yes! I was ready. I'd been dying to know what the Secret of the Gods was ever since she'd called me that in my dream years ago. I ran my tongue over my dry lips and swallowed nervously. And really, how much more could my life change? No more waiting.

I nodded at her.

She smiled and closed the distance between us, reaching out to touch my face. "At the dawn of the Rebirth, when the only sentient life in the Sangelis were the Gods of the New Age and the ancient ones, there was Sorin, Summoner of Light and Darkness. Next to Arazul, the Great Creator, he was the most powerful of the divine beings—wielder of dual, opposing forces of nature. Sorin was espoused to Jaraya, Goddess of the Night, who summoned the moons that lit up the night skies across the Sangelis."

As her melodic voice wove the story, I pictured the striking image of Sorin from A *History of the Gods*. And then Jaraya, the Goddess whose aura I sensed was cunning and cruel.

The Goddess Eolith continued. "Although Sorin cared for Jaraya, he did not love her. His heart, you see, belonged to me."

Okay . . . I didn't see that coming.

"Millions of years passed, and worlds grew and flourished in the vastness of the Sangelis, but Sorin grew tired of it all. He could no longer bear a life of secrecy, having to love me in the shadows, under the cloak of his darkness. He yearned for our love to flourish in the light—the more dominant side of his nature—to have me with him in every manifestation of his power. To live for eternity without me by his side was a future he could not endure. He vowed to proclaim his love to the Gods, and to make me his beloved over Jaraya."

Oh dear. That definitely didn't sound like a good plan. There were entire histories written of the fury of spurned women and Goddesses.

"Before his great proclamation, however, I learned the impossible—I was with child, which was a miracle and enigma tangled into one since celestial beings are made, not born. I shed happy tears that the Mavigos had blessed the union of our love with such a hallowed gift and saw it as a sign of the evolution of our kind."

My eyes widened. Another development I didn't see coming. Where was this all going?

"On my way to convey the news to my beloved, I was intercepted by Arazul, who forbade me from telling Sorin of the miracle I carried. You see, Arazul explained that the union between Sorin and Jaraya could never be undone, for if Sorin relinquished his union with the Goddess of the Night, it would bring about a cataclysmic event, plunging two worlds of the Sangelis into darkness for millions of years, bringing about the deaths of billions of life-forms. Arazul feared that if Sorin learned of the child I carried, he would put its life above all else. And so, I kept my silence, but informed Sorin of what would happen if he relinquished his union with Jaraya. He was honorable, and I believed that he would put duty and the fate of the Sangelis above me. It broke my heart to release him, but I willingly did so, convincing him that this was the only course of action. Although it took every ounce of strength he possessed to let me go, Sorin could not put the lives of billions at risk for his own happiness. For his own sanity, he let go of me completely, vowing that if he could not have all of me, he would have to live with none of me."

My heart filled with sorrow as I gazed at her. What would I do if that were me? If I had to give Ash up to save the rest of the world? And how difficult would it be watching him with someone else at his side? Would I make that sacrifice? I gripped his hand tighter and pushed that thought away.

Sadness clouded Eolith's face as she continued. "I was heartbroken, and I petitioned Arazul to release me to raise my child in secret, but the Great Creator knew the truth of the child growing within me. You see, the offspring of the Summoner of Light and Darkness and the Goddess of the Ethereal Harmonies had a powerful destiny—one written in the stars by the Mavigos long before the dawn of the New Age. Born of light and darkness, born of love and music, the miracle growing within me was the child of celestial love spoken of in that ancient star etching. Of this, Arazul was certain."

Wait. What? My mouth dropped open. It couldn't be. No fucking way! How was this even possible?

My eyes flew to Ash's and he gave me an imperceptible nod, his brows lifted slightly. He squeezed my hand gently, as if to say, "Let her finish."

Eolith brushed her fingers across my cheek. "But the signs had not yet aligned for this to come to pass—the signs spoken of in the celestial star etching. The Celusian Moon still shone brightly in the night sky and the light of Selayne still blazed a trail across the heavens. And so, after Arazul revealed the truth of my child's fate to me, together, we set into motion a plan. Arazul took the seedling child growing within me and ensconced it in the Cradle of the In-Between—alive, but not living, in a suspended state of slumber, not to be awakened until the Mavigos deemed it time."

My body went unnaturally still, flashing back to the first time she had come to me in my dreams. *I was robbed of what I awaited with bated breath for thousands of years*, she had said. At the time, I had no idea what she was talking about. *You are back where it all began—in the In-Between.* No. It couldn't be. This was crazy!

Eolith looked out into the distance, toward the harbor. "Although I understood that there was no other way, I mourned the loss of my miracle. The loss of my child and my love was a festering wound upon my soul, and Arazul recognized the grave danger it placed upon the Ethereal Harmonies. He gifted me with four fully-grown daughters, fashioned purely from my essence and the Harmonies I protected. My heart was filled with light and love once more. Strong names, I gave them—names to endure steadfastly across time: Medra, Caladra, Avaia, Zarra."

That's right. The Cloryals were her daughters. If Eolith was saying what I thought she was saying, then that would make them . . .

"As for my child with Sorin, Arazul and I understood the dangers of any other celestial being learning of its existence, and so thousands of years later, when the Celusian Moon dimmed and exploded into nothingness and the light of Selayne disappeared,

Arazul recognized the signs and was quick to act. He removed my child from the Cradle of the In-Between and breathed life into her fledgling lungs, shrouding her in protective magic. He transported her himself to a world far away, where the Gods of the Sangelis would not be able to find her should they ever learn of her existence. There, in the human world, she would live as a human child until the time arose—when the Mavigos would call on her to fulfil the purpose for which she was born. And now, here we are. Everything has come full circle."

Oh shit. She was saying what I thought she was saying. Never in a million years could I have imagined that *this* was the truth of my identity. There had to be a mistake. My parents were Kylie Satler and Jeff Maren, not powerful gods I'd never heard of until a few days ago. I was born to human parents, a human child. Wasn't I?

My mind was reeling. *A human woman, and yet not entirely a human woman*, Oletho had said.

Harwen Valkyse had taken me back to my birth. The image of the lifeless, blue child flashed in my mind, followed by the rosy-cheeked, alert baby the next. What did it mean? And I had been right. What I'd sensed in that room was indeed the Great Creator, Arazul. Based on what Eolith said, he had brought me there from the Cradle of the In-Between.

Holy shit! Eolith was my mother. *My mother!* The Goddess of Ethereal Harmonies—belonging to a part of the universe far removed from the one I grew up in—my mother? And I had a God for a father. This had to be a dream. My entire human life couldn't have been a lie.

Everything I had learned about the ancient star etching and my role in it was overwhelming and difficult to grasp, but this new revelation—it was completely implausible.

Deep inside, you know it's not that implausible, Catraia whispered into my mind.

Eolith stepped closer toward me, both her hands cupping my face. "Now you know the truth, leida mata. You are the child of my heart. Soladeo." *Daughter.*

She took me in her arms, and I sank into her embrace as the melody inside her wrapped itself around us both. I had been so young when my earthly mother died, I hardly remembered the feeling of her arms around me. But this—the utter and complete contentment I felt in the embrace of the Goddess of Ethereal Harmonies—it was the stuff dreams were made of.

Chapter 40

"E O, LOVE, RIGHT ON time." Tora glided toward us, making a beeline for the Goddess of Ethereal Harmonies, wrapping her in a warm embrace.

"Glad to see that in all the millennia, you haven't lost your fashion sense, Tora," Eolith said, surveying Tora's lime-green outfit with amusement.

"Fashion keeps life interesting, Mother Goddess." She took Eolith's hands in hers. "I am happy you came."

"Did you really think I wouldn't when I know the grave danger my daughter is in? When I know what must be done?"

I blinked. What must be done? I looked at Ash, my brows furrowed in confusion.

"By now, you must have heard, Asher," Eolith said. "Madio Averon has allied with Kaliope. And I have more news coming out of Brus-Winnd. She has turned WorDalg."

Ash stiffened next to me, an overwhelming feeling of rage and frustration emanating off him. A jolt of power rippled from him, and before I even grasped what was happening, a loud crash tore through the space behind me. I turned to see one of the stone columns of the pergola blown to smithereens and smoking.

Immediately, Tora lifted her hand in a quick wave, and the column was whole again, as if it had never happened. "It's all right, Smolders. We understand."

"I'm sorry," Ash said, running his hand through his hair. "She always seems to be one step ahead."

I stared at him, the muscle working in his jaw hard to miss. Why *was* she always one step ahead? What resources did she have at her disposal to give her an edge? And a Sovereign allying with her? That was nuts. Treachery.

"Who is WorDalg?" I asked.

"WorDalg is the ancient being who is bound to guard the burial place of Valkyse's Phantera," Ash explained.

Shit. I could definitely see why Ash had exploded. Kaliope was going after the Phanteras. Did that mean she knew about the celestial star etching?

Eolith's eyes blazed silver as she looked between the three of us. "I gave up a life with my daughter to preserve the future spoken of in the celestial star etching. With all my heart, I believe in the promise of the Light Age. I will do whatever I can to help."

Ash and Tora looked at each other. There was something I was missing.

Ash took my hand, reading my confusion. "Elle, I explained what Tora said about the darkness of the rebounding curse around your soul, and what that means for you when it comes to using your magic."

I nodded, a feeling of foreboding creeping up on me. "Yes. Because I am cut off from the light inside my soul, the darkness takes over when I use my power, and Catraia has to work against that to rein me in. I am not grounded in the light because I can't tap into it."

Ash nodded. "Above everything, the most important thing right now is destroying the rebounding curse—specifically Gargmoin's dark magic around your soul. From everything Tora has explained, as long as that remains, your powers are a threat to you. The only way to destroy the rebounding curse is for you to get your memories back, but the rebounding curse is what caused your memory loss and is keeping them trapped."

I stared at him blankly. What a complete mind-melt. Talk about chicken and the egg.

"What happens now, then?" I asked.

Tora furrowed her brows. "Listen, my love. Lorien Reo is the only one with the power to restore your memories and destroy a rebounding curse steeped in the dark sway of the Old, Arcane Magic—Gargmoin's magic. Lorien is the guardian of that great power here on Ariadna. Restoring your memories and destroying the curse is something he could easily do if you were in Brus-Winnd and connected to the power source of the Old, Arcane Magic—the light strain. In order to get to Dramhelm Manor, though, you must first go through the Territories, where the dark sway of the Old, Arcane Magic runs wild. As such, the darkness around your soul will respond to that immediately, causing the dark elements to overwhelm you before you can even get to Lorien. As a result, that path is closed to us."

"So where does that leave us?" I asked, a sinking feeling settling in my gut.

"You must go back," Tora said.

"Go back where?" I asked, afraid of what she was suggesting. "To Earth? I thought I was never meant to be there."

Ash squeezed my fingers, his handsome face so serious it filled me with fear. "No, not Earth."

Tora touched my arm gently. "We have to send your consciousness through the back door of your mind, to the past, Elle—to the last moment you remember. Your memories still exist—they're just trapped. You must relive it all through your consciousness—the events that sparked the will to live again, that

371

staunched and reversed the spread of the darkness and murk eating away at the core of who you were. You must relive Ash. Your time with him. How you grew to love him. Other revelations were laid bare during that time that you must also experience again, reveals that are too important for you to forget. It's all there, locked away in the recesses of your mind. You won't remember any of your time in Ariadna while you're there. Only after you've recaptured all your lost memories and exited the Void will everything weave together."

Wait. Shut the front door and back the hell up. What?

"I won't remember any of my time in Ariadna?" I blurted out, my eyes in a panic as I looked between the three of them. "All three of you, Gwynn, Catraia—gone?"

"Only while your consciousness is in the past," Tora explained. "Your mind will regress to the state it was in at the point in time you are sent back to. Only when you come back to the present moment after the rebounding curse is destroyed, will all the memories you had here catch up to you once more. Your time here will not be lost to you, Elle. You will remember everything again."

Although that filled me with a small measure of calm, my mind was swimming in questions. "Is this even possible?" I asked, fear seeping into my bones. "Do we even have the time for this? That's almost two years of my life you're asking me to relive."

The Goddess Eolith—my mother—smiled softly. "That is why I'm here, Eleyse. You need a plane of consciousness in the Void that is impervious to time. My sanctum in Solniess—the Divine plane—can host your consciousness while it journeys through time."

"This is our best option, Elle," Tora said. "Time doesn't exist in that part of the Void, which means that here, in the waking world, the time you're gone will pass for us in the blink of an eye. The only thing that remains is for Lorien to come here to trap Gargmoin's magic the moment your consciousness is reconnected with your body. I have already sent word to him."

I stared at the three of them with what I was sure was a deer-in-headlights look.

Tora squeezed my shoulder. "I know this might be confusing to you, Elle, but it will work."

"Explain it to me," I said. "I have so many questions. Like, can I screw up anything when I go back? Or do something that will alter what happens in the future? Can anything go wrong? Will I come back intact? Will I have Catraia with me? Will everything be the same when I return?" I turned to Ash, desperation in my eyes as I stood there trembling, the threads of my sanity rapidly unspooling.

He pulled me to him and I clutched the fabric of his vest, the cloying smell of the leather invading my senses.

"Can I have a moment with Elle?" Ash asked.

Tora and my mother nodded and walked to the other side of the rooftop.

The moment they left, I burst into tears. "I . . . I don't know if I can do this, Ash. I was in a dark place back then. I don't know if I'm strong enough to say yes to reliving that."

He tilted my face up. "Look at me, Elle."

I wiped my eyes and lifted my gaze to meet his.

He stroked my cheek gently. "I know you're scared, but you can do this, baby."

My heart fluttered at the endearment, but the love and reassurance pouring out of him only added to the panic rattling my nerves.

"And you won't be alone," he continued. "I'll be there. Your consciousness will travel back in time to the last thing you remember."

The last thing I remembered was going to Crusoe's after work for a drink. Ash had confirmed that that was where I'd met him for the first time.

"But I won't know you," I rasped. "When I got to Ariadna, even though I'd lost my memories, you were never a stranger to me. My heart and soul remembered who and what you were to me the moment I laid eyes on you. I can't bear to lose that."

Ash rested his forehead against mine. "Trust me, my love. Our journey is one that is worth reliving again. The moment we meet that night, the world around us turns electric, and just keeps igniting from there."

I intertwined my fingers with his. "Tell me what to expect. Tell me that I'll come back to you."

"I wouldn't be on board with this otherwise, Tialla." He curled a finger around a lock of my hair. "As for what to expect, Catraia and I will guide you through the Void and ready your consciousness for its return to the past. Catraia will send you back in your mind to the point in time where you need to go—the last thing you remember. Once your consciousness is back in that moment, you will move forward through your memories to relive the events of the past until the moment Gargmoin's magic hits you. When I say relive, that's basically what it is. You can't change anything or do anything differently. You won't have any awareness of the future or anything beyond the moment you're reliving. Your consciousness will become one with the past, and the flow of events will occur as if you're living through them for the first time. You will have no external awareness of being an observer. You simply sink into the past and relive it exactly the way it played out. Once Gargmoin's power hits you, Catraia will guide you out of the Void and back into your body. As soon as you open your eyes, Lorien will use his power to siphon the shard of Gargmoin's magic out of you before it can settle in around your soul and feed off any residual darkness that lives inside you. Only then will you be restored."

"What about Catraia?" I asked. "Will she be with me?"

"Catraia will be a witness, but she will not live in your mind the way she does now. She will be on the periphery of this experience, her sole purpose being to guide the flow of your consciousness."

I couldn't help the dull thud of fear that struck me. I was going to be alone again. Alone, with no purpose and filled with emptiness. The mere thought flooded me with nausea. Falling in love, only to

. . .

A slow shiver coursed through me, building in intensity until I was unable to control the tremors rocking my body.

Ash ran his hands down my arms before reaching up to cup my face. "Tell me, Elle," he said gently.

"I'm scared," I whispered, a sob building in the back of my throat. "You said you were gone from my life those last five months." I choked back a ragged gurgle. "I'm terrified of who I might have become in that time. Terrified for my own mental health and what losing you might have done to me. And what if," I said, my voice barely even audible, "what if when I remember, it changes how I feel about you now?"

Ash's eyes flashed with anguish and his fingers drifted down to caress my neck. "Listen, Elle. I'm not going to lie and tell you that everything was perfect for those two years. Life's not like that, as you well know. There were rough times in there, yes, but every moment with you was fucking worth it for me." He gripped my chin gently, forcing my eyes to meet his. "Getting to know you, falling in love with you, watching your fearless, beautiful spirit come back to life. Those are the memories that haunt my dreams, baby. You were a hollow specter when I met you. Trust me, you're not going to want to miss your own transformation, to witness how, once you felt the light on your face again, there was no stopping you. How strong and brave and invincible you became—a woman who was comfortable in her own skin. I might have led you out of the darkness and pointed you toward the sun, but the moment you realized you had wings, you were untouchable, my love. Pure magic."

Tears slipped feely down my face, and I lifted my hand to touch his jaw. Never in my wildest dreams could I have ever imagined that I would find someone who loved me with the intensity and devotion that Ash showered on me, who believed in me with the certainty that he did. Everything had a cost, and looking into those brilliant emerald eyes brimming with so much intense emotion, I was struck with the abrupt and unshakeable realization that what pooled in those shining depths was worth every bit of pain I might have to endure. If it all brought me back to this place, to him, I would gladly do it.

I wrapped my arms around his neck and buried my face in his chest. His hands clasped my waist, pulling me closer, his warm breath skating against my cheek. For a long moment, we stood entangled like that, basking in the heated emotion coursing through us, neither of us wanting to pull away.

Finally, I lifted my head and looked at him, running my tongue over my dry lips. "I know nothing comes without risk, Ash. What are the risks here?"

His brows furrowed. "The risks lie in the Void, with your shadow self that will remain slumbering in the present—if you get trapped or waylaid and it disrupts your journey, or if somehow you cannot make your way back to your body. Also, the moment your consciousness is reconnected to your body, Lorien needs to act. If he doesn't, then we will have failed and the darkness will continue to spread."

I swallowed, the lump in my throat hard and unyielding.

"Think of it like this," Ash explained. "Your consciousness is a sum of parts: the past, present, and in rare instances, glimmers of the future. In the Void, your shadow self is grounded in the present. It can be taken or be placed in danger, like you experienced with the God of Chaos yesterday. Once your consciousness journeys back to the past, however, you lose all awareness of what is happening in the present moment—you're essentially in limbo, in a state of suspended animation until you return to the present. That means that your shadow self in the present moment is still susceptible to danger. I don't want you to worry about that, though. I will make sure you're safe. I promise you."

I already knew the lengths Ash would go to protect me. I didn't doubt that he would keep me safe.

"I have one last question," I whispered.

"Ask me."

"Can anything go wrong in the past that didn't happen the first time around?"

"No. Your past has already happened for you. You are not traveling back in time like you did through the Senshifter, where you had the ability to influence things. You are just reliving events that have already been recorded and stamped in your consciousness."

I squeezed Ash's forearm, my nails digging into his warm skin. "Are you sure this will work?"

He squeezed my fingers gently. "It has to. It's the only way."

His eyes shone with assurance, love and resolve, filling me with conviction. "Let's do it then. Whatever it takes."

Chapter 41

WE STOOD IN A breathtaking bedchamber with wide balcony doors that overlooked a cerulean-blue ocean. My mother's sanctum in Solniess was stunning. God magic was definitely something else. At least my consciousness would be in a place of tranquility and beauty while I reclaimed my memories. I stared at the sheer expanse of the water against the backdrop of a cloudless sky, growing smaller in the vastness around me.

After we left the rooftop at Cazara Torannon, Tora had used her magic to teleport to Brus-Winnd, and a few minutes later, Lorien Reo had returned in her place. Tora had stayed behind at Dramhelm Manor to safeguard the core of the Old, Arcane Magic in Lorien's absence.

As guardian of that ancient power, Ash explained, Lorien could not leave the Territories unattended. Because he and Tora wielded the same type of magic, she was the only logical choice to act as a surrogate.

Everything afterward passed by in a flurry of activity—meeting Lorien; talking to Gwynn, whom Ash had brought up to speed; spending a few moments with my mother. The entire time, Ash didn't leave my side, and I was grateful for that. My mind was numb, my movements robotic, my body tense with the anticipation of what lay ahead.

"Enjoy falling in love with my brother again," Gwynn whispered as she hugged me tightly.

Ash made sure everyone understood what had to be done, explaining that from the time it would take me to get to the entrance of the Void, then enter the gateway to my mother's sanctum in Solniess, and then back out through the Void back to my body, only seconds would pass in the real world. That still blew my mind. Lorien assured him that he would be ready to trap Gargmoin's magic, destroying the rebounding curse the moment my consciousness reconnected with my body.

And then I was delving into myself, moving toward the source of my power as Catraia guided me to the entrance of the Void, where, a few seconds later, Ash joined me. Together, we ventured through a gateway that led us to my mother's sanctum in Solniess.

Now, as my eyes traced the path of a solitary bird soaring across the sky, my mother took my hand and squeezed it lightly. "You will be comfortable and safe here, leida mata. No harm will befall you. I will make sure of it." She clasped my face in her hands and brought her forehead against mine. "Once you return to us, it will be time for you to do what I said you would when I came to you in your dreams—to take to the heavens and fly, Renala Cielta." *Celestial Queen.*

She pulled me in an embrace and I let myself sink into her warmth. My mother. I wanted to know her. That alone was worth coming back for. Everything had happened so quickly that I hadn't had time to ask about my father and if he had ever found out about me, but it was high on my list for when I returned.

Slowly, she released me, and Ash's arms wrapped around me. My mother left the room to give us privacy.

"This is so surreal," I said, "I'm having a hard time wrapping my head around it all. My consciousness is here with yours in the present, while our bodies are sequestered in Cazara Torannon.

Catraia will guide my mind back to the past, while my shadow self stays here. I'd be lying if I said I wasn't nervous to the point of being sick."

Ash tucked my hair behind my ear. "That is why I will not leave you while you're here."

"What?" I said, my mouth dropping open. "Ash, you said it will feel like two years for me. I don't expect you to sit here watching over me for that long. You have more important things to do."

He intertwined his fingers with mine. "You forget, Tialla. Time is inconsequential here. And there is nothing more important for me to do than this—to ensure that you're safe and that you come back to me with your memories intact and the rebounding curse destroyed."

"Ash, I can't ask you to put everything on hold for me, even here in the land of no time."

"You're not asking. This is my choice. I waited almost a century to be with you again, Elle. This is but a blip compared to that. As well, I made a dangerous enemy today of the God of Chaos. I will take no chances with your safety."

"But my mother—"

"Is added protection. With the two of us watching over you and Catraia guarding the flow of your consciousness, you will be safe."

I studied his handsome face, noting the determined look in his eyes, the unwavering resolve that seeped from him. "I will do what Gwynn said," I whispered, brushing my fingers against his jaw.

"What's that?"

"I will enjoy falling in love with you again, my Gloweyen King."

His eyes clouded over with emotion, and he lowered his head and kissed me, his lips moving against mine slowly, reverently. I wrapped my arms around his neck and exulted in the intoxicating feel of him. He trailed kisses down my jaw, and I wound my fingers in his dark hair, reluctant to let go.

Slowly, he pulled away and brought his forehead against mine. "From the very first moment you stepped out of the Senshifter into my room, I knew the truth of who you were. And once that truth was confirmed for me, I carried it with me all these years, waiting patiently for the day when I could say it to you and the reality of it would fully resonate with you."

I frowned. "What do you mean? Who am I?"

He smiled. "What you've always been to me. Tialla mata. You are truly a Goddess, Elle. That is your heritage, the truth of who you are."

My eyes filled with tears. He was right. For the first time, those two words were more than just an endearment. My parents were both Gods. As unbelievable as it was, I *was* a Goddess. But more importantly, I was his. *Tialla mata. My Goddess.* I was proud to hold that title.

"Are you ready?" he asked, cupping my cheek with his hand.

I nodded, wrapping my arms around his neck, my eyes glued to his.

"I'll see you again soon, my love," he whispered.

My vision blurred, and I swiped at my tears, refusing to lose sight of him in these last moments.

Everything will be all right, Eleyse, Catraia said softly. *Time to go back.*

And just like that, the image of Ash was ripped away from me, and a vortex of light swirled in front of my eyes, sucking me in. In a rush of heat and howling wind, my mind unraveled, and the face of my soul's shadow—my beautiful love—faded, then disappeared, swept from my memory and launched into the far-flung reaches of the Void, leaving me empty and cold, a blank slate to start fresh again.

Acknowledgments

THIS BOOK WAS A long labor of love, and after five long years, I finally get to release it into the world. To my sister, Tams, I could not have done it without your encouragement and support. From an early age, your love of reading inspired mine, and I love that we still share that. You were always willing to read and re-read my drafts and provide me with your honest feedback. You loved my characters and story as much as I did and made me believe that I could be a *real* writer.

To Maegan and Stacey—my soul sisters—fate made it so that we were thrown overboard together, adrift in uncharted waters as the tempest life rained down on us battered us. I could not have made it through the storm without you both, and I'm so fortunate that we had each other. You are both my biggest cheerleaders, and I love you to the moon and back.

To Alex, my writing sister, I am so grateful that a random Facebook message in a writer's group spawned this beautiful friendship. I could not have gotten here without you. For all the times you peeled me off the floor, walked me off the ledge, slapped some sense into me, I will be eternally grateful. This thing called writing that owns both our souls—I am so happy I have you to share that with. This book would not have been what it is without you—your invaluable suggestions, feedback, support. I told you, you're my *May*, girl!

To my editor, Jess, I am so grateful for all your words of encouragement, for your painstaking attention to detail, and for cheering me on all the while, making me believe that my story was one worth telling.

To Sarah W, thank you for loving my story and the intricate world building, and for always being willing to read and provide feedback.

To my writing coven sisters, Gemma and Sarah, thanks for all the laughs, encouragement, and incredible feedback, and for loving Ash as much as I do.

To Andrew and my wildlings who believed in me and gave me the time I needed to pour myself into this story, even though it took me away from you on many occasions, I love you guys!

About the Author

L.S. TAAL IS A Canadian author who lives in Atlantic Canada with her family. A lover of the written word and vivid, lush storytelling from a young age, her biggest complaint is that there are not enough hours in the day for all the stories waiting to be read.

When she is not creating worlds and stories of her own, she can be found either spending time with her family, hiding from said family with her head stuck in a book, or writing music.

You can connect with her on Instagram @L.S. Taal

On TikTok @l.s.taal.author

On email lstaalauthor@gmail.com

www.ingramcontent.com/pod-product-compliance
Lightning Source LLC
Chambersburg PA
CBHW051316250626
47155CB00007B/2341